1884
No Boundaries

1884
No Boundaries

A Story of Espionage, and International Intrigue

A.E. Wasserman

ARCHWAY
PUBLISHING

Archway Publishing books may be ordered through booksellers or by contacting:

Archway Publishing
1663 Liberty Drive
Bloomington, IN 47403
www.archwaypublishing.com
1 (888) 242-5904

Because of the dynamic nature of the Internet, any web addresses or links contained in this book may have changed since publication and may no longer be valid. The views expressed in this work are solely those of the author and do not necessarily reflect the views of the publisher, and the publisher hereby disclaims any responsibility for them.

Any people depicted in stock imagery provided by Thinkstock are models, and such images are being used for illustrative purposes only. Certain stock imagery © Thinkstock.

Cover Art: Wassily Kandinsky, *The Blue Rider*, 1903 Private collection, Zurich, Switzerland

Map courtesy of Map©Cassini Publishing Ltd. All Rights Reserved

This book is a work of fiction and although based upon a true story, names, characters, places and incidents are used fictionally and any resemblance to actual persons, living or dead, is coincidental.

ISBN: 978-1-4808-1652-7 (sc)
ISBN: 978-1-4808-1653-4 (hc)
ISBN: 978-1-4808-1654-1 (e)

Library of Congress Control Number: 2015905544

Print information available on the last page.

Archway Publishing rev. date: 4/22/2015

Dedicated to Their Daughter
Florence
Born June 23, 1885

And in Memory of
Richard Warren Field

Anybody can sympathise with the sufferings of a friend, but it requires a very fine nature to sympathise with a friend's success.

- Oscar Wilde

NEW LEADENHALL MARKET.

PROLOGUE

The Rhineland, Prussia, Bullay, Germany
April 29, 1884

Reeking of ale, the German pushed his way through the crowd of merry-makers, stumbling toward the door of the beer hall. Karl shoved past one last heavy-set man and made it through the entrance, out into the cool night air.

He'd lost sight of his brother and worried Marc had left. He should never have told him; no one else was to know. *Verdammt,* his brother knew too much and was too stupid, *zu dumm,* to understand the necessity of what the others planned—the far-reaching implications. No choice now; his little brother *had* to join in.

Desperately looking up and down the dimly gas-lit street, he saw only a tall stranger walking toward him. Who the hell was this man? He knew all the people in the vicinity of the village. The German proceeded unsteadily to confront this outsider. *"Wer bist du?* Who are you? What are you doing in this village?"

Startled by the German's belligerence, the newcomer abruptly halted. After a breath, he calmly replied, "I'm headed to the train station."

The angry drunk staggered closer to block the way. At a couple inches under six feet, he stretched taller to be eye to eye with the stranger. "Is that your horse there—the one in the harness?

I see no wagon. Did you steal it?" Karl accused, hoping for a fight because he felt like one.

The stranger stood more erect, and with a dark look in his eye defiantly replied, "No. It's not mine. Now let me pass, *danke*."

Karl squinted harder at the stranger but failed to yield, and the two men stood eyeing each other. After a long minute, the drunken German broke eye contact, looking sideways. He took half a step back when he remembered why he'd come outside. Less threateningly, Karl asked, "Have ... have you seen a man come by here? A little shorter than me, with brown hair?"

"No, I've seen no one," the stranger said evenly. "Excuse me. I must go." With that, he stepped around the drunk and without looking back, continued toward the depot.

Karl glared after him, wanting to fight the arrogant bastard, but again remembered he was worried about his brother. He *had* to find Marc and force him to join the group. Otherwise, the consequences could be dire: death for one or both of them.

He staggered on down the street, attempting to hurry. Turning up a tree-lined lane, he spotted someone farther up whose silhouette resembled his brother. Then he heard the clip-clop of the harnessed mare behind him. Loose, she followed him as he went, much to his annoyance. Just as he was going to wave her away, he heard Marc calling. He left the horse and walked to his sibling. Now he would settle everything once and for all.

Five short minutes later, Karl rushed back down the lane, his veins coursing with adrenaline and a head clear of everything but what he'd just done. Racing toward the street, he spooked the little mare. The train whistle announced its arrival at the station, but he didn't hear it as he tucked the knife with its sticky blade back into its sheath. Wiping the blood from his hands onto his shirt, he hurried through the darkness to his home two blocks west. As Karl ran, his legs pumping fast and heart pumping faster, he heard the screams as men hurried from their homes, some even in nightshirts, and into the lane.

They found his bleeding brother sprawled beside bushes along the lane. One man clamped his hands tightly over the blood spurting from the dying man's chest. Another ran to get the town watchman. Someone else caught the mare and tethered her. Others hovered over the bleeding brother, asking who stabbed him. "Did you see who it was? Was it a robber?"

All they could hear in a whisper bubbling with blood was, "Bismarck ... a ... a plot ... stop ... kill him...."

PART ONE

The Prelude & Fugue

CHAPTER 1

London, April 23, 1884
Six Days Earlier

Langsford was bored. He tugged the corner of his stylish moustache as he rode in the carriage with his guests. A tall, handsome gentleman, his dark beard was neat and trim. Nearly twenty-two, he was an aristocrat, wealthy, and well-educated.

He knew his one companion, former school-chum Heinrich, was also bored because he sat and stared straight ahead, looking at nothing.

Youth and boredom—a delectable combination for trouble, but neither of them thought about that on such a lovely spring day.

They, along with Heinrich's father, *Reichsgraf Dieffenbacher*, rode in the coach from Langsford's home on Grosvenor Square, headed to London's financial district, the last place the younger two wished to be. The Reichsgraf, a mature, solid man with light-brown hair and piercing pale-blue eyes, was always a formidable presence. Guest or not, declining his order-like request to come along for the day wasn't an option. The young men sat in stilted silence.

Pulling up in front of the Bank of London, Pelham, their driver, expertly halted the pair of blacks, their hooves dancing on the cobblestones while Graf Dieffenbacher got out. "I'll be a while. Wait here," he ordered. He turned and confidently strode toward the massive bank.

As soon as the older Prussian disappeared through the tall embellished doors, Langsford exchanged glances with Heinrich, who looked dashing in his expensively tailored suit.

Langsford prompted his friend. "Let's escape—what say?"

"Yes! Anything!"

They both bolted from the carriage, pent up energies propelling them.

"Wait for us, Pelham," Langsford called up to his driver. "We need to stretch our legs."

"I have no doubt, m'lord," Pelham replied with the hint of a grin.

The two headed to cross Threadneedle Street, surrounded by banks of stone opulence that held their stoic wealth, standing firm and strong in the financial district that anchored the world's economy. Heinrich, clean shaven, tall and lean, took in a big breath of fresh air and sighed, "I don't care a whit about finance, but even walking here is better than sitting in a blasted carriage. I'd rather be astride a horse than have one pull me about."

"You always have. I prefer my feet on the ground, not my seat in a saddle."

"Of course you do. And poetry and anything with 'artistic merit,'" Heinrich teased. They worked their way through the maze of fancy broughams and barouche carriages, and paused for a passing phaeton. There were few merchant wagons on this financial street and even their elegant five-glass landau had failed to stand out among the many fine vehicles. They hurried and dodged forward, arriving safely on the other side amidst men in top hats and derbies.

"Let's go to Leadenhall Market," Langsford suggested. "The decrepit old place has been restored and now it's famous. Food, shops of all kinds, and a decent pub. All covered with a roof."

"All under one roof? It's that small?" They turned up Cornhill Street.

"Hardly. It's huge. You can find a quick gift for your mother there in one of the shops so we have an excuse for being there; then we'll get a pint or two to kill time while we wait for your father."

"I don't want to think about *Mutter* or anything in Prussia."

"You're in a mood. Like a woman with the vapors."

"You should know about moods, with your sensitivities," Heinrich retorted with a laugh.

"Not to mention my delightful vice of investing sterling, you might remember." Langsford laughed at himself. "But soon, you will need to be completely without sin yourself, so now is the time for fun and a few pints."

"Don't remind me," Heinrich groaned.

At Gracechurch Street, they turned right and spotted Leadenhall just up ahead. Entering the immense marketplace, Heinrich looked up. The roof structure towered over the throngs of merchants and buyers, sheltering an entire intersection and beyond of two streets. Arched high above their heads, the "roof" was wrought ironwork with glass panes bouncing jeweled light. Turning full circle while he gazed upward, Heinrich pointed. "*Sapperlot!* Look at that!"

Not yet lit, for it was the middle of the day, the gas lamps hung suspended from the great height of the ceiling, each throwing dancing sunbeams from their six panes of beveled glass.

A young boy in dirty overalls and cap pushed a heavy crate on a two-wheeled wooden dolly. "Make way! Make way," he cried from behind the rattling load.

Langsford and Heinrich leapt up on the sidewalk where the

market shops lined a seemingly endless street that curved left. At small tables, their linens draping to the pavement, one lady read her book with gloved hands while others sat sipping tea or nibbling pastry. In the middle of the street, vendor carts stopped here and there to sell their wares.

Shoppers, unlike the serious businessmen in the financial district only blocks away, exhibited lively energy, eager to get the freshest meat, newest bauble, or gossip from the next vendor. The two men passed a window of upside-down pheasants dangling beside freshly plucked ducks. Men laughed in the open doorway of the Lamb Tavern pub.

"Let's grab a tankard or two when we leave," Heinrich suggested, peering inside.

"That's what I had in mind. I haven't been up this far. See the sign on that millinery? Even the Queen shops at stores here." Langsford pointed across the street to a small, pretty storefront opposite them, boasting a sign that read, By Appointment to Her Majesty the Queen. "Let's get your mother a hat pin or scarf. Then to the pub!"

Crossing to the right side of the street, they entered the open door in the maroon-and-cream storefront. Once inside, Heinrich removed his top hat, letting his eyes adjust to the dimmer light. Surrounded by colorful displays of shawls, feathers, and hats, he wove his way around the merchandise, boot heels clicking on the wooden floor until he arrived at the counter. He placed his hat on the glass counter, looking down at the merchandise on display ... then a girl's voice said hello.

Heinrich looked up and saw her.

She was beautiful and young. She had dark hair, and green eyes, and that wonderful English coloring—a light peaches-and-cream complexion set off by her crisp white high-necked shirtwaist, a brooch at her neck.

He loved her the moment he saw her, completely unaware that this meeting was the catalyst for everything that lay ahead.

CHAPTER 2

Leadenhall Market, London

"Good day, sir," the shop girl greeted. "May I be of assistance?" Her eyes sparkled as she spoke.

Heinrich's knees wanted to buckle. Her soft voice was as beautiful as she was. Quickly he looked back down at the counter and slightly shook his head.

"Yes, miss." Langsford's round voice filled the small shop. "We are in need of a hat pin or scarf as a gift for his dear mother, a countess back home in Prussia. I suggested a nice British trinket."

Heinrich did not hear what his friend was saying. He had stopped thinking and only felt his heart thumping.

"Of course, gentlemen." The shop girl sorted through several scarves and picked up a deep blue silk scarf to show. "Do you know if she prefers blue? That is my favorite color. This is a very beautiful silk."

Heinrich, recovering from his initial reaction, looked at her, marveling at her green eyes, and asked, "What is your name?"

"I beg your pardon?"

"Your name. What is it?"

"Anna Boardman." She blushed, making her English complexion even more beautiful with her green eyes and dark hair.

Heinrich placed his hand on top of hers as she held the scarves on the counter. He felt the need to touch her, to reassure her in some fashion. She did not pull her hand away, although he expected her to. He watched her catch her breath and blush.

"My dear girl," Langsford behind him said. "I apologize for his lack of manners. I do." The lord then turned to Heinrich. "You shouldn't flirt. You've embarrassed the poor thing."

Heinrich did not break his gaze from Anna, or acknowledge Langsford.

"Will you have tea with me, Miss Boardman?" Heinrich's tone was a blend of imploring and demanding.

She stood there, her hand still under his. "I am afraid I cannot leave the shop, sir." She paused to catch her breath while she looked down at the counter, at his large hand encompassing hers that still held the blue silk scarf she'd intended to show him. Quickly she added, "While I am honored by your invitation, I must decline." Then she looked up at him, her green eyes melting his heart.

"I'm Heinrich, or Henry to you British," he belatedly introduced himself. "And this is my dear friend, Lord Langsford. I apologize for being bold, but I am not in London for long." He paused. He had gone too far to retreat now. He picked up her hand in both of his. She looked back down at the now abandoned scarf. "I would like to have tea with you. I am a well-behaved gentleman, am I not, Langsford?" He asked without looking at his friend.

"That he is, Miss Boardman. Most of the time," Langsford laughed without Heinrich or Anna noticing.

As Heinrich held her hand, she looked at him directly for a mere moment. Quickly looking down again, she suggested with hesitation, "I suppose I might walk with you briefly this evening after I close the shop. You are, after all, a visitor to London, so it would be proper for me to tell you about our city." She took a large breath, while he was holding his. "In fact, if you would be so kind, you could walk me to the underground railway. Of course it would only be proper that your friend accompany us. I would be uncomfortable without a chaperone." She gently withdrew her hand, picked up the scarf, and folded it, then replaced it back inside the counter. "I close the shop at six sharp." She stood silent, standing quietly behind the counter, her trembling hands clasped behind her.

Heinrich picked up his hat, then took two steps backwards from the counter. "Fine. I shall be here to escort you to your train." He half bowed, turned, and headed for the door while putting his hat on. Langsford, puzzled, looked back and forth between the girl and his friend, then followed Heinrich out the door.

None of them realized what trouble they were headed for.

CHAPTER 3

Leadenhall Market, London

Walking back through the market, Langsford was baffled. "What are you doing? You can't meet that shop girl later."

"Indeed I shall."

"Just what do you think you'll do? Gentlemen socialize with ladies. They carouse with ladies of the evening. She is neither!" Across the street, a round-faced green grocer was selling cabbages to an old woman in a tattered scarf. Heinrich watched them rather than meet Langsford's eyes. The shopper waited while the man wiped mud off the green heads and onto his apron before carefully placing them in her sack. "Why flirt if you have no ill-intentions?"

"It's not as you suggest. I'm honorable. Forthcoming. Direct."

"There are other ways to describe you."

Heinrich looked directly at him. "Yes, but I have never seen such a beautiful woman."

Langsford laughed and shook his head. He couldn't deny that. "Thank God I don't have a weakness for women."

"And yet, ironically, you are the one now married," he chuckled as they walked toward the front of the market and Gracechurch Street, drinks at the pub long forgotten. Fixated on his conversation with Anna, Heinrich continued. "Did you hear what she said? We can escort her to the …"

"The Met. The underground train."

"Yes, I shall walk with her there."

"I think not."

A vendor in shirt sleeves and suspendered trousers hawked pans as they passed.

"What? Of course I will."

"Why would you even venture ... and your father?"

"Forget him. Forget the future. Today I'm a visitor and she is duty-bound to show me London." He beamed at his flawless argument.

"Because you are a visitor ...?"

"Yes."

"And you know she wants to show you London."

"Indeed. She does. She said so."

A few doors down, a restaurant's new special advertised itself with its wafting odor of fish and chips.

"What would your father say about this?"

"Nothing if he does not know."

"That's how it is?"

"That's how it always is. Works best. I do something; he yells at me afterward then goes about his life."

An aproned fish monger called out his catches of the day. The wooden wheel of the flower girl's cart clunked on the cobble-stones as they waited for her to pass. "Hardly a serene life."

They exited the market and crossed Gracechurch Street, dodging wagons and carts.

"My life with *Vater* has never been serene." Heinrich stopped walking. "So it is settled, then? You'll be my chaperone at six? She won't go without you as a chaperone. She said as much."

"Apparently you need me."

"As my host, you said yourself it was your obligation to show me a good time."

"You twist my words, friend."

"Did you not say just that this morning?"

"Yes." Langsford sighed. He knew he'd lost the argument.

"As you say, 'there it is.'"

Langsford pursed his lips and pulled the tip of his moustache. "Mock me, do, but I have a suspicion you would go anyhow, without me. Heaven only knows what type of trouble you'd find yourself in if I were to leave you to your own devices."

"Imagine the trouble you would be in if I had left you to ... well ... *your* own ... devices."

"So you won't let that go, will you?"

"Not when it suits me. What are friends for?" he teased.

"It's okay for you to get muddled up with a girl, your soon-to-be forbidden fruit, and yet I can never taste my own?"

"Seems as though you are correct. The world is unfair."

"That it is." Langsford shook his head. "I give up. Six o'clock it is."

"Excellent!" Heinrich grinned widely as they walked up Gracechurch Street toward Threadneedle.

"Slow down. Slow down." Langsford tossed his hands in the air. "My legs do not stride as long as yours."

"That is because they are short," Heinrich laughed.

"They are long enough to touch the ground," Langsford retorted. "And going fast will not make six o'clock come any faster."

CHAPTER 4

Leadenhall Market, London

Perplexed, Anna Boardman watched as the two gentlemen left her shop. Typically only ladies were her customers; rarely a man. At sixteen, she knew better than to allow a gentleman to flirt in the shop. She tried to tell herself to feel indignant, to be insulted, but in fact she felt quite the opposite. She was flattered, honored, and rather enjoyed feeling flushed as her heart raced. She felt as though she were floating off the floor.

Marriage and boys. Topics she and her girlfriends always chattered on about. Since she had no dowry and her prospects were slim, she had realized early on she might well end up an old maid and need to support herself. Still, she dreamed that someday a handsome man would come courting.

Dreams or not, she was practical and had learned enough at school to be able to work quite competently as a shop girl. For four years, finishing school at age twelve, she'd worked in various shops, helping to put merchandise on the shelves, fold clothing, and serve customers. A year ago the owner of this fine millinery shop had hired her, giving her a great deal of responsibility, including decorating hats. She was very grateful for the chance to succeed as a salesgirl and to work in the preeminent Leadenhall Market. Plus, there were many decent men working in and around the area who would make good husbands. She might eventually

be courted by a green grocer's son or a cab driver. Serious courting; not flirting.

Talking with Henry felt like more than flirting. There was
something honest and sincere about his demeanor and words;
much more than a wink or a whistle. Oh Mercy! What was she
doing? She reviewed the scene over in her mind.

His name was Heinrich. He was tall, with brown hair and the
deepest blue eyes she'd ever seen. He'd touched her hand, shocking her. His touch, his gentle touch on her hand. Even though his
presence made her heart pound, he made her feel safe. There was
something about him ... he was so confident. Capable.

After Henry and his friend—a lord no less!—had left the shop,
and without even buying the blue silk scarf, she found herself
a bit peeved. Worried for some reason. Then it struck her that
perhaps they had come from a pub and were just pulling a prank,
teasing her.

For the rest of the day the incident bothered her. She convinced herself that no true gentleman would in fact speak to a
mere shop girl like her, let alone wish to escort her to a train. She
realized she wouldn't be seeing either of them again. They never
intended to return. Disappointment swept over her.

As the day wore on, the entire situation grated. By mid-after-
noon she was absolutely indignant and angry at herself for falling
for their tomfoolery. Imagine! She would just have to be on her
guard when gentlemen, or any men, came into the shop. She could
not let them disrupt her days.

CHAPTER 5

Leadenhall Market, London

Outside the millinery shop, Anna turned the key in the lock just as a coach pulled up. She spun toward the sound of horse hooves and saw Henry leap from the carriage. Surprised, she froze in her footsteps, dropping the key from her hand.

Quickly Henry was by her side, picking it up. "*Ach*, my lovely Anna," he breathed. *My lovely Anna*, she heard. Her heart skipped a beat. He put the key in her hand, and she simply dropped it in her drawstring purse without looking.

She glanced over at the open carriage and saw the other Englishman who nodded with a wave and a lopsided grin. Looking back at Heinrich, she tucked a tiny lock of stray hair under her bonnet.

"I am here to escort you to your 'Met' train." Heinrich offered his arm, which she simply stared at, still unable to move. He took her hand and placed it on his arm. "*Kommen Sie*, let's walk. This direction?" Anna looked down at her hand on his arm and nodded, letting him guide her down the street toward the market's exit.

She stopped two doors down beside a shuttered book shop already closed for the day, finding her voice. "I'm surprised you came." She smiled, looking up at him as her shawl slipped off her puffy sleeves. She tried to grab the end and missed, but Henry caught it and gently lifted the shawl back into place.

"I said I would and with a chaperone, just as you requested." He gestured toward the coach, grinning from ear to ear. They started walking again. "You thought we wouldn't come?"

"I thought you were teasing." With this confession she glanced up at him and saw his dark-blue eyes looking at her. Her stomach flipped and she immediately looked away.

"Never about seeing you." He smiled.

She laughed from relief as well as embarrassment, feeling awkward. *This is not proper*, she thought. *Oh, but I want him to like me. No. I have to tell him this is improper for us to walk ....* This was a predicament she did not know how to handle.

Smiling, he reassured her. "Miss Boardman, I apologize for upsetting you. My intentions are honorable." It was as though he read her mind.

"I believe you, your lordship." She glanced over at Lord Langsford who sat squarely in the carriage and nodded again when he saw her look. The driver held the horses under tight rein, keeping the coach close behind, following as they left the shelter of the Leadenhall Market's famous roof. The finest shops were in Leadenhall itself. Lesser shops circled outside the newly designed marketplace, offering cheap merchandise or older meat and poultry. They passed a green grocer still hustling to gather his displays of food from under his awning.

He chuckled again. "Call me Henry. I like my name in English and am bored by titles."

"Henry," she said softly.

As they walked closer to the Cannon Street Station, the street snarled with cabs, omnibuses, and other carriages. Pedestrians pressed forward on the sidewalks, anxious to get home to the London suburbs. Anna was normally one of them, rushing to her home in Bermondsey, but tonight she was content to walk on

Henry's arm. He steered them skillfully out of the way of rushing men and women.

"It's quite busy. People can shop at many places around here."

"You were going to purchase a silk scarf from me," she reminded, a teasing tone in her voice. "I do hate to miss a sale."

"I confess. I completely forgot about the scarf."

"For your mother, too."

"*Ja*, my mother. I forgot *her* as well!" he teased back. "Then I will buy it, but not for her. For *you*, because it matches your eyes," he laughed, his laughter contagious.

"The scarf is blue and my eyes are green."

He stopped abruptly, jostled by other pedestrians, then turned her to peer closer. "Yes, they are indeed the most beautiful green. You mean the scarf is not green?"

"The scarf is deep blue—more like *your* eyes, your lordship."

"Henry," he corrected, then drew her beside him again as they continued walking. "You said blue is your favorite color. If it matches *my* eyes, then you can remember me when you look at the scarf. That settles it. I shall come by tomorrow and purchase it."

"Then I shall sell it to you." They chuckled together.

"Where do you catch your train?"

"The station is just a ways down. I live across the Thames in Bermondsey. It is too far to walk but it is a short ride on the train."

"Ah. It's fascinating that here you have so many trains in the city itself. In Prussia we have trains from town to town, to the big cities, but I have never seen a city with so many trains just to go from one part to another."

"Well, London *is* a large city. It might even be the largest city in the world. Most of us Londoners have no carriage, so we take the omnibus or a train to work." Still in a humorous mood, she continued, "After all, I would not want to live above the shop in

Leadenhall Market." She described herself hanging out the first-story window, hollering down to the ground floor that she would be at work in five minutes.

Henry laughed with her. She was glad when he laughed—it sounded nice. "I've never worked, so I must confess that I don't know anything about it. I began school at thirteen—had governesses until then—so learning was my work, I suppose."

"That's curious. I finished school at twelve. Will you always be in school? Surely you will have a trade—no, of course not! I so apologize!" She blushed at her huge faux pas, remembering who he was. Her stomach knotted. "You're a nobleman—your mother a countess!"

They stopped beside a building just before Cannon Street, before the main crush of hurrying commuters. The carriage halted, blocking traffic, forcing cab drivers to yell obscenities. She looked again at Langsford and saw he was leaning back in his seat, top hat low over his eyes, arms folded as though he dozed. Heinrich took both her hands in his, regaining her attention. "I don't want to talk about my mother. It's you I want to talk about. Plus, I'm not anxious to take you to the train and say goodbye."

She dare not admit she did not want the walk to end either. Could it be that he indeed found her attractive? A commoner? Would that even be possible? "We should go or I may miss it," she suggested, suddenly wishing she weren't walking at all with him. She then remembered her justification for allowing the gentleman to escort her. "Do you have questions about London? You *are* the visitor."

"No. You have answered them all."

"You've not asked any."

"I already know what's important. I know your name is Anna, and you work in that shop back there. What else could be important about London?" She giggled, and he smiled. "Then tell me what else I should know."

She talked about the society ladies who came into the shop to order special items for the balls and events during the society's high season in London. She had listened to them talk about this lord or that lady, she admitted, and was up on all the latest fashions. She recounted stories from the London newspapers and asked him if he had English books. "Have you read Dickens? I love his stories—we read a lot at home." He listened intently while she spoke. She was excited for him to learn about her London world. "Sometimes we go to Hyde Park for a picnic, or visit Westminster and listen to Big Ben—that's a huge clock tower. Someday I would love attend the Royal Albert Hall. It is so beautiful! There is just so much here in London. I do hope you have a most enjoyable visit, my lord," she concluded. They were at the station.

"Wait!" Henry said so sharply she startled.

"Instead of taking the train," he offered, "we should drive you all the way home in the carriage. My friend Langsford is with us, so it is all aboveboard and proper."

She tried to protest. "Oh dear, no. That would not be proper—not at all." Yet she stood still. She lost her argument to Henry, because of his smile. She lost her argument to herself because of her heart.

CHAPTER 6

No. 12 Grosvenor Square, London

The next morning, young Langsford stood in his foyer, unable to ignore the tirade echoing from his upstairs library. He wasn't sure what to do. He was embarrassed and sad as well. He knew Heinrich's father had a vile temper. This morning that temper was unleashed yet again on Langsford's former school chum, and it was his fault.

The words tumbled down the staircase.

"*Du machst uns Schande!* You bring shame upon us. You defy all that our family stands for!" Graf Dieffenbacher raged above.

Langsford looked out the opened door where the day threatened to drizzle and tugged the corner of his moustache.

He'd tried to be a good host for his guests, even with his bride away visiting her sister. Arising early that morning, he had dressed in his worsted wool morning coat with lighter gray trousers, anticipating a casual brunch of fine food and lively conversation: talk about Prussia, the economy, and news from the financial district where Heinrich's father had been the day before. Instead, he faced a warring father and son. He never argued with anyone. Discord made him uneasy.

Langsford attempted his best to ignore the uproar above. His responsibility as a host was to make everyone happy. Obviously he'd failed, for the Dieffenbachers were leaving London immediately, their trip canceled.

And it was all his fault.

Well aware that his friend's future not only loomed in front of him, but over him, oppressing him, Langsford, unfortunately, had managed to make everything worse for Heinrich, who had come to London not only to visit but also to attempt to change his father's mind and to alter the family's demands of him. None of that apparently mattered now, Langsford thought, listening to the yelling above. Heinrich would not be able to rationally converse with his father, at least not today from the sound of it.

His father stood inches from Heinrich, bellowing in his face about Heinrich's current misdeed. Calling upon the female commoner, Anna Boardman, was conduct completely unacceptable.

The usual serenity of the library, with its tall shelves of leather-bound books, was shattered by the Graf's rage. He spat his ire and his voice crescendoed in the high-ceilinged room. "You are stupid—stupid—to try something like this!" Heinrich refused to wince when his father's sausage-tinged breath smacked his nostrils. "How dare you defy me! You have no thoughts in that empty head of yours!"

Heinrich glared back at the older man's contorted expression and watched the bulging vein in his forehead turn purple. The Graf's anger pummeled Heinrich, but his words failed to penetrate. He stood defiant, immobile, and silent, refusing to flinch. He simply endured this barrage as he often did. At six feet plus, he was a more handsome version of his stately patriarch: taller, with darker hair and deep-blue eyes that were sad.

His father turned and marched out of their host's library, heels resounding on the parquet floor, anger echoing in his wake. Heinrich remained where he stood, staring straight ahead as though his father had not left. After several long heartbeats, he exhaled a drawn-out breath, then turned and walked over to sit on the velvet horsehair settee near the tall windows. Leaning back with his hand gripping the maple arm, he let his knees shake as his heart raced.

Heinrich had always tried to oppose his elders. He knew he'd been a willful child and an even more defiant youth. Nearly an adult, maturing had not erased these traits. His father used to be able to prevent his son's disobedience because his demanding will overpowered Heinrich's ability to defy. Not this time. Meeting Anna had awakened something deep within him. He had always feared his father, but now? He didn't know. He felt confused.

The young man sighed, leaning forward to place his head in his hands, and wondered if he would ever be able to break loose of his father's—and family's—demands.

Hearing the rat-a-tat of shoes descending the mahogany staircase, Langsford turned to find the Reichsgraf coming down to the foyer. "We shall be going now, my friend. I must apologize for my son and his crassness. *Gut,*" the Prussian said, looking outside. "I see the footman is nearly finished strapping on the luggage."

Langsford turned to observe the last of the bags being buckled onto his landau in front of No. 12.

"How Heinrich talked you into being a part of this mess, I have no idea, for you have good sense. I know how beguiling he can be, however, so I've no fault with you."

Langsford pursed his lips and nodded silently. He believed he was to blame for not stopping Heinrich when he had a chance and knew the Graf did as well, but fine manners dictated he dare not voice his true opinion. There were layers to social decorum, and this abrupt departure was an overt message, the opposite of the Graf's words. It was intended to be an affront to Langsford, their young host.

His driver, Pelham, would take them to the train station as soon as all was loaded. Still early, there was not much traffic around Grosvenor Square. The carriage was the only vehicle nearby besides a few hansom cabs.

"When my son manages to come down, please inform him that I await in the coach."

"I regret you must leave so soon. I'd welcome it if you would reconsider …"

"*Nein*. The boy must learn, and I do not want him making a fool of us on foreign soil."

"There it is, then. I understand," Langsford replied, although he knew it was far more complicated. "Please do return any time with Heinrich." He wanted to add something favorable about his friend, for they had a firm bond between them, but he held his tongue. His instincts told him to say no more.

"I am, as always, delighted to come to London; however, Heinrich will not be back. This was to be his last trip before…. . He won't be returning." The Prussian's tone was firm and his words clipped more than usual. Quickly his demeanor changed. "And you, of course, may come to our estate any time. In fact, I wish you would. Visit with me and Gerhard, who is closer to your age anyhow. I always enjoy offering you our Prussian hospitality."

"Indeed, I shall plan a trip to the Rhineland soon, while Heinrich and Gerhard are still home."

A quick little bow between them, and the Graf turned on his heel and trotted down the steps toward the waiting landau, leaving Langsford feeling guilty for his part in this. He'd thought it had been merely a harmless flirtation with the shop girl, something

Heinrich might briefly indulge in before proceeding with his life's plan; a flirtation that Langsford himself would never be able to do. He was wrong.

Neither of them could indulge, but for very different reasons.

CHAPTER 7

The English Channel

Heinrich's journey home to the Rhineland was excruciating. He had not wanted to leave Anna, but to return to her shop as he'd promised. She'd drawn him to her like a magnet does filings, and he wanted to cling to her. Never had he felt such attraction. But his father refused to listen. Furthermore, he hated leaving London and Langsford, who was more an older brother to him than his own. Langsford understood, especially now that he was married.

His father sat silent as their train traveled through England. At Dover they boarded the large steamboat that would take them across the English Channel. As they sailed leaving the white cliffs behind, Heinrich sat opposite the elder Dieffenbacher, not daring to speak, gazing out the porthole at the choppy waters. The boat pitched up and down, gray water churning swiftly along the hull, mirroring his mood while his mind struggled. Home. Prussia. The Rhineland where the Dieffenbacher family had emerged during medieval times as one of the landowning noble families, privileged, wealthy, and powerful.

A family with power, though he himself had none.

With the time in London cut short, this trip back was his best chance to try to broach the treacherous topic of his future, but now was not the time. His father sat reading his book, and interrupting wouldn't do. He needed to wait for his father to speak first. Excusing himself, he went out onto the deck where a misty breeze keenly buffeted his face and he inhaled the sharp salt air, remembering his yesterday in London ....

Heinrich found himself fascinated by Anna. Fresh, unpretentious, and unlike any girl he'd met either on the continent or in England. She was smart, direct, and lovely, with a sweet sense of humor. A commoner, without formal education, she floated on the outskirts of better society, keenly aware of the world to which she did not belong. Still, she had poise, spoke properly, and was well-read. There was nothing stiff or superficial about her. He wanted her presence to envelop him. He'd been ecstatic when she agreed to be driven home last evening.

He'd longed to sit beside her in the carriage, but being a gentleman, he sat instead beside the tobacco-scented Langsford, hardly his first choice. He watched as her gloveless hands nervously smoothed the folds of her black skirt. Oh! To hold one of those white hands, breathing in the smell of her perfume.

She accidentally knocked her drawstring purse to the floor and he picked it up for her, earning her smile. He thrilled how she looked around the inside of the carriage, its double top now closed. "This is so beautiful," she exclaimed. "To think my lady customers sit inside coaches like these, wearing my hats."

"You, as well as your hats, sit beautifully in this coach." Langsford grinned.

"That is sweet of you to say."

"He's just the chaperone. Ignore him. I'm your escort and I say you grace this carriage with your fine charm and beauty." Watching her take in this new experience gave him great joy.

"Thank you, m'lord."

"It's Henry to you."

"But you are titled. Your mother a countess. Could you explain your Prussian titles, my lord?"

Heinrich had felt the pit of his stomach lurch like the carriage he was sitting in. He did not wish to think about home. Not Germany, and certainly not Prussia. His escape to Great Britain was just a brief respite of what was to come. He'd forced himself to answer her question.

"My father has the title Reichsgraf, which is like your English count, and yes, that makes my mother a countess. *Karl der Große*, the Holy Roman Emperor, conferred the title on our family."

"He means Charlemagne," Langsford corrected.

"Charlemagne," Anna repeated, nodding her head. "I've heard of him. France. I thought you were German, but you are French?" she asked, cocking her head to the left.

"Lord no!" Heinrich exclaimed; Langsford chortled.

"Karl der Große and Charlemagne. The same person," Langsford gasped between laughs as Heinrich pursed his lips and gave him a look.

"And you would have me, and poor Anna here, think of him as French when in fact—"

"It was the Frankish Kingdom ...." Langsford shrugged, winking at Anna, who seemed completely confused by the two of them. "The Rhineland was not always part of Prussia, Miss Boardman. It belonged to France when Charlemagne lived." Langsford chuckled with a wide grin.

"So you *were* French?"

Langsford chortled louder at Heinrich. "No one dared to make that observation before, my Prussian friend!" The Englishman was having too much fun.

Heinrich tossed him a look. "It was the *Frankenreich*, ole chum. Germany."

He then responded to Anna. "Ignore him. We've been Catholic in the Holy Roman Empire regardless of political rule. Today we are Catholic *and* German." He realized how little history she knew. His sister also had that adorable ignorance since history was not a subject taught to girls.

"I do know King Henry VIII didn't like the Catholic Church so he started our Church of England." She smiled, attempting to continue the conversation.

Her white high-necked blouse and black skirt did not diminish her loveliness. He tried not to stare at her, but couldn't help himself. He watched as she turned to include Langsford in their conversation as well. How polite she was. Though uneducated in the fine graces of a lady, her genuine sincerity and kind manners nonetheless added to her natural charm.

He was staring and Langsford elbowed him, forcing him to continue the conversation. "We've been Catholic long before your King Henry VIII. The Reichsgraf even voted in the General Assembly of the Holy Roman Empire."

"Is this General Assembly—is it like the House of Lords?"

Thoroughly amused by this time, Langsford interrupted before Heinrich could answer. "Suffice it to say that the Dieffenbachers are an influential family." He smiled and winked at Heinrich. "And politics is not a topic for the ladies, I should remind you."

She put her hand up to her chest and gasped, "Oh how important you and your father are, your lordship." She bowed her head quickly as if in a curtsy, dissolving Heinrich's heart again.

"It's Henry," he corrected, "and the title goes to my older brother, Gerhard."

She smiled at him, making him feel warm inside. He never wanted to leave her.

But he had left her. His father, and tradition, had prevailed again. The spray from a large wave misted his face as the steamer ploughed through the choppy waves, taking him farther away from her. Forbidden by his father to send Anna a message, Heinrich had left without explanation or apology.

He shivered as the steamboat rose and fell, the cold sea air slapping his cheeks, and bringing him back to the present on the English Channel. The fog was lifting and the dark line of the French coast was now emerging on the horizon.

CHAPTER 8

London

Unaware that Henry's trip was cut short, Anna happily arrived at the millinery shop the next morning. Henry had promised to buy the scarf, so she set it on the counter, loosely rolled to avoid creases. Unsure when her new friend might arrive, she kept looking over at the door, hoping to see the young Prussian every time it opened.

The morning went slowly with few patrons. She refastened ribbons and feathers on the hats in the window. She selected a recently arrived broad-brimmed hat and began to trim it with a copper ostrich plume and netting. By lunchtime when he had not arrived, she chose to forego her packed meal and remain at the counter, not wanting to be found with her mouth full of food when he walked through the door.

The afternoon dragged on, although there were more customers. Ladies needed spring hats or tiaras to match a new gown for a social occasion during the Season. She presented a cheerfulness she did not feel as she showed them her merchandise. She forced warm smiles when they handed her their engraved cards so she would know where to send their purchases.

Her normal world was small and safe. She helped society ladies select the proper hat, brooch, or scarf. She listened to them talking to one another about various social engagements of the Season, and gossip about one lady or another. Other than what she heard in the shop and read about the Queen and Prince Albert, Anna had no experience regarding the rich and powerful upper classes beyond bits of fashion. She was an observer on the sidelines of a more elegant society which she could only watch from afar.

Listening to Henry in the carriage the evening before had been fascinating. *Imagine going so far back in time that Germany was a Frankish Kingdom and they gave away titles to families. Did the British do the same thing a long time ago?* Her mind swirled.

The clock ticked on. By five, her heart stopped singing. The Prussian gentleman had not shown up. She was peeved with herself for ever thinking he would.

Upset, she decided to do what she had never done before. She organized the books and deliveries quickly, tidied up the counter for the umpteenth time, put on her bonnet and shawl, and then walked out, locking the door behind her. Early. It was five thirty.

Unlike yesterday, there were no sharp hoof beats on the cobblestones behind her. No deep voice calling her name. Tears welled up in her eyes as she left with her head down. She walked so quickly that she could see the tips of her toes swinging out from under her long skirt.

Leaving the underground Met, she hurried passed the new Bermondsey Town Hall and then turned down a narrow side street. Her home looked like all the others, tied together with repetitive front doors and yards. Though a few stout structures from Elizabethan times still endured, the old slums around them were recently demolished, replaced with these modest row houses that dominated this solid working-class neighborhood. She opened her gate and ran up the walk to unlock the front door, rushing into her small, tidy home.

Agitated and disappointed, she untied her bonnet, tossing it aside on the little table by the door, and tore off her shawl, which landed on the back of a parlor chair. She went into the kitchen to brew a pot of tea, banging the copper tea kettle down on the range. Waiting for it to boil, she thought about her life.

Here in the sanctuary of home, she shared a room with her childhood friend, Charlotte, whose aunt and uncle rented the structure. They had kindly taken her in when her parents died of typhoid six years earlier. Both girls were extremely fortunate and grateful to have such stable and healthy living conditions. Because of her job, she was able to pay her portion of the rent and other necessities, so she should be happy, but she wasn't. *Am I destined to be a spinster?* She had no genuine prospects. Even the green grocer's son was courting a pretty teacher whose working-class father offered a dowry.

The kettle gave in, its lid dancing with steam. Using a dish towel, she held the handle while she poured the boiling water over tea leaves at the bottom of the pewter pot that had been her mother's. Setting the kettle to the back of the range, she placed the hand-knitted tea cozy over the pot to keep it warm while the tea steeped.

I am stupid to be upset just because a ridiculous flirt failed to show today, she scolded herself. At the same time, her inner voice told her how kind, wonderful, and smart Henry was.

The front door creaked open and Charlotte entered. "Hallo, dearie. You home already? 'Tis quite early for you."

"Lottie! I am so glad you're home. Come. Please. Have tea with me."

"Is Auntie about?" Charlotte came into the small kitchen, gently placing her shawl and bonnet on the wall hooks. She wore a simple dress with a high lace collar and lace cuffs on her long sleeves. Her reddish-brown hair frizzed out from her bun and her freckled face and impish nose made her appear like a young school girl even though she was sixteen, the same age as Anna. She turned to the exposed shelves and took down two cups and saucers.

"I haven't seen her," Anna replied. "Perhaps she's at the butchers or green grocers. It's too soon for Uncle." Anna instantly dismissed the topic of who was where. "Oh Lottie, I must talk to someone, for I'm simply beside myself. I just—I don't—"

Charlotte stared at Anna. "You're upset! Come. Sit. I'll pour and we'll talk."

She ushered Anna onto the closest ladder-back chair at the table, then opened the tin-fronted cupboard where they kept the small white milk pitcher. Sniffing it, she set it on the table with the sugar, and sat down. "What's happened? You were utterly happy this morning."

Anna stared at the sugar bowl in front of her. "Yes. I was happy until Henry didn't …."

Charlotte poured a bit of milk into the bottom of each cup, followed by tea.

"He didn't what?"

"He didn't come." Anna covered her mouth with her hand.

"But you had such a lovely time driving home last evening."

Anna mindlessly stirred the sugared tea that Lottie had placed in front of her.

"It sounded all so romantic." Lottie sighed, holding her teacup midway between saucer and her lips.

"I am far too trusting. I am stupid, stupid, stupid!" Anna snapped.

"Who is stupid?" Aunt Bess called from the front doorway, returning from market. Bess Miller, a middle-aged woman with a thick waist, sparkling blue eyes, and gray hair, entered the kitchen carrying a knitted string bag bulging with a cabbage, four potatoes, and a lamb shank wrapped in paper, all of which she emptied onto the counter. Folding up the string bag, she turned to the young girls sitting at the table, raising an eyebrow at their silence. "So now, just who is stupid and why?"

"Let me pour you some tea, Aunt Bess." Lottie got up to reach for a cup and saucer.

"Sit down, girl. I'll get my own cup, thank you. And while I do, I'll have you both tell me why dear Anna is stupid, and why both of you are wearing these two pitiful faces."

Aunt Bess took down her cup and saucer, and sitting at the table, poured in some milk and tea. As she stirred her cup, she looked expectantly at the girls, first at Lottie, then at Anna.

Reluctantly, Anna told the entire story. "You see, Aunt Bess, I so wanted to see him again, but now I am unsure of his intentions."

Lottie, ever the romantic optimist, chimed in. "Maybe Henry meant to come by and, well, the carriage broke a wheel."

"Hardly, girl." Aunt Bess shook her head. "First, Anna, you should never have accepted that invitation. No gentleman is the German; *that* is for sure." She paused and sipped her tea. "Then riding in a carriage with two men like a ..." She left her sentence unfinished.

"But Aunt Bess, Henry walked with me, while the landau; it was truly a landau with glass windows, it was oh, so beautiful—"

"None of that matters," Aunt Bess interrupted. "Do you think that wealthy gentlemen have nothing but honorable intentions? Do not think that for an instant," she sternly scolded. "It's best you put it out of your mind." With that she stood up. "Now you both help me with supper before your uncle Maxwell comes home."

CHAPTER 9

No. 12 Grosvenor Square, London

While Heinrich sailed back to France, Langsford remained uneasy. His bride had yet to return from visiting her sister in the north and he was at loose ends. He missed Heinrich, the only person with whom he could just be himself without anything to hide. He walked with his Border Collie, Tweed, through the mews that led to his cobbledstoned stable yard behind No. 12. There he found his coachman grooming one of the black horses tied to a post adjacent the tack room.

"Good afternoon, m'lord." Pelham stopped brushing to greet his employer. In his early thirties, Pelham wore stained, green cloth pants; a white broadcloth shirt with rolled up sleeves showing his muscled forearms, and a brown leather vest that stretched across his broad chest. Clean shaven, his warm smile showed genuine pleasure to have company.

"Turned into a beautiful day." Langsford wished his mood matched.

"Indeed it did. Thought to take advantage of this weather to give the ponies a bit of a thorough grooming."

Langsford chuckled at the word *ponies*, for the carriage horses were tall, fine-boned animals, and with well-sculpted muscles, quite the opposite of a round pony. "They look shiny and sleek to me."

"Well, m'lord, they are black and they show every bit of dust and dirt." Pelham went back to his meticulous work, a brush in each hand swiping one quickly after the other to flick any dust specks from the gleaming coat. "It's the groom's day off, but if I waited 'til tomorrow, the weather mightn't be as nice."

"I should feel badly for liking only blacks since they are more work, but I do like the looks of them, and these boys are a good team."

"Not complaining here, m'lord." He whisked the brushes against each other to clean them. "In fact, I do feel proud driving 'em. A bit spirited at times, but nothin' I can't handle."

"You do well, Pelham." He reached down and unsnapped the leash from Tweed, who promptly began to circle the horse.

"There he goes, thinkin' the horse is a sheep to herd."

"Yes. I suppose I should take him back to the estate where he can work again. His ribs from the cow kick have healed well."

"It was kind of you to bring him here while he mended," Pelham picked up a coarse rag and wiped the horse's face.

"The dog's a fine companion and someone to talk to," he laughed, "when I don't have Lady Regina or you around to complain to."

"Aye, I suppose, though I have yet to hear you complain, m'lord."

"Today may be the beginning." He pulled out a crude chair that sat just inside the tack room door. Brushing off some loose hay, he sat on the wobbly thing. Tweed moved so that he was directly opposite his master, the tied horse in between. "Tweed, that'll do. Come."

Reluctantly the dog gave up "herding" and came to sit by his master. Langsford scratched him behind his right ear.

Pelham leaned against the wall, arms crossed on his chest. He was muscular and fit. On several unfortunate occasions, he had come to the defense of his employer, warding off a dipper or two who were intent on lifting a pocket watch or money clip. On trips to the country estate in Kent, south of London, Pelham was adept at preventing dragsmen from cutting the luggage from the carriage. After Pelham's wife had been taken by illness in the bloom of life, the two men began to spend time together, and especially now, whenever Lady Regina was gone. An odd pairing, they enjoyed their unusual yet symbiotic relationship.

"I'm disappointed in myself, Pelham. I permitted Heinrich to go and get in serious trouble with his father."

"Without you, m'lord, Master Heinrich might have gotten into more trouble, and certainly it would not have been good for the young lass to be alone with him; so to my way of thinking, you did them both a huge favor."

"I had no idea how to stop him." He sighed. "And now, I've committed a faux pas and find there's nothing I can do." *I should have interfered*, he chastised himself, smoothing Tweed's fur. "There it is, then, boy." The dog listened intently. "I let Heinrich convince me with logic, but truth be told, it was seeing how he felt about her.... I gave in to my good friend and made a muck of it, didn't I, fella?" Tweed nosed his hand again, offering another opportunity for therapeutic petting.

"We were right there; you in the carriage with me drivin'."

"The problem is Heinrich's father was irate about it. It's my fault for letting him pursue mischief. I'm not able to reconcile myself to my own judgment."

"If the man is mad at his son, that be between those two, not yourself, if you don't mind my sayin'."

"I'm not sure ...."

"Because you never raised a son, if you don't mind me

saying something so personal. I've seen how my nephew's mother worries."

"It's no easy task, I'm sure. My father would agree, if he were alive today. Lady Regina could probably weigh in with her wise thoughts. She's a good woman and I'm fortunate to have found her."

"It's more difficult for gentlemen like you, having to select the proper lady and have society approve of your choice."

"I have Lord and Lady Stanley to thank for that. Did I not tell you the story?"

"Can't say that you have. Isn't Lord Stanley an earl?"

"Indeed. The Earl of Exeter, and a friend of my father's, whose wife, Lady Clementine, actually paired me with my future wife; a dinner where she seated me across from Lady Regina."

"These women are very clever."

"That they are. It's interesting, as lovely as my Regina is, I've never seen a more beautiful woman than the current Countess, Lord Stanley's second wife. Very gracious, Lady Clementine. She is the same age as Lady Regina; close friends—you would think she and my Regina were sisters. I shall be forever indebted to her for finding me my wife."

"A good wife is worth her weight in gold, I'd say. I was fortunate to find darlin' Margaret, a lady's maid, whose father approved of our match. She turned me into a man, she did." He looked down at his dusty boots.

"I remember her with great fondness, Pelham. A fine woman. You miss her a great deal, I know." Langsford had watched three years ago as his coachman struggled with grief after his wife was taken during the cholera epidemic. He'd turned to drink and neglected his duties. Langsford had hired another driver for a while, allowing Pelham to sort out his sorrow.

"I am grateful to you for keepin' me on when you shoulda fired me." The man looked back up, his eyes bright with held back tears.

Langsford's father had passed during the same epidemic, the loss a huge hole in his own life. He felt the grief every day as he moved through it while learning to handle all the responsibilities as the new lord of the estate, property and title combined. The last thing he would have done was dismiss any staff during that time.

"Nonsense. I would never have let you go. I understood. We were going through the same trial." He ruffled the dog's fur more. "I knew eventually you would sort it out."

"As you have managed as well, m'lord. I'm always proud to be in your employment." Clearing his throat, he abruptly changed the subject to the previous topic. "I'm sure Master Heinrich will find his way with his father. You did nothing wrong, and I apologize for expressing my thoughts on the matter."

"Of course not. I appreciate your opinion, for you were there."

"He is so smitten—he would have gone without us. Taken a hack or walked even. He's young and hot-blooded, he is. Like a young stud colt."

"That's an apt description." Langsford smiled. "Plus he's a stubborn Prussian." His smile faded as he stroked Tweed's head, still worried about his friend and knowing he could do nothing to help him with his father, or save him from his fate.

CHAPTER 10

France

As they docked in Calais, Heinrich watched the steamboat crew moor the vessel with massive rope lines, tying them to the pier. He felt he was tied just as securely to his own forced future.

The Graf assured their baggage was properly transferred to the correct train. They would change trains twice more, first in Lille, France, and again inside the German border at Thionville. The final leg, along the river Demichbach in its wooded valley, would be by coach to the Dieffenbacher estate. The entire trip from London took three to four or more days, depending on the unreliable French train schedule.

Sitting in the plush first-class compartment across from his father, Heinrich watched the French countryside through the dirt-speckled window as the train rattled and rocked rhythmically along its metal tracks. Fences whizzed by as he stared at nothing through the glass.

Finally the Graf spoke. "You fail me yet again." He shook his head in disappointment. A silence followed as his father sat back in his tapestried seat to light his ivory pipe, the train gently rocking. "I worry for the church," the Graf's tone had become soft and confidential.

Surprised, Heinrich turned from the window and faced his father, heartened by this change of mood. His father leaned forward, elbows on knees with unlit pipe in one hand, capturing

Heinrich's full attention with his passion. Heinrich met his father's piercing eyes full on, waiting.

"We owe God's Church our utmost devotion and—" His father sat up, making a fist in the air, "we shall always defend it. I and others in the Centre Party stopped Bismarck's *Kulturkampf* when he tried to cut the church off at the knees. You know all this. You grew up with our work in the Centre Party. We had no violence, no fighting. We stopped Bismarck with our *political* force."

Heinrich's youth was surrounded by this culture war as it unfolded. Bismarck had feared the church's power and he responded by passing anti-Catholic laws in Prussia. Men often came by their estate late at night to report on the imprisonment of priests and bishops. As a young boy, Heinrich would creep to the top of the stairs and listen to disturbing news about the parishioners' arrests as well. He'd recognize the names of those jailed—a family friend or a priest.

"No one ever stopped such an ugly movement as the Kulturkampf without war, but we Catholics did. *We* beat Bismarck."

Heinrich nodded. He had to admit that the Graf's influence was great, and when he had thrown his political weight into opposing Bismarck's policies, the Kulturkampf ended. The son had always been impressed. "It was a fine accomplishment, Vater." Heinrich also knew the popularity of the Catholic Church waned afterward, especially in Kröv and smaller towns. The Iron Chancellor may have backed down, but he had successfully weakened the church.

Perhaps now, Heinrich thought. *After all, with fewer churches, it needs fewer priests.* Heinrich felt a surge of hope with this small argument. He opened his lips to speak, but not quickly enough.

The older Prussian pointed his pipe stem for emphasis. "We are *not* done. The church was weakened throughout all those years.

Now more than ever, it is important *you* be ordained, Heinrich. The church needs to regain power until it is as strong in Prussia as it ever was."

Heinrich was seven when his father first told him he was to be a priest. "Our divine agreement was made between the Roman Catholic Emperor in the eighth century in exchange for our title. You, Heinrich, my second scion, will be our next priest. You are a link in our chain within the Catholic Church that *will never* be broken." At the time, he didn't understand, but as the years passed, the realization of his fate dawned on him, and the weight of this chain his father spoke of grew heavier. Inwardly Heinrich shuddered. The day was not far off now.

"Once you are a priest, son, I will see that you will be able to go on to be a great and powerful bishop. You are a *Dieffenbacher.*" His father sat up straight, his tone emphatic. Heinrich stiffened. "*You* will be powerful in the church. Pope Leo will be grateful. With your brother powerful in the army and later Parliament, the family title will soon be *Margrave,* or even *Herzog.* For all our efforts I will have led our family to higher rewards."

Heinrich's resilience drained. He knew anything he said now would not be heeded. His father had grand, ambitious plans that included him first in the role of priest, then ultimately bishop, and the title equivalent of duke, or earl, for himself, and ultimately Gerhard. Heinrich had no choice but to do as his father commanded him. As a Dieffenbacher, he was bound to his fate.

In resignation, Heinrich nodded assent. The elder Dieffenbacher sat back and lighted his pipe. "*Es ist gut.*" Smoke curled from both corners of his mouth as he puffed it to life.

Heinrich's pipe dreams went up in smoke. He'd permitted himself visions of returning to London and Anna, the requirements for his priesthood absolved by his vater. He saw himself as her husband, sitting across the table from her lovely presence, much the same as Langsford dined opposite the beautiful Lady Regina. He and Anna would walk arm in arm through a park while his heart sang. He'd envisioned his father understanding his love for this woman—a suitable allowance allotted to them. Living perhaps on a section of the family estate in a newly built mansion and driving into the local village for Sunday Mass; showing her what living the noble life meant. She would buy hats from someone else and fine dresses .... The sound of flipping pages brought him back to the present. His father was reading again, finished with their conversation. The mention of Anna had never come up. The issue of his priesthood, finalized.

Heinrich was defeated in spirit and soul. He would never lay eyes on Anna again.

CHAPTER 11

France and Prussia

Father and son sat in silence for hours on the second train while a landscape cluttered with windmills gently rolled past. Silently Heinrich counted them, lulled into a mindless stupor by the rhythm of the train.

Unwillingly, he thought of his brother who would be a military officer, destined afterward to enter the German parliament. Both positions were his birthright—a very different destiny mapped out for a very different man. Gerhard, the first born, was selfish, and seldom showed an interest in anyone else, especially Heinrich. There was, however, one exception.

His older sibling insisted he accompany a group of friends into the village of Flußbach. The Graf was gone from the estate for a few days and Gerhard knew they could sneak out after supper. "Whenever Pa-pa is gone, that is our chance."

Heinrich, always glad for adventure, joined them one night as they sat down at the local beer hall, steins foaming over. Sitting in the dark, cramped tavern, they laughed, joked, and drank ales, one right after another. The place was packed with noisy people along with loud festive accordion music that reverberated around the smoky room.

"Ah!" exclaimed Gerhard. "Here come some beauties." A round girl with nearly exposed bosoms laced tight within thin fabric walked by as several similarly attired girls wandered around other tables. Gerhard reached out and grabbed her by the wrist. She stopped, smiling at them all, pulling the already low bodice of her dress lower to show nearly her entire bulbous bosoms. Instantly, the young men began flirting with her, making lewd comments and sounds as she did a wiggle of her hips at them. Gerhard let go of her wrist, grabbed her waist, and pulled her onto his lap, kissing her fully on the mouth.

Heinrich expected her to pull away and slap him, but instead she kissed back. Gerhard's slightly inebriated entourage cheered him, clinking their beer steins, spilling ale on the plank table and quaffing so fast that more spilled onto their chins. Heinrich and the others watched as Gerhard began kissing the girl's neck, his hand kneading one of her breasts.

The girl leaned into Gerhard's groping hand, whispering into his ear, laughing. Then she abruptly stood up. "*Komm' mit.* Come outside and bring your friends." She smiled over her shoulder at the men sitting there.

Gerhard immediately stood up, inviting the others to join him. They laughed. "No, not that one," one answered.

"I shall wait for that blonde over there," replied another, "but take your brother. He needs to, for he will not have a chance later!" They all laughed again, urging Heinrich.

"Yes, go, go."

Reluctantly, Heinrich followed Gerhard, whose arm was around the girl's thick waist. The three of them went out the back door of the small German saloon into the cool night where the bright moon cast sharp shadows in the alley.

"I'll get her juicy for you." He laughed, backing her up against some barrels along the wall. He kissed her hard on the mouth as he squeezed her right breast. He grabbed her blonde hair in his fist and pulled her head back so he could kiss her neck. He moved down to her exposed bosom, the nipple finally springing from the laced bodice. Gerhard spun the girl around and splayed her across the large barrel top at the same time lifting her skirts high around her waist. Only her toes could reach the ground.

She wore no underwear and the white globes of her buttocks reflected in the moonlight. Gerhard spread her legs farther with his knee as he unbuttoned his trousers.

Heinrich had seen many farm animals breed so he knew what to expect, but he had never seen so much of a naked woman before.

Gerhard took his erection out and with one hand guided it toward her opening; the other pinned her down at the waist. He thrust and thrust hard. She cried out. He moaned.

Heinrich felt himself tense and thicken inside his own trousers, his eyes glued to the copulating pair in front of him. His hand found his own erection through the cloth of his pants, rubbing and moving his own pelvis as he watched his brother act like a farm bull.

Gerhard thrust again, quicker this time, then again and again. The girl kept moaning and saying how good it felt. Gerhard gripped her hips with both hands, pulling her up onto him each time he thrust forward, smashing into her white flesh. Heinrich pressed hard on his own erection, shuddered, and froze, unable to focus. Gerhard thrust several more times, shoved hard with one final thrust that arched his head backward and grimaced with a loud groan. The girl, who had been bracing herself the best she could off the metal rim of the wooden barrel, pushed backward so that her feet could touch the ground.

"Ah, that was good," Gerhard finally said, slipping out of the girl and slapping her left buttock.

"Ja," she said, turning around and pushing her skirts back

down, adjusting her bodice so both breasts were fully exposed. "It was *sehr gut*. Now for the other ..." She looked at Heinrich, who was still standing there, frozen.

Gerhard, too, looked over and then laughed so hard he doubled over before he could button his own trousers. "Look! Look!" He pointed at Heinrich standing with the moonlight on him. "You are not going to have your turn, now are you? Look at yourself. You are wet already, you fool."

Heinrich was humiliated. Watching was such a stimulation he had ejaculated before even touching female flesh.

"I thought you could handle this. Go home! You don't need a woman." He finished buttoning himself back into his pants.

"I should still get the price of two, for he had pleasure watching—" the girl began.

"No, you *fotze*, you cunt, you don't." He tossed a handful of *pfennigs* on the ground at her feet. "That's all you get, so get on your knees and find them." Turning to Heinrich he said, "You. Go home. You won't be able to go back inside, not looking like that. It is bad enough that I will have to explain to my friends. You're no brother of mine. Go home."

Heinrich had walked home. It wasn't far, but every step made him feel worse. He didn't want *prostituierte* like Gerhard. He didn't want to be like Gerhard at all. But he also didn't want to be himself—destined to be a priest.

A priest. The word echoed in his head, bringing him back into the present. He rubbed the bridge of his nose as the train clacked along its tracks taking him closer to home. He didn't want women. He only wanted one girl to love, but he'd failed to even discuss Anna with his immovable *vater*. The Graf was not to be defied—his power far-reaching. Heinrich had no choice but to comply. The church, the family, and his father would never permit him to leave

Prussia permanently. No one in his position had ever refused their duty to the birthright. No one in hundreds of years had turned away from the honor of priesthood.

They finally arrived at Thionville, just inside the German border where they boarded the next train through the Rhineland, one of the most picturesque areas of Prussia. Peaked-roofed cottages and orchards with white or fragile pink blooms blurred by. In the fields peasant women wearing large hats and curtailed petticoats, stopped work to watch the train rattle along, its dark smoke plume a streaming banner as it chugged past. Heinrich stared at nothing, nature's beauty lost on him. He shoved any thoughts of Anna from his mind, instead wondering what fun Langsford was up to.

Two hours later, the locomotive pulled its five cars into the Wittlich station, the end of the Dieffenbachers' train travel. The opened landau, driver and footman sitting high on the seats above the horses, arrived just as their baggage came off the train. In no time, the gentlemen seated within, the carriage rolled over the rough cobblestones and out of town toward Flußbach, the small village of stone cottages with straw-thatched roofs near the estate. The carriage wheels splashed long-standing green puddles where pigs, ducks, and young children played before scurrying out of the way. A withered old man hobbled out his front door to see who was trotting by. The landau left a wake of excitement as it passed by three shops, two beer halls, the church, and a windmill on the rise just beyond.

The driver wheeled a tight right turn onto a narrow dirt lane with grasses growing between the wheel tracks. The horses walked, tossing their heads for they knew they were close to home, while Heinrich's stomach knotted with tension. A tall stone wall imposed alongside the lane until it gave way to the wide entrance of the estate where they turned left into the large paved courtyard, the *hof*, which anchored the important buildings.

To the left of the entrance sat the stables. Flies and chickens were busy in the manure pile stacked in front. Its roof, the tallest, lifted a weather vane. The coach parted a gaggle of geese and agitated more chickens as it passed the carriage house. On the right, opposite the granary, a thatch-roofed cottage, tucked under a sweeping linden tree, was the home of Dirk, the estate's farm manager.

The *schloss*, or castle itself, was nearly hidden from view, veiled by a stand of horse chestnuts whose spiked blooms dropped a rose-colored carpet of petals. Less a castle and more a mansion, its modern architecture featured a red-tiled roof topping three stories, with dark arched windows peering from the walls.

The original feudal schloss, once a genuine castle, lay abandoned far beyond. Cows now grazed around and frequently inside, for the wooden doors had long since decayed along with most of the ancient roof, leaving only the stone walls of the previous fortress to fend off nature. It had been a wonderful place for Heinrich to play as a child when he had loved every corner of the estate.

The driver halted the horses at the modern schloss' front entrance. Everyone had been on alert, listening for clip-clopping hooves on the cobblestones. Family members, along with key servants, lined up to greet the returning travelers.

The Graf superficially nodded his greetings, walking quickly. *The Gräfin* smiled pleasantly at her spouse as he reached the fourth and top step of the entrance where she waited. He offered her his arm and together they entered the broad hall of the mansion.

Heinrich was sullen and silent. For him the stone buildings with their rough walls were now the prison of his heritage.

CHAPTER 12

Bermondsey, London

One evening shortly after Henry had failed to return, Anna sat on the bed brushing her hair while Lottie slipped into her nightgown. "Lottie, Henry looked at me so adoringly... ."

"Last year I was at Monday Market, and a man looked directly at me, but it's very dangerous to look into a man's eyes."

"It is? I don't know why. I liked looking into Henry's and I liked it when he touched my hand. He is so strong and yet gentle. I felt a tingle throughout."

"He *touched* you?"

"Yes, I know it isn't proper, but honestly, what harm ...?"

Lottie quickly sat on the bed beside Anna, leaned in closely, and said, "If you look at a man, and he touches you, you are likely to, well, you know ..."

"What?"

"You know, as they say ... you can be ..." Lottie turned her head and in a hushed whisper said in Anna's ear, "in a family way."

"Ooohh," Anna stiffened, brush in midair. "Oh no, oh no! I'm not going to be just a spinster, I'll be—Oh what have I done?" She began to sob.

"It's only what they say." Shocked at Anna's reaction, Lottie attempted a retreat from her statement. "Maybe it doesn't always happen."

On the verge of hysterics, Anna couldn't calm herself. Within minutes Aunt Bess knocked on the door. "Girls! Girls! What *is* the matter?" She cracked opened the door a few inches, then wider as she saw Anna's heaving shoulders in Lottie's arms.

Anna's words were disjointed, so Lottie took over. "I told her that if you look at a man and he touches you, you can ... well ... a baby ...?"

"Oh there, there, my sweet," Aunt Bess sat beside them and turned Anna, wrapping her arms around her. She held her to her ample bosoms while Anna quieted. "You girls," she tisked. "I can tell you've never set foot on a farm." She wiped strands of hair off Anna's forehead. "A bit of a glance at the right man will do no harm if you want to find a husband, and as long as it's just your hand he touches, you'll be fine."

"Oh, Aunt Bess, I truly liked his touch. I liked his face, his eyes ..."

"But this is *not* the man for you. There will be a better one, an Englishman. Once you are engaged, then you can hold hands all you want. I didn't know very much at sixteen, either, but you'll learn. And you, Lottie, don't be telling tales when you don't know anything yourself. You got poor Anna all upset and she's already unhappy. You mind your p's and q's."

Both girls now sat still looking at Aunt Bess, Anna wiping tears from her cheeks, and Lottie chastised.

"You both behave and do as you are told. Be good girls."

Aunt Bess left the room, gently shutting the door behind her. The topic was closed.

CHAPTER 13

The Dieffenbacher Estate, Prussia

Reluctantly stepping from the carriage and walking by the servants, Heinrich sighed as he began to climb the steps. Then he saw his older sister, Gisela, who always elicited a smile from him, emerge from the doorway. A short wisp of a girl with light-brown hair, she wore a yellow frock with a brown bow beneath the collar. Beside her on the top step was her two-year-old daughter, little Ilyse, whom he immediately swept into his arms, kissing both her fat cheeks to make her giggle, as the three entered the mansion.

"Oh Heinrich, it's good to have you back so soon! We have missed you, haven't we, Ilyse?" Gisela prompted. Heinrich gently handed the child to a servant who came to take her back to the nursery.

"It's good to see you, too, dear sister, but not good to be here within these walls."

Together, the siblings walked down the broad hall with its black-and-white tiled floor. The hall itself extended through the mansion. Bisecting the hall was another, just as broad and with the same tiled floor, creating a cross so the downstairs kitchens, maids' rooms, governess's room, and footmen's rooms easily connected. Before the intersection of these main halls was the grand staircase, and it was this that Heinrich and Gisela ascended, arm in arm.

"Oh, tell me, did you talk to Pa-pa?" Gisela inquired of her younger brother.

"No. His mind is the same as the stone walls of this house— immovable and solid."

"Oh, Heinrich! I hoped you two could speak civilly. Though I must admit, I did not hold much hope that you would sway him."

Heinrich was silent until they reached the upper hall where the salons, dining room, and private family rooms were.

He sighed. "I have no choice, even though ..."

"Even though, what?"

"Oh. Nothing ...." He turned from her and walked down the hall into his suite. In the sitting room, he glanced around at his horse-hair-stuffed sofa with its mahogany trim and the cherry table with its hammered-bronze edge. He liked the masculine furnishings, especially the pair of antler chairs upholstered with fox skin and deer hides. Even a gilded-framed oil of horses and riders gliding over stone walls in pursuit of a bounding deer spoke of his keen love of the hunt. This room was his welcomed retreat, but even this he would soon leave behind for a stark existence within the church.

He entered the adjoining bedroom where his heavy-framed bed stood, its dark velvet drapes tied back on each of the four posts. In contrast to the interior, the windows were hung with yellow silk curtains, letting filtered light offset the darkness.

His servant was already unpacking, hanging a suit in the tall wardrobe.

"Good afternoon, Herr Heinrich."

Both his rooms felt dank, for the thick walls kept the April warmth at bay. He shivered. "Is it lighted?" He pointed toward the rectangular porcelain stove that stood nearly two meters tall. A hawk with gold-tipped wings and beak surmounted its top and a cast-iron ivy twined over the heat vent at the bottom.

"Ja. The room will warm." He helped Heinrich out of his coat and hung that as well. "I'll go light the sitting room stove." He bowed slightly and left.

Heinrich relaxed, feeling the warmth spread. He parted the silk curtains to look out briefly, then dropped them and returned to his sitting room, which had views in three different directions. There he dragged an antler chair over to the east window and sat. Soon he'd enter the seminary, and his life as he knew it would be concluded, but he no longer cared. He dozed.

Heinrich's servant awakened him in time to dress for supper. At exactly seven thirty it was time for the *abendbrot,* the last of the five daily meals. Reluctantly he left his suite to walk the length of the hall to the large dining room. Everyone was already seated so he quickened his step to avoid the wrath of his father, slipping in to promptly take his place.

The entire family was present. His parents sat at opposite ends of the table, his brother Gerhard, stockier and blond, on the left beside his sister, Gisela, who sat between her brothers. His father's youngest sister, and husband, along with their young sons, Fritz and Johann, who also lived at the estate, were across the table facing him. The young boys, ages five and six respectively, sat squarely on their chairs and held their hands in their laps awaiting grace. Too young for family meals, little Ilyse remained in the nursery.

Heinrich pretended to listen to his father's prayer and then mechanically took the proper portions when the servants offered trays of food. Once everyone was served, his father nodded permission to eat and simultaneously they picked up their forks and knives.

Heinrich found the food tasteless and the conversation uninteresting, but the youngsters caught his amused attention. Not at all fond of the sauerkraut on their plates, Fritz and Johann quietly made faces as they each picked up a single strand of the fermented cabbage, trying not to giggle. Unfortunately the Graf noticed and glared at his brother-in-law, the boys' father. Silently and swiftly the younger parent rose, snatching Fritz by the back of his collar and grasping Johann's arm, and dragged them to their feet. One chair thudded to the floor while the older boy whimpered, and his younger sibling screamed. Without a word their father removed them from the room. A servant instantly removed each boy's plate. Another righted the tipped chair. The family remaining at the table took no heed of the commotion or the boys' empty places. Polite table conversation continued.

Heinrich, however, did notice the boys' predicament for as a child he'd experienced the same treatment many times. As he ate his own sauerkraut and potatoes, he remembered being removed to his room. Over his bed was the well-tied bunch of sticks and twigs. The bundle, inappropriately called a "tickler," smarted and stung when his father switched him, creating welts on his buttocks and legs.

Tonight Heinrich could hear little crying voices in the distance as they felt the tickler. Just as he had as a child, the boys would go to bed without their supper. For breakfast they would find the same plates of sauerkraut placed in front of them, for food was never wasted. Usually young Heinrich refused to eat his food the morning after disobeying, and he would be required to eat alone at the small *Katzentisch*, or cat's table, for at least a week. Remembering now, he sighed and took another bite of the sauerkraut he still didn't care for.

With the meal concluded, they gathered as usual in the salon to read aloud while the women knitted or embroidered. As Heinrich went to sit in a chair near the piano, his father gasped.

"This window's still open!" He called for the head servant of the household, who instantly came running. The Graf pointed at the two visible thermometers—one mounted on the outside of the window, the other inside to the right. Typical of Prussian houses, the opening and closing of windows was strictly regulated. On spring evenings, once the outside temperature dropped below the interior, windows were shut tight against the stagnant, toxic night air. In the morning, at precisely the correct temperature, all windows were opened to warm and air the house.

The head servant immediately shut the open window. "I apologize. This window somehow was missed. I'm afraid it's been open the entire time." He turned, and with a slight bow, suggested as an inquiry, "Shall you all leave the room until the night air disperses?"

"Everyone adjourn to your rooms," the Graf answered by ordering his family. "Gerhard, escort your sister to safety. I will take your mother and the rest of the family. I'm afraid it is too unhealthy to remain here this evening." He turned to the servant. "Find who made this error and be rid of him."

The man hurried away to find the errant help who now had no employment.

Glad to be alone in his rooms, Heinrich dismissed his own man, donning his heavier cotton night shirt by himself. Going into the sitting room, he chose one of the deer-hide chairs beside a closed window. *A good man, my own servant*, he thought. Heinrich watched the sliver of a moon peek through the silhouetted trees.

He forced himself not to let any wrenching sobs escape from his situation. The "tickler" hanging over his childhood bed made the lesson never to cry extremely clear. He brought himself under control and watched the moon lift higher above the trees, suspended from the shadow of a cloud.

CHAPTER 14

The Dieffenbacher Estate, Prussia

Tuesday morning after the usual second breakfast that followed Mass, Heinrich wandered to the stable. He wouldn't be able to ride once he became a priest-candidate at the seminary a week hence—or do much else, truth be told. He shoved away the thought, wanting to enjoy today and ride.

As he passed the carriage house, a horse and rider barreled into the hof, the young man atop yelling, "Hey boy! I just heard you're back early." It was Klaus in all his exuberance coming to see his friend. Dirty blond hair messed by the wind, brown eyes that matched the leather of his tall boots and billowing shirt, he laughed as he reined in his mount, allowing it to half rear. For fun, he spun the horse in a tight pirouette, ending in a prance. The girls all loved Klaus, who dashed in and around their lives. This laughing daredevil was a favorite with his peers. At the moment, he was exactly what Heinrich needed to lift his spirits.

"It's about time you showed your ugly face." Heinrich laughed. "I thought you had been killed in the woods while hunting dangerous bunny rabbits."

"I nearly was," Klaus jested. "I've come to have you join me in the *Krieg der Kaninchen.*" War of the rabbits. "Quickly!"

That was what Heinrich liked about Klaus. Nothing was ever too serious, nor did it need to be, for there was never anything looming over his head. He was heir to his family title and fortune and there the expectations of him ended. His life was simple. Heinrich envied that.

Klaus dismounted and a groom came to take the horse. "Walk him out a bit, but keep him nearby," he instructed. "My friend is waiting for a horse he can handle." He threw his wide grin at Heinrich.

The main groom already had Heinrich's horse, *Preis*, in the cross ties for brushing and saddling. This Trakehner-bred mount was the breed the Prussian cavalry had used for more than 150 years. More refined than the heavy artillery horses, they were for officers and dragoons, bred to be fast, athletic, and easy to handle.

But Preis was an unusually marked animal deemed undesirable for the military. A cavalry unit rode matching horses so the unit was mounted on one color. Should a soldier on a different color appear, the odds were he was the enemy.

Heinrich's rare horse was tobiano-colored: brown with large white patches and white stockinged legs. With too few available for a matching military unit, the animal was sold off as a riding horse. Heinrich laughed at the thought, for he did not match anything, either. Not Klaus. Not Langsford. He and his horse were both misfits.

"Of course odd Preis shall frighten away all the rabbits. The little buggers will think he's a spotted shorthair pointer."

"You're just jealous because Preis jumps over the fences while you look for the gate to open," Heinrich taunted.

Once his horse was tacked, Heinrich swung up into the saddle, and the two horsemen clopped side by side through the hof, out behind the carriage house and down the dirt road that led behind the schloss. There, stretching out in front of them, were fields with woods beyond.

Both prudent horsemen, they knew Heinrich's gelding needed a good kilometer to warm up or risk bowing a tendon or straining a ligament in its legs. Walking easily along the dirt road, they passed groups of farmworkers preparing the ground for the spring seeding. Draught horses leaned into their thick leather collars, steadily pulling the ploughs through the heavy dark Prussian soil.

The farm manager, Dirk, recognized them and his hollered "ha-low" echoed across open land. Heinrich waved a hand above his head in reply. He was Heinrich's favorite worker and had taught Heinrich to ride his first pony. Dirk always had time to stop what he was doing to answer a question little Heinrich had or to help adjust his stirrups.

Klaus relaxed on his horse, his feet dangling out of the stirrups. He leaned back until his head rested on the horse's rump, then began sit-ups. "I might as well take advantage of you ambling along on your spotted dog of a horse," he teased, breathing heavier as he sat up multiple times.

"Just as well," Heinrich retorted, laughing. "You need to work your weak muscles." He was glad to have his friend with him, but seeing Dirk encouraged the ache deep within. Perhaps because he was older now, he saw how different men were and how varied their lives. Dirk's world, Klaus's world, his father's world, Langsford's world, a priest's world, and although he didn't want the thought to invade his mind, it did—a world with Anna.

The pang deep in his stomach hit again. "Race you!" he yelled, urging his horse into a gallop as he leaned forward over Preis's neck.

"Cheat!" Klaus howled, sitting up fast and grabbing at his reins. The two horses breezed down the dirt road with long flowing strides. Grazing cows looked up to stare from the other side of a wattled fence, its interlaced leafless limbs keeping them con-tained. Along the other side of the road, an open field spread wide. Heinrich shifted his weight to the right, asking the horse to turn. Preis lifted up and over a small ditch of dry cattails and reeds, Klaus's horse close on his heels. Landing smoothly on the other side, the pair galloped harder through the field. They sped across the land, stride for stride.

Heinrich let out a yell. He was no longer racing Klaus but the ache in his gut—to gallop on forever, away from his father, from traditions. Away.

The horses and riders easily sailed over a barrier of fallen tree trunks and continued toward the woods on the far side of the field, flying over the damp ground and jumping another fence.

What if he just kept on going? Heinrich's internal voice asked. Preis lifted up and over a low stone wall without breaking stride. His father would send servants after him to bring him back. Maybe even the police. Horse and rider turned left, picking up speed. The church would excommunicate him. He would disgrace his family. Quickly the trees became closer, forcing Heinrich to sit back in the saddle and slow. He couldn't run away any more than he could gallop through these trees.

Klaus circled his horse to slacken his speed, unable to slow quickly enough. Heinrich waited for his friend and they wove their way through the saplings.

Heinrich reached out to pat his horse's neck and let his reins hang loose as they wandered through what now was quickly be-coming forest.

"I let you win, you know, Dieffenbacher," Klaus declared, mov-ing his horse around a larger oak. The trees were becoming so thick they picked their way through, streaks of sunbeams blink-ing between the thick trunks. "I pulled up so I wouldn't run your spotted dog into a tree," he laughed good-naturedly. The day was beautiful, with the smell of spring lifting from damp earth.

"You mean you avoided a fallen tree you couldn't leap over." Heinrich's horse danced sideways.

The woods opened up again as the land gently descended until they arrived at a fast flowing creek, a tributary to the Demichbach River. "Let's stop here a bit," Klaus suggested. "Give the horses a break." He winked. "I brought some cigars."

Dismounting, Heinrich looped the reins over his horse's head and let him walk into the stream to take a few deep draughts from the flowing water. Not letting him drink too much while still warm from the gallop, Heinrich led him over to an outcropping of rock where he leaned back, reins in hand, beside his friend.

He and Klaus each lit a fat cheroot, puffing and coughing on the strong tobacco. "Why are they called cheroots?" Heinrich asked, pretending to enjoy it.

"Dunno. It's an American savage word, my vater said. He said these are from a little island off America. Cuba. Claims they are the best." Klaus cleared his throat and inhaled again.

"If these are the best"—Heinrich spat some tobacco from his tongue—"I would hate to smoke the worst. This is awful."

"True, but manly. Maybe if we had brandy to drink with them."

"It doesn't matter. I won't be drinking anything but wine or smelling anything but the smoke of incense."

"*Was?* Your vater still won't relent?"

"Nein."

"Verdammt!" Klaus spat. "I wouldn't stand for it."

"You don't have to."

Preis, with one hind foot cocked under him, dozed, his tail brushing an occasional fly. The other horse chomped some fine grasses at water's edge, content. The sounds in the forest were soft and steady: the soothing gurgle of the stream, the breeze through the treetops, a calm within the trees.

There was no calm within Heinrich. "What choice do I have? I can't even talk to him. I met a girl in London."

"No! He let you?"

"Of course not. I went without his permission, and now I will never lay eyes on her again."

"*Mist!*" Klaus stood up and threw the cigar on the damp weeds. He dug it into the soft earth with his boot heel. "Heinrich, you must act a man if you ever hope to be a real man. Stand up for yourself!"

"It's little use. I have to follow tradition. My birthright."

"*Scheiße!* Do you let your vater tell you where to ride your horse? Or do you take the reins yourself? Which?" Klaus was adamant. "I've watched your father boss you all your life, and I, for one, am tired of it. Going to school in England made you a *feigling ohne rückgrat*." A fainthearted coward.

"It is easy for you to say because he is not your vater and you do not have to live with him."

"Well, you won't either, once you leave for the seminary."

Heinrich hesitated, seeing a certain logic emerge.

"You're right; I won't see him."

"So why obey him if you will be gone from him regardless? Don't you want to do what you wish?"

Yes I do, he thought. But dare he? Was he truly a coward? He sat silent. Klaus was correct. When he rode his horse, he took command of where he was going. He didn't let the horse decide. He had to determine his own fate and take the reins of his own life, except ... "If I leave, he'll send servants after me—or worse."

"So outsmart them. You're clever."

"I could go to London. Anna! Langsford ... but I would be disinherited, penniless."

"Make your own money, then. You have brains. The question is do you have the guts?"

Heinrich sat silent for some moments, then said more to himself than Klaus, "Obeying him has always been something I've done except for small things. Until Anna, I never thought I could leave. I only hoped to change his mind. I've always wanted his approval, but I've never had it. Only entering the priesthood would please him. Then he'd be granted a higher title—he'd be a *herzog*, a duke, and I'd be a priest." He buried his head in his hands.

"So you sit silently and let him make decisions for you. Makes no difference to me. I'll simply see you at confessions and tell you about all the fun I'm having."

Heinrich could hardly breathe. It would not be easy or simple to defy the Graf. He had to find courage he had never found before, but he knew what Klaus said was true. He must take charge of his own life or he would be forever lost. Not just to Anna, but to himself.

"Thank you, Klaus. You are right."

"Of course I am, except about these awful cigars. Next time I'll steal a pipe or two along with port," he laughed, going to his horse. "And I'll confess about it to you, friend!"

Heinrich walked up to Preis, ready to return to the schloss. He knew what he wanted to do. No, *had* to do. Today!—or never.

CHAPTER 15

The Dieffenbacher Estate, Prussia

The entire schloss was in an uproar.

Family members and servants alike attempted to go through the motions of a normal weekday afternoon, quietly holding their breath, straining to listen.

The tension started in the dining room during the midday meal. Rather than leisurely sitting back to enjoy coffee after lunch, Heinrich demanded he speak privately to his father. That was unheard of, for no one made demands of the Graf. Heinrich insisted and persisted until the family patriarch gave in. Gruffly the Graf motioned his insolent son into the library across the hall. The father rolled the library's sliding oak doors shut with a bang, he and Heinrich behind them. At first there was silence, but within minutes the yelling crescendoed through the doors. Semi muffled echoes reverberated throughout the first floor and down to the ground floor where servants quietly moved about.

The family was silent with expectant fear and slowly moved from the dining room into the salon next door opposite the library. Gisela tiptoed in and sat beside Gerhard in one of the armchairs.

"Heinrich is getting in trouble again. The boy is a fool." Gerhard smirked.

"Shhh, stop. Let us listen. Perhaps it's not so bad ... maybe Pa-pa will be nice," his sister offered, not convincingly.

Their father's voice came from across the hall. "How dare you defy me! *Du solltest tot sein. Tot!* You should be dead. For centuries it has been thus and you think you can change this tradition? It is your birthright to be a priest. A blessing! God's wish!

They could hear Heinrich's much quieter voice attempting to speak. "No, Father. I shall not ... no ... this tradition ..." Finally he blurted out, "I will *not* be a priest!"

His father's bellowing voice overpowered his. "The Holy Roman Emperor himself handed us God's gift of nobility. For hundreds of years—hundreds!"

The voices simultaneously resounded, blurring words into a loud cacophony. The shouting rattled the sliding doors. Next a fist pounded, perhaps on a desktop, followed by the crash of glass or crystal smashing into smithereens against, what? A wall? A bookcase?

The family sat in stunned silence, not daring to move. *No one* confronted the Graf. Heinrich's mother sat with mouth open, her hands holding her flushed cheeks in utter dismay. Even Gerhard had lost his sardonic expression and was horrified. Gisela cast her eyes downward as they filled with tears for her beloved brother. The little boys sat frozen, clinging to their mother. Downstairs servants crept up the wide staircase from the ground floor, stopping to hold the curved walnut banister while they looked up.

A long silence, the air suspended without sound, without breath. A grand pause.

Finally, Heinrich's softer voice. "I would honorably serve in the military and do the family proud. *In der Armee.* If you cannot agree to that, then I shall leave the family—I cannot, and will not, follow the family tradition."

Another long unbearable pause as the household remained frozen.

A deep, threatening reply, "If you refuse, I could have you arrested. Defy me and you will regret it, I promise, so help me God!"

The Graf slid open the doors with a thunderous bang, making everyone jump. The servants in the stairwell scurried back to their tasks below. The Gräfin picked up her embroidery needles as everyone quickly attempted a pretense of normalcy, but the Graf marched into the great hallway, pivoting away from everyone in the salon and heading toward the now-vacant stairwell.

Heinrich took a deep breath, straightened his shoulders, and with pounding heart, left for his rooms. He tried not to shake, willing himself to be steady. Even though his father did not accept his declaration, Heinrich had said what he intended. For him, it was over and done.

The coast clear after the Graf descended the grand staircase, Heinrich's mother and Gisela ran down the hall after Heinrich, tears streaming down their cheeks. Already at his doorway, Heinrich turned to the distraught women. "Don't worry. I know what I'm doing."

The women were sobbing, and he took each one in his arms. "I am sorry, *liebe Mutter*, dear mother, *geliebte Schwester*, beloved sister. I have never fit in this family as father wished, and I have always caused much angst and grief." He gently kissed each of them on the cheeks. Their sniffling eased and he continued. "Father bellows and rages like an old bull, so we will all be happier once we no longer argue."

"It is difficult for everyone, yes, when you two argue," his mother gasped, the tears still running down her white cheeks.

"I know. The arguing will cease, I promise. If I became a priest, I would not be here to argue. So should I leave for a different destination, I still shall not be here to argue with him."

His mother began to sob again. Gisela looked at him, tears still filling her bright eyes.

"I would make a terrible priest. The difference is now I can find my own way."

"Oh, my boy," his mother wailed and he hugged her tight.

"Please be glad for me, Ma-ma."

He looked at his sister. "Take care of her. Go back to your day. Vater will cool down."

He touched his mother on her cheek. "I love you." He sent them on their way, assuring them he would see everyone at supper, then entered his room, closing the door behind him.

It was best to leave immediately, he decided, even though it was late afternoon. He knew he needed to be out of his father's reach and influence. He was not afraid of highway robbers in the dark. Preis could easily outrun any of them. Quickly he changed back into his riding attire, pulling on his high leather boots. Standing up, he moved around his room, gathering items to pack. His coat, hat, gold watch, a purse full of five and ten gold marks, plus a jumble of smaller coins including a few pfennigs. It was fortunate the money was left from his London trip along with papers he might need for traveling. He grabbed a small valise and quickly stuffed extra clothing inside. Looking at his pocket watch, he knew he had a few hours before the abendbrot. That would give him a head start because he wouldn't be missed until then. His father didn't realize they had just had their last argument.

Heinrich looked out his sitting room window where he saw the workers still ploughing as they worked their way down the field closer to the hof. Peering out the opposite window into the hof itself, he saw his father speaking to the stableman who was bathing Heinrich's gelding. Damn. He'd have to take a different horse.

Picking up his small valise, Heinrich went into the hall to the very rear of the mansion and down the servants' plank staircase. He slipped out the servants' door into a back yard where two geese honked at him. He held his valise and hat under his morning coat, doing his best to slouch and look like the rebuffed youth he was. A pig, busy rooting in the torn-up grasses by the edge of the brick yard, ignored him. He passed a good distance from several servants hanging laundry. They looked away because, while they already knew he had been redressed by their master, they attempted to hide any knowledge of family matters.

Rounding a corner of the schloss, he hurried along a back wall lined with flowering bushes. Once he reached the end of the wall, he turned, cutting into the adjacent woods. There he stashed his valise, with his hat and coat, behind a moss-covered log. Unbuttoning the top of his shirt, he smeared damp moss and earth on his shoulder, and rumpled his hair a bit to make his pending story more plausible. Then, much as he hated doing so, he walked out into the future rye field toward the men who were ploughing, his eyes searching for the farm master.

Again, Dirk spotted him first. The seasoned farmer never missed anything. "Well, Herr Heinrich. You look to be on foot. Where did your fine steed head without you?"

Heinrich smiled, for he was genuinely glad to see Dirk, making it all the more difficult for him to lie to his old friend.

"We seemed to have had a parting of the ways," he fibbed. "I took a fall at a fence and Preis headed off west. I was going to walk back to the stables then I thought maybe I could borrow one of your horses to go after him." He added to his plea. "I'll make sure Vater knows so you won't have to explain if you are short in the rows you ploughed."

Dirk laughed. "Of course, lad. We can spare one from that

team over there. The mare is good for a bit of a ride and the gelding she's teamed with can pull the plough for a while alone. He's young and strong ... like you." The older man grinned at Heinrich. "Steffen, go to unhitch the mare there and bring her over. She needs to give Herr Heinrich a ride."

Within minutes, Heinrich was astride the short, plump *schwarzwälder fuchs*, Black Forest Draught mare. Bred on the estate, these horses were used for all the farming work. Shorter and rounder than Heinrich's Trakehner gelding, her deep burnished coat blended into the woods as she walked with long slow strides, still wearing her harness as she carried her rider. Heinrich stopped to gather up his hidden belongings and then moved farther east, deeper among the trees.

From the fields, from the hof and the schloss, there was no longer any sight of Heinrich.

CHAPTER 16

Prussia

The moment Heinrich left the estate, he felt utterly free. After skirting through fields to avoid local roads where he might be seen, he rode northeast on a main thoroughfare. It was past nightfall when he arrived in the little town of Bullay hours later. There he planned to catch a train back to France, and return to London. To Anna.

He abandoned the pretty mare, leaving her at a watering trough on the street. Her pine tree brand would make it easy to identify her as property of the Dieffenbacher Estate, as it was well known they bred them. Confident she would be found and returned to Dirk, he patted her shoulder as she put her nose in the water for a deep drink.

Heinrich walked a few blocks to the small station depot to catch what turned out to be the last train of the night. Other than a short encounter with a town drunkard, his journey thus far was uneventful. His father would have checked at the Wittlich station but would never think to look this far for him. Relaxed, he settled down in his inexpensive third-class seat and stretched his long legs out for the three-hour train ride southwest to the French border.

Once there, passengers lined up on the German side of the border to change trains at Thionville. While there was still a late train scheduled, Heinrich was tired and hungry. He opted to stay the night and catch a morning train. He grabbed some bread and cheese at a small café that was just about to close and found a vacancy at an inn near the station. Once in his room, he pulled off his boots and lay on his bed without undressing. Emotionally he was drained after riding through the woods from the estate earlier that afternoon, worried his father would send servants to chase him and somehow force him home. Here, on the French border, he felt beyond his father's grasp. Confident in his unfettered return to England, he fell into an exhausted sleep.

Heinrich could not know the Prussian police were closing in on him, tracking a stranger from Bullay whom they believed to be a *mörder*, a murderer. A *polizist,* interrogating the Bullay station-master, learned the stranger had purchased a ticket to Calais and boarded the last train to Thionville. The *polizisten* had a complete description not only from the stationmaster, but also from the murder victim's brother, Karl, who saw him on the street shortly after the killing. The man was rushing to the train, Karl reported. No one else was around. His brother was discovered stabbed immediately afterward.

The murderer they sought was tall, a good six feet, clean shaven, with brown hair. The stationmaster, who had the better look at him, guessed he might be twenty years old. The man wore riding attire and tall leather boots. All he lacked was a riding crop and a horse, the stationmaster said. Instead, he was curiously traveling by train.

The polizisten assumed the mörder was planning to escape across the English Channel at Calais. Two of them were assigned to pursue the suspect on the first morning train out, while two others, suspicious the abandoned mare they'd found wandering the street was connected due to his attire, and most likely stolen, were dispatched to find who owned her.

Thus, early the next morning the uniformed pair, High Grade Otto Brauer and his subordinate, Low Grade Herbert Ritter, booked themselves straight through to Calais, boarding the first train. "The *drecksack* definitely went to France," Brauer proclaimed. "And so we shall too." Within three hours, they pulled into Thionville, the transfer point. While they waited for the next train to France, they asked the ticket master if he had seen their *mörder* the night before. He hadn't. The *polizisten* both shrugged their shoulders. "Such a shame not everyone is observant," Ritter lamented.

"If they were, you, my friend, would be out of a job."

"I want the job, but I'd rather be home with my wife."

"And lose the chance to drag this *verbrecher* back to be hanged? And impress the Police Ministry in Berlin? Don't be a fool."

The Prussian train system ran like clockwork, and inside fifteen minutes, right on schedule, they boarded their train to Lille, France. As their train chugged out of the Thionville depot, they had no idea that they had just passed the man they sought.

Heinrich was in no rush at all as he sat in a Thionville café the next morning. He planned to catch a later train once he finished his breakfast. He'd heard the trains arriving and departing over at the station. He'd already missed the first Lille train since he had allowed himself the luxury of sleeping longer than normal. He could board the next one scheduled for early afternoon.

When it was time, Heinrich walked along the station platform, waiting for his train to pull in. He sat on the bench along with a dozen or so others. Rested, he was impatient to be on his way, his thoughts focused on Anna. A train stopped for a different destination and he watched travelers climb down from the large metal cars, the steam from the engine blowing back over the train. Within minutes, the heavy hands on the station clock pointed to its departure time. The engine groaned, building its momentum, and pulled the train out of the depot.

There was only a brief quiet, then Heinrich's train arrived exactly on time. Most of those who had been waiting on the platform were also heading for Lille. Heinrich, clutching his valise with his few articles of clothing, followed the line of passengers. He climbed the three steps and then walked through the last car where he found a seat in third class. He noted that the same grime-covered windows were on all the trains regardless of class.

Miles in front and several hours ahead, the polizisten, Brauer and Ritter, were well on their way to Lille. They'd settled in on the longest leg of the trip, their arrival time still hours away. Once they changed trains in Lille, Calais was only three hours farther. High Grade Brauer was looking forward to grabbing the drecksack there. The mere thought of it gave him great pleasure.

Heinrich, behind the police, was also on his way to Lille. His seat was small and cramped. The stuffy car was crowded, yet he would much rather be riding in this car jammed with strangers than in the lavishness of a first-class compartment with his vater.

He needed to have a plan by the time he arrived in London. *I'm smart*, he told himself. Well educated. He would find a position teaching in a boys' school. *Yes. That will work.* Inwardly he laughed, recalling his initial conversation with Anna about her job, admitting he had never had one. He would work in a private school and teach Latin, mathematics, and German to support his family. He would be a common working man. This new concept excited him. He could tell Anna they were now equals. *Once I have secured work and a salary, then I will have an audience with her father and receive his permission to court her.*

The train rattled on as it sped along, clacking on its tracks.

Hours later, the train carrying the Prussian police pulled into Lille. The two raced to catch the final train to Calais. They congratulated themselves on their luck, for the French locomotive, running late, still puffed at the station. They hopped on board this last one of the day to the port. "We'll nab this man in the morning." High Grade Brauer rubbed his hands together. "His description has been telegraphed to Calais by now, I'm sure."

"It's possible the French police have already detained the murderer, holding him for us," Low Grade Ritter replied hopefully.

"That would be a shame—to miss out on the fun of his arrest and beating."

They settled in for the last leg of their pursuit.

Arriving in Lille much later, Heinrich discovered the last train to Calais had departed long before. He again found a small room at an adjacent inn, but anxious now to get to London, he was unable to fall asleep and lay in bed refining his plans. He'd stay with Langsford who, he was sure, could assist him in obtaining a position of some importance. Langsford had connections.

Yes, Langsford, like Klaus, is a friend I could trust with my life, he told himself.

Heinrich finally drifted off to sleep, dreaming of Anna and London.

Chapter 17

Leadenhall Market, London

After her bitter disappointment and embarrassment, Anna regained her sense of comfort in the rhythm of her daily routine. She kept busy with women who purchased new spring hats. Tears welled up in her eyes as a matron left with the blue silk scarf, but Anna decided it was better to be rid of the reminder.

On Wednesday she counted a week and a day since Henry's visit and decided to never think of him again. As she designed new trim for a hat, Mr. Thompson, the owner of the shop, arrived to look over the inventory. Always pleased with Anna's work, her employer told her to take an extra half hour for lunch that lovely day while he worked.

Taking her lunch, she stepped out into the market where the spring daylight streamed through the sparkling glass panes high overhead. She sat on a small bench on the side of the street to enjoy her bread, cheese, and ripe plum and to watch shoppers, horse-drawn carts, and vendors go by. She'd eaten only a few bites before the boy from the Hopson's Boot Maker Shoppe up the street walked over to greet her. Robbie, a young cobbler, had spoken politely to her several times before and seemed nice enough. A tall, lanky fellow, he always smelled like good clean leather, which Anna rather liked. He was wearing his cobbler's apron, and sure enough, his work clothes smelled like tanned hide. She could see his lean forearms below his rolled up shirt sleeves.

"'allo, Anna." He removed his gray cap, his dark blond hair falling askew into his eyes. Nervously he rubbed his other hand on the side of his trousers. "'Tis a pleasure to see ya. I seldom spot ya outside yer shop."

"Hello, Robbie." She gave a little laugh. "Mr. Thompson is counting inventory today, so I have a longer lunch break."

"Well 'at's nice. 'Tis a pleasant day. Sunny." He fidgeted, standing on one foot then the other. "And no rain," he continued, running his fingers over the bill of his cap. "I'm on me way to the tanners to pick up a batch of leather. A good thing, too, since I've five pair of ridin' boots to be made in no time." He grinned broadly.

"That's a great deal of work."

"I've earned a nice reputation for fine stitchin'," Robbie boasted. "And I've started usin' either calf skin or Spanish Cordovan if I can get it. The ladies who ride like 'ow soft it is."

"Yes, I would want comfortable boots, but I've never been on a horse, so I don't speak from experience."

"Perhaps someday I'll take ya ridin' and ya can wear me boots." He looked down and blushed. "Well, 'ave a nice lunch. I must take me leave." He donned his cap.

"Thank you, Robbie. Good day to you."

Anna watched him stride down the street toward the exit of the market beyond the curve. She chewed her piece of cheese slowly. She sighed. *He is nice*, Anna thought, *but Robbie is a fraction of the man Henry is.* She took another bite of cheese. *How I wish ...*

Chapter 18

France

Heinrich rose early in Lille the next morning and purchased a coffee and croissant. Though not as filling as his favorite rye breads and cheese, the twisted sweet roll would have to suffice. The sun burned away morning clouds, and he was eager to begin his journey to Calais. His morning train on time, he boarded with buoyant purpose. In three hours he would be at the coast to board the Dover steamer. Every minute now brought him closer to Anna.

Arriving in Calais the prior evening, the polizisten rushed from the station platform to the adjacent boat docks. Everything was deserted at that late hour and there was no word their man had been detained. Brauer had stood there, both pleased and seething. While he didn't want their man to escape, he wanted to be the one to take him.

A couple of men walking along the dock told them a spring storm made the tides difficult and no boats had left the port that day. "Good news, Ritter," Brauer smiled. "The mörder could not possibly have left. He'll have to try to board early morning."

"Shouldn't we look for him tonight if he's here?"

"No, stupid. Why make it harder? We can rest tonight and begin watch early in the morning. I guarantee we'll arrest him at the docks before the first boat sails."

The next morning Brauer and Ritter returned early to the ticket office. Yes, the telegraphed description of their man had been received. No, no one recalled seeing him. Thus, they waited with the patience of any predator, watching trains arrive, bringing passengers from all parts of Germany and France.

People began to jam into the ticket office, which quickly became too crowded for the policemen to remain. They walked outside where they encountered more commotion.

A small fishing vessel had arrived from Dover reporting to the harbor master that the deep water channel off the English coast remained too shallow for the large eighty-foot steamboats. Even though the Calais harbor dredged a deep water channel to allow the boats access, Dover's landing along the White Cliffs of Britain was a challenge when the channel filled up with silt pushed by stormy tides.

The first boat scheduled to depart was canceled.

Before long, the place was aswarm with waiting passengers. All the chairs and benches were taken. Impatience spread throughout the crowd as people asked one another questions that had no answers. *When would the ferries sail? When would one arrive?*

It was this swirling humanity that greeted Heinrich as his train pulled into the Calais station just before noon. Not far from the pier, Heinrich looked through his smudged window at the crowds. He saw people attempting to work their way toward the ticket office. Some stood crowded in one spot, while others pushed and milled about.

"What's happening?" he asked the conductor as he prepared to disembark. He paused by the top step, not yet climbing down from his car.

"Il y a une attente de la marée haute à Douvres." There is probably a wait for high tide in Dover.

Heinrich looked around at the throng of people. It would take him a great amount of time to purchase his boat ticket with all of this going on.

"Les bacs ne s'exécutent pas si le port de Douvres est pauvre, monsieur," the conductor explained." The ferries are late when it is like this.

The young Prussian wanted to be on his way to England and his disappointment was bitter. He briefly remained on the top step.

A split-second hesitation. That's when he saw them.

The two polizisten, in full Prussian uniform, brass-buttoned coats, and *pickelhaube*, spiked helmets on their heads, were just leaving the ticket station. Why would they be here? Prussian police in Calais? Were they looking for him? There was no reason for them to be here in France. German police did not cross the border, let alone police from Prussia. Why were they here, if not sent by his father? He panicked.

The polizisten were working their way through a mass of people just outside the ticket office and into a very thick crowd, not looking up at the train. Not yet, anyway. Heinrich's instincts took over. He quickly turned to reboard the train, literally pushing his way past the French gentleman behind him waiting to disembark.

"I am so sorry for ... I have something I forgot ... pardon, monsieur. *Pardon. Excusez-moi.*" Heinrich turned sideways and slipped between the Frenchman and a heavy-set German woman. After everyone else disembarked, Heinrich found a seat on the opposite side of the car, away from a window where one of the polizisten might see his face from outside. All he could hear was his own pounding heartbeat. Certainly the police were there for a different reason. *It had to be,* Heinrich told himself. *The thought that Vater threatens me makes me this afraid?* He tried to laugh at himself. The other voice in his head advised: it is better to avoid the police ... just in case. His vater was angry enough to have sent them. He has both the temper and the power to do so. Heinrich hunched farther down in his seat, shocked and scared. Could it be that refusing priesthood is an actual crime? He wondered. *Will the polizei take me back to my vater or put me in prison for running from the church?* He never knew he could be this frightened. He was trapped on the train, yet dared not get off with the polizisten on the pier. A shiver ran up his spine as he thought how easily they could find and arrest him.

New passengers boarded the train, squeezing by one another to find seats, chatting and politely excusing themselves if they accidently trod upon another's toes. Heinrich kept his eyes on the station platform, praying that the two polizisten would not decide to search the stationary train. He glanced around, seeing how far it was to the back of the car. He should have seated himself at the rear so he could move back a car should they board the train at this door, but all the seats were taken. *Stupid fool*, he thought to himself. *It's this lack of thinking, this panic that will get me caught.* The train whistle pierced his ears. His eyes remained glued to the car's door as the conductor stepped up into the car, and the door closed. The train jerked its loud way forward, inching then rolling as its momentum increased. No polizei. He sighed in relief until he thought they might have entered the car behind him and could walk into this one from the rear where he would not see them.

Fear spiked up and down his spine once more.

The train pulled away from Calais and the conductor walked down the aisle calling for tickets. The Frenchman sitting in the aisle seat beside Heinrich paid the fare to Boulogne. Not knowing where else to go, Heinrich decided that he would also purchase a Boulogne ticket. Many people would be at that port. A ferry from there would take him to Folkestone. With luck, he could *still* escape to London.

Were the polizisten on board, ready with their cuffs and leg irons? He felt new respect for the Catholic clerics and clergy imprisoned by Bismarck. How ironic that they were jailed for faith and he may be jailed for lack of it.

After a nerve-wracking twenty minutes in which no police came into the car, the train clacked into a small depot in the village of Saint Inglevert. Heinrich impulsively decided to leave the train. A tiny station, no one waited to board and only two others got off with him.

He couldn't get off the platform fast enough, worried a lurking policeman would spot him. Panicked again, he hurried to the narrow main street in front of the little depot and immediately turned down the first side road until he was out of sight of the station. Breathless, he worked his way west through the little town and back to the railroad tracks. He'd heard the train depart minutes before, so feeling safe to do so, he stepped onto the graveled bed. Worried about robbers and not knowing where he was, he decided it was safest to walk along the tracks. The empty rails stretched out before him, appearing to converge into one.

Heinrich walked in the French countryside, the midday sun warming his back and shoulders. Suddenly he was ravenous, for he had eaten only the small French breakfast back in Lille. There were no cafés in the middle of nowhere—no servants calling him to the table. He had no bread to eat—only some crackers in his pocket. He had no idea where he was, had no horse and no one to help him. He trudged along, stepping from one railroad tie to the next.

For the first time, the weight of genuine helplessness descended upon him. He was alone, worse than a peasant. Once his money was gone, he wouldn't have even a pfennig. *I will be locked up in the poorhouse if my London plan fails.* Or locked up in jail if the police catch him.

The day was beautiful, with a few white clouds hanging lazily in the blue sky overhead. Birds sang their joy from young saplings and gnarled trees, which had all leafed out in tender green. With each step he analyzed his plight. Dare he consider turning back? *Back to what? My father? The police?* Back is to nothing. Here is nothing. Nothing. He could only go forward. He had to get to Langsford. *He will help me with Vater and the polizisten. He'll know what to do.* Talking himself into a better mood, he stepped up his pace, valise in his left hand by his side, coat held over his shoulder by his other. Knowing Langsford would help him, he again felt hope he'd soon be with Anna.

Chapter 19

France

Back at the Calais pier, the polizisten still anticipated the Prussian's arrival. By afternoon, two boats had sailed and the crowd dissipated but the men spotted no one. Bauer and Ritter then gave up and checked nearby inns, asking if anyone had seen the verbrecher, but the only responses varied from a casual no, to fear of a dangerous German at large. Their search brought no results. Thus, as Heinrich walked the tracks west, the two police were continuously coming up blank. "Damn. It's as though the mörder has not been in Calais at all," swore Bauer, feeling like a fool. "Where *zum teufel* has he gone?"

Heinrich stopped where a road crossed the tracks. His stomach had given up growling, but his booted feet were sore. He leaned against the wide trunk of an old tree and within minutes he heard hooves clopping beyond a bend in the road. An old farmer driving a small cart pulled by a shaggy horse slowly appeared. In the back of the cart were two calves, probably heading to market in some nearby village. The driver brought the horse to a halt when he saw Heinrich. "Pourquoi êtes vous ici par vous-même, jeune homme," Why are you here by yourself, young man? Do you need help?" The French farmer seemed kind.

"Je suis pour se rendre à la gare plus tard." I have to get to the

train station later. He told the man how he got off at the wrong
stop and did not want to wait for the next train to come, purpose-
fully speaking awkward French, hoping to appear a naive traveler.

The Frenchman laughed. "Ah, youth! Too impatient to wait,
were you? You must learn to listen and learn your French better."
He patted the board of the spring seat. "Come. Sit. I will drive you
into the village and you can catch your next train there, jeune
homme."

Heinrich gratefully climbed up beside him. The old man
clucked to the old horse, which obediently leaned into the worn
leather yoke and pulled them forward at a clip-clopping walk.

"Je vous remercie, monsieur." Heinrich settled in with his
valise in his lap and his coat folded neatly on it. Both he and his
boot-clad feet were grateful.

The road paralleled the railroad track, and after an hour, they
arrived in the little village of Marquise. The train station sat on
the edge of town where the farmer let Heinrich off.

"Je vous remercie beaucoup. Je suis très reconnaissant de bien
vouloir monsieur." I am most grateful. He shook hands with the
farmer and climbed down, putting his hat atop his head with a
pat. He nodded as the farmer clucked to the heavy little horse,
which clopped slowly away.

Crossing the dirt street, Heinrich looked around, watchful
for police. He had no idea how they caught criminals. He'd heard
descriptions of Catholics arrested in their beds in the middle of
the night. He cringed at the thought. Entering the dusty station,
Heinrich went to the ticket master and explained he had been
dozing and misunderstood the conductor who'd announced the
stop. It wasn't until the train left that he realized he had disembarked too soon. Would his ticket still entitle him to journey to
his original destination, Boulogne?

"Oui, bien sûr." Yes, of course.

"And would it be possible to purchase a second ticket through to England as well?" Heinrich inquired, hoping that buying only one ticket now would eliminate the need to buy another in Boulogne, helping him to stay out of the sight of police.

The Frenchman explained that if he were going on to London by way of Boulogne, Heinrich would actually save money with one ticket straight through to the city itself.

"Both Boulogne and Folkestone are good harbors, *bons ports*, though it is a longer crossing than from Calais." The man smiled. "But you will still arrive in London."

As Heinrich stood there with opened purse, he had an idea. The polizisten would look for a man without much money, which is how it appeared. He had galloped away on a borrowed horse, traveled third-class on a train, and as his aching feet reminded him, walked. His vater had no idea how much money he had with him. If he traveled first-class now, the polizisten might not even look in the first-class compartments.

"How much is a first-class passage straight through to London?" Money would do him no good if he were arrested, and traveling first-class would help him hide.

The fare was exorbitant by comparison, but he paid with a Prussian gold mark and carefully watched while the ticket master counted out his change in francs. He now had first-class passage on the train, the steamboat, and the train up to London. Excited and relieved, he wanted to wire Langsford, but wiring from France might alert authorities, so to be safe he would wait until he landed in Folkestone.

He had more than an hour to wait for his train so when his stomach growled a reminder that it had been empty all day, he donned his coat, restored his hat to his head, and carried his valise to a small café. He sat in the corner so he could see while he ate a quarter of a chicken and an artichoke along with a small beer. *Once I'm in England I won't need to worry about police.* Langsford will convince his father to call off the police. His father had always been fond of Langsford.

He checked his watch. It was about ten minutes before the train was due so he picked up his valise and returned to the station. The train's whistle and screeching brakes announced its timely arrival. Heinrich held his breath as he watched people step from the cars, fearing there might be police. Stepping up he quickly found his private compartment in the first-class car. He smiled, for it was a perfect place to hide.

CHAPTER 20

Bermondsey, London

While Heinrich sat on the French train, Anna sat on her bed attempting to tat lace for a blouse she'd sewn. Lottie sat in their bedroom chair, working on embroidery

"Just let me make my own mistakes tatting."

"I was just trying to help because you're clumsy."

"I'm only clumsy when I'm nervous or frustrated," she said defensively. "I want this to look perfect."

"Just make a kerchief so you can drop it in front of a boy." Lottie giggled at the thought.

"Don't be silly. I need to dress appropriately to wait on the ladies," she said, exasperated.

Lottie huffed, slamming her embroidery down onto the armchair. "You will never get a husband if you don't try. Just because Henry disappeared ..." She didn't finish the sentence. "You're going to be an old maid and it will serve you right."

Lottie could be irritating, but Anna felt ashamed when she let herself be annoyed. Had it not been for Lottie and her aunt and uncle, Anna would not have this secure life. Lottie sat silent and Anna's irritation receded. "Forgive me for being cross. I'm perplexed about everything right now."

"I should think before I speak." Lottie looked forlorn as she sat on the bed beside her.

Anna smiled. "Well, thus far, you don't have that tendency

and I wouldn't know you if you did," she laughed and flashed an endearing smile, making Lottie giggle. "I do have something I want to tell you, though, about a young man."

"Who? Did Henry return?"

"No." Anna shoved thoughts of Henry from her mind. "It's a boy at the leather shop, Robbie. He's very sweet and kind and I think he might like me. He's a cordwainer."

"What on earth is a cordwainer? It sounds dreadful."

"It's just a fancy word for a cobbler is all. He makes shoes and boots from fine leather. He's quite good; has to be if he's working in a Leadenhall shop."

"Oh, this is doubly exciting!" Lottie beamed and bounced on her feet.

"I don't understand?"

"Well, you have been so distraught about Henry, I was afraid it would upset you if I told you when you have been so ... so sad."

"What didn't you tell me?" Anna's eyes widened.

"Francis Blackwell from church! He tipped his hat and said hello." She giggled. "He wants to ask Uncle Max's permission to call on me." She bounced on the bed, jiggling Anna along with her tatting. "Oh, I dreaded not telling you, but I was afraid it would hurt your feelings."

"I'm happy for you. I know who Francis is."

"I don't want you to be sad."

"I'm not," Anna said and smiled.

"Let's hope your Robbie asks Uncle Max, too. It's time you had a beau. We can row along the Serpentine together on Sundays."

With Robbie? She suddenly had second thoughts. He was awkward, not self-assured like Henry, the dashing Prussian who walked confidently into her shop—a man who made her feel weak, so out of breath. His touch burned her skin and weakened her knees. Now he was gone. Not a word. Nothing. Involuntarily, she sighed and stood up so Lottie couldn't tell what she was feeling. She would never see Henry again. Would some other man ever have the same effect on her? It certainly wouldn't be Robbie.

Regaining her composure, Anna realized Lottie had still been talking. "If Francis seems nice, then I will let him call on me once a week for a year. No, for six months. Well, maybe a year. Then we can become engaged for the standard two years and by the time I am nineteen I can be married. Who needs to wait until they are twenty-one? And if you begin seeing Robbie, why, we can have a double wedding in three years. Wouldn't that be wonderful?"

"You've not even formally met Francis. What if you find you don't like him?"

"That's just like you, wanting to ruin everything. That's why I didn't want to tell you in the first place. You *are* jealous."

Anna defended herself. "You seem to be planning for three years from now, and you have no idea what might happen this week. I'm not jealous, just sensible."

"Well," Lottie sat in the chair and picked up her embroidery. "It's just so fun to think about Francis and being courted, and engaged," she giggled. "He *is* dashing."

Anna began tatting, letting Lottie prattle on while her own thoughts of any marriage prospects preyed on her mind. She was expected to marry or be an old maid. The latter didn't bother her as much as having to remain with Uncle Max and Aunt Bess, continuing to be a lifelong burden when they had invited her into their family home to help an orphan. She had no right to impose herself on them in that way, but unmarried, she would have no choice. She could never earn enough to be able to pay for her own lodgings, even if she became manager of a shop. An unmarried woman, a spinster; one of the worst spots for any girl to find herself in—dependent on family forever. As much as she loved her adopted aunt and uncle, they were not her family and she could never subject them to her permanent care. But Robbie? He might be her only chance for marriage.

She sighed as she tatted with her shuttle, wondering if she should really make a lace edged handkerchief to drop in front of an interesting boy. Wasn't she pretty enough to attract someone on her own? Henry had thought so ....

CHAPTER 21

Boulogne, France

"Boulogne, prochain arrêt, Boulogne," the conductor announced. The brakes wheezed to a stop along the platform, and Heinrich peered out the window. Throngs of people milled about the depot area and beyond. Boulogne was seldom quiet. As the largest fishing harbor and port in France, lined with gorgeous beaches for tourists, the town bustled with activity.

The boats to Folkestone weren't until morning, but the through-ticket entitled him to lodging, the conductor advised. Heinrich took a tram to the hotel listed on the backside of his ticket.

Late in the day as Heinrich had continued along the French coast, back in Calais the polizisten Bauer and Ritter had come to the conclusion their man had either left a train prior to Calais or continued westward. Bauer shifted their strategy. With a reward for capturing the mörder, the ranking policeman would not let any possibility go unexplored. His sense of pride was at stake, along with the gold marks he wanted. It was better this way. When he grabbed his man, he wouldn't have to share the reward with Ritter after all. So High Grade Brauer sent his partner to backtrack from village to village, east toward Thionville, in case the man departed the train prior to Calais. Brauer, then, continued west in case the Prussian had simply bypassed Calais to go farther on to Boulogne. Perhaps he'd planned to cross the channel there, hoping his ticket to Calais would throw the police off—the mörder was smarter than they thought. Brauer caught the next train headed to Boulogne, a relatively short train ride away.

The hotel was more luxurious than Heinrich expected. The room had starched linens and a decent bed with a down-filled comforter. Wishing he had more clothes other than the few he'd hurriedly stuffed into the valise, he dusted off what he wore, brushed his coat and threw water on his face. He felt somewhat better. The hotel restaurant was still serving so he trotted down three flights of stairs, enjoying that he was in such a large hotel. The maître d' seated him off to the side at a small table for two. In the new French style of courses, the waiter first brought onion soup with crusty bread followed by thin asparagus fresh from a nearby garden. He followed with a blue ling, probably caught off shore early that morning; the fish melted in his mouth. The French food was much lighter than what he was accustomed to but excellent. Next the waiter presented a small plate of Welsh rarebit, an English influence. How grand it would be to dine here with Anna, he thought. His heart warmed. *I shall take her out to dine once I am settled in London.* In high spirits, he finished the final course of fresh fruits with cheese.

Afterward he decided to walk in the cool sea air. He doubted any polizisten had followed him here. He felt confident in his safety. Strolling down Grande Rue, the breezes came in off the water as he mingled with people in the exciting port town. Gray winter days over, the town buzzed with tourists dining in restaurants, browsing inside the small boutiques that were open late for their benefit, or casually strolling in the evening air.

He walked toward the docks. The moonlight illuminated the masts of the fishing boats as they gently bobbed in the harbor. In only a few hours, well before sunrise, fishermen would be swarming the docks and boarding the boats to sail out to sea for their early morning catches. Tonight the empty boats patiently waited.

Heinrich turned up a smaller lane just past Rue de Lampe where two gentlemen with their ladies were out on the town. He felt a pang, for he wanted Anna to be with him. He would walk with her along these cobbled streets... .

His feet hurt. He had already walked too far in these boots. He wished he had brought shoes with him. He'd buy some in London. For now, it was time to return to his room.

Lone polizist Brauer arrived in early evening, planning to check all the ferries in the morning. If no one fitting the drecksack's description had been seen or if the ticket office had no information, he would backtrack to Calais, train stop by train stop, to ask if anyone had seen or spoken to the wanted Prussian. The reward made the effort worthwhile.

Otto Brauer had eaten in Calais and rested on the short train ride, so when he arrived he was alert and ready. The policeman was like a hound on a scent and he would not easily give up. He walked the nearby streets, checking restaurants, stopping in hotels. He walked up Rue de Lampe for a few blocks. He walked around the general port area, checking the more modest hotels and restaurants.

He did not turn and go up Grande Rue. That was farther from the port and closer to the old town and the Basilica of Notre-Dame de Boulogne, a place more likely to attract the tourists and people of means. His man was not in either category.

Although he had funds from Berlin allotted for this pursuit, he chose in his usual fashion not to spend much. He was no fool. The pfennigs and marks were better off in his pocket than in someone else's. He checked into a small place near the docks. He wasn't sure it was clean, but the proprietor guaranteed no bed-bugs or rats. He removed only his helmet, coat, and shoes, then lay down on the thin blanket atop the straw mattress where he immediately fell asleep.

By three a.m., men clad in heavy slickers and canvas hats readied their nets and lines. Muffled voices carried across the harbor. Oars splashed, for they needed to be away from the docks before their luffing sails would fill with wind to sail them farther asea. By five a.m., all the boats had gone and the slips sat vacant.

The steamer ferries slowly came to life next, as captains and crews readied them for the day's crossings. The first was not scheduled to leave until eight, but there was much preparation.

Brauer was up and out the door by six. He found a small café where he purchased bread and coffee as the sun rose above the horizon for another beautiful spring day. He walked over to the debarkation office to watch and wait. Few, other than the steam-boat crews, were up, but soon droves of passengers would descend on the docks.

His instincts told him the verbrecher was there and he'd grab him fast. He smiled at the thought of the arrest, filled with the satisfaction of doing his job. He would beat the mörder ... not so much that he couldn't walk, for he needed to be able to travel, but a good beating—inflicted pain kept a criminal in line. Once he got his man back to Prussia, the reward would be his. He grinned at the thought, licking his lips at the same time.

At six o'clock, Heinrich awoke. He stood at the bureau and washed his face and torso with the water he poured into the basin. Drying with a linen towel, he felt refreshed. He took a clean shirt from his valise, and quickly buttoned it. He had no other pants, so he shook out his one pair and wiped the dust from his riding boots, wanting to be somewhat presentable when he arrived at No. 12 Grosvenor Square later that night. By six thirty he was sitting downstairs again at a small table eating a light breakfast. He headed out of the hotel and into the street by seven fifteen, eager for this last part of his journey.

The town was already awake. The first steamboat was due to leave in less than an hour. He spotted a tram on the busy Grande Rue and caught it at the nearby stop. He counted the exact fare in francs and asked to be advised of the proper stop for the steamboats. The driver nodded as he whisked a light whip gently across the broad rears of the horses.

Polizist Brauer watched as the port activity increased. Now seven thirty, travelers scheduled for the first and second steamer ferries arrived, with later departing passengers straggling in. Many were buying tickets, and the little office quickly became crowded. He stood and arched his back to stretch, then walked through the incoming passengers, stepping into the flow of people, scanning the crowd. Brauer had acute vision and remembered nearly every face he had ever seen, but he still only had a description. At least, thanks to a telegraph received last night from Prussia, he now had a name: Heinrich Dieffenbacher.

People arrived at the docks on foot and by wagon, train, and omnibus. It was less than a half hour until the first steamer sailed, and travelers with tickets stood in a queue by the gangplanks.

The polizist scanned the line but saw no one remotely fitting the description.

Heinrich's tram arrived and he stepped off along with six others. He made small talk as they walked to the dock, chatting about travel and the weather. He suddenly felt nervous and walked in the middle of the group, which seemed safer. Just in case.

Unfortunately, the others hadn't purchased tickets. He bid adieu to his companions as they headed to the ticket office, leaving him alone, physically exposed. Automatically he scanned for polizisten and was relieved not to see any. The "First-Class Passengers" gangplank was open for immediate boarding. With his valise in one hand and ticket in the other, he walked up the wooden incline, anxious to board and leave the continent. He'd be safe once they sailed.

Simultaneously, the lower-class travelers were now permitted to board their respective gangplanks, and all crowded forward at once. Additional passengers rushed from the debarkation office, tickets in hand, to join the crunch.

Heinrich walked straight up on deck and directly inside. Separated from second class by the galley, the first-class restaurant with its mahogany tables and plush chairs remained empty. Beyond, a glass skylight cast pale light into the main oval-shaped lounge. The majority of first-class passengers were already gathered, surrounding a heavy stove that squatted in the center of the room. Firmly reinforced to both floor and ceiling with long slender rods, it emanated heat, offsetting the sea air chill. While the men stood, women sat on the red velvet cushions of the cast-iron chairs.

The lone polizist kept scanning the crowd. Brauer glanced toward the station house where the queue to purchase tickets for later departures grew longer. No one.

Heinrich stood behind a group of fellow passengers as they talked about Boulogne. He noticed one particular couple because they appeared to adore each other. The gentleman stood beside the chair of a very attractive lady. He beamed at her with great affection. Heinrich found himself watching the pair.

The man spoke. "I'm so pleased you enjoyed Boulogne. I knew you would."

"Yes, my dear husband. You are always right." She adjusted her gloves and looked up at him with adoration. "I think my favorite's the Basilica of Notre-Dame; the dome is so beautiful."

"I like the old walls—so ancient; they go back to the Romans." The husband leaned over close to her cheek, placing his hand on her back, and whispered something.

"Oh," she lightly gasped. "We are in public." She giggled her reprimand. Looking at him with moon eyes, she said, "You take advantage because it's our honeymoon."

"Precisely because it's our honeymoon, sweet girl," he replied, grinning broadly, standing straight again, his hand now resting on her shoulder.

Heinrich wanted to honeymoon with Anna, just like this couple.

Lost in daydreaming, he realized the boat had been released from her moorings, steam engines rumbling down below turning the massive paddle wheel. They were leaving the pier and France. His massive worry lifted. He had done it. He was actually free!

The couple decided to go out on deck to see the magnificent

Dome of the Basilica one last time. *A good idea*, Heinrich thought. He hadn't seen much. He would go on the deck and take in the view, still thinking about returning here someday with Anna. He followed the honeymooners through the carved walnut doors; the steamer's crest etched into their oval glass panes. They climbed a few steps to the upper deck and the panoramic view of the port city.

Brauer had not seen the man he searched for. Perhaps the next boat. He stood on the pier watching as the first steamer departed: the massive rope lines already cast off, the smokestacks belching white into the sea air, the huge paddle wheel turning. Slowly the boat moved a few feet from the pier.

Brauer looked up at the deck above where people stood at the railings.

Heinrich had been looking out, gazing at the beautiful dome. Then, for no reason, he looked down. It was then he saw the polizist!

Brauer saw Heinrich, a man on a boat wearing riding boots. Most importantly he saw his expression: one of abject surprise and fear. He knew that look, for he always saw it on the face of the wanted just before he closed in on them.

The two men locked gazes, staring with wide eyes: one angry, one shocked.

As the steamer moved farther away and down the dock, Otto Brauer walked quickly beside it, but the boat was a half dozen or more meters from the dock. He knew he couldn't board now. Dammit! He'd just missed his quarry! He was furious. How did this man board the steamer? He quickened his pace as the steamer increased hers, moving her farther toward to the deep harbor waters. His instincts would not permit him to stop. He yelled as loudly as he could.

"Ich werde dich bis in die hölle verfolgen, Heinrich Dieffenbacher!" I will follow you all the way to hell! He knew his man heard him. He saw him flinch at his shout. He saw his hands grip the railing.

The boat was moving faster. The policeman ran parallel. He yelled. He yelled a threat. Or was it a promise? "Bis in die Hölle!"

The words hung in the wind.

All the way to hell.

PART TWO

The Quagmire

CHAPTER 22

No. 12 Grosvenor Square, London

Langsford, with plenty to concern him, slowly trudged up the grand staircase to the first floor. Heinrich had shown up on his doorstep the night before, disheveled and apparently homeless. The whole story sounded astounding, and now this morning, Langsford faced a very difficult situation. Tweed trotted up the wide steps beside him. "What am I to do?" he asked the dog. "He's my friend. We've always looked out for each other, ever since we met. But this ..." He folded a piece of paper in half and placed it in his pocket, remembering another time six years earlier at school.

The Prussian brothers were attending the English school, sent there by their father so they would become more "worldly." Both Gerhard and Heinrich were younger, but Langsford had been assigned by the headmaster to help the younger boy settle in. One afternoon Heinrich couldn't find his older schoolmate, so he looked in the play rehearsal room even though the rehearsal had ended a half hour before. He'd swung open the door and found two actors: Langsford and an older blond student whose muscular arms surrounded Langsford as they passionately spooned.

At the sound of the young boy's entrance, Langsford pushed the other boy backward, shoving himself away from the embrace in the process. "I was running lines ... We're a bit late here."

Langsford wiped his mouth. "George and I were, uh, going over his cues."

"That's a *verdammte Lüge*! I saw! Don't lie to me!" Heinrich was three years his junior and new to the school. Langsford knew the younger boy didn't understand how it was at a boys' school here in England where everyone lived together. There were no private governesses here wiping noses. The housemaster, Johnson, was in charge of their group and he had advised Langsford, "Don't protest when George shows affection. You're a fortunate one should he find you worthy." Heinrich was too new here to realize what often went on outside of class.

"It's—it's—" Langsford couldn't find the right words as Heinrich came closer.

"It's wrong. It's sinful!" Heinrich glared at George, determined to defend his new English friend. He knew passages from the Bible. "You're an abomination." The young Prussian bristled, tall for his age, his hands already in fists. "Get out!" And George picked up his shirt, spat at the thirteen-year-old and quickly left the classroom. Langsford, picking up his own shirt, walked over to the desks and chairs shoved up against the walls, and sat, ashamed.

"I know it's supposed to be wrong. But it's not uncommon. George said even Housemaster Johnson kissed him."

"The housemaster? That ugly old man? And he *let* him?!"

"Apparently."

"Eeew. Why?"

"It's not so bad, a man kissing another man. The Greeks did it all the time."

Heinrich made some odd noise and shuddered. "It's beastly, you know. And it leads to sodomy."

"I know."

"Then don't do it."

"It can be difficult to resist with some of them."

"Well, resist it! You are one of the good fellows around here. One of the few I can tolerate. But if you are going to do ... this ...I don't *want* to know you."

"I think I have demons." Langsford looked at the floor. "I never told anyone until now."

"I don't want to hear it."

"It's true."

"You're crazy. That's only because your mother died when you were little. But you are kind, smart, and you kicked my brother's arse. He deserved that."

"Well, Gerhard *is* an arse. No one likes him and he bullied you and took a swing at me. What was I to do?"

"Most people at home run from my brother. But you didn't back down. That's one reason why I like you. I want to be just as smart and clever and brave as you when I'm as old as you."

"You're just a little boy. I don't know why I even talk to you."

"Because I'm a friend, even if I *am* younger."

"I suppose you're all right. I just can't tolerate the bigger boys beating on the likes of you little ones. But you, you stand your ground."

"I learned early on to hold my own against my own brother and his friends."

Langsford's shirt rebuttoned, he pulled on his coat and walked with Heinrich out of the classroom heading over to one of the quads. "Let's not speak of this again."

"I won't if you keep those demons in check. Or you'll end up in jail and your father will pay a big fine and then beat you at home. Spooning never has a decent ending. Bulls don't rut with bulls."

"You're right."

They walked along the stone walls of a school building, remaining silent.

Langsford spoke in a whisper. "I know I shouldn't." And though
there were moments when he wished he could, even when he
longed for a male embrace, he did his best to keep those demons
in check. Even when he fell in love—his own forbidden fruit, he
refrained from pursuing the man.

A few months after this incident, Housemaster Johnson
suddenly departed the school and students referred to him as
"Mandrake Johnson." George was abruptly absent—sent home.
Heinrich had been right about that type of spooning never re-
sulting in anything good. A solid lesson, but one that led to many
frustrating moments for Langsford since. After that incident, he
and Heinrich had become fast and loyal friends, never speaking
of this seriously again. Vague, joking references were the only
mention as their lives continued. Langsford finished school before Heinrich and returned to London, although they'd stayed
in touch.

Last year, Langsford had married lovely Regina, hoping that
having a wife would keep his demons at bay. It seemed to have
worked. His wife was a blessing.

He reached the top of the stairs. What was he to do about
Heinrich now? A friendship torn between loyalty and what was
legally right? He couldn't find an answer. He was heartbroken, for
he loved Heinrich like a little brother. He straightened his smoking jacket and walked down the wide hall, Tweed's nails clicking
on the floor. With a deep sigh he entered the library where the tall
multi-paned windows encouraged gray morning light.

Langsford remained in the doorway looking with concern at
Heinrich who sat at the desk at the far end of the room, elbows on
the inset leather, head in hands.

"Ahemmm," Langsford cleared his throat and walked into the room. "We best talk." He stood beside the desk obscuring what light the tall windows cast.

Heinrich looked up with a bright expression. "Yes, I really need your help."

Langsford motioned Heinrich over to the chairs opposite the fireplace where they both sat in the matched wingbacks. The levity of their friendship nonexistent for the moment, they sat in serious silence, staring into the fire.

"I was grateful you were my chaperone on my earlier visit," Heinrich began. "I don't know if I told you."

"That was nothing," Langsford replied, glossing over the apology. "Today we've a real problem."

"Yes. My vater. I cannot believe he wants me arrested. This entire situation has gotten out of hand."

"Explain precisely what happened."

"I ran away," Heinrich confessed. "I couldn't remain home and become a priest."

"You didn't change his mind?"

"For hundreds of years our family has had a priest."

"You never had a choice, did you?"

"Not if I stayed in Prussia. Vater threatened me if I disobeyed. So I left. I got as far as Calais when I saw the polizisten my vater sent." He described his attempt to outsmart them by staying on the train, walking along the train tracks in France and boarding the steamer in Boulogne. "They nearly caught me there."

Langsford bit his lip, picturing it.

"I thought I would be safe here in England, away from my father. Away from the police. I worried police might be on the boat at Folkestone so when I got off, I quickly got in the waiting queue of passengers ready to board. I figured the police would only look at people leaving the ferry."

"That was clever."

"I was lucky, because I heard someone yell my name. Three bobbies stood calling at the gangplank, 'Anyone seen Heinrich Dieffenbacher?' He shook his head. "I was terrified. Vater must have telegraphed the English police to arrest me! How far does his influence go?"

Heinrich went on to describe how he slowly slipped away and out to the street. "I knew if I could get to London, you would help, but with the bobbies looking for me, going by train was out of the question. Between getting wagon rides and walking, it took me several days, but I managed to get here. I don't know what to do next. I don't want to be arrested! I don't want to be a priest!"

It was this tired, disheveled young Prussian that Langsford found when Mr. Barnes, his tenured butler, announced a visitor's arrival the night before. Langsford graciously welcomed him and after listening to a brief version of why he'd unexpectedly shown up, had the house staff show him to a guest room, assuring him they would speak in the morning. Langsford, shocked and worried, hid his concern, knowing he had a tough decision to make.

Now the two friends sat beside one another in front of the fire that was warding off the damp spring chill. Each man had a different agenda: Heinrich wanted help with his father. Langsford had to figure out if that was the truth.

"Will you contact my vater?"

Langsford abruptly cut off his request. "You need to read this. It arrived yesterday morning." With that, he took the paper from his pocket, carefully unfolded it, and handed it to Heinrich who read it several times with an ever-increasing frown. It was a telegraph, scripted on the official Post Office form:

POST OFFICE TELGRAPHS
NO FEES TO BE PAID UNLESS STAMPED HEREON
Time sent *9:27* From *Commissioner Henderson* Dated *May 5ᵗʰ* 1884
Telegraph for: *Lord Langsford*
Grosvenor Square No 12

Advise Prussian Secret Police seek Heinrich Dieffenbacher
for murder. Believed to be your acquaintance. Now in
England. Dangerous. Contact immediately if seen.

"I ... *Ich ... Was ist das denn?*" Heinrich struggled to understand.

Langsford had already known what Heinrich did not when he arrived last night—he was wanted for murder. They were friends; he couldn't just contact Scotland Yard. He needed to give his friend a chance to explain, and this morning he watched closely. An alert businessman and keen poker player, he'd learned how to read people, plus he knew Heinrich well. The young Prussian's reaction showed no clue that he was aware of why the police wanted him. He appeared to honestly believe his father was responsible.

Heinrich stared at the small flame flickering within the embers in the fireplace, the telegraph hanging limply in his right hand. "I don't understand. I thought my father sent the *Preußische Geheimpolizei.* The Prussian Secret Police and Scotland Yard want me for murder?"

He groped, trying to make sense of what he'd just read. "Me? *Mord?* How?"

"I don't know."

"*Vater* did not send the police?"

"No."

"Why do the police think I have anything to do with a murder?"

"I don't know."

"Who did I murder?"

"I don't know."

A long silence hung in the library.

"Heinrich, old chum, I don't know why, but you are an international fugitive."

CHAPTER 23

No. 12 Grosvenor Square, London

Langsford reached for his *Bruyère* pipe and gazed into the fire while Heinrich absorbed the telegraph's contents. He anticipated Heinrich's inevitable question.

"Do you believe the telegraph? Do *you* think I murdered someone? Are you going to turn me into Scotland Yard?" Anxious, Heinrich stood, hands fisted at his side to challenge his English friend.

Drawing on the pipe, Langsford puffed a couple times. "No, I don't believe you are a murderer. Not you. You wouldn't even let me kiss a schoolboy, years back. You've been schooled to be a future priest. How could *you* ever break a major commandment?" he grinned.

The tension left Heinrich's shoulders and he exhaled with relief as he sat back down. "*Gott sei dank!* An ally."

Langsford took another puff. "You realize your father has probably disinherited you, even if he didn't send the police. With this charge of murder, you are in dire straits, old chap."

Heinrich nodded, looking down at the parquet floor.

"Did you come to London to run from the Preußische Geheimpolizei, or to the pretty face at the Leadenhall shop?" Langsford quizzically raised an eyebrow.

"My only thought was to leave Prussia for a future with Anna. My plan was to come to London, find employment, and court her."

He stood again, picked up a poker, and pushed back a fallen log, sending sparks up the chimney. "Everything fell apart when I spied the polizisten in Calais." He replaced the poker in its stand. "The question is: What am I to do now about the Secret Police? Anna?"

The Englishman stood, leaning on the mantel to face Heinrich. "It appears I am in my home with a fugitive. If I fail to turn you over to the authorities I, too, will be in quite a pickle with Scotland Yard."

Heinrich turned pale.

"Don't worry," Langsford laughed. "I won't let them arrest you. We'll think this through, you and I."

"What if someone here contacts the police?"

"We mustn't breathe a word of it to anyone here. No whisperings amongst the servants." He puffed his pipe. "Do you have any idea why you are accused?"

"Nein."

"Then you want to escape?"

"I won't run from something I did not do. I'll have to take my chances and turn myself into Scotland Yard, I suppose."

Langsford removed his pipe from his lips and Heinrich paced back and forth. "You *will* be dragged back to Germany where you could be hanged, you know."

"It's a chance I must take." He stopped in front of the fire. "Disobeying Vater reflects poorly on me but to be accused of murder? *That* mars the Dieffenbacher name throughout the State of Prussia and Germany. You know it does."

"Yes. Heritage brings large and heavy responsibilities which you *cannot* leave behind. You can only escape your father's demands."

"The family land, the estate, everything, could be taken by the

State! What would become of my mother, my sister, my little niece and cousins?" He shook his head. "I cannot imagine ...."

Langsford recognized Heinrich's set jaw. He'd seen it many times before when Heinrich had made up his mind, but this time it was ill-advised. "You can't rely on the polizisten or Scotland Yard to look for the truth. The Prussians are convinced you are the murderer and they won't search for anyone else once you are arrested."

"Won't they want to find the truth?"

"No."

"I won't run. I'll stand up like a man."

"There *is* a third option. Solve the case, and clear your name."

"Solve it? I have no idea how."

"Return to Prussia. Prove your innocence."

Heinrich held Langsford's gaze as he thought about the Englishman's words.

"I'll help you."

"Ja?"

Langsford knocked his pipe against the side of the fireplace to empty the bowl of ash. "I do owe you a rather large debt that goes back to a nearly misspent youth," he confessed with a chuckle. "Besides, ever since I consented to your crazy idea to visit Anna, I've been on your side there. The forbidden fruit, you know. My favorite kind."

For the first time, Heinrich smiled. "I'm glad. We've always stood by each other." He echoed Langsford's earlier thought. "But what can I do, assuming I don't get arrested?"

"Simple. Find out who was murdered and by whom. And don't get arrested."

Heinrich walked over to the tall windows, staring out at the gray day. "Can I manage that?" He turned to face Langsford. "All I want is to be with Anna. Dare I visit her now?"

"I wouldn't. Too great a risk."

"No. You're right. I'm a fugitive. I have to solve the murder first."

Langsford joined him at the window overlooking Grosvenor Square just as the sun penetrated the gray. "We'll make a plan. I'm good at that."

"Yes, you've always been the smartest of the lot. I don't know what to do."

"First, we need to explain your presence here. The staff doesn't really know you, only my driver Pelham and he can be trusted. You were barely here last visit and you hadn't been in London since before I finished school. You are now my ... Let's see ... not a Prussian schoolmate. A Westphalian cousin."

"Westphalian?"

"Close enough. Still German."

"What about your wife?"

"Regina was gone to her sister's when you were here. She's never met you. That's to our advantage."

"But she's back now and certainly knows you have no Westphalian cousin."

"She won't question me. I'll buy her a new necklace to distract her. Besides, she'll be leaving for our country estate this Friday. We don't spend much time together," he sighed.

"So when do *we* leave?"

"As soon as you've grown a beard."

"What? And look furry like you? I actually was thinking of a stylish moustache, myself."

"No. A beard." He stroked his own and smiled. "Something posh, fashionable, to match mine."

"Hardly! The fox hounds should chase you. But I suppose ... something to hide behind so no one recognizes me." He touched the stubble already on his chin. "All right."

"I'll go to Scotland Yard tomorrow and ask the commissioner for more details since he sent me the telegraph."

"Do you know him?"

"Yes. Through my father, rest his soul. Because of him, I know most of the ranking men in London."

"You'll find out who was murdered?"

"Yes, and where. Then we'll know where to go." Langsford looked out the window, his hands clasped behind him.

CHAPTER 24

No. 12 Grosvenor Square, London

The next morning, Heinrich went into the library where he knew he'd be alone. Lady Regina never entered this particular room, it seemed, and the servants only if someone rang.

Langsford would join him when he returned from Scotland Yard, although Heinrich was not sure how soon. The Englishman enjoyed staying up until early morning hours and slept late, none of which his father would have approved. Yet here was a nobleman who did not need to work but did because he enjoyed the business of investing. What his vater would call lack of discipline in a daily routine did not appear to be to Langsford's detriment.

Heinrich sat stretching, his long legs sprawled out in front of him. He'd slept little and was tired. He daydreamed how Langsford would return shortly to tell him that the entire telegraph had been a mistake and no one was murdered. They'd have a good laugh and a drink ... and Anna would drive up in a carriage... . Then Langsford ...

But his reality didn't go as his daydream had. An hour later Langsford sat again in the adjacent winged back. "I have facts." He lit his Bruyère. Heinrich sat at rigid attention, eager. Langsford spoke between puffs as the pipe began to draw. "There were two brothers." He pulled a small note from his waistcoat pocket to read, setting the pipe in its stand. "One is Marc, the other is Karl."

He looked at Heinrich. "Marc is who you are accused of murdering. It seems his brother Karl saw you on the street." Looking back at the note again, he continued. "The last name is Gülker. Live in Bullay, Prussia. Never heard of it."

"It's north of our estate."

"Do you know the Gülker brothers?"

"Never heard of them."

"Were you ever in Bullay?"

"That's where I caught the train—instead of Wittlich. It's the same *Koblenz-Trier* railroad line."

"I don't understand."

"Vater threatened to force me to stay. I figured if he sent someone to stop me from boarding a train, he would expect me to go to Wittlich, the closest depot. So I went to Bullay instead. The stop just north."

"How much farther is it?"

"At least four hours' ride. Maybe more. I arrived in time to catch the last train."

"The brother claims he saw you on the street after the murder."

"I don't remember anyone.... Oh, I passed a drunk, I think."

Langsford cut him off. "What do you remember about this drunk?"

"Nothing much. Harmless," he recalled. "I walked around him and went on to the depot."

Langsford nodded, "Well, someone saw you. The police only had to ask the stationmaster where you were going. They began hunting for you before you were barely on your way."

"Why would they accuse me? How do they know my name, even?"

"That's what we need to find out. Now we know where to go—Bullay." Langsford paused to pick up his pipe as he set the note on the side table. "Scotland Yard, as you saw from the telegraph, believes you are here in England."

"Ja. The polizist saw me aboard the steamer to Folkestone." Heinrich described the polizist running alongside the boat screaming, "All the way to hell!" They are here in England hunting me right now, I know."

"No. As Commissioner Henderson pointed out, the Prussian police won't come here. They don't need to because of our extradition laws. If Scotland Yard finds you, they'll send you back. But think about this: Scotland Yard is searching for you *here*. No one expects you to return to the continent. That's exactly where you'll be, back in Prussia."

CHAPTER 25

Leadenhall Market, London

Anna was putting the finishing touches on a hat display when the bell over the door tinkled. She looked up to see Robbie, cap in hand and a wide grin on his face. He wasn't wearing his usual cobbler's apron.

"Ahem," he cleared his throat.

Anna smiled back. "Hello. How is your boot-making?"

"Good, thanks." He awkwardly shifted his weight from one foot to another. "I came 'ere, 'oping not to be a bother, but I wanted to speak abou' a private matter." He fiddled with his cap.

Anna quietly smiled, hands folded in front of her.

"I wish ta inquire if I may pay a visit to yer father ta ask permission so I can call on ya." He blushed as he spoke.

This is exactly what I didn't want, she thought. Robbie was pleasant, but that was all. Still, no one else has spoken to Uncle Max on her behalf, she told herself. What if no one else ever does? *I must say yes.* "Robbie"—she forced a wider smile—"you need to speak with Maxwell Miller, my friend Charlotte's uncle. We live with him and his wife."

Emboldened now that he had begun, Robbie blurted out his rehearsed speech, "Dear Anna, yer a most beautiful girl and yer kind and ya like me. I spend nights thinking about 'ow we can be better ac-quainted. Just standin' 'ere in this room with ya makes me 'appy." His face radiated his excitement. "You'll speak to yer uncle to tell 'im I want ta make an o-fficial call this Sunday?"

"Of course. How nice of you, Robbie." She turned to the counter so he could not see her face. She couldn't tell him he didn't hold her heart. Instead she managed to utter, "I shall tell Uncle Max."

"Oh, that'd be wonderful, Anna! I would never call on ya without talkin' to 'im first." He donned his cap and nearly skipped out the shop door, so excited he didn't say good-bye.

Anna sighed as the door shut. If Uncle Max did not agree, then Robbie would obey and not bother her. Henry, on the other hand, did not care what anyone thought. He'd looked at her, and in that commanding manner of his, declared he would visit her again. He was like a storm, surrounding her with his presence. Robbie? What could she call Robbie? *I suppose he is more like a slight breeze. Pleasant, but easily ignored, and even a bit of a nuisance.*

The issue was that Robbie was here and Henry wasn't, and she couldn't ignore that fact.

CHAPTER 26

Calais, France, to the Rhineland

Langsford and Heinrich, with trustworthy Pelham traveling in second class, took the train from London to the channel. The weather was beautiful in Dover, and as they sailed, they could see Calais nearly the entire way. The ancient French town was bright in sunlight when they docked. Once disembarked, they waited for customs. Langsford advised Heinrich, "Don't show your passport with your real name. They haven't required them since the end of the French war, but should they ask, say you don't have one."

"I didn't know that. I always present it."

"Well, don't."

They passed through customs, answering negative to the only question asked—"Do you carry any tobacco or spirits?"—in spite of the pouch of pipe tobacco in Langsford's jacket pocket. He winked at Heinrich as they exited the door leading to the French trains. Pelham joined them from his customs line to see to their baggage. Once the train ride ended, he would be Langsford's official driver.

Most travelers were going on to Paris and wanted the train to Amiens. The trio walked down the platform for the eastbound train to Lille. Once seated in their private compartment with the doors latched, Heinrich lowered the windows to let in the spring air. Langsford settled into the comfortable seat opposite.

"No offense, but I wish Anna were here; you, of course, as chaperone."

"I imagine you do."

"I may never see her again," Heinrich lamented.

"I find that hard to believe."

"The first moment I saw her, I knew ..."

"Ah, there it is."

"Surely it was love like that with your wife."

"Must I talk about it with you?"

"Why not?"

"Because my first love was not Regina."

"Oh?"

"My feelings were toward someone who, like your Anna, would have been unacceptable to my father."

"Really?"

Heinrich doesn't fully appreciate the demons that fight me, Langsford thought. He would have no idea how difficult it was to control them, for they were always there, hidden in the shadows. "Even though I *was* in love ... not marriage material for me."

"Regina is perfect for you, love or not. Position, wealth to match yours. Once I marry Anna, you won't wish to allow us to grace your table; we will have no position or money."

"If that bothers you, then why pursue it?"

"It doesn't bother me; just that I'll miss you. Still, being with someone I love makes it all worthwhile. My sister married the man Vater chose; she's sad most of the time." Heinrich fell quiet for a moment. "I miss Gisela. And Mutter. Now I have a fading hope of being with Anna."

"Let's resolve this police matter first. Then you'll call upon Anna." Langsford felt sad for his friend.

"What are we going to do first in Bullay?" Heinrich suddenly refocused on their mission.

"We aren't going there directly. We get off at Wittlich. You stay at the hotel and remain inside lest someone recognizes you."

"Then why have I let my beard grow to hide my face if you think I'll be recognized?"

"Even though you've a beard, people in the area know you well."

"I think I look quite different."

"You'll be on their minds. I'm sure there's talk in all the villages. Tongues wag."

"I want to get on with it and find the real murderer, not hide in a hotel."

"You want to blunder like a fox into a trap? Stay in the room. I've send word ahead to your father that I'm coming."

"You're going to the estate?!"

"Yes. The police will have spoken to your father. I want to find out what he knows."

"What good will *that* do? Won't he think it strange you ask?"

"It will appear as normal curiosity. The more I know, the better our success. We'll just have to see what happens and play it as the cards are dealt."

"I prefer not to think of this as a game," Heinrich moaned at the Englishman's reference. They'd played quite a few hands of the French game poker, waiting those days for Heinrich's beard to grow. He'd lost nearly every game to Langsford.

"I'll stay inside but only for a short while. We're wasting time."

"We *shall* go to Bullay," Langsford sat back. "But I strongly suspect your father can shed some light first."

Unbeknownst to Langsford as they rode the train through France, a man wearing a derby hat and a long brown coat walked up to the entrance of the grand residence on Grosvenor Square. When Barnes opened the heavy front door, the old butler conversed briefly with the man.

"I regret that Lord Langsford is presently not in. Have you a card?"

"No card," replied the man. "Do you know when I might find him in?"

"I'm afraid not, sir. He's on the continent at the moment. Whom shall I say called?"

"Just Mr. Abberline, Scotland Yard."

Barnes nodded.

As the door closed, the man turned and walked away.

CHAPTER 27

Bermondsey, London

Robbie and Mr. Maxwell sat talking in the parlor. The girls and Aunt Bess waited nervously upstairs.

A few evenings before, Anna sat at the table after supper, tracing the lace pattern of the cloth with her fingertip as she told Uncle Max about Robbie. Her uncle was a slight man, wearing his favorite soft black leather vest, rolled up sleeves, and twill pants. His trademark was a permanently ink-stained index finger. An editor at *The Daily Telegraph*, he was intelligent and hardworking. Self-educated, he wanted "his girls" to have decent educations and encouraged them to remain in school until it was concluded. Anna had come to love him very much.

"I've been waiting for this moment." He smiled, setting down his tea. "Aunt Bess and I have managed to put a few shillings aside for your dowry. That will help encourage the young man."

She was surprised. "Oh, Uncle Max. You are far too generous." She ran around the table to hug him, his lamb chop sideburns tickling her cheek.

"My dear child. All the money you make goes into the household. You have none."

"But without your kindness these past years, I wouldn't have been able to finish school or had you all for a family. I'd have lived in an orphanage and I would never have been able to have this job at the shop without your help."

Uncle Max smiled broadly and patted her hand. "I know you are grateful. That's who you are: caring and good. I want you to belong to a man with those same qualities. You, and Lottie both, have given us much joy and light in our lives."

Now it was Sunday and Anna sat upstairs on her bed remembering that conversation. She felt guilty now, because she wished there were no dowry. Without one, Robbie might be deterred.

Aunt Bess fussed with her hair and gave her more advice about how to act around a suitor. Lottie, beside herself with excitement, listened eagerly. When she finished with Anna, their aunt went back downstairs to check on the men. After a minute or two, she called upstairs. "Anna. You've a gentleman caller." Filled with dread, Anna got up, limply accepted a hug from Lottie, and went down.

Robbie, standing at the foot of the steep stairs, greeted her. He was wearing his best clothes: a starched cotton shirt with a thick, coarse bow tie and a somewhat rumpled tweed suit. He still had that clean leather smell about him.

"'allo, Miss Anna." He was stiff and formal, unlike the Robbie she knew at the market. "I brought these for ya." He handed her a small bouquet of flowers—an extravagant purchase from his small salary.

"How nice, Robbie." She sniffed them. "They're lovely."

"Let me put them in water for you, dear." Aunt Bess took the flowers and disappeared into the kitchen.

Uncle Max, who was standing nearby, spoke up. "Anna, Robert here has asked permission to call on you and I have happily given it. So, you two may sit and talk, with Aunt Bess's and my blessings."

"Thank you, Uncle Max."

He winked at her behind Robbie's back then left to join his

wife in the kitchen where they could chaperone from afar. Robbie and Anna stood alone in the foyer.

He spoke first. "I'd be surprised if we 'ad any rain." He touched her hand and she flinched. Immediately Robbie drew his hand back, slightly embarrassed. Instead, he stepped aside and gestured so that she may walk first into the parlor.

"Yes," she said. "Let's sit and talk." She perched on a chair, leaving the settee for Robbie, to assure distance between them. Just as in the shop the other day, Robbie seemed awkward and unsure, quite boyish. He was already twenty-one, she'd discovered as they chatted. A bit younger that Lord Langsford, but older than Henry. *I cannot compare him to Henry*, she reminded herself. Henry was just a fantasy. She forced a smile and listened to Robbie describe new boots for a lady about her size and age, but who wasn't as pretty. "If titles were bestowed by beauty, you'd be royalty." He spoke his line by rote.

"What a sweet thing to say."

Robbie spoke of a new man at work. "He be older than me, but he ain't experienced in leatherworkin'. His stitchin' is coarse and uneven. Ya'd think a leatherworker from Germany'd be exact. In an odd way I'm glad 'e ain't."

It surprised Anna that the new worker was German. "Why would he come here to work?"

"Well, 'e says there's no work over there. A bunch of 'em, including a Frenchman, come over here. It's good we're in London and we 'ave jobs, you and me."

She wondered why skilled workers would have left Europe, and asked Robbie what he thought.

"I don't really care as long as they don't take me job. But I doubt they could—I'm much better than any of 'em foreigners."

He changed the subject. "Someday I plan ta buy a beautiful shawl at the shop so ya can wear it like the fancy ladies."

"That would be lovely."

"I'll save me pennies, then," he smiled. "I've fine skills, ya know."

She listened carefully as he talked about his abilities. She asked him if he liked to read. "Naw, I don't fancy that stuff. Readin' distracts you girls from fulfilling your domestic chores. It's a dangerous thing, women readin'. I've been warned about 'at."

"I see," she nodded. "I did enjoy *Alice's Adventures in Wonderland*, by Lewis Carroll. It had beautiful drawings. Uncle Max didn't mind my reading it. He likes it when we read. What do you enjoy, then?"

"A good round of ale with me boys. A game or two of cards. Nuthin' better than bein' with friends, don't you agree?"

"Yes, friends are good. I'm blessed to have my best friend live here, too. Lottie and I are very close."

"I wouldn't know 'bout family, much, but I'm glad you have Lottie, I suppose."

They continued to talk about nothing specific because she couldn't find a topic he was enthusiastic about except his cobbling skills. After a proper amount of time, she stood. "It was nice of you to bring the flowers and to call on me. You are very kind, Robbie." He seemed a bit dull, she thought ungraciously. Maybe next visit she could get him to engage in a serious conversation much like she had with Uncle Max—or like she had with Henry ....

As if on cue, Uncle Max came out of the kitchen and into the foyer. Robbie turned to him. "Might'n I be so bold as ta request yer permission ta return Sunday next for another pleasant visit with yer lovely niece?"

Before he could reply, Aunt Bess joined them. "We would love to have you, Robert, but you must come for dinner."

"Yes, son. Come for dinner," Uncle Max agreed.

Oh dear, Anna thought as her heart sank.

CHAPTER 28

The Dieffenbacher Estate, Prussia

A message to Langsford from Heinrich's brother, Gerhard, had been waiting at the hotel in Wittlich. Langsford had read it aloud.

> *My dear Langsford—*
>
> *I fear I must inform you of the death of my beloved father. We buried him only days ago after he was killed by robbers as he traveled to Berlin. Now I have the burden of holding this wretched household together. The entire place and everyone in it is done up in damned black. I welcome the very sight of you. Do come for dinner and leave that hotel to stay with us for the duration of your kind visit.*
>
> > *Your faithful friend, Gerhard,*
> > *Reichsgraf Dieffenbacher*

"*O mein Gott!* No!" Heinrich stood paralyzed in shock. Langsford wasn't much better off. This was the second time Heinrich had bad news—just when he thought nothing could be worse than an accusation of murder.

He stumbled back onto the bed, sitting. "*Nein, nein!* Vater!" he gasped, his face ashen. "This ... no ... my vater ... I defied him and now ..."

"One had nothing to do with the other."

"We fought ... his last thoughts of me now ... I thought in a year I could come back... ."

"I understand. There is nothing as wretched as losing your father." Langsford knew too well the raw feeling of the loss of a father. The void filled with seemingly endless ache. An unsteady aloneness like a building without underpinnings, a rudderless skiff. He felt dizzy remembering the impact of the loss of his own father.

"Of course, I'm sorry. I know you've been through this, but this is worse ... He hated me."

"No, he did not hate you. He was upset because he wanted to control you and he couldn't. He was demanding, pushing you into the priesthood, but it certainly was not hate."

"I'll never be able to tell him I am sorry to be such a disappointment, such a failure." Heinrich caught his breath, unable to cry because the man he would weep for had sternly taught him to never shed a tear. "He will never know I am not a murderer."

"He wouldn't have believed you were."

"I can't stand this," Heinrich put his head in his hands. "Everything gets worse and worse. My vater!"

"I'm sorry. Truly. I have to go. Pelham and I have to go."

"Go."

"I'll be back as soon as I can. Just stay in this room."

Heinrich looked up at him. "I need to clear my name more than ever. If I can, then Pa-pa will know about it in heaven, don't you agree?"

"I've been told that those in heaven see everything." *There it is, then. That should help give him solace.* He couldn't think of anything else to say. He picked up his hat. "I'll find out as much as I can and hurry back." He tore himself away to go to the estate. There he planned to give his condolences to the family and see what, if anything, he might learn to help the murdered man's youngest son. His heart was heavy.

Everyone at the Dieffenbacher estate was in heavy mourning, mirrors draped, black figures moving slowly about, shadows within shadows. They'd already felt a devastating loss over Heinrich's disappearance; now on the heels of that, the death of their patriarch. Indeed, the nearby village also mourned, he'd noticed as Pelham drove him through in the rented coach. The burden of tragedy weighed heavy on everyone here. Except, it seemed, Gerhard. "Wretched household" he'd said in his note that was devoid of even a hint of grief on the part of the eldest son.

Several hours later, after a muted welcome, Langsford sat outside with Gerhard in the wicker chairs under the spreading limbs of the linden tree. He'd felt like an intruder during the abendbrot where conversation had been forced and polite, the house's sober mood sinking deep within his own core. The Gräfin had not joined them but remained in her room, mourning. Gerhard, now sitting at the head of the table, had ordered his uncle to take his two small cousins back to the nursery, declaring that children should no longer dine with adults. Gisela had only pushed her food around on her plate and was admonished by her brother for being wasteful. It was not only a sad table, but a disharmonious, unhappy one.

Glad to be outside and alone with Gerhard, Langsford settled back, enjoying the slight breeze. The late afternoon shadows stretched long on the last of this sunny day and he felt his mood lighten. "That's quite a pipe you have there," he remarked, packing tobacco into his own short Bruyère as Gerhard picked up his.

"Yes, it was Vater's. Look on the porcelain bowl." He held the long-stemmed pipe by its arched cherry wood stem to show the decoration. "This is a 'regimental' pipe. *Zum Gedenken* of the Battle of Sedan back in 1870 where he fought." On the front of the bowl a small hand-painted soldier sat on a horse at the battle site.

"A fine commemoration of that decisive battle. Worthy of him."

"Ah, but the darn thing is the devil to keep lit." He began lighting the tobacco and a wisp of smoke curled above the miniature soldier.

"I've nothing fancy here. Just a Bruyère wooden pipe. Popular in London although they're from Saint-Claude. A simple horn mouthpiece and straight stem." Small puffs of smoke rolled from between his lips as his teeth clenched the stem. "Quite plain by comparison."

While he never cared much for Gerhard and truthfully still didn't, the undeniable connection one feels with old schoolmates remained. He felt for him. Gerhard had just lost his father, and even if he didn't show it outwardly, he knew it had to affect him deeply. Langsford himself had emotionally staggered under the responsibility of carrying the family title along with estate and the wealth. He would have gladly traded it all for another afternoon with his own father. He always felt he was far from ready to carry on where his father left off. *Enough!* he told himself. *I don't need to wallow in my own self-pity from three years ago.* He forced himself to return to the present. "So, tell me, how will the estate fare now?"

"I don't imagine anything much will change, except I plan to make everything more profitable. My farm manager has to do more, that's all, which is why I pay him as much as Vater did, only now he'll have to earn it."

Langsford noted that everything was "I" now that Gerhard was the new Reichsgraf, and he seemed to relish the role. "Then that bodes well for the family."

"They have no complaints. I had planned to go into the military, but not now. I shall go directly into Parliament. There's more power there."

"That makes sense."

"Well, there aren't any wars now, are there? So I have to make a name for myself somehow. Vater had all the luck. Things happened in his time. Wars. Kulturkampf. Opportunities for him to gain his powerful reputation."

"Each generation has its own opportunities, though."

"I haven't seen any of late, have you? Plus my little brother, this *vollidiot*, has ruined everything with the church. Our name's severely tarnished in the eyes of the bishop." Agitated, he flung the porcelain pipe into its stand. "Might as well be a bloody lurker."

"Where *is* Heinrich? Is he already in the seminary, unable to come home?" he bluffed.

"He was supposed to go this month, but he refused. Refused!"

"Maybe Heinrich felt life as a priest was too limiting." He refrained from mentioning Heinrich's red-blooded attraction for the opposite sex, something he knew Gerhard enjoyed to the fullest.

"It's not a question of what *he* wants. It's a question of what is *expected*. Duty to the church, to our family. You don't see me stepping away from my duty!"

No, but you only gain from this and don't have to give up your life and freedom. "You certainly have stepped up into your title and its responsibilities," he truthfully observed.

"It is a great burden, but I was raised for this."

Langsford steered the conversation back to Heinrich, a difficult thing to do with Gerhard, who preferred talking about himself. "So where is your brother if not at the seminary?"

"He ran away, the coward. Failed even to do that well. He's wanted by the polizei."

"The police?" He feigned shock, pulling the pipe from his mouth and sitting upright.

"Ja. They came the day after Heinrich left. They want him for a murder up in Bullay."

"My good God! Murder? Heinrich?"

"The police came to the estate to talk to everyone, but Vater ordered them away. No one questions the integrity of the Dieffenbachers."

"Did they say why they accused Heinrich?"

"No. But we thought that a murder in Bullay has nothing to do with anyone here."

"There it is, then."

"But it wasn't. Shortly afterward, the Preußische Geheimpolizei, the Secret Police, arrived. Very high-level polizei demanding to arrest Heinrich, who, of course, was not here."

"Did your father ask them to leave as well?"

"Nein. They are the police who arrested Catholics. Even we cannot send *them* away. So they searched the entire estate. They spoke to everyone. Not just the family, but all the servants, the field workers, grooms, household staff. Even my manager, Dirk."

Langsford remained silent, hoping he would continue.

After a pause, Gerhard stood. "I'm thirsty. We need some fine ale. I forgot the bell—let's go flag a servant." Together they walked toward the side entrance. "It took a while to learn the facts, and it was quite by accident. Father demanded he be present as the Preußische Geheimpolizei questioned everyone. He was the Reichsgraf, so they permitted it. That was how we were able to piece together facts, just from the questions they asked of the men here."

"Clever."

"They wanted to know who Heinrich was friends with and

where he went. They asked if he went to Bullay often and how he knew a Marc Gülker. They asked how he felt about Bismarck. They even dared question both my father and me about our role in the Centre Party." Gerhard was angry and red-faced as he recounted their interrogation.

"They are the Secret Police. They distrust one and all, my friend. It sounds as if they were testing to see if you were involved in whatever this murder was."

"Ja. I agree. Verdammte polizei."

A house servant saw them and immediately came to see what they desired. "Bring full *Theresienthal* steins out to us in the garden." Satisfied, he led Langsford back to their seats under the massive tree. Langsford's silence allowed the new Reichsgraf to continue speaking frankly.

"Because the servants were questioned so intently for lengthy periods of time, they have all talked about this throughout the village and farther. The Dieffenbacher name has been smeared and all because of Heinrich. *Dieser Dummkopf!*"

"Did the police discover anything?"

"That's when everything unraveled. Heinrich had stolen one of our plough horses for his escape, though no one realized it at the time. It was found in Bullay the night of the murder, which proves he *was* there. Stabbed a man to death." Gerhard took a long draught of ale. "He should spend eternity burning in hell for murder and for ruining the Dieffenbacher reputation. *Zur Hölle mit ihm!*"

Langsford realized Heinrich had been in the wrong place at the wrong time and it was looking worse and worse. He had to find the real murderer because he knew Gerhard would not do anything to help his younger brother.

CHAPTER 29

The Dieffenbacher Estate, Prussia

A slender man in a gray-green shirt and dark-brown trousers held up by aging suspenders approached them. He stopped a few feet opposite their chairs and removed his cap.

"Herr Dieffenbacher, könnte ich bitte mit Ihnen sprechen?" *May I speak with you?*

"Ja?"

He smelled like a combination of fresh hay and earth. The thick soles of his ankle-high boots were caked with black soil. The farmer stood stiffly at attention, cap in hand.

Hired help did not rate introductions and none were made. Gerhard carefully replaced his pipe on the table when he realized it had gone out and then began to talk with the man. Langsford followed the conversation but politely looked away, gazing out at the stand of trees adjacent to the hof. There was a structure beyond. He squinted, spotting stone walls as he listened to the Germans' conversation.

The man was the *gutshofleiter*, Dirk, who managed the farm, and he was talking about a hay field and two milk cows. Langsford recalled Heinrich speaking fondly of him. *Maybe he'd be useful.*

When the two were wrapping up their conversation, the Englishman interrupted. "Darf ich ihn um einen Gefallen bitten?" *May I ask him a favor?*

Gerhard nodded quizzically. "Ja."

"I negligently left a bag at the hotel." This "forgotten" bag was his premeditated excuse to return to the hotel. "If he could retrieve it for me I'd appreciate it." He'd intended to send Pelham back, but Dirk could prove more useful. Langsford knew his host would accommodate him to be polite, even if it were inconvenient.

"Dirk, drive a cart into Wittlich for the bag. Others can fill in for you—work a bit harder today for their usual wages."

Dirk replaced his cap. "I will hitch a horse and lea—"

"Could I see your stables, if I may ask?" Langsford interrupted, standing to stretch. "I've never seen them and you two brothers always bragged about your horses." He grinned.

His request proved well timed. Before Gerhard could answer, a house servant came to ask about a broken chair. Frau Dieffenbacher couldn't decide if a workman should repair it in the house or send it to the furniture maker. Irritated, he waved off both his guest and manager. "I must take care of this, so go with Dirk, while I handle things my mother apparently cannot."

Langsford and the farmer set off toward the stable.

"Do you understand English?"

"Ja. I understand better than I can to speak."

"Good. Gerhard and I are former schoolmates. I also know Heinrich, who speaks well of you." He saw the man's subtle reaction as his leathery face lit up at the mention of the younger brother.

"Ja. Heinrich was a *guter Junge*, a good young man." He reminisced. "I helped to teach him his own pony to ride. We always had a gute time when he came to help with the plough or the seed."

"You spent a lot of time with him?"

"Ja, I did. He liked the animals. I had him bottle-feed orphan calves and once a colt. He turned into a fine horseman."

"You are proud of him."

"I thought he was a fine boy, with good *herz* ... character. Now I do not know."

Langsford probed to see what Dirk thought about Heinrich's situation. "He's in trouble with the police now, I hear."

"The idea that he murdered a man—he would never do that. Even though Heinrich lied to me, I still cannot believe."

"He lied?"

"I didn't know Heinrich wanted to run away. He lied to get a plough horse. I heard gossip later that Herr Dieffenbacher and Heinrich had a terrible argument. That might explain the lie to steal a horse, but certainly not ...."

"Murder."

"Ja. I am very *traurig* for Heinrich." Sad.

The path curved behind a large tree. When the pair was no longer visible from the mansion, Langsford stopped. "I know for a fact that Heinrich did not murder anyone."

Dirk stopped short and stared at Langsford. "How on earth do you to know this?"

"Heinrich arrived in London a few days ago."

"You saw him?" Dirk's face lit up in a wide grin.

"Yes. He didn't know he was wanted for murder until I told him." Langsford, carefully assessing how strong Dirk's loyalty was to Heinrich, saw both surprise and relief in his face. *There it is. Dirk will help.*

"You must not tell anyone that Heinrich came to me in London. It would adversely affect my friendship with the entire family and prevent me from helping Heinrich."

"Ja. Ja," Dirk immediately agreed. "I will tell no one."

"Good, then I can trust you. Actually, Heinrich is here in Prussia with me."

"He is here? Now?"

"Yes. We intend to find the real murderer to clear Heinrich."

Dirk smiled a huge wide grin. "That's *wunderbar!*" The farmer suddenly showed concern. "If Heinrich is here, he's in danger. Where is he now?"

"He's at the hotel in Wittlich, which is why I left my luggage behind. I need you to go retrieve the bag *and* bring Heinrich here."

Dirk's eyes widened. "If he comes to here, his brother will give him to the police. I know Gerhard."

"It will be fine. I've figured a way."

"*Einen Weg?*"

"You get Heinrich from the hotel. Before you turn into the gate of the hof, drop him off along the road. He can hide in that old stone building past the trees."

Dirk thought for a second. "You mean the old stone schloss?"

"Yes. He'll be safer than in the hotel."

"That might work—no one goes near there these days."

"Can you find a way to smuggle what he needs?"

"Ja. I can do that. It won't be a hotel, but he can be comfortable. Safe.

"Only a short time, hopefully a day until we leave. We are going to Bullay."

"*Bullay?* Where the murder was?"

"Yes. That's the only way we can find out what really happened and prove Heinrich's innocence."

"Let me come with you. It's a bit of a distance, but there are times when I go there for to sell a horse. We can use that as a reason to go. I have a yearling colt to sell to a man near there."

"An interesting thought. It would help me have a reason other than the real one."

"You can be looking at horses, ja? And I am helping you find one."

"We can't leave Heinrich here alone with both of us gone. Could you use him as, say, your stable boy, helping with the horses you're buying or selling?"

"But people will know him. He'll be arrested!"

"He's grown a full beard and looks quite different. We'll have him wear farmer's clothes. People won't recognize him, especially if he is working for you. Out of context."

"I do need help. I'll think of something to say to Gerhard."

"I always travel with my driver, Pelham. He'll come with us. A good chap. In fact, he's at the stables right now. He's excellent both with horses and thwarting any thieves."

"It's too bad he wasn't with Heinrich's father," Dirk looked down at his heavy boots, his mood darkening. "The robbers killed him and left his own driver for dead. Just for the marks he carried with him. Senseless. He only had money because he was heading to Berlin to convince the head of the Secret Police they were hunting the wrong man. He was going to the Wittlich depot for the train north but was attacked just down the road here outside Flußbach ...." Dirk shook his head and pursed his lips. "He didn't believe Heinrich was a murderer, and then he himself was murdered!"

"This is the first I've heard details. Do they know who the robbers were?"

"Nein. The people in the village said they saw several strangers around for a few nights, but no one has seen them since. I think they were watching for someone to rob. Our driver, Hans, landed in a ditch of water when the horses bolted up the road. He was stabbed, but he'll recover."

"Did he get a good look at the robbers?"

"No. They wore masks."

"He was fortunate he wasn't killed as well."

"Gerhard didn't think so. He blamed him for not protecting his father and dismissed him. Now I'm short-handed for help, so it's a good thing you brought your own man, and an excuse to pretend to hire Heinrich. Then the four of us go? It will be far safer on the road, especially if there are robbers in these parts."

"Yes. Safety in numbers. But for now, the first thing is to get Heinrich hidden in the old schloss. Can you do it so no one sees?"

"Ja. I can."

They continued on to the stable, the private conversation over.

"In the meantime, tell me about these horses," Langsford pointed to several who hung their heads over the Dutch stall doors.

Their silent conspiracy had begun.

CHAPTER 30

The Dieffenbacher Estate, Prussia

It was nearly nightfall by the time Dirk dropped Heinrich off by the cherry trees, well before the stone wall of the hof. He headed to the ruins of the fourteenth-century castle, through the woods and along a field, following its fencerow. He slipped through a second wood with small trees. Emerging, he crossed a meadow filled with lowing cows and jogged over to the old stone ruins. In the dusk he was sure no one saw him.

He'd played there as a child and knew the interior of this fortress-like structure well. The walls were a meter thick and still held a few inhabitable storerooms near the backside. These had no windows, which was probably why they had held up. Most of the wood had long since rotted except for massive beams spanning the ceilings. Years back, part of the roof had been replaced so the ancient storerooms were useful again, but they had since been abandoned and forgotten once more when new barns were built. No one would suspect anyone was inside.

Dirk had found a door somewhere and reattached it with newer hinges. Likely it had served as a barrier to keep cows from wandering too deep inside. Heinrich yanked it open and found a small room set up for him. A milk-glass kerosene lamp threw light into the corners. A straw mattress and blanket lay on the dirt floor. Dirk had even dragged in a crude wooden chair with a small plank table to hold the little lamp. Who knew where he had found even one piece of furniture—forgotten items stored within the schloss perhaps? Dirk knew the estate better than anyone. For the moment, this was perfect for his needs.

Shortly after he settled in, Dirk arrived with a basketful of cold meats, cheese, and a jar of sauerkraut. He had extra bread and cheese for the morning along with coffee. He unpacked the basket in awkward silence. They hadn't had a chance to talk because Heinrich had hidden beneath a tarp in the wagon coming back from Wittlich.

"How did you get all that?" Food was always locked in cupboards after each meal to prevent servants from helping themselves.

"I have my ways." Dirk grinned. "I'm glad to see you, Master Heinrich."

Heinrich paused, uncomfortable and unsure what to say about stealing the mare. He sat a minute without a word.

Dirk broke the tension. "I understand why you lied to get the mare."

"I'm sorry ..."

"I wasn't angry. Now I understand."

"I'm unsure of anything I do now."

"So often in life, we aren't sure. I would have let you borrow the mare even if you were truthful. I don't mean to speak ill of the dead, and we all mourn him, but I do know how your father could be especially strict with you. I'm sorry. For you. For your family."

Heinrich's guilt ebbed away. Dirk had forgiven him.

"You'll be safe here. I just need to get one more thing." The farm manager left, showing up a few minutes later with a small contraption Heinrich had never seen. "It's full of kerosene. Simply light it like a lamp. See this top is a burner," Dirk explained. "Set your coffee kettle on the top until it's hot."

Heinrich examined it curiously.

Dirk chuckled, and the awkwardness in the room eased. "I learned about this little stove and thought it would be good to have when we are hunting."

"You don't have to build a fire to heat coffee or food?" He picked up a piece of the rye bread.

"Nein. We set up one or two of these at the camp when we hunt elk. Use both it and your lamp sparingly. Your brother measures how much kerosene we use."

"I'll be careful."

"One other thing." He unrolled a bundle he had under his arm. "Here are clothes Lord Langsford wants you to put on. This way if someone sees you, you'll look like a farmhand." Dirk unrolled a bundle containing an old shirt, dusty pants, and worn boots.

"Good idea," Heinrich set his bread aside and looked over the sad attire, "I think." He pulled off his boots and stood up, unfastening his trousers. "Well, no reason to wait. I am now a farmer," he laughed, pulling on the baggy pants that were too loose in the waist.

Dirk handed him the coarse-woven shirt and the suspenders. "Will keep your pants up."

He watched Heinrich finish dressing and laughed. "Now you look like a real worker. I wouldn't know you myself." Heinrich stood in front of him, bearded, a cotton shirt tucked into loose-fitting britches, a sweat-stained cap and scuffed boots. "Master Heinrich, farmer!" He pointed to the discarded outfit. "Make sure you take those fine riding boots of yours and wrap them in the burlap sack along with the rest of your own clothes to tuck away. Lord Langsford said you are only a farmer from here on, no longer the well-dressed gentleman."

"I can see that."

"Drink your ale, and get a good night's rest. You are safe here. *Gute Nacht.*" He left the door ajar behind him.

Early the next morning, after everyone else left for daily Mass in the village, Langsford sent Dirk to get Heinrich at the schloss. Dirk found the youth sitting near the crumbling stones, looking across the fields.

"Hurry before they return. We're leaving. Everything's packed."

"Didn't my brother think it strange you are going with Langsford?"

"No. I told him I had a possible buyer for a horse up there, which is true, and he is all for turning everything into marks. Gerhard already knew Langsford wanted to see horses—something about it being for his earl friend who has horses in England. No mention of you, of course, but in Bullay, should anyone ask, you are my stable boy."

"All four of us are going?"

"Ja. And if the horse sells, all the better. My time is well spent." He winked.

Dirk and Heinrich rushed to the cobblestoned hof where a farm wagon and two chubby horses stood ready. Heinrich climbed onto the seat beside Pelham. Langsford, now also clad as a farmer, clambered up.

"You even make a farmer appear dashing, Langsford," Heinrich smirked.

"I can't let you out dress me, now can I?" The Englishman picked off a piece of straw from the front of his shirt.

Dirk swung into the saddle astride Preis, holding the lead of the untrained colt. Pelham clucked to the horses and they moved through the hof, out the gate, and onto the country road, leaving with time to spare before the family returned. Bullay and the real murderer were only a five or six hour wagon ride north.

That afternoon when they finally arrived in Bullay, they left the horses and wagon at the livery, and walked to a simple *gästehaus* nearby. Once ensconced in their room, Langsford brushed the dust off his trousers and poured water from the pitcher into the bowl, splashing his face while the others settled into the crowded room with its four cots.

"Pelham, tomorrow you and I will check around town while Heinrich and Dirk are off to sell their horse." He grabbed a rough towel and began to dry his face.

"Wouldn't it be easier to ask the night watchman about the murder?" Heinrich sat in one of the ladder-backed chairs to pull off his boot. He shook out a small stone.

"Of course," Pelham realized. "Watchmen, not police like London."

"That's right," Langsford rolled down his sleeves, feeling more refreshed. "Cities like Berlin have the *gendarmerie*, but villages usually just a single watchman, if that."

"Go to Trier if you want to talk to actual police." Heinrich pulled his boot back on.

"We're here to find Karl Gülker, not any police or watchman," Langsford reminded them. "He's the one who accused Heinrich." Langsford lifted his satchel onto his cot where he gave a skeptical look at the straw-stuffed mattress and its lumps. "But whatever we do, we can't be obvious in asking anyone questions, and you, Pelham, won't need to say anything really. Just stay handy in case the murderer discovers why we're here and wants to slit *my* throat." He laughed as he drew his index finger across his neck.

"You're worried about *your* neck? It's *my* neck at stake here, old friend." Heinrich grimaced.

"True, but tomorrow you'll be up to 'horseplay' with Dirk," he teased. "'Tis your English friend, yours truly, who takes the risk." He bowed.

"Sometimes you are worse than my brother." Heinrich stood to take his turn at the basin.

Dirk chuckled. "Heinrich, you make a raggedy farmer, in those clothes and with your scraggly beard."

"If I fell over him in an alley, I wouldn't know him," Langsford assured with a grin.

Always practical, Pelham ignored all of them. "I'm hungry. Let's go eat."

Over potatoes and cheese, along with pints in the local beer hall, they sat idly talking about their favorite horses.

"There's no horse in the world that can match an English Thoroughbred," Pelham bragged, his mouth full of potatoes.

"Except my Trakehner who excels at jumping anything, thank you," Heinrich challenged, ready for a friendly debate.

Langsford contributed little, as he watched the locals file into the place.

Dirk took a swig of his beer. "I prefer a sturdy little horse, one that never goes lame and gets *real* work done."

Their banter continued while Langsford watched patrons come and go. A group of loud young men arrived and took their beers to a long table, talking and jesting, jabbing one another.

"Do you recognize any of them?" Langsford asked behind his stein. Heinrich shook his head.

Other patrons arrived as the evening progressed. Pelham,

the foam on his beer overflowing onto his hand, came back from getting another tankard and sat. Women laughed, taunted, and teased. With the arrival of an accordion, violin, and horn ensemble, the music infected the hall's rising energy. Langsford kept wondering who might be willing to talk about the murder two weeks ago. He couldn't just sit there like a bump on a log. He needed to pick someone and strike up a conversation.

A tableful of farmers on their right was quieter. They leaned in to hear one another, hunched in discussion. When one of them rose to get another ale, Langsford followed behind him to order one himself. Leaning on the bar, the man looked friendly. He wore a coarse cotton shirt with a black wool vest that remained unbuttoned. *Here goes*, Langsford thought, knowing he had to ask someone and it might as well be this man.

"*Hallo.* A friend mentioned I might find Karl Gülker here. Do you know him?"

"Haven't you heard?" The Prussian turned to face Langsford. "Karl disappeared right after his brother was murdered. He owes me some pfennigs. Other than that, good riddance, I say."

"He disappeared?" Langsford was speechless. After a beat, he extended his hand. "I'm Mr. Langsford, here with friends looking to sell a horse," he tilted his head toward the three left at his table. "Thought I'd look up this friend of a friend and have an ale."

The man nodded, offering his hand as he returned the introduction. "Ernst Schmidt."

"What happened to Karl?"

"No one knows."

"Did something go awry?"

"Well, the polizisten think so."

Langsford called over for two beers, one for Ernst, and one for himself.

Heinrich followed casually to join them. "Make that another," he held a finger up to the barman.

"This is ..." he began to introduce Heinrich.

"Gerhard," Heinrich jumped in, providing a pseudonym.

"Come drink with us," Ernst invited, "since you can't have a stein with Gülker." Leaving Pelham and Dirk at their table, the two followed Ernst back to his. The men there nodded a welcome as Langsford and Heinrich swung over a couple empty chairs from an adjacent table and sat as Ernst introduced them.

Heinrich turned to the man on his right, saying, "A lively beer hall, this."

"Ja, it is. You come from near here?" he asked Heinrich.

"Just north of Wittlich. Brought a colt for a buyer near here."

"That so? Wish you luck in this economy. Your price best be fair."

"It is, for it does us no good to set a high one and keep a horse to feed." Heinrich laughed. The others at the table agreed.

"I see you are no fool," stated one of them.

"I try not to be," he replied, taking a gulp of his ale.

"It's hard to sell anything let alone earn much these days," a third man joined in, having returned to the table with another stein. Their talk turned to the depression and how more and more men had begun stealing just to get by. Crime was on the rise, from petty theft to highway robberies.

"And murder. I hear there was a murder here," Langsford prompted, forcing back thoughts of Heinrich's father and that highway robbery, knowing Heinrich must ache at this talk.

"Ja." The Prussian across the table answered. "First one brother murdered, and now the second. The polizisten are convinced the same man killed both."

"What?" Heinrich exclaimed, only to have Langsford's boot crush hard on his foot.

"He disappeared right after he told the police who killed his brother," one of the other men clarified. "They haven't found Karl's body yet."

"A shame about Marc," commented another. "I thought he was a promising youth, though Karl wasn't much good—that temper of his. Too quick to fight."

"True. Beat up his own brother as well as others more than once. A shame." Ernst raised his stein. "Here's to the dead men. May they catch the killer." They all toasted while the music and gaiety abounded, the noise level rising. Langsford swigged his beer. It tasted bitter, like his mood. He felt they had just hit a major wall—finding Karl was no longer their solution.

His stein dry once more, Langsford stood. "Well, it's an early morning for us; time we say *auf Wiedersehen.*" Pelham and Dirk rose when they saw him, taking their cue to leave. All four exited the beer hall and walked out into the cool night air.

Walking to the gästehaus, Heinrich sputtered at Langsford, "What do I do now? They think I killed Karl as well! I needed him to confess he lied!"

"Even if you had found him alive, he probably wouldn't have confessed. He may have truly believed you killed his brother."

"So then how do I prove I did not kill either man?"

"By finding the man who did. You know it wasn't you." Langsford wished it were that simple, but for the moment, he himself wasn't sure what to do next.

CHAPTER 31

Bullay, Prussia

The next morning, after Heinrich had left with Dirk to sell the colt, Langsford and Pelham checked on the remaining wagon horses at the livery. The two Englishmen planned to snoop about the village afterward, expecting this to be a quick errand. When they walked into the barn, the proprietor, Johann Schneider, welcomed them, assuring that the horses were fine under his care. "The night watchman comes by every evening to double-check. You've no reason for concern."

Pelham bent over and picked up the horse's front leg, checking the shoe.

"Does he bring any more news about the murders?" Langsford wanted to ask everyone he came across today the same question. Something or someone was bound to have some information, or so he hoped. "The men at the beer hall told us. Frightening."

"Well, that's what I'm meaning to say. The watchman won't let me release these two horses or your wagon until either he or the police talk to you, seein' you're strangers."

"Talk to *us?*" Pelham set the hoof back on the ground and patted the horse's neck, glancing uneasily at Langsford.

"With the trouble of late, I'm afraid, he's a bit edgy."

"I see," Langsford answered, his mind spinning. Bullay was big enough for a policeman? Did they suspect Heinrich already? Were they all in jeopardy of being caught? Or was this just a simple precaution as a result of the murders? He took his time formulating his words. "Because we're new here." He wanted to reassure Pelham and at the same time show Johann he had no concern. "Where do we find your watchman?" He'd prefer to avoid any police.

"Caspar Severs? He's probably at home since he works all night. But the policeman, Joachim Wulff, is still here. He's been here weeks. Sent by the Royal Guard with several other polizisten to track a thief here from Berlin. Shot him dead, they did, that one afternoon. Right here in town. So they were already here when the first Gülker brother was murdered—that very same night. Good thing, too. They chased that murdering devil clear to France, I'm told."

"Then we can all rest easier." Langsford smiled at the livery manager, knowing that the wanted man had actually landed in London on his very own doorstep. Uneasy that someone from the Royal Guard was in town, he quickly decided he needed to head the police off as soon as possible. "We should go find policeman Wulff and introduce ourselves today."

"You don't need to find me. I'm here," a commanding voice behind them announced. Turning, he found a short, broad, uni-formed man in tall boots polished to a glaring shine, brass but-tons on his coat buttoned to his neck, and a *pickelhaube*, a spiked helmet, strapped on his head. He made an intimidating figure.

Langsford, with a boldness he did not feel, stepped forward to shake the policeman's hand. "Mister Langsford, from England, Officer Wulff. Mr. Schneider just told us the night watchman or you wanted to meet us. This is my friend, Tom Pelham." The man gave no response, so he continued. "We heard about the murders in town."

"I'm not here to talk about crimes. I just need to know who is here and why. What is your purpose to be in Bullay?" Wulff was all business.

"This is my first time here. Journeyed up from Wittlich, actually, after visiting with an old friend," he began, making small talk both to feel at ease himself and to get the glowering Wulff to relax. "Here looking at horses with Tom, who knows far more about horses than me." It seemed strange to use Pelham's first name, but to do otherwise would reveal they were not equals.

The polizist scrutinized him thoroughly, and Langsford thought he would be a worthy adversary in a poker game. The man's face was unreadable. Pelham, standing beside the horse, nervously stroked the animal's head.

Wulff looked at Johann. "These are the men who came in yesterday then?"

"Ja."

Langsford was waiting for someone to mention that four men had arrived, but Johann said nothing more and Wulff seemed to be satisfied. It was fortunate Heinrich and Dirk, both Prussian, were allowed to take their two horses earlier and had already left town. Maybe the livery man hadn't been awake yet, but this "wolf" was sniffing too close for Langsford's comfort.

To occupy Pelham, Langsford pointed to the horse and asked, "Check that left hind. I'm worried that there might be an abscess brewing in that hoof."

Pelham turned to the horse's rump and picked up the hind foot, facing away from Wulff, exactly where Langsford wanted him. No need risking a reaction from his driver to alert this polizist during Langsford's next dangerous move. He couldn't let Wulff walk away without finding out more. He summoned his bravura. "I had hoped to see Karl Gülker while here, as we have a mutual friend, but I understand he was one of the murder victims. So shocking!"

"Yes. And his brother—both murdered."

"Johann said you chased the man who did it clear to France."

"Ja, one fled."

"One? There's more than one?"

"Yes, which is why I am still assigned here. I'm checking everyone because of a large plot to assassinate Chancellor Bismarck."

Langsford sharply caught his breath. "I'm afraid I don't follow. Why do the police think the murders are involved with an assassination plot?" He was frantically trying to sort out how two murders in a small village turned into treason.

Wulff relaxed, his feet spread shoulder-width and his hands behind his back as he recounted the situation. "The first murdered man confessed as he died, admitted to being part of this group."

"More men are involved?"

"We have evidence several were involved. The man you wanted to see, Karl, reported that his brother had admitted to the plot, less than an hour before his murder. He apparently feared for his own life from others in the group, and rightly so. We suspect because Karl knew about it, the same traitor murdered both of them."

"Frightening. And tragic." Langsford had trouble believing his ears. The police not only accused Heinrich of double murders but wanted him for treason.

"Not as tragic as it could be if we don't shoot them before they shoot Bismarck."

CHAPTER 32

Bullay, Prussia

"Heinrich." Langsford shook his friend's shoulder. It was late afternoon, and he'd just returned to the gästehaus where Heinrich slept in the one of the straight-backed chairs after a long day helping Dirk. Pelham had gone on to the livery, unused to being so far from the horses in his charge. "Heinrich!"

"Ja, natürlich ja—" Heinrich startled. "Was ist das?" he muttered as he sat up.

"Where's Dirk?" Langsford was nervous not knowing where everyone was.

Heinrich looked around the sparse room, slow to remember. The other small cots were empty as was the other chair. He found the answer. "He went down to the livery once more ..." He rubbed his bleary eyes.

"Good. He's with Pelham then." Langsford pulled up the vacant chair from the corner and sat. "I spoke with a policeman this morning."

"A polizist?"

"Don't worry. He only wanted to meet newcomers. There was no mention of you specifically," Langsford answered the worried question. "That isn't the issue. You've a bigger problem, not just—"

The door swung open at that moment and Dirk appeared. The big smile on his face widened when he saw them. "*Ein guter Tag!* I have marks in my pocket for the yearling. Heinrich's brother will be very pleased." He hung his cap on a wall peg and removed his coat. "This horse brought our price because Heinrich did a fine job showing him." He sat on the edge of the cot and pulled off one of his hobnailed boots, rubbing his foot. "Pelham will be here in a minute so shall we get a quick supper... ." He held his boot suspended halfway to his stockinged foot as he caught the Englishman's concern and Heinrich's face scrunched with worry.

"Is there a problem?"

"Serious trouble." Langsford leaned forward in the squeaky chair, elbows on knees.

Dirk remained on the edge of the straw-filled mattress, looking back and forth between the two. "What? Did they find Karl's body?"

Langsford exhaled a long sigh and slowly shook his head. "No. Police discovered Marc was in with a group planning to kill Bismarck. They believe you, Heinrich, are part of that plot."

Heinrich's mouth dropped open. He stared blankly, brow knitted in a perplexed frown. "*Wie bitte?* Why on earth ...?"

"Karl told the police his brother confessed, explaining that he'd changed his mind, wanting no part of it. When he tried to leave the group, the other conspirators threatened his life."

Heinrich stood, confused and frowning.

"The night he died, Marc asked Karl to protect him, but before Karl could learn who the others were, his brother ran outside into the street. Karl thought his brother must have seen one of conspirators in the pub where they were and was scared. He tried to catch up with him and was searching the streets for him when he saw a stranger heading toward the train depot."

Heinrich's breathing was in short gasps.

"Are you all right?"

"... The drunk I saw... . That had to be Karl."

"Obviously Karl saw you, later concluding that you murdered Marc."

Heinrich began to pace within the small room, but could only go a few steps in either direction. He turned around at the little bureau, leaning back against it, hands on the cold marble top. He found a thread of a voice. "I *was* here ... but—"

"There's more, I'm afraid. The police confirmed the story. Marc's dying words, a 'deathbed confession,' they call it. Marc admitted to the plot when he died."

The room froze in silence as the significance sank in.

"Two men, brothers, independently confirmed an assassination plot, with you a part of it." Langsford was grim as he whispered, "Mord und verrat." Murder and treason.

Heinrich staggered, jarring the bureau, the pitcher on top rocked water into the porcelain bowl. "Mein Gott!"

His head swirled as he gripped the marble top behind him. "I—I'm not in any plot." His voice began to rise, "You understand? I have not conspired to *kill* anyone."

Langsford put his finger to his lips. "Don't let the rest of the *gästehaus* hear. You don't need to convince us."

Heinrich spoke in a loud whisper. "Why do the police think I am involved in a plot because a dying man said so?" He looked back and forth between the two men. "This is wrong! Treason?" He gave an imploring look at Langsford.

"Yes. If convicted ... capital punishment," Langsford uttered. "Bismarck himself reinstated it to execute traitors."

"I remember," Dirk recalled. "Max Hödel was executed when he tried to shoot Emperor Wilhelm."

Heinrich turned ashen, and collapsed into the chair. "Und was mache ich jetzt?" What do I do now?

Logic dictated Langsford's words, not wanting to frighten

Heinrich further. "What we *do* remains the same. It's just that the odds are stacked higher. More police diligently searching."

"That explains why the secret police are involved." Heinrich's voice shook.

"Police who think *you* are in England. Otherwise they might think you even murdered your own father. Still we must be even more cautious."

Dirk still sat with boot in hand. "We've already been seen together here in town." He leaned over to finally replace his boot. He tugged on the bootstraps and then stood up, stomping lightly to get his heel down. "No one is suspicious of you here. I wouldn't worry right now." He bent to tie them.

Langsford gave Heinrich a hearty pat on the shoulder and rose. "I say we go find Pelham and get something to eat. My stomach takes priority, right now," he smiled, forcing his worry to the side. "We'll have supper and figure out what's next."

He hoped it wasn't going to be Heinrich's arrest.

Chapter 33

Bullay, Prussia

Returning to the gästehaus from a café where they'd finished off sausages and beer, the four walked along the street down toward the wide ribbon of water, the Moselle River, wanting to discuss facts in private.

"Let's review everything," Langsford began. "What did Karl say to you that night?"

"It seems like a year ago." Heinrich tried to recall. "I can barely picture the drunk."

"What happened when he saw you?"

"Not much. He blocked my way briefly, is all." He paused. "Oh, right—I thought I saw the bone handle of a knife or dagger. He was too drunk to do anything and I just walked around him. He staggered on, probably back up the street."

"Did he say anything to you?" Langsford stopped, wanting Heinrich to concentrate. Dirk and Pelham leaned on the low wall beside them, letting Langsford ask the questions. The river current beside them reflected a silver moonlight.

Heinrich thought a long moment, leaning, too, against the stone wall. "Yes. He asked if I'd seen someone who looked like him. I remember now."

"What did you say to him?"

"I lied and said no."

"You lied? You *did* see someone?" Langsford was trying to get a picture in his mind.

"Yes. I didn't want to talk to the drunk. And I only saw the other man in passing."

"How long before did you see this other person?"

"I'd say less than a minute."

"Did this other person look like he could have been Karl's brother?"

"He might have been about the same build, but it was dark. I don't really know."

"What happened after you encountered Karl?"

"I went to the depot and purchased my ticket to Calais."

Langsford stood stoking his moustache while he thought. "You saw someone who could have been Marc alive. He was probably still alive when you encountered Karl."

"There! I didn't kill him!"

"Not exactly proof, but it does clarify things. The facts are different than the police think."

"Of course the facts are different. Someone else killed Marc!"

"Here's what we know." Langsford started to count on his fingers. "First, Karl, drunk, was looking for his brother. Second, Karl has a reputation for fighting, even with his own brother."

"Marc tried to kill Karl?"

"No. Picture what happened. You head for the train station, passing Karl. He goes the other direction toward a man who, most likely, was his brother, Marc: still alive."

"All right ..."

"What if Karl is the one who is part of the conspiracy, not Marc? After all, he has the reputation for fighting and perhaps the personality to be an assassin. Karl finds his brother and to keep *him* quiet, stabs him in a drunken rage. What a perfect opportunity to blame a passing stranger for a murder that he himself committed."

"*Karl* is the murderer?"

"There it is."

"Kain und Abel," whispered Dirk.

"It's perfect. Karl gives the police not only the reason for the murder, but a murderer as well. He himself gets away with murder and can continue with his plans to kill Bismarck."

Heinrich protested. "If he is part of the plot, why would he tell the police about it?"

"He had to because Marc had already told them about it as he lay dying, just not enough to implicate Karl—maybe in order to protect his brother or maybe because he died too soon. Either way, it was nebulous enough to be unclear. Karl then wove his clever story to set the police on a wild goose chase—after you."

"But Karl's dead."

"Karl is devious. Remember, the police have no body. I imagine he left town without telling anyone so his disappearance seems suspicious. He'd already told the police what he wanted them to know, so before they could question him further, poof, he's gone."

Dirk pursed his lips. "And everyone thinks, 'Poor Karl. He's been murdered, too.'"

"But he's really alive and under no suspicion whatsoever." Heinrich stood, running his hand through his dark hair. "The police have a suspect to chase—me!"

"The real assassin is loose and no one suspects."

Heinrich scratched his head. "How do the police know who I am?"

"Did you tell the stationmaster your name?"

"No. I only bought the ticket."

"He rode here," Dirk reminded them. "He tricked me into letting him have a draught mare."

"Yes, she was slow. I got here so late ..." Heinrich blanched. "Mein Gott! I left her at a watering trough just before I saw the drunk. Karl. He asked me if the mare was mine and I denied it, but he saw me with the horse."

Heinrich looked at the farmer. He and Dirk simultaneously exclaimed, "The Black Forest brand!"

"The what?"

"The breed brand," Heinrich explained. "I knew she would be returned to Dirk because of her brand. I never dreamed that assuring she would be taken home would lead the police to me for something I didn't do!"

"Hold on now. Your father's horses have a brand that people recognize?"

"Yes," Dirk interjected. "We breed the Black Forest Draughts and we brand them on their hips with a simple pine tree sign. People in the general area would recognize the horse as belonging to the estate."

"Where is the mare now?"

"She's home," Dirk answered. "The police brought her back."

"Did you tell the police Heinrich took the horse from you?"

It was Dirk's turn to pale. "I did. I didn't want them to think he was a horse thief, so I made sure they knew Heinrich had my permission." He blew out his breath. "Instead of keeping you out of trouble, I did just the opposite, didn't I? I thought they were just returning her and I had no idea they thought a murderer had left her behind."

Heinrich rubbed his eyes. "If you hadn't told them I took her," he sighed, "someone else would have, since other workers were in the field. None of this is your fault."

"When did they bring the horse back?" Langsford asked, trying to fit all the facts together.

"A day or so after he rode out," Dirk answered.

"Thus the police confirmed it was Heinrich, and they wired Scotland Yard." He now understood the chain of events.

"But when I got to Calais, the police were already waiting for me."

"They were in Bullay, already chasing a criminal from Berlin. After Marc's murder, all they had to do was ask the stationmaster where you were going. The police started their hunt for you before you were barely on your way," Langsford explained, "because the stationmaster gave the police a solid description of you. They discovered your name later when they returned the horse."

Dirk frowned. "If they knew the murderer was leaving on that train, how could Karl have been murdered by the same man later?"

"Exactly." Heinrich seconded, also confused.

Langsford reached into his jacket for his Bruyère. "Didn't you say you stayed overnight when you transferred trains?"

"Twice. Thionville and Lille."

"That's why the police arrived in Calais ahead of you. They traveled straight through. Because you took longer to arrive, they thought you'd doubled back."

"And murdered Karl?"

"I'm afraid so." He paused. "Gentlemen, we have figured out what actually happened. Karl is my choice as the murderer, and he is alive. Somewhere."

"He knows the truth and we can still find him!" Heinrich brightened. "But where do we look now?"

"Someone around here probably knows," Langsford answered.

or barns around town. Rumor has it the Gülker boys are in 'cause they don't like the new laws."

"New laws?" Pelham asked.

"All workers have to pay for health and disability insurance. None of us can afford these payments, and no one likes them. The party tried to protest, I guess, but our Iron Chancellor has declared it illegal."

There was a general pause at the table, then Langsford spoke. "You know, Karl Gülker was a friend of a friend, and I'd intended to have a beer with him. Shocking to hear of his death from Ernst Schmidt last night. Maybe I should find one of his friends—still have that drink. Would you know any of them?"

"Well," Schneider replied rubbing his chin. "There's two I've seen him with: Fritz Kastner and Helmut Bär. Seems they might be members of the Social Democratic Party, too. Haven't seem 'em lately. Probably laying low with our Officer Wulff lurking about."

"No one wants a copper after him, now do they?" Pelham grimaced.

Langsford pulled the tip of his mustache. "We should pay our respects," he told Pelham. "... the right thing to do, given the circumstances. Does either man live in town?"

"Don't know about Bär. He seems to drift about. Kastner's folks is over on Zehnthausstraße. Number two. You can ask 'em, but it's not really worth bothering about," Schneider advised. "I wouldn't get involved. Police, you know. Stay clear of Officer Wulff and any Social Democrat folk."

"You're probably right. Karl's death weighs on my mind more than it should, I suppose."

"Let's toast to those of us alive, then." Schneider lifted his stein, sloshing a bit of ale onto the table.

"Yes, alive, breathing, and no police chasing us." Langsford clinked his mug with the others. He was curious what tomorrow would bring.

"Fascinating how much information you can gather over a drink or two and some good luck," Langsford said to the others returning to the gästehaus. "We ran into the livery master. Had a few tankards with him and his friends."

"What'd they tell you?" Heinrich was sitting on his cot, polishing a boot while Dirk leaned back in one of the chairs, listening intently.

"Found out who two of Karl's friends are: Fritz Kastner and Helmut Bär. Seems they are both members of the Social Democratic Party here."

"What does that have to do with the murder?" Heinrich sighed, sounding irritated.

"The party's illegal and meets secretly around town. A protest against the new insurance laws."

"Ja, I know," Dirk nodded. "I have to pay for insurance now. Heinrich's vater paid, too. Now I have less money, the estate pays for insurance instead of hiring men we need, and I must do more work. It's a not a good situation."

"Your Iron Chancellor is taking money from everyone's pockets." Langsford sat on his cot, pulling out his pipe. "He's not any more popular with the Social Democrats than they are with him. And that might be a reason why they want him dead. Not a good reason, but a reason."

"Where can I find Karl's friends?" Heinrich asked, standing up and pulling on his boot as though he was readying to head out the door.

"We know where Kastner lives, or at least his parents."

"Then let's go. They'll know where Karl is."

"Slow down. No point in doing anything tonight. You'll only draw attention to yourself. Best to avoid the night watchman. You and Dirk go in the morning, but be careful."

"You two aren't going?" Dirk frowned, looking between Langsford and Pelham.

"We'd stand out too much as Englishmen, but I don't want Heinrich to go alone, so you'll accompany him."

"Is it safe for Heinrich to go at all?" Dirk asked, still frowning.

"As safe as it's been so far," Langsford replied. *Which means until the murder is solved, it's always a gamble,* he worried silently.

CHAPTER 35

Bullay, Prussia

The next morning, Dirk and Heinrich knocked on Kastner's cottage door a couple streets up from the river. A middle-aged woman answered, "Hallo?" She opened the door a crack, eyeing the two men suspiciously.

"Hallo. I'm Gerhard," Heinrich began, "and this is Dirk. We're looking for Fritz Kastner. Do you know him?"

"Ich bin seine Mutter." I'm his mother. "*Weshalb?*" Why do you want him?

Dirk answered, "A friend told us he was looking for a horse."

"He's not here." She began to close the door.

Heinrich's hand interrupted the door's swing. "When will he be back? We just want to talk to him before we leave town," he fibbed.

"He went to find work." The woman let the door open a bit more, and the daylight exposed her tired face and brown, graying hair. "My son can't afford a horse. He has no job." She shook her head.

Dirk stepped closer. "Oh, a shame. Maybe we can help him. We know several people who are hiring, ma'am."

"Nein. Too late. He went to London."

"London?" Heinrich asked with surprise. "Why London?"

The mother stood almost sagging in the doorway. She wasn't as old as she first appeared, but was instead worn with worry. "A shame he must go so far to find work. I didn't want him to go, but there's money to be earned. His friends in the party guaranteed it. You know, those democrat people."

"Social Democrats?" Heinrich offered.

"I know an Englishman with horses," Dirk spoke with empathy, "who needs good workers. I could send word to Fritz. After all, we Prussians should look out for one another. How can I find him?"

"That's kind of you." The corners of her mouth turned up in a tiny smile and briefly she looked younger. "But him and his friends will be working in them British factories over in London," Frau Kastner explained. "I don't know exactly where, but he'll send word back. Fritz is a good boy."

"Your son and his friends are wise to go." Heinrich wanted her to tell them more.

She smiled wider at them. "Ja, Fritz is smart. Smarter than his friend, truth be told." She paused, looking past them to the street, talking more to herself than to them. "I don't much like Karl... ."

Did she mean Karl Gülker? Heinrich audibly gasped. Dirk coughed to cover his surprise, but she failed to notice and kept talking. "I'm sorry about his brother, but Karl's mean. Helmut, he's all right. He's the one that said those democrat people guaranteed jobs. As long as they got work, I got no reason to fuss about them going to London." She wiped her hands on her apron for no reason except to be done with her visitors. She began closing the door again. "Sorry I can't help you more, but I know he's not buying no horses."

Dirk tipped his wool cap and thanked her. "I hope your son and his friends do well, Frau Kastner. Auf Wiedersehen."

Smiling but looking down, she quickly shut the door on them.

They walked down the street, Heinrich barely containing himself. "Did you hear that? Karl definitely isn't dead! He's in

London! Do you think his friends are part of this plot? Where did they go in London? Did they get jobs?"

"Slow down. You ask too many questions. You heard exactly what I did. I have no idea what the three are doing, other than working in factories."

They returned to the gästehaus where Langsford sat cleaning his pipe while Pelham laid on a cot, one leg atop his knee, his hands behind his head. "They went to London!" Heinrich blurted out, swinging the door closed behind him.

"Who?"

"All of them! Fritz's mother told us he went to work in London factories. With Karl and his other friend." Heinrich began stuffing his few possessions in his bag. "We have to leave for London!"

Langsford put down his pipe. Standing, he straightened his vest and checked his pocket watch.

"Frau Kastner said the Social Democrats promised them all jobs in London," Heinrich said impatiently.

Langsford raised his eyebrows. "A melding of Prussians and British with the Social Democrats. It makes perfect sense for Karl and his friends to go to London."

"How?" Heinrich frowned, confused.

"Something I overheard, actually. While Pelham did whatever he does with the horses, I went out to get more tobacco while you were gone. Stopped at the market on the way back for some cheese and rolls and was stopped by a couple men on the street. Asked me if I wanted to be part of Social Democratic Party where it's legal. Seems members have left for Sweden and England where it *is* legal. I declined but there were some Germans who were interested and said they were willing to go to England, so I listened in. I overheard the name of the man who runs the party in England. That's a start."

"So you think Karl went to London for the party and not jobs?"

"Perhaps. We can ask the man in charge."

"Who?"

"An Earl, Lord Contracross. I'm not familiar with him, although I thought I knew all the earls, but it's easy enough to find out who he is."

"Great news! Someone in the Social Democrats can tell us what factory Karl works in." Heinrich began packing up his bag. "Then let's head back."

"We shall." Langsford grabbed his valise from under the cot. "We'll all go back to the estate and, Heinrich, you and I will catch a train to London at Wittlich in the morning. Let's not chance anything by staying longer here in Bullay."

Pelham drove the wagon back to the estate with Langsford sitting beside him and Dirk in the back. Heinrich rode Preis, happy to be in a saddle again and they were all glad to be away from Bullay and Officer Wulff.

"How will you find Karl in London?" Dirk asked. "Go to each factory there?"

"That part doesn't make sense," Langsford answered. "London has only minor manufacturing—very few factories. Manchester and other cities have far more. It's odd they told Frau Kastner the factories were there."

"Then why go to London?" Heinrich queried from astride Preis who pranced beside wagon.

"Perhaps a cover story?" Pelham held the reins in one hand. He clucked to the team and the men stayed silent with their own thoughts for the next few kilometers as they trotted through the rolling farmland.

Heinrich glanced around "Look at these fallow fields. Why weren't they planted?"

"No market," Dirk said. "We planted for ourselves again this season, with little to sell."

"Is that wise? Vater always boasted how many marks the crops brought in."

"We cut back, both in crops and livestock for the past few years. You just never noticed. It's the depression. That's why there aren't many jobs. Anywhere."

CHAPTER 36

The Dieffenbacher Estate, Prussia

That evening Heinrich sat in his hidden schloss room when Langsford unexpectedly appeared in the doorway. "I brought some port. Your brother has gone out for the evening and I thought you'd enjoy the company."

"Good. I hate being holed up in here."

"I would, too, and I'm afraid I won't boost your spirits any tonight."

Langsford's expression was tense, making Heinrich hold his breath. He sat on the straw pad on the floor with Langsford in the crude chair at the wood table.

"I've learned more about your father. You need to hear this. That day, when he left for the train, your father took the trap cart. His driver, Hans, survived the attack, though the robbers probably thought he was dead. Afterward, Gerhard fired him for not protecting your father. Tonight, though, Hans returned to get a recommendation from Dirk and we three had a long conversation about what actually happened."

"What'd he say?" The candlelight bounced odd shadows on the stone walls.

"He and your father were outnumbered. Hans was stabbed severely in the arm and ribs while trying to fend off the three men, but they managed to drag your father from the trap causing the horses to bolt. Hans was flung from the cart into the boulders beside the road. Knocked out," Langsford continued, "except that as he was coming to, he heard someone say, 'Come on Helmut, hurry! We got the money. Let's go!' He was aware of them running away. He managed to drag himself over to your father, but they'd already slashed his throat."

"He was a *guter mann*, if a strict *vater*." Heinrich's voice caught.

"This is difficult," Langsford continued, "but you, we, must focus here. This was not a case of highway robbers."

"What else would it be?"

"Murder." Langsford held up his hand as Heinrich started to open his mouth. "Hear me out. I asked Hans what horse was pulling the trap and he confirmed it was a Black Forest draught, branded like the mare you rode to Bullay. I asked him how sure he was that he heard the name 'Helmut,' and he was very sure. He also confirmed there were three men. He'd seen them around a day or so earlier when he went out the hof's entrance and figured they were walking to the village. He recognized them when they jumped out at the cart that morning. And in broad daylight right on the other side of Flußbach. They were not trying to hide who they were. The three intended to kill the men they were robbing."

"Three?"

"Yes, three." Langsford pursed his lips. "And one named Helmut, the same as one of Karl's friends."

Heinrich shook his head. "Merely a coincidence. Helmut is not an unusual name. You're imagining things."

"No, think about it. Three men, and only a few hours from Bullay. *And* the day of the robbery fits right in with when police think Karl was murdered."

Heinrich fell back down in the chair.

"Karl talked to the police probably more than once and

learned the mare came from the estate. He would have no way of knowing the police thought you were in England. On his way to London, he came here with his two *kameraden* to kill the man he thought he saw in Bullay that night. The man he falsely accused. With you dead there would be no way anyone would ever point a finger at Karl. A simple highway robbery to cover his final tracks."

"They watched for my vater to ambush? Mein Gott!"

"Yes. Karl only saw you in the dark. You're similar to your father in size and looks."

"It's because of me Vater is dead."

"No. Don't get confused. It's because they are killers. And we will find them."

"Are they still here or did they really go to London?"

"My guess is that they headed to London after killing your father."

Langsford watched Heinrich set his jaw when he spoke. "I won't rest until we find them."

The next morning, Heinrich pulled up the collar of his work shirt and yanked his cap down over his eyes and watched as the horses were backed into the shafts of the carriage.

Dirk walked closer. "Be well, my boy. You will soon catch those three."

"I'm grateful the estate is in your good hands, Dirk."

Dirk turned and coughed, his kerchief to his mouth, but swiping a damp eye. He turned to the Englishman, "He has a good *freund* in you."

"Hopefully he and I will return together once the Prussians are caught."

"Ja, it would be good to have him here with family again."

Pelham climbed up to drive them to the Wittlich train depot. Langsford sat with the other two, determined more than ever to find not one, but three murderers.

CHAPTER 37

Bermondsey, London

The following Sunday came too quickly for Anna. Robbie arrived, scrubbed and shiny, wearing a freshly starched blue work shirt, tweed trousers, and a woolen coat. Aunt Bess cooked an extravagant leg of lamb, with roasted potatoes, peas, and a scrumptious mint sauce—a delicacy that they seldom permitted themselves to enjoy except for a holiday. *Leave it to sweet Aunt Bess*, thought Anna. The table was laid out with the best lace cloth. They ate the delicious meal in an awkward silence. Everyone felt uncomfortable, on their best formal behavior to impress Robbie, who in turn wished to impress them. Even Lottie tried her best to suppress giggles.

Anna's stomach was in knots and she ate very little of her favorite meal. After a dessert of port-laced trifle pudding, Aunt Bess stood and announced, "Lottie will help me in the kitchen. Anna, why don't you and Robbie visit? After all, you're his hostess." She began clearing the empty plates.

Robbie awkwardly pulled out Anna's chair. Uncle Max rose and reached for his pipe so he could smoke in the parlor while the young couple joined him to attempt a strained conversation. They were soon saved when Aunt Bess returned from the kitchen. "Lottie has graciously offered to finish the washing up so that I may visit, too," she smiled.

Uncle Max stood. "Then I suggest we four go for a stroll and get some fresh air."

"What a marvelous idea," Aunt Bess replied. "Let me fetch our shawls."

Anna, at a loss with this awkward boy, was grateful for a diversion. Practical, she wanted a suitor, but she still pined for Henry, or at least someone who made her feel as he did.

The four left, Uncle Max and Aunt Bess walking a discrete distance behind Robbie and Anna. They passed along the lengths of brick row houses and she thought of her walk with Henry, the carriage rolling beside them. She tried to shove the thought of him, his name, his demeanor, his person, from her mind. She needed to pay attention to what Robbie was saying. He was apologizing for not having a pony and cart so they could drive somewhere interesting. "We're limited to a walk this fine day. But then I don't need anythin' more than to be with you."

She smiled. "Thank you. I do enjoy a nice walk along the streets of Bermondsey, especially when I don't need to rush to be somewhere in particular. No need to ride at all." She wanted him to feel better.

"I think 'bout ya every day. I've spent this last week wishin' every day fer Sunday ta come sooner."

"The week seemed to go quickly, perhaps because I was so busy at the shop."

"Work at my shop is never ending." Robbie segued into boot making. They strolled over to the Leather, Hide and Wool Exchange on the corner of Leathermarket Street so he could show her where he came for the hides he needed. "It's a bit of a trek from Leadenhall."

"I knew this was here, but never knew this is where you came.

I've always thought of Bethnal Green as the shoe-and boot-making center."

"I've friends who work at Bethnal Green, but it don't compare to my shop," he boasted. "The high-class clientele come ta me."

"Yes, it's an advantage of Leadenhall."

They walked aimlessly for another half hour. Daylight was long that time of year, and with Sunday dinner over, there was no reason to hurry. She still couldn't find anything to engage Robbie in a conversation outside of boot making and leather working. She finally searched for an excuse to return home. "We probably should begin back. Aunt Bess may not be up to walking so long." She hated herself for her white lie, for Aunt Bess and she both loved long walks.

"Of course, sweet Anna. I'm not familiar with how ta properly attend ta a girl I'm escortin'. I mean, I've been given advice, but this is a bit new ta me. Wouldn't want ta cause Mrs. Miller no distress."

"I understand. We're both learning about courting." She hoped she would warm up to him eventually. Surely he had some thoughts about something other than cobbling. She'd just have to find one of interest to him.

As Robbie reluctantly departed later that evening, he suggested that perhaps they catch the underground train the following Sunday to make their way to Hyde Park for a picnic. The whole family could come with them.

"I will ask them, Robbie," Anna reassured him as she ushered him out the door.

Aunt Bess pronounced him a nice young man. Lottie, as usual, was especially curious, but Anna avoided both direct and indirect questions. She didn't want to dwell on the topic of Robbie.

During the next week, she found herself staying inside when

Mr. Thompson made another visit to the shop. "Oh, I am happy to help while you are here. There is no need to miss customers simply because you're working on the books," she insisted, not wanting Robbie to see her outside and come over to visit.

By Thursday, she realized how much she was avoiding him and felt ashamed. She lectured herself as she rode home on the Met. *He's real flesh and blood, not a dream.* Not someone who showed up one day, then disappeared. He was a nice boy, employed and with a fine craft—a solid future in his trade. If leathers and boots were important to him, then they will have to be to her, too. Time to face reality and stop pining and learn to appreciate Robbie. *No one else wants me and he does.* She had little choice if she didn't want to be a burden on the Millers for the rest of their lives.

The next day she locked the shop at break time. Not wanting to be gone unduly long, she hurried, carrying both her lunch and one she packed for Robbie as a surprise. They would eat together from now on. *After all, he is the man I will spend the rest of my life with.*

PART THREE

The English Hunt

CHAPTER 38

Pratt's Club, London

The carriage rocked as it turned right, eight hooves rhythmic on the cobblestones. Langsford sat across from Heinrich who held the overhead strap firmer, his tight grip matching his jaw. "This is a wild goose chase, looking for *some* man at a stuffy club who just *might* hold a meeting where *maybe* the three Prussians *might* show... ." Heinrich's impatience was overt. "We would do better to inquire at the factories where Karl and his friends have gone."

"The idea is we find the earl, we find the Social Democrats, we find Karl and his friends."

"Just because someone's mother mentioned the Social Democrats?" Heinrich snapped.

"Yes. That and the fact we know they are in the party."

"Why *not* the factories?"

"We don't know where." Langsford leaned forward to peer out the dark window. The rain-smeared view of street lamps cast long wavy lights on wet pavers.

Heinrich, too, looked out briefly. "What if we are missing the chance to find them?"

Langsford leaned back in the tufted leather seat. "We aren't."

"So we go to an exclusive club to learn who runs the party in England?"

"Indeed. The earl is the best lead we have at the moment, so we ask."

"That's why, in all this rain, we are headed to Pratt's?"

"It's one of the important clubs in London. Membership is limited to an influential few," Langsford grinned, putting his thumb in his lapel. "Excuse my immodesty but I am one."

"You sound pompous."

"Then I've succeeded. Thank you. Someone will know this earl and we ask at Pratt's."

"If it's so important, why weren't we there yesterday?"

"They were full."

"You can't dine whenever you want?"

"No. It's small. Only fourteen at the table."

After a brief silence, Heinrich piped up again. "Wasn't Pratt's where we were originally supposed to go the day we went to Leadenhall Market?"

Thoughts of Anna, Langsford realized. "Perhaps we should have gone to Pratt's then."

"And avoided the market and the chain of events that triggered my predicament?"

"A hard truth. Yes."

"No. If I'd never met Anna, I would never have been able to defy my vater. Wanting her gave me courage."

"There it is, then."

They stood in Pratt's foyer and handed their dripping umbrellas and coats to the steward, then walked into the sitting room where smoke wafted from pipes and cigars.

"Would either of you care for a beverage?" another steward inquired.

"Thank you, George. I'll have a port, as will my friend."

"Of course. I shall bring your beverages right in, your lordship."

The mahogany walls had a lusty sheen in spite of the hazy air. A tapestried hunt scene hung on the far wall and dark oil portraits peered down from the other walls. Gentlemen sat smoking and reading or quietly chatting. Too early to be tippling alcohol, they were subdued.

Langsford introduced his friend as his cousin, using his pseudonym. "Gerhard, may I introduce Lord Arthur Westchester—has the fastest race horses in all of England. In fact, Arthur, I should tell you about some of his horses I just saw in Germany."

Westchester shook Heinrich's hand and laughed. "I'm sorry, but English horses are the fastest in the world, and I own the fastest of those."

"Perhaps you do, but ours jump higher," Heinrich quipped, eliciting a chuckle from the older Englishman.

"This is Lord Henry Albert Norbiton, who always manages to beat me in chess."

"Someday," the old baron joked, "I may let you win." He clasped hands with the young Prussian.

"The clever Lord Edward Nevel." Langsford gestured to the gentleman on his left.

"It is my pleasure to meet you." About the same age as Langsford, he too, shook Heinrich's hand.

"And Lord Charles Wofford, whose art collection is second to none."

"Lord Wofford," Heinrich nodded, carefully shaking the old gnarled hand.

Heinrich recognized these were all powerful men, both young and old, as he settled into a leather wingback.

"So Langsford," began Norbiton, a tall, thin man with little hair and a pince-nez perched on his nose. "Are you following the Argentinean investments? I've not seen you here at Pratt's lately so I thought you'd gone to Argentina yourself to buy the entire country." He chuckled at his own humor.

Heinrich grinned at the good-natured jab toward Langsford.

"Alas, no," Langsford happily retorted. "You care to join me, though, when I do?"

"To invest? God no!" Norbiton exclaimed. "And be confused for a mere businessman?"

Langsford laughed heartily. "Just offering you one last opportunity to have fun with your own pounds instead of letting your banker have it all, in addition to his percentages."

"I dare say," Westchester joined in. "He'd have more fun betting on my horses."

"And he'd have nothing to show for that fun after your slow steeds lose," Langsford jovially quipped. "He'd have no return on his lost sterling."

The servant, George, arrived with a round silver tray holding two crystal glasses of port. Langsford nodded a thank-you, taking the stemware, handing one to Heinrich. After several sips, he set his glass down to fill his Bruyère pipe. As he tamped the tobacco, he turned to Wofford. "And what fun have you been up to, Woffie?"

Heinrich sipped his port and watched the exchange.

"I dined the other evening with Professor Marks. You know, the head of the West London Synagogue. He was a friend of your father."

"I thought he was a Hebrew professor or something."

"He teaches at London University, too," Nevel confirmed.

Norbiton nodded. "I met him once. Brilliant man."

"Jews are fine as long as they aren't those newcomers from Russia. Have you been to the East End to see those ragamuffins? Ikeys. Cheats and beggars," Nevel opined.

"You forget Disraeli was a Jew, as is our under-secretary," retorted Norbiton. "Class indeed makes the difference." He turned to Langsford. "Jews are good with money. Perhaps you should partner with your pounds," he chuckled, adding to the constant ribbing the young Englishman always received.

"Ah, but I do invest with Jews. The Rothchilds," Langsford retorted with a wink, raising his glass in a mock toast. "My father did not raise a stupid son."

Heinrich enjoyed the back-and-forth banter, laughing in amusement. He was having fun.

"The Rothchilds kill in the market," Wofford laughed.

"It is kill or be killed in the markets these days," Norbiton declared, "and I personally prefer not to be involved. That is what my banker is for. To make me sterling without worry."

"And your wife spends it all," Nevel replied sardonically.

"Leave the baroness out of this," growled the baron.

"Now, now," teased Westchester. "I'm sure your wives are your best advisors."

Nevel laughed. "My wife knows not to interfere."

"Lady Regina would have no interest, so the issue is moot for me."

"Lucky you," Wofford added. "My Lady Evelina is interested in everything."

"You must control her," Nevel advised, becoming serious. "We are responsible for what our women think and do."

"Why, pray tell, are we discussing wives?" Langsford remarked through teeth clenched onto his pipe stem.

"Indeed. There are better topics to pursue if we are to speak of females... ." Norbiton winked.

Heinrich sat silent, watching this exchange between the men, and drank his port.

Langsford removed the pipe from his mouth. "I've another topic that might be of interest."

"Oh," perked up the earl. "Do tell."

"Does anyone here know an earl, Lord Contracross? I heard mention of him while I was on the continent. For the life of me, I can't place the name."

"Lord Contracross? I don't think I'm familiar with him," offered Nevel.

"He is not in the House of Lords, I can tell you that," stated Wofford.

"I can't say I've heard of him, either," chuckled Westchester, puffing on his cigar.

"If someone comes to mind, I'd appreciate knowing."

"Why are you interested?" Nevel asked, known for prying.

"Nothing important. I understand he's interested in German politics and as I've both family and friends in Germany, I thought it would be a worthwhile discussion with him, that's all," he downplayed his reason. "Just bothersome I can't place him."

"Should I recall, I shall tell you," Nevel assured, then turned the conversation to the prospect of new colonies in Africa. "We've done jolly well with India. I expect we shall do the same on that continent."

"It seems everyone wants to get in on Africa. I read that Belgium intends to colonize a portion as well." Thus the conversation continued with international politics.

Heinrich leaned over to Langsford and whispered, "This is boring, and we are getting nowhere. We should be searching for Karl in English factories and not be wasting time here."

"Shhh. Give it some time. The night is far from over."

Three other gentlemen arrived one after one another. Langsford again introduced "Gerhard." The Earl of Exeter, last to arrive, garnered great respect from the others. He greeted everyone and, pleased to meet Langsford's cousin, remarked, "A great time of the Season to visit London. Some of our best weather, May is. You'll have a jolly time. You young people always do."

Westchester laughed. "You can see our Lord Edward Stanley, here, is a sensible sort. A chap that is up on his weather."

"Yes, Stanley, you are," Norbiton agreed. "So tell me. We were discussing this earlier. Are our ladies too bold, trying to tell us what to do? Does yours?"

"Well, this is certainly a topic for discussion," Stanley flippantly responded. He turned to George and patted his pocket. "Bring me a brandy. Damn. And a cigar. I forgot mine." Turning to his gentleman companions, he smiled. "I shall need fortification for *this* conversation!" he joked. "Lady Clementine is in fact smart. Plus, she's a redhead, but"—he paused for drama—"she obeys me without question." He laughed heartily. "And she found Langsford, here, his lovely bride. I shall give her complete credit for that …. sorry, son, but you surely needed help in that department."

Everyone had a good laugh, and Heinrich watched as Langsford mildly blushed. No one else, besides himself, knew why courting a woman had been so difficult for his English chum.

"Some women are now so bold as to voice opinions in the papers," exclaimed the newly arrived Lord Woodhill, Member of Parliament. An avid reader of London publications, he seldom missed anything current in the political winds. "I was astonished at—I believe Eleanor Marx—writing about the popularity of the socialist movement. She should be married and tending to babies."

"Yet who would want her?" Westchester retorted. "Unfeminine."

"Well, Lady Regina is pleased for me to make the decisions

and she is pleased to spend the results of those decisions. I would say she is the smartest of them all, with the exception of perhaps lovely Lady Clementine who was smart enough to tell her to marry me." Langsford toasted with his glass held high. "To our ladies. May we always love them!"

"Hear, hear," they all chimed in. As the toast ended, George announced dinner. Langsford and Heinrich accompanied twelve others to the dining room. Once seated, Heinrich looked around the table as a footman placed a bowl of julienne soup in front of him.

"There's definitely a problem with importing so many goods from America," Nevel continued an earlier topic on the depressed economy. "We should never have allowed so much trade," he railed.

"Now, Nevel," soothed Norbiton. "It is actually good to have trade with both of the Americas, north and south."

"What does not help, particularly in Europe," the Earl of Exeter added, "is Bismarck's stance. It was far from the ideal time for his Tariff Act."

"Now, let's not get onto the topic of Bismarck," Nevel warned.

"He's proven to be aggressive, stubborn, and unable to steer Germany in a beneficial direction," the earl retorted. "He should follow Parliament's example. There is a reason why the sun does not set on the British Empire."

"Hear, hear," they all chimed in, raising their glasses as they did when on the rare occasion they unanimously agreed. "God save the Queen!"

"George," summoned one of the members. "I'm less fond of this soup. Does Cook have another?"

Heinrich leaned over to Langsford and in German inquired, "Heißen alle diener George?" Are all stewards called George?

Langsford laughed, spilling soup from his rounded spoon. "Yes, everyone is George. That way we don't need to remember names."

"True," Lord Stanley, the Earl of Exeter chimed in. "We come to relax and be away from the day to day. We don't have to remember any names but our own."

"Drunk or sober," Norbiton laughed. "Which can be a challenge."

"We do what we wish," the Earl of Exeter scowled, "which I personally prefer to be with restraint."

"Nothing goes beyond these walls," Nevel sighed contentedly.

"Ah, these sacred walls," repeated another diner.

"We only let in the problems we *want*."

"I don't have a problem, but a puzzlement," Langsford began. "I risk boring some of you since I posed this earlier, but I wish to quiz the rest of you now."

"I love puzzles," said Lord Stanley. "What is it?"

"I was on the continent recently and heard others mention an earl, who for the life of me, I cannot place. Maybe I heard the name wrong since it was spoken in German, but it sounded like 'Contracross.'"

"Lord Contracross?" The earl looked over to the other gentlemen further down the table. "I don't believe so."

"No," another gentleman replied, shaking his head.

"Certainly not in the House of Lords."

"Can't say I recall anyone. An earl, you say?"

"Well, it was worth asking." Langsford was getting nowhere.

During the second course, conversation was interspersed between forkfuls of red trout with *canard à la rouennaise*. By the third course of quail and peas, they ate more leisurely.

"Does the Queen trust Gladstone to handle European issues? She favored Disraeli, but now... ."

"Gladstone will attend the Berlin Conference this November next. What's interesting is that Bismarck believes the Germans and the rest of Europe can colonize the entire black continent of Africa."

The table became silent as they consumed their cherry compotes with the fine Madeira wine served alongside. As they lingered, appetites sated, a more wine-induced conversation continued.

"Only we British are able to manage, and quite well I might add, a great deal of colonies. Germany simply doesn't have the power or wealth." Stanley was adamant. "Pardon to your cousin, Langsford, but Germany is *not* Britain."

"Yes, I, too, have your skepticism," Nevel agreed. "Only we could rule 'Darkest Africa' adequately. Why look how well we have done with India, taking an uncivilized area and guiding them into civilized ways."

"They certainly know how to make a fine cup of tea by now," another jested.

The Earl of Exeter stood, the signal for all to adjourn.

Langsford and Heinrich also stood to follow when a 'George' approached, towel on arm and liqueur bottle in his right hand. "Excuse me, your lordship. Might I offer you both an after-dinner drink? And as I pour, I would be pleased to share some information with you."

"By all means, George."

"Thank you. You are most indulgent." With a nodded bow, he adeptly poured from the cut-glass decanter into crystal stemware, then offered them from the tray. "As I was serving tonight, I could not help but overhear your question about Lord Contracross, an earl, my lord."

Langsford pulled on his moustache in anticipation.

"It occurred to me that you may be searching for a place, not a person."

"Is that so?"

"I'm from up north, Essex, your lordship. Perhaps if a German said 'Contracross' might it sound like Countess Cross? 'Tis a hamlet in Essex. A nearby village is Earls Colne, so I put two and two together and thought the German may have referred to these two towns. You simply heard what sounded like an English name and title."

"I dare say!"

"I apologize for speaking so directly, but I felt it my duty to offer my opinion."

"Not at all. You might have something there after all, by George," Langsford laughed at his pun. "Thank you. Well done. There it is."

While not the information Langsford expected, it was another concept to investigate. Rather than linger at cards and champagne as originally planned, he bid good evening to the remaining gentlemen who were now feeling their drink and embarking on the topic of naked ladies, delighting Heinrich. Langsford excused himself and, dragging Heinrich with him, hurried back to Grosvenor Square, eager to discuss what they had just learned. In the privacy of the library, Langsford settled comfortably in front of the library's fire. "A place, not a person. Countess Cross. Earls Colne." The Prussians could be in one of those small towns.

Heinrich stood in front of the fireplace. "How far? How do we know the Prussians are there?" Heinrich reeled off questions. "Why would the Social Democrats be there?"

"One question at a time." Langsford rose and walked over to one of the bookshelves behind the desk at the far end of the room. "Let's see if I can find a map of that area." He dragged his right index finger along a series of book spines on a shelf at eye level. He kept scanning the books, then on the shelf just below, pulled out a thick volume. "Ah, this should have what we need."

He returned to his chair and began flipping through its pages of maps while Heinrich looked over his shoulder. "These hamlets are in Essex, an easy journey north by train." He held the book up. "There, nearly side by side."

"That's Countess Cross," Heinrich pointed to tiny print. "But we don't know if the Prussians are there," Heinrich fussed. "We're on a wild goose chase."

"We'll see when we get there."

"Another trip to find them?" Heinrich was skeptical. "Why would they come all the way to England to go to a tiny place like that?"

"Maybe they did and maybe they didn't."

"Why don't you go, since it's your idea, and I'll stay in London and search."

"Don't underestimate the British police," Langsford warned. "Scotland Yard will ship you back to Prussia in a heartbeat. Staying with me is your best bet."

Heinrich sat down with a huge sigh. "So I have to go to these towns in the middle of nowhere."

"Tomorrow, the middle of nowhere, my friend," Langsford laughed and picked up his pipe.

CHAPTER 39

Countess Cross, England

The next day, Langsford squirmed in his third-class seat. Squeezed in beside Heinrich, he rode the Colne Valley-Halstead train north to Countess Cross. The wood seats were small and hard. "Damn, this infernal wool itches."

"*You* are the one who said we should look the part," Heinrich laughed.

"I did. But I didn't mean to feel the part, too."

"I have my scratchy beard and worn clothes, so it's only fair."

"I don't have to *like* it."

"Those clothes build character."

"And I suppose this infernal cap does, too."

"Look on the bright side: the car isn't packed." Heinrich tilted his head. Several passengers sat scattered throughout the coach, either reading or sleeping. The adjacent seats remained vacant, affording them a modicum of privacy. He moved to the seat in front, turning around to continue. "I was packed in like a sardine in France. We have all this space to ourselves." Heinrich looked around one more time and then whispered, "You don't think anyone from Scotland Yard has followed us, do you?"

Langsford looked at the other passengers. "If they have, I think they are being very blasé. They'd have arrested you already."

Two hours later they arrived at the village of Earls Colne and hired a small livery to travel the final two miles to the little hamlet of Countess Cross. When they arrived, they found nothing more than a crossroads. Across from them on the right side of the street was a pub that served as both restaurant and inn. A total of eight houses, one little school, and a small church made up the rest of the hamlet, which was surrounded by farmland as far as the eye could see.

They crossed to the pub. The Ox & Plough was a hazy, crowded little place that smelled like spilled ale and stale smoke. The old barkeep eyed them suspiciously as they sat at a rough-hewn plank table. The room was close, with three tiny windows stuck in the dark walls. Unlit lamps hung on grimy chains suspended from the low ceiling.

The old man came over. "Ya want the special?"

Langsford, unsure what the special was, confirmed. "Two," he said holding up a pair of fingers.

In a few minutes the barkeep plunked down two plates. Langsford surveyed the food in front of him: cheese, bread, pickled onions, and gherkins. "Out in the middle of nowhere, I suppose I cannot expect this to be the fare of a London pub."

They ate in silence, watching and listening to the few men around them.

Heinrich ate quickly. "If you English served five normal meals a day like we do at home, I wouldn't get so hungry." Finished, he pushed away his plate.

"It's good you're hungry or you wouldn't eat this," Langsford laughed, wiping his mouth.

"Let's find this trio fast and leave."

While Langsford agreed, he still wasn't sure what they'd do once they did locate the Prussians. He was saved from replying when the barkeep came back to their crude wooden table and began clearing the empty dishes. "What brings you blokes here?"

he asked, stacking plates on one arm. "We've had strangers of late and it don't sit well with the decent folk of Countess Cross. Not sayin' that I have any sort of thing agin' you, but yer two more blokes I dunna know."

Langsford ignored the insult and answered with his version of a working-class dialect. "We want to be catchin' up with acquaintances. Germans."

Heinrich choked on his laugh before Langsford's sentence was finished and quickly took a sputtering swig of ale, making him choke more. Langsford kicked him under the table.

"Ouch!"

"There be a lot of men, English, German. All strangers," the barkeep scoffed. "Claim to be lookin' for work. Does this place look like we've jobs?"

Langsford exchanged glances with Heinrich.

"We're lookin' for friends from Bullay, Prussia. They're 'bout our age. Would ya know 'em? Karl Gülker, Fritz Kastner, or Helmut Bär?"

"I pay no mind to the names of strangers."

"Well, we'll ask 'round. For now, let's 'ave a pint or two. Oh, and we'll be takin' a room for the night, too."

The proprietor's face lit up. "Ya can stay here as long as ya spend money. I've got no bone to pick with you 'bout that, mind ya." He turned to fetch more ales, calling over from the bar. "Oh, an' sorry fer callin' ya 'blokes.' Too many strangers. I never know who's gonna knap."

"Knap?" Heinrich asked.

"Steal. He's not exactly a trusting sort."

Heinrich looked around at some of the other patrons. "Maybe he has a reason."

The barkeep came back with their ales. "A few men met here

a couple nights back. They ain't stayin' here, which is what they should be a doin'." As he returned to the bar, he loudly added for the benefit of all in the room, "And unlike you two, most folk don't drink as much as they should for the time they sit at me tables." He shook his head as he wiped glasses.

They remained at the table, talking about London and Prussia and recalling various school pranks of the past, but Langsford kept watching the locals. There was no place else in the tiny village to go.

For supper they ordered bubble and squeak and more pints.

The Ox & Plough quieted as people began to leave. Only a few patrons remained, the hour late for the farming community. Langsford and Heinrich, convinced they were getting nowhere, were about to go upstairs for the night when a grizzled farm laborer came over from the bar and sat himself down, wobbling the crude wooden table.

"It's someone you're looking for, is it?"

CHAPTER 40

Countess Cross, England

The man had few teeth, creating a lopsided smile. He smelled worse than the pub. "I might be able to help ya." He plunked down his nearly empty beer glass.

"Just how?" Langsford didn't try to hide his disgust at the filthy little man.

"I mighta seed them three you be lookin' for ... from Bool-lay." He smiled, pleased with himself. "One's Karl." His smile broadened.

"How do you know him?"

"I keep my eyes an' ears open. For a gen or two, I can open my mouth as well, 'specially if me glass is filled to the brim with gatter." He smacked his lips and tapped his glass on the table. "And sumthin' in the stomach as well as me pocket."

Langsford called over to the barkeep and ordered three lagers, along with a slab of cheese and bread. The scrawny little man beamed.

"We already mentioned Karl and Bullay, so that's worthless. Tell us something useful and I'll decide if your facts are worth anything."

"I don't usually let someone insult me intelligence like that," he feigned indignity. "And I don't do no business in this manner, but I like ya. I'll do you gents a favor this one time." He scratched his scraggly beard.

"We're so honored."

"I were sittin' 'ere a couple days ago, mindin' my own business, and these three Germans, they come in to meet a man who were here tonight."

The barkeep set down the plate of bread with a square of cheddar along with the ales, sneering at the grizzly man. When he left, the newfound "friend" grabbed a chunk of bread and stuffed his mouth until his cheeks bulged.

Chewing with his mouth open, he continued. "The man on the fer side by hisself tonight. Left a little bit ago or I wudda come ov'r sooner." The food muffled his words. "Name of Lentz. Him with your friends the other night. Three of 'em huddled with him, talkin' German they was."

"Sie sprachen Deutsch?" Heinrich asked, his palms holding his glass.

The man stuffed his dirty face with cheese. Talking with his mouth full, he exclaimed, "I heerd German but can't lower meself to speak nuthin' but the Queen's English." Langsford winced. "But I did heerd the name Bismarck and the word mord. Don't that mean sumptin' bad in German? Murder?"

"Yes. Murder. And you heard them say Bismarck?" Langsford asked as if the name were a mere curiosity.

"Sure as I'm sittin' 'ere. They want ta kill 'im. Can I have my gen now? A bob, a shillin' for me troubles?" He beamed his toothless grin.

The last remaining patrons got up from a table near the front and walked out the door, leaving just the three of them and the barkeep who was busy counting money, not listening.

"People often say they'd like someone dead," Langsford replied, indicating he had no interest, as he drank some ale. "We don't really care what they say in any language," he lied. "We want to know where they are."

"Maybe stayin' at a boardin' house over in Earls Colne... ."

"Maybe?" Heinrich pushed. "You aren't telling us anything." He leaned back in his chair and scowled.

"I need sumthin' jiggling in me pocket now, don't I?"

Langsford reached for his purse and pulled out a thruppence, which he tossed on the table. "That'll do for confirming they're near here."

"One thruppence won't be jingling." The man flashed another huge, toothless grin. "'At's not all right, now is it? I need ta hear the jingling. There's a mate for it, in't there? So it won't be lonely?"

"Only if you can tell me about this Lentz. Then your coin may get a mate, though you'll spend it all on ale, I'm sure."

"Oh no! I'll be getting flowers for me mother." He laughed hard.

Langsford pulled out another coin and put it on the table in front of him, quickly covering it with his palm. The dirty man looked at Langsford's hand as though he could see through it to the silver coin. He licked his lips and continued.

"Well, this Lentz, he been 'ere maybe near a week. Had meetings 'ere in this pub 'til this tosser kicked 'em out." He nodded toward the barkeep. "The bloke does the same ta me if he don't see no money first."

"Never mind that. Go on about Lentz," Heinrich glowered at the scrawny man.

"He speaks English good. Said he be going to London and see them three there at meetin' in a gattering." He chewed on the remaining bread crust.

"Gattering?" Heinrich raised his eyebrows.

"Means pub," Langsford explained. "Which one?" he asked the little spy.

"A pub I nev'r heerd of, I swear. They's going to a committee meeting. There weren't nuthin' more."

"Where's Lentz now?" Langsford demanded.

"Probably at the Lion and Boar ov'r in Earle Colne." He eyed the Englishman's hand. "Tomorrow night for sure fer a meetin'. Him an' a gent called Summerhill."

"Who's Summerhill?" Langsford glared.

The man broke his gaze. "He were here a few times, too. Talkin' with Lentz. Before they was told not to come back here. His partner. 'At's worth sumthin' now, ain't it?"

"How do you know this?" Langsford kept his hand plastered over the coin.

"Well, let's just say I followed 'em ... better chance of getting' a free pint ov'r there. Weren't nobody left 'ere. Then the blokes kicked me outta there, too. Even when I had me money." He tried to look pitiful. "I go where I'm welcome, so I come back 'ere."

"So, Lion and Boar?"

"My coin needs a mate now, for the jinglin' ..."

There was a decent chance Karl and his friends were actually in the vicinity. "We're done here." He lifted his hand off the thruppence.

The spy snaked out gnarled fingers to snatch it, laughing, and then downed the dregs of his lager. "Maybe 'Hair' Lentz and Mr. Summerhill be givin' an engraved invitation to you gents." He dragged his coat sleeve over his mouth. "I'll be seein' ya at the next roy-al ball." He stood, tipped an imaginary hat, and staggered out.

Langsford watched the seedy little toe-rag with his "jingling" coins disappear through the door. He smiled at Heinrich; Lentz, Summerhill, and the Prussian murderers were likely in the next village only two miles away.

CHAPTER 41

Hyde Park, London

While Langsford and Heinrich posed as out-of-work laborers, Anna and her family strolled in Hyde Park for a pleasant afternoon. "What fine young Englishmen we have here, Aunt Bess," Uncle Max said and winked at both Anna and Lottie who were accompanied by Robbie Wells and Francis Blackwell. "I'm so glad handsome young men enjoy my company." Everyone laughed as they settled in on the grass along the Serpentine water in Hyde Park. Sitting on quilts, they all relaxed on the gentle slope while couples smoothly rowed by. Ducks paddled near the shoreline, frequently dunking upside down.

"It's a taste of heaven," Aunt Bess sighed blissfully, sitting back on her hands, face tilted toward the sun.

"I remember coming here as a boy," Uncle Max reminisced.

"You came here often, didn't you?" Aunt Bess prompted.

"I did. I must have been ten when we came to the opening of the Great Exhibition. The Queen and Prince Albert were here. I wanted to see them, but there were so many people, we could barely walk. Never got near."

"We're lucky to live 'ere," stated Robbie. "So much in London town." No longer the shy boy, he was emboldened ever since Anna had shown her interest. While Robbie was not the man of her dreams, she knew he was sincere and she accepted him as her only hope for a secure future.

Anna listened to the others relate their favorite London experiences while she helped Aunt Bess empty the picnic baskets. Freshly packed that morning, they contained sliced boiled tongue, a steak-and-kidney pie, a veal-and-ham pie, strips of cucumbers, stewed fruit with pastry biscuits, ginger-beer, and lemonade. She set the sponge cake for dessert off to the side along with the fresh fruit and cheese.

"A picnic fit for a king," declared Uncle Max, rubbing his hands together in anticipation.

"And enough to feed an army," red-headed Francis laughed, and picked up a piece of meat pie.

"Food tastes better on a picnic," Aunt Bess said with a smile.

"Yer food is good anywhere," Robbie answered, his mouth full.

A breeze wafted up from the Serpentine as they became intent on the food spread before them. After they'd finished, Francis stood and extended his hand to Lottie. "Let's stroll along the water." Lottie giggled and took his hand, letting him assist her.

Uncle Max batted his eyelids. "I don't think I can, Francis. I ate too much," he joked in a falsetto, patting his belly.

"Oh, Uncle Max," Anna laughed.

"Anna, we'll go, too." Robbie hopped to his feet, brushing crumbs off his trousers.

"And I"—Uncle Max winked—"want to sit and gaze at the beauty of your lovely Aunt Bess. It's time you four left us alone."

His wife blushed and laughed. "I do believe that Mr. Miller is simply too lazy."

"'Tis a good day to feel lazy." Robbie defended his host with a smile and then took Anna toward the sun-glinting water. Lottie and Francis trailed behind, giggling.

The couples ambled along the water's edge. Anna shaded herself with her newly purchased parasol, feeling like an elegant lady while Robbie chattered on. "I've a new stitch to flatten the top of a boot so it don't rub the leg. People know I take a lot of pride in me work."

"It's good to have happy customers." Anna smiled.

"Soon I'll stitch purses, vests, and leggings. And I'll sell leather goods to the Queen's household. Earn a Royal Warrant with a sign out front just like your shop."

Anna pictured it: By Appointment to Her Majesty the Queen written under the royal seal depicting the lion and unicorn. It had been hung long ago in front of her shop, but she knew a business had to earn the right from the Royal Family in order to display it.

"When that 'appens, I'll 'ave a good living for me wife and family." He stopped to look at her. "A girl like you deserves me."

He reached for her hand, but she moved it next to her other on the handle of her parasol. She wasn't yet engaged, she thought, remembering Aunt Bess's words. Only slightly rebuked, Robbie walked on. "At lunch, we all told stories but ya didn't. What'd ya do as a girl?"

Anna shuddered. "I prefer not to remember my childhood, for it ended sadly."

"Yer 'sposed to tell me everything."

"I didn't know that. I apologize."

"What are ya hidin'?"

"Nothing. I often think of my parents, I miss them... ."

"Ya 'ave your uncle and aunt."

"Of course. I'm grateful for them and love them, too, but I still love my parents."

"What 'appened to 'em?"

"They departed this world when I was ten. Typhoid. I was at school when they died within hours of each other at the hospital."

"Well, people get sick and pass over all the time. Ya was old enough even then to know that. Yer being silly now."

"I suppose. I suppose my parents protected me."

"Well, ya turned into a nice girl, Anna. It ended fine and now ya 'ave me."

They stopped at a bench where a large tree overshadowed both the walkway and the water. The boaters passed nearly at arm's length and Anna smelled the mud-luscious earth as the water lapped the bank only feet below.

It saddened her that Robbie didn't understand how she felt about her parents. She'd been staying at their neighbors' home while her mother and father were at the Fever Hospital. The day she learned she was an orphan, she came from school to the neighbors' house where they gently but firmly told her she could spend one last night, but would have to find a relative to live with, for they could not take in another person to feed and clothe.

She'd stood on the stoop of their house and looked over to her old home, where her father had waved to her only days before, where she'd played games with her mother.

"It was strange," Anna spoke more to herself than Robbie. "I looked at our house and realized it was empty. My parents weren't there and never would be again. Seeing the house like that ... Its emptiness looked exactly how I felt." She could see the past as she looked at her old home. What she couldn't do was see her future.

"What'd ya do?"

"I had no relatives and no idea where to go except an orphanage." She remembered she went back inside the neighbors' house to pack her meager belongings and thought, *Tomorrow I'll ask my teacher where the orphanage is.*

Even then, she knew she had to be practical and "face facts," as her mother had taught her. At the tender age of ten, she abruptly faced very difficult ones.

"'Twas time for ya to grow up. You 'ad it easy. I've been on me own since seven."

Anna gazed beyond the Serpentine.

Robbie was still talking. "Parents are 'sposed go on to their own reward, Anna. Nothin' to be sad about."

Lottie and Francis strolled up to join them on the bench. Lottie, always curious to know what people were talking about, instantly picked up on Robbie's words. "You're sad, Anna? Why on earth?"

"She misses 'er parents. I told 'er dead is dead, ya know."

Anna stiffened but said nothing.

"Her parents died, and it *was* sad, Robbie. But it ended up wonderful, didn't it, Anna?" Lottie sat beside her, their skirts bunching up between them. Francis perched on the edge at the very end, bookending the girls with Robbie.

"Yes, it did, all thanks to you." Anna looked at her friend and blinked back tears, her nose and forehead giving her quick throbs from the effort.

"I told my aunt and uncle about Anna's parents," Lottie picked up the story. "Of course they knew one another because we were best friends. I'd always dreamed of a sister like Anna, so they decided she could live with us. It's like I wish for something to be true and it just happens." She bounced on the bench, remembering her excitement. "Look at us now, with beaus at the same time. You would think we were maybe twin sisters, to be married at the same time." Lottie giggled, and covered her face, embarrassed by what she'd just said.

Deep down, Anna sometimes felt she had traded her parents for a sister. As much as she cared for Lottie, and when a child also wished they were sisters, she thought she had been punished for wanting something she didn't have. She vowed she would never ask for anything again. She feared if she did, it would exact a huge price.

I shall never wish for someone to love that I don't have, she thought, shoving away a mental image of Henry. *That's when I lose what I do have.*

CHAPTER 42

The Lion and Boar, Earle Colne, England

The Lion and Boar was a large Tudor-era public house, its black timbers in-filled with rough plaster. It sat just past Burrows on High Street, where houses and shops lined both sides of the main thoroughfare and side streets branched off into this larger village.

Once Langsford and Heinrich entered the establishment, they found themselves surrounded with the caramel glow of the gas wall lamps. At the bar they ordered two lagers and a pork pie apiece. After Langsford paid, he asked the barman if a man named Lentz was around.

"Bernd Lentz? No, but his partner is," he answered, setting their full glasses in front of them. "'At's him, over at the table, sittin' by hisself. Harold Summerhill."

"Thank you."

"That was easy," Langsford said under his breath to Heinrich.

Their pies not yet up, they carried their pints over to the lone man, who sat at a shiny varnished table.

"I beg your pardon. Would you be Mr. Summerhill?"

"Yes. Harold Summerhill." The man stood to shake hands. He was of normal build and better dressed than they in his tweed coat. His trousers were new and his shoes recently shined but his ruddy face gave away the fact that he'd worked extensively outdoors. "And you?" He smiled, a pleasant sort of man.

"Langsford," he replied, dropping his title.

"Gerhard," Heinrich fibbed.

"Sit," Summerhill invited, gesturing to the empty chairs across the table.

Langsford settled in the seat and explained their presence. "We're looking for Bernd Lentz. The bartender said you know him?"

"Yes. He's my assistant. We're both in the Social Democratic Party."

There it is. "That's why we've come."

"You're from 'round here?"

"No. South of London," Langsford replied, for his country estate was indeed there. "My cousin Gerhard's from Germany. And you?"

"I was born here but worked buildin' track for the Met down in London. That work's done, it is. Like others, I've needed new work, but it's scarce. So I joined the party. Figure if we stick together, eventually we'll be strong enough make sure there's plenty of work for everyone." He looked at Heinrich. "With fair pay, here *and* in Germany."

"You guarantee jobs, then?" Langsford asked.

"No, but I help organize the men for a united front. I ran a large crew while we laid track, so I knew I could run a few party meetings here in England. The party's illegal in Germany"—he looked again at Heinrich—"which is why you're here, if I'm to guess." He paused with a friendly smile. "A large group of socialists went up to Stockholm, too," he added.

"So I've heard. Legal there, too." Langsford smiled, wondering how the man could afford nice clothes.

"The laws just got to catch up in Germany. Socialism is the new way."

Summerhill's explanation seemed logical. He held meetings

and recruited for the party. It wasn't clear what Lentz did exactly. Could the German assistant be leading a subversive plot behind Summerhill's back? Could he be connected with the three Prussians?

"There's a small meeting in a little while at nine. Why don't you attend?"

Langsford looked over at the bar. "Our pies are ready but we'd be interested in the meeting. Be glad to stay."

"You'll find it useful." Summerhill nodded good-bye as he rose to greet another man walking over to his table.

They ate their pies, and within a short time, men started to gather. About a dozen ended up at several tables pulled together. They joined them and Bernd Lentz arrived right at nine o'clock. He introduced himself with a heavy German accent, while Summerhill sat off to the side.

Heinrich didn't remember what the drunken Karl looked like, so they were dependent on hearing someone say his name. So far, no one referred to him, let alone a Fritz or a Helmut.

Lentz spoke. "This long depression hits all of us hard, year after year. I've come from Europe where the market is too weak for most crops to sell." He paused, looking at the men sitting around the tables. "Normal farm work isn't there again this year because less is planted." He gestured with outspread arms as though he were embracing that empty farmland, and Langsford pictured the fallow acres in the Rhineland. "And even if the fields are cultivated, they're planted by machines, ploughed by machines, and harvested by machines."

Lentz shook his head, pausing while those listening commiserated among themselves. "Then after harvest, there is almost nowhere for the crops to be sold. Now the governments have added taxes and tariffs and continue to ruin the economy."

Summerhill walked to the front of the group. He further painted the bleak picture. "The markets generally are ruined everywhere, and here in England we're no different. England imports food, tobacco, and cotton from the United States. Europe imports from South America. We have switched from selling crops to products. As a result, there are factories, but workers don't know how to run the machines. Even the farm equipment is hard to work. We have to learn, but how? The governments have to teach us. It's time they helped."

"But I cannut work in a factory that in't here," complained one man.

"A good point, my friend," Summerhill nodded. "It is difficult to relocate where the factories are."

"The government should pay to move us."

"That's right." Another voiced his opinion.

Langsford watched the men nodding and clapping when they agreed. Some were angry, clenching their fists.

Summerhill held up his hands for order. "The world is different. The middle-class worker must be skilled. You have to learn new ways and someone has to teach you."

"Then teach us!" yelled another farmer.

The paradigm was shifting in the economic world. Langsford sat watching these middle-class laborers. He hadn't viewed this through workers' eyes before. *I see the world economy from a completely different vantage point.* These men's daily concern was having a job, while his was figuring out where to put his pounds to make more. *The layers of classes—fascinating.* He pulled himself from his thoughts to listen.

Summerhill continued. "You have to be different, too."

"We don't want to be different. We just want to work!" cried out another.

"And you will. United, we can force our governments to help us so we *can* work!"

One man pounded on the table. "No tariffs so there'll be work again at the ports!"

Summerhill calmed the men as he raised his hands, palms out, urging several who had sprung out of their seats to sit down. "The solution is socialism, not just in Britain but in Germany, France, Austria—all of Europe," Summerhill reassured them. "The Social Democratic Party has power. The best way to get our governments, and especially the German chancellor, to cooperate is to play the game of politics. More and more of our party members are gaining seats in the German government, and Bismarck can't stop them."

As the meeting wound down, many of the men remained around the table, excited about the issues and chatting with Lentz. Langsford took Heinrich back over to the bar. As he'd hoped, Summerhill quickly joined them.

"Did you hear anything interestin' tonight?"

Langsford nodded. "It's a lot to think on."

"That's a fact. Without the party there's no way to protect us working men. We need to join together to demand fairness from both employers and governments."

"Makes sense." Langsford paused to order another pint. "Speaking of workers, maybe you can help. Gerhard has been trying to locate his friends."

"Ja," Heinrich spoke up. "Fritz's mother told me they came here for the party. Maybe you know them?"

"Possibly. Who are they?"

"Karl Gülker, Fritz Kastner, and Helmut Bär."

"I might know them." He set his own beer glass down on the bar. "Did one of them have a brother?"

A jolt shot up the Langsford's spine.

"Ja. Just before they left for England, Karl's bother was murdered. Terrible."

"You're from Bullay?"

Langsford's poker face belied his excitement. *He knows them.* "He's Prussian," he answered, figuring the three thought Heinrich was dead, having no idea it was his father they murdered, so it was safe to reveal this.

"You know where we can find them?" Heinrich spoke up.

"I might." Summerhill sounded falsely unsure.

"They're on a committee," Langsford prompted, recalling what the grizzly old man had said—a bold bluff.

"Did they tell you what committee?"

Heinrich took the cue. "Ja, they did, but I can't say. This is, how do you say ... not to tell?" Heinrich was doing a fine bluff of his own.

"*Secret* is the word you want," Langsford offered, playing along, liking that Heinrich acted as though he knew more than he did.

Heinrich nodded. "They wouldn't like me to say more. A friend in Bullay said I should fill in for the dead man."

Summerhill countered with a blunt question. "What was the dead man's name?"

The hair on Langsford's neck stood up.

"Marc Gülker," Heinrich answered. "He was my friend, more so than the others."

Another good answer, Langsford thought, drinking from his glass to hide his sigh of relief.

"His brother is Karl Gülker."

Summerhill rubbed his chin, thinking. "The others names again?"

"Fritz Kastner and Helmut Bär."

"Ah, yes," he bit his lips. "If I recall, they *are* on a party committee." He paused to stare directly at Heinrich who held his gaze, then continued. "They've left for a committee meeting in London, so you've actually just missed them."

"A committee meeting in London? Excellent!" Langsford took the conversation back. "We're headed there tomorrow."

"Well, it isn't quite that simple. Party members must be assigned to a committee," Summerhill explained. "If you're serious about joining one, then we'll have to see. I'm returning to London myself, so Gerhard, why don't you meet me there Tuesday? We can discuss your role in the party. There may be other tasks more fitting for you."

Langsford wasn't thrilled if Heinrich were assigned to a different committee, but there was little choice. Getting involved in any way would get them closer to the Prussian trio.

"Gut," Heinrich replied. "Where do we meet?"

"At the Lamb Tavern pub. I'm sure you can find it. Six o'clock."

Langsford spoke up. "We'll meet you there, but six thirty is better."

"Six thirty is fine, but no need for you to come because I'm only talkin' with him. Need to see if he's suited for this committee's work."

"I don't understand."

"Englishmen have different roles than Germans. I can meet privately with you at a later date if you want. There'll be another meeting there Tuesday night at nine." Dismissing Langsford, Summerhill turned to Heinrich. "In London, then?"

"Ja, London," Heinrich answered.

"Then I'll see you Tuesday." Summerhill, the apparent leader of both the party here in England and the committee, nodded and walked away to speak to other workers.

Langsford and Heinrich, calling it a night, left the pub.

Heinrich was jubilant. "Finally! Karl will be there. What that seedy little man told us last night was worth the six pence."

Langsford chuckled. "The chase is still on. The hounds, meaning us, have circled and are closing in."

"States the man who would never sit on a horse long enough to ever chase a fox."

"As long as men like you are willing, then why should I bother?"

CHAPTER 43

No. 12 Grosvenor Square, London

Back home in London the next day, Langsford sat in front of the library's fire, watching as Heinrich paced. "Karl will be here Tuesday to meet with Summerhill—"

"Finally," Heinrich interrupted with a sigh of relief. "We've finally made progress."

"Yes. We've confirmed they're in the party and here in London." Langsford tamped tobacco in his pipe.

Heinrich walked faster. "We should have Scotland Yard arrest those four and Lentz."

"The police have no reason to arrest them. We need proof they are up to no good."

"I can tell them."

"And be arrested yourself, or murdered by them like your father? No, we need to *prove* Karl is a murderer and that they are plotting an assassination. We need facts or confessions."

Heinrich looked deflated as he plopped down in the adjacent wingback.

"That's why you need to get on this particular committee to see what they are up to. Dangerous or not, only you can gather the facts we need since Summerhill seems to only want Germans. I can't do it."

"I really have to meet with Summerhill? Alone?"

"He was adamant about just you."

"Summerhill didn't seem to be so vile. Would he plan to murder someone ...?"

"You're far too trusting. While I would prefer to believe what people say, I learned that, sadly, men are far more complicated." After pondering a moment, he spoke again. "You were clever to tell him a friend suggested you take Marc's place."

"The problem is I don't know Marc's friends. If he asks who, I won't know what to say."

"It doesn't matter if you don't know his real friends. You can say you spoke with ... What was the name of that man in the beer hall in Bullay?"

"Let me think." He paused. "It was Ernst. Ernst Schmidt."

"Good. You can say Ernst Schmidt. Never claim you know the others directly. Just tell Summerhill that Ernst thought you'd make a good replacement for Marc."

"Simple enough to remember. I'm getting good at pretending to be someone else."

"We both are." Langsford fingered the silk lapel on his smoking jacket, remembering the scratchy coat from yesterday. "Just be on the committee long enough to get facts. Then I can go to Scotland Yard."

"What if Summerhill isn't alone?"

"That's crossed my mind, too. It may be wise for me to go ahead of you before the meeting. Maybe give us a heads up about who and what to expect."

Dressed again in worker's clothes, Langsford had more than a scouting mission in mind when he went to the Lamb Tavern Tuesday. It was close to five o'clock when he departed the cab at Leadenhall Market's main entrance and headed up toward the public house. He found it odd that Heinrich's meeting with Summerhill was here. This made him uneasy on a different front: the proximity to a certain millinery shop.

While it was true he wanted to see what men might already be at the pub, he worried about Anna being in the vicinity. He'd purposely changed Summerhill's meeting time to six thirty, wanting Anna to be long gone for the day. He chuckled, remembering she closed the shop at six. *Then, my only concern was etiquette,* he thought. Not police or assassination plots. Now he was worried Heinrich might falter while talking to Summerhill if Anna walked by, saw him, and called him by name. That could be disastrous. It was best to check everything ahead of time. He had a good hour and a half to scout around.

Walking toward the pub, he spotted Anna's maroon-and-cream shop up on the right, but he turned left into the pub, swallowed by the dark interior. As his eyes adjusted, he could see it was larger than the ones in the little villages he'd just visited. This one was geared to a higher class of patrons and served fine food and drink. The walls were paneled; the oak tables stood on turned legs. Langsford walked over and ordered an ale at the mahogany bar, admiring its polished carvings. Scanning the interior reflected in the beveled mirror he faced, he watched as businessmen chatted and imbibed. Since coffeehouses and cafes had dwindled in popularity, the public houses had replaced them as the preferred meeting places. These days, important business decisions were made over a pub's pint or two.

Langsford didn't recognize anyone. He downed his drink, wondering how he could protect Heinrich during this critical meeting. His friend proved he could hold his own so far, but this would be the first time Heinrich was left on his own, and that was a worry.

As Langsford stood at the bar, a nondescript man in a long coat and derby entered. Scotland Yard Inspector Abberline slipped over to a corner after getting a drink, scanning the room much as Langsford had done, only much more subtly, curious to see if the English lord was meeting anyone. For some strange reason, Langsford was dressed in old clothing as if in disguise. He knew the man was up to something, but he couldn't sort it out just yet. He was waiting for his superior at the Yard to confirm Lord Langsford had a Westphalian cousin named Gerhard. If not ....

Langsford left the establishment. He hadn't seen Summerhill, Lentz, or anyone he recognized from Earle Colne. He'd check again on his way out of the market. He walked out into the late afternoon on the sheltered street. Anna was his next stop.

CHAPTER 44

Leadenhall Market, London

On a late Tuesday afternoon, Anna stood outside the shop's door for fresh air. She knew Robbie was picking up an order of leather and might not be back before closing so she'd probably miss him today. She was becoming fond of Robbie, even if he was overly eager and a braggart. He meant well. She enjoyed his Sunday visit, although truth be told, she enjoyed the outing with her entire family. She watched the shoppers hustle along the street, hurrying to finish before the shops closed. Suddenly she did a double-take. Right across from her was that lord. She was sure of it. He looked funny in a worker's coat and suspendered trousers, but she recognized his handsome face. She wasn't sure what to do—slip back inside, or stay and say hello. Her indecision decided for her. He spotted her, waved, and crossed the street, weaving his way through the vendors and buyers.

"Anna!" He tipped his cap. "What a welcome surprise to see you!"

Anna gathered herself and replied stiffly, "Hello. This *is* a surprise. I never heard from your Prussian friend ... or you."

"Yes. You are correct. May I extend apologies? Heinrich ended up in a great hurry those weeks back," he explained. "He was forced home before he had an opportunity to even say good-bye to me." Langsford laughed, attempting to make light of it.

"In his rush," Anna bristled, "he must have forgotten his impeccable manners." She gathered her shawl up around her shoulders, intending to say good-bye, but dropped the end of it. She grabbed at it and missed.

"When he returns, he'll give his apology in person." Langsford reached down to pick up the dangling shawl and placed it over her shoulder.

"That won't be necessary. I have no desire to see him."

"I understand. You have a right to feel peevish."

"I never gave him a thought, if you must know," she lied, and stuck her nose in the air, accidentally letting the shawl slip off her other shoulder. She tried to get the errant shawl under control. "His actions tell me the opposite of what you report." She hung onto the shawl with a tight fist and tipped her nose in the air again. "I am aware when someone is sincere and when he is not. Your friend, I fear, is no gentleman."

Suddenly a man raced at them. Startled, she stepped back with a flinch. "Robbie!"

"Anna! Is this bloke disturbing ya?" the cobbler gasped. He wore his leather apron, the sleeves of his work shirt rolled up high on his biceps. He panted from his short run. "I saw 'im bothering ya."

"No, Robbie, I'm fine."

"I saw ya arguing when I took me leather to the shop."

"It's only a former friend." She glared at Langsford. "He stopped by to look at some scarves a few weeks back but didn't purchase any."

"Touché," Langsford laughed. "You are correct. I apologize a second time." He turned to Robbie. "Nice to meet you, Robbie. I trust you work in one of the shops here? A cobbler?"

"Uh, Hopson's Boot Maker Shoppe, up the street on the left."

He relaxed then, reassured the man was no threat to Anna. "If yer ever needin' custom-made boots or a bridle, I make real fine ones." He offered his rough hand to the man who was about his own age.

Langsford matched the firm shake.

Robbie smiled. "Of course if ya got a scarf for yer gal from Anna here, that would be good, too. But ya need to do it soon, 'cause if I 'ave anythin' to say, Anna will be quittin' her job afore long. A girl like her's destined ta become someone's wife, she is." He looked over to her with puppy-dog eyes and a longing that could not be mistaken. Anna blushed.

"That certainly *is* news." Langsford nodded to Robbie. "Nice meeting you. I'm headed to the tobacconist so I'll take my leave. He tipped his cap again. "Anna, a pleasure." He continued up the street. Robbie lingered briefly and then went back to his work. Anna turned without a word and went back into her shop, feeling a mixture of horror and hope.

Inside, Anna stood confused. Frustrated. Why couldn't Robbie make her feel the same as Henry? Seeing the lord brought up her memories of that day when he was chaperone to the two of them. She hung up her shawl and returned to the counter where she wove satin ribbon into a spring hat. At least she could handle this, she consoled herself, trying to be pleased with her work. But if the lord were nearby, wouldn't Henry come back soon, too? She tried humming a tune to make herself feel better, only to discover it did not.

Minutes before closing, the door jingled open and she turned to greet the last-minute customer. Her eyes widened when she saw Lord Langsford. Again. She found herself scanning behind him for Henry but no, no one was there. Still, in spite of herself, she was thrilled Langsford had returned. He was a link to Henry.

"Ah, Anna." Langsford removed his cap. "I've returned to purchase that scarf as promised, albeit weeks ago."

"I don't wish to shame you into it." She smiled though she knew she didn't mean it. He should buy a dozen scarves for the grief she'd felt. She sorted through a pile of scarves on a side display, accidentally dropping half the stack. "Oh dear." She leaned down to pick them up. He bent down to assist.

"This is similar." She held up a blue square from the pile on the floor.

"I shall purchase it." He scooped up all the rest and placed them on the counter. "It's a gift from Heinrich to you." She looked up, wondering if Henry planned on coming in.

"I don't understand." She looked at the door and then realized Langsford was buying it on Henry's behalf. "I can't accept a gift," she heard herself saying. "It's, er, Robbie," she stuttered. "We're courting. It's not appropriate. Although"—she paused in midprotest to catch her breath and gather her wits—"I could sell you this hat for Lady Langsford." She pointed to the one she just finished.

He laughed. "You are quite the salesgirl."

She reached for it and knocked over the spindled stand, sending the hat scooting along the counter. Why was she so clumsy whenever Langsford or Henry was around? She was irritated with herself.

He stood the stand back up so she could replace the beribboned hat. "So you are engaged, then?"

"Not yet." She hesitated. "But soon. As soon as ...as ..." She faltered, unable to continue.

"So you prefer to keep his company over Heinrich's then?"

"Oh no," she gasped without thinking. "I mean. That is to say ..." She hated that she was so flustered. "To be truthful, I was upset when Henry didn't return, but it's for the best he didn't.

I must allow Robbie to court me." She shocked herself with her bluntness.

Langsford's demeanor changed to serious. "Listen closely," he spoke quietly, causing her to catch her breath. "Heinrich was punished because he called upon you without his father's approval. He was forbidden to contact you, ever. As a result, because he cares for you, he rebelled and fled Germany to come here—to London. To be with you."

Anna tried to grasp what he was saying. Henry had left London in a rush after she met him. Then he fled from home. She got that far in her head. But "to be with her" ... She couldn't believe her ears. *Fled? Why?* Words failed her.

"In returning to London, he got caught up in some, shall we say ... business? As soon as he can, he will come call on you."

Henry *did* care about her! Her heart fluttered and she couldn't breathe.

"You need to understand all that since that cobbler thinks he's courting you."

She pictured Robbie, steady, tried and true. And Henry, going away, coming back. Visiting her later. Uncertain. She didn't hear anything else. She hung onto the counter. In her wildest dreams ... Henry!

"Anna, are you all right?"

She looked up. "Oh, yes."

"Now," he joked, "I am a matchmaker."

"Oh dear ..." She tried to focus, but she couldn't.

"Please wait for him before you agree to any engagement promise. He wants to assure everything is in order before he calls."

"Oh, how do I know what you say is true? Robbie is here." She was babbling but couldn't help herself. "I have no real dowry. I'm an orphan." She couldn't stop her unladylike and forward words. "I don't want to be a spinster... ."

"Heinrich will proceed in the proper fashion. I promise."

She took a breath, managing a smile. "Are you sure?"

"Yes," he smiled back. "I have another thing to ask, however. Should you see him over the next few days, please don't acknowledge him. It could distract him from his, uh, business. Interfere."

"I wouldn't want to do that."

"You need to wait until he speaks to you first. Even if you see him. Do you understand?"

"Of course. But how soon do you expect him to come by?"

"Probably before too long."

Langsford paid for and left both the scarf and hat on the counter. "From Heinrich," he said and left, closing the door gently as she stared down at the counter and what it held.

She didn't see a man wearing a derby and a long brown coat watch from the other side of an apple cart when Langsford left. After the door closed, Inspector Abberline crossed the street but Anna had already locked the shop from the inside. She'd put on the hat and twirled behind the counter while her heart raced.

CHAPTER 45

Leadenhall Market, London

While Anna twirled, Heinrich hailed a hansom cab near No. 12 and told the driver his destination. He'd been surprised to learn the meeting with Summerhill was at the pub in Leadenhall Market.

"Anna's shop will be closed," Langsford reminded him. "She won't be there."

"You changed the meeting time because you knew she would be locking up at six and I might see her."

"There it is. The last thing I want is for Anna to spot you. What if she called you by name?"

"To see her once again ..."

"You need to be focused."

But Heinrich couldn't keep Anna from his head. He pictured her the day the carriage had pulled up while she locked the shop. In her bonnet with wisps of mahogany-brown hair peeking out, caressing her fair cheeks, her green eyes sparkling.

His mind flickered with images of Summerhill, mixed with those of Anna. He forced his meandering thoughts to dissolve when the cab stopped at the market. He hopped out to pay but before he could step away from the curb, Harold Summerhill was beside him.

"Good evening, Gerhard. You're on time."

Heinrich startled. "Guten abend, Mr. Summerhill." He felt prickles of fear. Immediately he chastised himself for hiring a cab. What if Summerhill asked him where he was coming from and how he could afford a hack? Out-of-work Prussian farmhands would never hail a cab.

Summerhill waved to the driver. "We'll hire you again." Looking at Heinrich, he explained, "We can talk in private." He opened the cab door for the youth.

Surprised again, Heinrich climbed back in while Summerhill softly spoke to the driver high up on the rear of the vehicle. Heinrich couldn't hear their destination, which made him nervous. What if Summerhill asked the driver where he'd hired him? Quick, think.... He'd been caught off guard twice within the first minute. He wished Langsford were here. He'd know what to say.

Summerhill climbed in beside him in the one forward-facing seat. The older man spoke softly and Heinrich knew the driver above couldn't hear over the traffic noise of the cobblestoned streets.

"I have to be cautious for a variety of reasons. First, I've concerns. The Prussians you named claim they don't know you and that you're not from Bullay. So I have to ask: Why did you lie?" He glared, no longer friendly but with a sinister air about him now.

Heinrich went into the defensive mode that he'd perfected whenever chastised by his father, instinctively adopting a stone face, staring directly at the Englishman but not seeing him.

"I'm sorry," he replied with a forced calm. "I didn't mean to imply that I'm *from* there. My English might need to be better." He spoke awkwardly, hoping that excuse would cover any slipups in his story. "I was in Bullay to sell a horse. I work on a farm south of there and sometimes I go to Bullay for my employer." Almost true, he thought, though the huge Dieffenbacher Estate could hardly be called a mere farm.

"Go on."

"I've several friends like Marc Gülker in the Social Democrats, and I wanted to join the party, so when Ernst Schmidt ..." *Slow down. Langsford told me not to rush my story*, he warned himself. "Er, he's a mutual friend ... when he told me"—he took a deep breath—"Ernst told me I would be perfect to take Marc's place on your committee. It was hard to talk to anyone about it without being arrested."

"I see." Summerhill had no reaction. Immediately he asked the question Heinrich feared. "The driver said you hired him at Grosvenor Square. And just why would a peasant like you hire a hack, especially from there?"

Verdammt. He hoped this lie would work. "I, well, *gestern abend*, last night I went with a, uh, lady of pleasure. I am not sure what she is called in English." He feigned his struggle with the language.

"Laced mutton, unless she cost a pretty penny—a toffer."

"Yes. Toffer. I was at, I think Carpenter Street?" He recalled the street name from a walk he'd taken a block or two south of the square during his earlier visit. "You see, I've been with her and was just now late." Heinrich looked down in mock embarrassment. "She told me to find a cab at that square." He attempted to appear relatively ignorant of the area and hoped saying he spent the night with a *prostituierte* was believable. It was definitely something his brother would have done, and after all, he was going by his brother's name.

"The tails are much cheaper in the East End. Keep that in mind."

Heinrich nodded, hoping it meant he bought his story.

"How come you can afford a night flower and a hack?"

"I sold a horse," he smiled, pretending to brag, relieved he came up with such a quick reply.

"For your employer?"

"Well, he's not my employer now, is he?" He grinned bigger. "And he's still rich there and I'm less poor here."

"You'd mizzle your own mother of everything in her purse, wouldn't you?" Summerhill appraised him for a few seconds. "Why do you want to be on this committee?" Another abrupt subject change.

"We want things better, and fast. We don't have time for parliament, but we can make a quick difference if ..." Langsford had told him to lead Summerhill into finishing this thought if possible. Heinrich stopped, hoping Summerhill completed his sentence.

He did. "If ... we take care of Bismarck. So. Marc confided in your mutual friend. Perhaps too much." Summerhill sat back, his shoulder now touching Heinrich's. They both looked out over the horse and traces.

Heinrich waited, wanting Summerhill to explain more. When he didn't speak, Heinrich impatiently broke the silence. "I am ready, Mr. Summerhill, to do my part."

Summerhill sat quietly for another long minute and then spoke. "How do I know that the police haven't sent you to spy?"

Another unexpected question. "I don't know," Heinrich answered truthfully. "I have no idea how I prove I am not with the Polizei." He knew it wasn't possible to prove a negative. "All I can do is tell you I don't know police anywhere, Prussian or English, nor do I want to." This latter part, he thought, was most definitely true. "They'd arrest *me*"—he winced for real—"for selling a horse I didn't own."

To his great relief, Summerhill laughed. "That's good, boy. You're too naïve to be in with officials, that's for sure. You do stupid things like steal horses and spend too much money on whores and hacks, but I hope you're smart enough to know how dangerous it'd be to lie to me."

Heinrich let his huge sigh of relief show. If the Englishman wanted to think him a naïve farmworker, all the better. "Then I can work alongside my *freunde*?"

Summerhill's laugh was ugly and a shiver shot up Heinrich's spine. "You'll meet the committee tonight after the party meeting. They'll decide then if you join them."

Startled that he needed to pass the others' scrutiny, Heinrich could only croak, "Ja, gut." His heart pounded. Tonight he would finally come face-to-face with the real murderers.

The cab halted at the entrance to the market where they'd began their conversational journey and the two stepped out. Summerhill spun around to face Heinrich. "The hack's my treat. Take it back to your cousin's. I'll see you both tonight for the meeting."

"Danke." Heinrich touched his cap ever so briefly in thanks, but Summerhill had already turned and left.

"Where to?" asked the driver. "Be quick. Your friend there wants to know I get ya back without delay."

Alarmed, Heinrich wasn't sure where to go. Obviously Summerhill wanted to know where he and his cousin were staying but he couldn't allow this driver to take him anywhere near Grosvenor Square. Summerhill was definitely not to be trifled with. The Prussian answered with the first place that came to mind: Bermondsey, remembering Anna's neighborhood. He reentered the cab and it rolled off toward London Bridge. He wiped the perspiration from his forehead. It was only pure luck the driver accidentally tipped him off. Heinrich needed to get rid of this cab and return for Langsford in a different one. Just before crossing the Thames, he spotted a dreary-looking pub, a hole-in-the-wall place, and told the driver to pull over. "I've time for a pint, so stop here."

The horse halted a few doors down. "I'll wait, but I've only so much time or I'll 'ave ta charge more," the driver warned. "Yer friend paid jest so much."

"I may be a while. Keep your fare"—Heinrich handed him several coins—"and take this tip." The driver pleased, he clucked his horse on. As the rig pulled away, Heinrich walked directly into the drab pub.

Drinking an ale while he let his nerves settle, he saw a man in a long coat and derby enter shortly after he did. The man didn't stay long and Heinrich paid little attention. He finished his glass and felt calmer. Suspicious that Summerhill might have someone following him, he picked up his cap and slipped passed the casks of ale to the alley door. He turned left down the dirty twitten onto the next traffic-filled street. There he crammed onto an omnibus jammed with people leaving work at the end of a work day. He rode a few blocks and then spotted a waiting cab. Jumping off the bus midblock, he jogged over and asked the driver to take him to Oxford and Duke Streets just north of the square. He would walk back to No. 12.

CHAPTER 46

No. 12 Grosvenor Square, London

"Were you followed?" Langsford, still wearing his least favorite clothes, met Heinrich in the foyer when Barnes admitted him. Tweed danced a hello.

"I don't think so. Summerhill's slick, though." He sounded rattled. "He paid the driver to tell him where I came from and where I was going. I had the cabbie drop me off at a pub near London Bridge and sent him on his way."

"That was smart. Did anyone follow you?"

"I doubt it—one man in a long coat who seemed out of place, but he left before I did. I'm just overly suspicious."

"And no one followed from the pub?"

"No. I left by the back door, rode a bus, then took another hack. Got out a few blocks north of here and walked back."

"Likely you're safe. Now fill me in while we eat."

"I could use beer more than food," Heinrich confessed.

"We both could. Let's eat outside to include Pelham. I want him with us tonight, should we need help. He's a good man, a lot like your Dirk."

They walked to the rear of the residence, where Barnes stood supervising a servant setting out their picnic-supper. Over ham sandwiches and oysters in the stable yard, Langsford and Pelham listened as Heinrich recapped his encounter. Unable to remain seated on his wooden chair, he stood, leaning against the wall, his foot nervously tapping. "Summerhill seems to be the decision-maker, but he's leaving it up to the others to decide about me. I meet them tonight."

Pelham finished his sandwich and placed his empty plate beside him on the bale of hay where he remained seated. "They could be settin' up a trap."

"We have to be ready for anything Summerhill throws our way," Langsford warned from his rickety chair. Tweed thumped his tail in agreement.

"You're right when you say never underestimate your foe." Heinrich gulped some ale, still unnerved. "I shudder when I think how Summerhill snuck up on me at the market."

"We're taking the omnibus tonight, Pelham"—Langsford turned to his employee—"but you're coming along. An extra set of eyes and ears and possibly muscle."

"My pleasure, m'lord." The coachman smiled, scratching the dog's ears. "I won't let anyone put a hand on either of ya."

"Just don't go and join the Social Democrats," he teased.

"Don't worry. Your black 'ponies' won't allow it."

"You worry about Pelham?" Heinrich choked on his beer. "*I'm* the one who has to join the infernal party with its murdering committee."

"It's your neck we're trying to save, so it's only fair it's yours we risk." Langsford grinned. He stood, pulling out his watch fob. "It's time we best go."

They entered the Lamb Tavern, anxious to finally meet up with the three Prussians. The businessmen who'd been there in the afternoon were long gone, replaced by middle-class workers who gathered to relax, talk, and let off steam.

Langsford walked over to the side of the pub while Heinrich went to the bar for ales. Workers pushed a couple tables together. Pelham sat down with them. Heinrich joined Langsford along the wall, handing him his glass. The room was expectant.

Lentz strode in right on time to begin the meeting. As before, Summerhill led the last portion of the meeting. As it wrapped up, Langsford heard someone say "Fritz." He looked over to see two men standing together farther down his side of the room. Were these two of their trio? A third approached them. The man Fritz said, "Hallo, Helmut," and slapped Helmut on the shoulder. Helmut greeted the third, "Karl, mein freund."

There they are! Langsford raised his glass to his lips and caught Pelham's eye. He tilted his head toward the three. Pelham glanced at them and then gave Langsford a nod.

Summerhill concluded the meeting. Leaving the men to talk with Lentz, he escorted the three Prussians to a table in the far back corner. Pelham moved to sit closer to the dark table, pretending to be involved with the remaining men, but Langsford knew his coachman's attention was focused on the corner. He walked to the bar to chat with a pub patron, keeping his eye on the group with Summerhill. Heinrich, holding his drink, remained along the wall, waiting.

Lentz abruptly rose and joined the group. *There it is,* Langsford thought. *The German is part of the committee, as I suspected.*

A fourth young man also stood and went to sit in the corner. He looked vaguely familiar, but the face was shadowed by the bill of his cap pulled low. *I've seen him recently!* Maybe up at Earls Colne? Langsford wasn't sure and it bothered him.

Summerhill leaned into the group, elbows on the table, whispering to the five: Lentz, Karl, Fritz, Helmut, and the unknown man in the cap. Then he gestured to Heinrich, "Gerhard! Come join us."

The moment had come. Langsford watched as Heinrich slowly walked to the table in the dark corner. Langsford held his breath.

CHAPTER 47

The Lamb Tavern, London

Summerhill stood and Lentz greeted, "Willkommen, Gerhard." Everyone at the table nodded. That was good. They think of him as Gerhard, plus with Ernst Schmidt's fake recommendation, Heinrich had credibility he couldn't have otherwise. The cover story had worked nicely. An added layer of protection was that they had no idea this was the man Karl framed.

Karl didn't look up but merely shrugged, not letting his face show. Neither did the man whose cap shaded his. Langsford could only see his profile. They sat in the deep shadows of the corner, staring down at their hands holding their glasses.

Heinrich sat beside Summerhill, away from Karl. *A good spot,* Langsford thought as he watched them huddle closer. He leaned with his back against the bar, elbows supporting him, and kept an eye on the table while he pretended to converse with other patrons as they alternatingly complained or boasted and quaffed their pints. Alert, he was ready to step in if Heinrich raised his voice to say "Ernst told me," a signal that he needed help from Pelham or Langsford.

The men remained huddled. Occasionally one or more nodded. Summerhill seemed to do most of the talking, but Langsford was too far away to hear anything. After twenty minutes, they nodded to one another and broke apart. Lentz and Summerhill rejoined several party members who sat around the middle tables. The other four committee members left the pub separately. Heinrich walked over to the bar for another ale, though his old one sat untouched back on the corner table.

I wish I could follow the badgers, Langsford thought, but it was unwise to leave Heinrich. He'd have to wait for another time.

They remained, allowing other members to depart, not giving anyone an opportunity to follow, waiting in silence until they were the only ones left from the meeting. According to plan, they rode an omnibus to the Strand where they hired a cab to take them northwest beyond Grosvenor Square. Getting out near Providence Court, they walked back to the stable off George Yard.

"I have a lot more information," Heinrich effused, "and—"

"Wait until we're inside. We'll talk in the library. You too, Pelham. You're in on this."

The three quickly slipped into the back entrance and trotted up the servant stairs. Finally ensconced in the library, they were safe to begin their own serious discussion. Langsford motioned Pelham to sit and he pulled the chair around from the desk. Heinrich paced while Langsford settled into a chair by the fire.

"Quite a long meeting the seven of you had."

"It didn't feel long. A lot of information. Summerhill began by asking everyone if they wanted me to replace Marc. No one objected. Karl never looked my way."

"So I noticed."

"I'm officially on the committee."

"Excellent! A large committee, too. I recognized everyone but the fellow in the cap. Who was he?" Langsford was still perplexed where he'd seen the chap.

"I don't know. Summerhill didn't introduce the others."

"Is he Prussian?" Pelham asked. He leaned with his elbows on his knees, cap dangling in his hand. "Summerhill may be the only one who's English."

"It would make sense for all the others to be Prussian since their target is Prussian," Heinrich agreed, "but he never spoke, so I couldn't tell."

"What did Summerhill say after you were accepted by the others?" Langsford brought them back on topic.

"He announced we have the 'go ahead' for the plan but didn't say who gave it. Probably a man high in the party. The older German, Lentz, will be in charge when the committee goes to Germany."

"The committee is going to Germany? When?"

"They, er, *we* are going to Berlin, and I have a problem, because they're going on Tuesday next." Heinrich ran his hand through his hair. "We're to assassinate Bismarck in November at the Congo Congress."

"What's this Congress?" Pelham stopped twirling his cap.

"It's a meeting of European leaders to decide what colonies their countries will have in Africa. And significantly enough, it's in Berlin," Langsford answered.

"Summerhill said we are all to get jobs there that will be situated within Bismarck's own residence. By going now, we'll be established within the staff and gain trust before November. I'm to be a stable groom since he thinks that's what I do."

"I'm thinking many leaders will be in Berlin. Bismarck may not be the only target."

"He didn't mention other heads of state. He did say that a contact at the residence will slowly be able to hire each of us."

"This is well planned," Langsford mused.

"Now that I'm on the committee, the polizei will believe I *am* guilty."

"Your job is to gather information. Mine is to handle the police." Langsford stroked his moustache.

Pelham spun his cap on his fingers. "My job is to physically protect you, but I can't do that in Berlin."

"Does the committee meet in London again?"

"We meet separately with Lentz, Monday, to hear the details for each of us. Because I said I sold a stolen horse, Summerhill said I need to change my name."

"Ironic. Just don't call yourself 'Heinrich.'" Langsford grinned. "See if you can find out from Lentz who the fellow in the cap is. I didn't get a close enough look at his face, though he seemed familiar. Probably saw him at Earls Colne. We're close to having enough information but we need all the names, if not addresses, and fast. Monday I'll go to Scotland Yard. We need to stop them while everyone is still here in London."

"We will have exposed the plot and Heinrich will be a hero," Pelham grinned, slapping his knee.

"Indeed. The traitors will be arrested and you, Heinrich, will be exonerated. We just have to make it happen fast. Monday is critical, then."

CHAPTER 48

Leadenhall Market, London

The next morning, Heinrich bounced out of No. 12, smartly dressed, his full beard neatly trimmed. He hadn't told Langsford he was leaving because the Englishman would have said no, and that was unacceptable. Ever since Langsford had said he'd run into Anna yesterday afternoon, Heinrich had planned this visit. He *had* to see her.

The sky held a bright sun and few clouds. Everything around him was especially keen and brilliantly alive. He walked with long strides. Everyone on the committee will be arrested Monday or early Tuesday at the latest. *There is no reason to wait*, he reasoned. *By Tuesday I'll be free.* He quickened his pace as each step brought him closer to Anna. Across the square he hired a cab, not wanting Pelham to know what he was doing, either.

Once at the market, he was a man with a purpose, dodging around the early-afternoon shoppers. He rushed up the roofed street, passing vendors and carts. Going right passed the pub, he scanned across the street for the cream-and-maroon shop. *There, up on the right.* He darted across and skipped up on the curb.

He straightened his jacket, removed his hat, and opened the door. His eyes adjusted to the dimmer light and he quickly spotted her. Alone, Anna was placing brooches in a display case when the bell tinkling over the door announced a customer. She stood to say hello.

Midturn she froze, and any welcome failed to leave her lips. Instead a small audible gasp greeted him.

"Anna."

She stood speechless, but completed her turn, facing him fully.

"Anna! I am back. I'm here!"

Her hand rose to her chest, covering her heart, and she dropped a brooch on the floor.

He stepped toward her.

"Anna. I have so much to say to you. You must think the worst of me because I left—"

She found her voice. "Oh, Henry! I understand ... Lord Langsford was by ..."

"He told me he saw you."

"Yes, he made a purchase and explained how you had no choice but to leave England that day, unable to send a message." She looked down, smiling. "He also said as soon as your business was complete you would visit. I am so pleased you're here, Henry."

He stepped closer to her, hat in hand, smelling her perfume. He lifted her chin so he could see her face. "I need to apologize for being rude. I gave you expectations and failed to meet them." The words could not tumble from him fast enough. "Please forgive me, dear Anna."

She smiled and rapidly nodded. "I forgive you, Henry."

"That means everything to me." Heinrich placed his hat on the counter, then took her hand, the one over her heart, and held it.

"I must be frank. I do not know when I can properly begin courting you, but I intend—"

The door tingled open and Robbie, holding a small leather purse, excitedly burst into the shop. He drew up short as Anna looked over at the door. She jerked her hand away, her eyes widened. Surprised at her reaction, Heinrich turned to see a strange man with a horrified look on his face. He looked back at Anna, who herself looked aghast. He stepped aside, unsure.

Anna faltered in her attempt to greet the newcomer. "Robbie." Flushed, she stepped forward, taking the lovely little purse he handed her. Made of fine textured leather and fully lined with silk inside, the leather was intricately stitched on a delicate silver frame with a small clasp closure on the top and a linked chain handle. It was a stunning little masterpiece.

"This is beautiful, Robbie. So intricate ... I've never seen ... Your work is so lovely," she swallowed, uneasy. "I am sure Mr. Thompson will be happy to sell these."

"This ain't for yer boss. 'Tis a gift I made for *you*, dear." His tone sounded normal but his countenance struggled between a smile and a scowl as he glared at Heinrich.

"How kind. I am honored, and"—she turned to Heinrich, apologizing—"please excuse my poor manners. Henr ...ah ...Heinrich, I would like you to meet a friend of mine. This is Robert Wells, a superb leather worker. Robbie, this is Herr Heinrich Dieffenbacher," she carefully pronounced the name. "He's visiting from Prussia." She smiled when she said his German name, melting Heinrich's heart.

Both men stiffly shook hands, Heinrich saying, "Pleased to make your acquaintance, Robert," as he tried to sort out why this man had called Anna "dear."

"'ow do?" Robbie stiffly muttered, looking intimidated.

Anna turned their attention back to the purse. "Robbie, this is exquisite. Henry, you should see his riding boots. You would appreciate them since you are a horseman."

"Well-made boots are always a pleasure, especially if they are fine leather," Heinrich politely responded, still puzzled why this man was here giving Anna a purse.

"I'm pleased ta hear ya say so. I've a growin' reputation with me work. I'm doin' so good, I'll soon be able ta support a family, which is why I'm courtin' this maid. I made the purse jest for 'er," he beamed.

Heinrich felt sucker punched in the stomach as if all the breath were knocked from him. He inhaled, his nostrils flaring, and looked at her. Her expression was horrified and shocked.

This worker, this man who smelled of leather and neat's-foot oil like a stable boy in a barn, was courting Anna? How could she be ...? But he knew. He'd not returned in time.

Her hands holding the purse were shaking. She had not stepped closer to Robbie but stood her ground equally between the two men.

Heinrich squinted at Robbie. "*You* are courting her?" He wanted to punch the scrawny cobbler through the wall, but as a gentleman, he would not engage in fisticuffs. He held his hands clenched at his side.

"Yes," Robbie snarled. "We have just begun a beautiful court-ship—with the blessing of her uncle," Robbie boasted, throwing a verbal punch.

"Is that true, Anna? Is he courting you?"

Put on the spot, Anna looked down at the floor and softly an-swered, "Yes, we just started the courtship. Robbie came once to Sunday dinner and we had a picnic ... but only once. Completely chaperoned!"

She looked up, and her eyes brimming with tears. "We've never held hands... ." Her voice cracked. "Henry, you left. I thought I would never lay eyes on you again." Her shoulders shuddered and she turned away from both of them.

"Anna? What's this? Herr Deaf-an-baker?" Robbie stepped up to Heinrich. "Who are ya and 'ow do ya know me Anna? She's spoken fer and you can't … can't …can't …speak ta her." Robbie stuttered as his temper swelled.

Heinrich stood his ground and smiled slightly. It was obvious she cared for *him*, not this leather stitcher. "You heard. The lady has spoken, and in fact has demonstrated which of us she holds affection for. She mistakenly thought I was gone." He kept his voice even and his tone respectful, like the honorable gentleman he was raised to be. "I am here. And I will continue to be here. For her and with her."

Anna turned and took a step toward Robbie. "I am so sorry. He's right. I did think he was gone, otherwise I would never have accepted your kindnesses. I have been most flattered by your friendship."

Robbie's face reddened. When she attempted to hand back the little purse, he refused. "It's worthless. Jest throw it away."

He turned, rushing through the still opened door. Going part-way after him, Anna called out, "Robbie, I'm truly sorry."

Heinrich went to her and turned her shoulders toward him until she was looking at him. "Though I've not spoken to your uncle, consider yourself being courted by a Prussian whose name is Heinrich Dieffenbacher," he emphasized his name. "Or, as you say, Henry." He laughed and made a little bow. "At your service."

She burst into laughter, the tension gone. They walked back to the counter where he leaned down and retrieved the fallen brooch, handing it back to her. "Henry," she repeated, and smiled at him. "Please speak to Uncle Maxwell right away. I don't know what he will say or think, since he has given permission to Robbie—"

With an impulse he could not control and did not try, Heinrich put his arm around her tiny waist, and with his left hand caressing the back of her head, brought his mouth to hers. He kissed her with an incredible gentleness. Then he stood back, his fingers trailing down to her cheek. "I love you, Anna Boardman."

The pretty little purse dropped to the floor, forgotten. She steadied herself with her hand on the countertop.

"I shall speak to your uncle this very afternoon. Our courtship will be official." He made a sweeping bow.

Delighted, she laughed again, and followed him to the threshold of the door. She stood and watched as he did a little dance step on the sidewalk, backing up as he went. "I, Heinrich Dieffenbacher, shall return!"

She was vaguely aware of Robbie standing up the street outside his shop, watching. She was vaguely aware of two other men across the street watching: a constable and a man wearing a derby and, in spite of the warm weather, a long brown coat.

Without warning, the two rushed Heinrich. "Halt there! You're under Queen's arrest, Heinrich Dieffenbacher!" yelled the constable. He grabbed Heinrich and locked his arm up behind his back. The other man walked up and looked at him squarely. "Aside from the beard, he fits the description."

Heinrich resisted, struggling to free his arm, but his wrist was already in the flexible handcuff.

Anna flew into the street, grabbing the constable's arm. "No! No, no, no! This is a mistake. He's not done anything wrong. Well, one kiss, but that's not against any law, in truth ..." Her mind was a tumult.

Robbie arrived, racing to intercept her. "Anna, get back. He's a criminal!"

"No, Henry! Tell them this is a mistake. You gentlemen are

wrong!" She tugged at the constable's arm. Robbie grabbed her by the waist and dragged her back, holding her tight.

"Sorry, miss." He successfully snapped the handcuff on Heinrich's other wrist. "Scotland Yard's been huntin' Heinrich Deaf-en-baker for some time. Treason."

"He's been going by Gerhard, but he just admitted his real name to the lady," the inspector confirmed.

The bobby smiled at the man in the long coat. "Ya did a real fine job, Inspector Abberline." He spun Heinrich around. "Back to Germany and the gallows!"

They jerked Heinrich away, dragging him between them down the street. Heinrich strained to look back, attempting to stop by planting his feet sideways on the cobblestones. "Anna!" he shouted "It's a mistake!" The Inspector yanked him along another few feet. "Go to Langsford …. Grosvenor Square …"

The two grabbed Heinrich tighter and the bobby knocked him on the side of the head with his baton. Their prisoner's knees buckled as he fell unconscious and they dragged him away.

PART FOUR

Frenzy

Chapter 49

Anna struggled against Robbie. She fell to her knees sobbing, pulling the cobbler down with her. Robbie stood and tried to yank her up. "Anna! He's bad. Arrested for treason!"

Arrested! The voice inside her head screamed.

She found herself on her feet. She pulled loose from Robbie's grip. People gathered on the market's street, gawking and pointing.

"It's a thief they caught, they did."

"Nah, worse'n 'at. They's takin' him to the gallows they said."

"Oh, a murderer then?"

"He almost killed us!"

"He woulda if'n we'd been closer."

"Didja see the body?"

The police and their prisoner disappeared through the crowd.

"Get inside, Anna," Robbie ordered. "I 'ave ta get back ta work and so do you. Go!"

Wordlessly she turned and hurried back into her shop. Slamming the door, she grabbed her shawl from its hook and yanked open a small drawer behind the counter. Riffling through it, she picked up the key and after a brief hesitation, took two shillings. She tied her bonnet slightly askew in her rush and walked out to lock up. She *had* to get to Lord Langsford! Henry said to!

She peeked up the street to make sure Robbie was gone, then shut and locked the door.

The crowd milled about, witnesses telling others what they saw. They craned their necks to see where the police had taken the bludger. Anna hurried into the street where she was quickly swallowed up among strangers crushing in as they tried to get a glimpse of the murderer. *Lord Langsford. Grosvenor Square.* She dodged a cartful of flowers and pushed her way through the crowd. She rushed toward the market entrance, the same direction Heinrich had been dragged.

She had no idea where Grosvenor Square was, though she'd heard of it. *Hurry! Lord Langsford will know what to do!* She passed a pub, the confectioners, and a butcher shop. Once outside the market she ran up Leadenhall Street frantically looking for a cab.

Abruptly she remembered the word *treason. Treason? Henry? No, that's wrong.* He had business like what is done at a bank. Her head was swimming in confusion as she hurried toward Gracechurch Street. She looked left and right, hunting for a cab. *There!* The horse stood with its neck parallel to the ground, dozing like its driver.

"Pardon me," she said, unsure how to address the driver. "I need to go to Grosvenor Square. Please. It's important."

"Eh?" The driver shook his sleep off, adjusting the cap atop his head. "Grosvenor Square?"

"Yes. Can you tell me what the fare is?" She wasn't sure she had enough.

"Ya want ta go ta Grosvenor Square and yer concerned about me fare, Lass? If ya need money, pay when ya get 'ome."

"I don't live there. I have to find someone." She was flustered, fighting back tears.

"I cannut take ya there if you dunna 'ave fare."

"How *much* is it?" She trembled, terrified she couldn't afford it. *Not be able to get to Grosvenor Square. Henry would be ... They shoot men for treason!*

"It be three six," he looked down at her and she realized that was more than she had. She started to visibly shake.

"Aren't you takin' advantage of the lady here?" a deep voice behind her asked. She turned and saw a bobby, baton in his hand, in his tall domed helmet and six shiny buttons in a line down his barrel chest. She startled, for she thought he was going to arrest her for knowing Henry. The police were suddenly the enemy.

"Oh, no, Squire. Miss, where is it yer goin'?"

Anna looked back and forth between the men, one up high on the cab and the other on the sidewalk beside her.

"She wants to know the fare to Grosvenor Square, and you made a mistake."

"Oh, did I? I musta not heerd right. Sorry. The fare be two bob six."

"Better. You're still within the Charing Cross radius and you charge the same as every other cabbie. Otherwise"—he looked at Anna and winked—"if you turn out ta be a buck-cabbie, I'll 'ave to take you in."

Anna attempted a smile, wiping a tear off her right cheek with the back of her bare hand. "Two, six. Yes, I have that." Relieved the two borrowed shillings she had taken from the shop, along with pennies in her purse were enough, she smiled at the policeman as he assisted her up into the cab.

"Good 'ay, miss." The policeman touched the brim of his helmet.

The driver smacked his horse awake with his whip and the rig jolted forward.

Once seated, Anna tried to calm herself. *Lord Langsford will clear up everything.*

The cab started down Gracechurch Street, but she paid no attention when they turned onto Cannon Street and went by Saint Paul's Church or passed around Trafalgar Square. The trip seemed like forever as they rolled along the streets, turning here and there. She had no idea where she was. Finally turning left onto Grosvenor Street, the driver halted next to the curb at the corner of St. Charles. "Here ya are, miss. Grosvenor Square."

"Thank you," Anna said, softly stepping out. She paid the fare. Looking about her, she failed to notice the tip-less driver's sneer. He thumped the horse's rump with his whip and moved on.

Anna stood facing a huge oval park surrounded by opulent houses, three stories tall and sporting grand facades. One after another, standing shoulder to shoulder.

She had no idea which one was the Langsford residence.

CHAPTER 50

No. 12 Grosvenor Square, London

Number 51 was on her left. Her heart sank. How would she ever find the right house?

She crossed the street to discover No. 1, relieved there were no more than fifty-one. She stopped in front of No. 2 and turned toward the park. The square was beautiful. She looked at the broad streets about the park. *There has to be someone I can ask*, she reassured herself.

After a few minutes she saw no one enter or leave a house near her. She crossed to the park and walked along the southern side where several hacks were parked along the curb. "Pardon me," she inquired at the nearest. "Would you know which is Lord Langsford's residence?"

The driver looked down at her. "Sorry. Don't know the chap." Then he added hopefully, "Where do ya need to go, miss?"

"I only need to find Lord Langsford."

Disheartened, she continued up the street to another cab. The horse chewed oats in the feed bag hanging on his nose and the driver stood nearby. "We're not in service, I'm afraid, miss."

"I'm not in need of a ride, but maybe you can help? I'm looking for Lord Langsford's residence. He lives somewhere here on Grosvenor Square." She opened her arms wide, gesturing at all the houses.

"Aye, that he does. This is me regular route, so he's hired me from time to time when he leaves 'is own carriage in."

"Which house?" she asked eagerly.

"Number twelve. You'll find 'im there." He pointed north across the park. "The red brick."

"Yes, I see it. Thank you kindly."

"My pleasure, miss." He tipped his hat. "If'n you wait a few minutes, I'll take you up there for ha'penny. It looks as it might rain."

"It's still a lovely day," she replied, wanting to save her remaining pennies. "I can walk across before any rain falls. Thank you."

Tightening her shawl around her shoulders, she walked through the oval park on one of the winding paths north toward No. 12. Its red-brick front sported three rows of windows dressed with white jambs. Four white balustrades stood in between the upper windows of the second and third stories, proudly lifting its gable. It was a lovely façade, warm and welcoming. The front entrance was diapered with arching white brick, and its large door bid one to come knock. She crossed the wide street and walked up, ascending the two steps to the door. Gathering her nerve, she twisted the ornate turn handle to ring the brass bell on the inside. She looked back at the square while she waited for someone to answer.

Coaches, hansom cabs, and privately owned broughams and phaetons rolled along. The streets were so wide, the traffic seemed sparse. The door opened, startling her.

An ancient butler answered. "Good afternoon, miss."

"Good afternoon. I'm looking for Lord Langsford. Do I have the correct residence?"

"Yes. Do come in." He stepped back, allowing Anna to enter the foyer. "Are you expected?"

"No. A friend sent me. It's urgent, I'm afraid."

"Do you desire an audience with both Lord and Lady Langsford, miss?"

"No need to bother Lady Langsford. But it *is* urgent I see his lordship."

The stooped butler gently clicked the large door closed behind them.

"It's just as well, as Lady Langsford is on holiday. But he is in. Have you a calling card?"

Anna swallowed a nervous giggle. "No, I have no card." *And probably never will.*

"What name shall I say?"

"My name is Anna. Anna Boardman. Lord Langsford knows who I am."

"Very well then. Follow me." He led Anna up the large staircase to the first floor. There in a broad hall they turned back toward the front of the house to a set of double doors on their left. He opened one and they entered a library.

"Lord Langsford prefers to meet his guests in here, his favorite room, while Lady Langsford is more traditional and prefers the drawing room, more formal and conventional on the ground floor," the butler apologetically explained.

Tall windows overlooked the street at one end and a large fireplace was opposite the double doors. The rest of the walls were filled with bookshelves reaching to the ceiling. The room, like the house, was warm and inviting.

"Make yourself comfortable, Miss."

Anna sat on the edge of a chair opposite the fire, holding her drawstring purse in her lap.

"I shall go alert the lord of your arrival." He left, softly shutting the library door.

Anna took deep breaths. *Henry might have been in this very room.* She looked around, amazed at how many books lined the shelves. She admired the beautiful desk, wishing she could wander the room, exploring and touching, but it wouldn't be polite.

The door clicked open. She turned, rising as she did. Langsford entered.

"Hello, Anna. What a welcome surprise."

She felt relief at the sight of him and the mellow sound of his voice. "It's Henry!"

"Henry? Oh, Heinrich." Langsford laughed. "Here, please. Be seated while we talk," he gestured. She sat down.

"Yes. Heinrich. I call him Henry, because that's his name in English and I teased him once... ." Her mind was muddled again and she couldn't think straight.

"So what about Henry? I can ask him to come join us."

"Oh, he's not here." Tears welled up in her eyes and one escaped down her cheek. "He's been arrested!"

"Arrested?" Langsford felt fear expanding from his gut.

"Yes. By a bobby and a normal man. They said something about treason. Henry yelled for me to come tell you."

"I had no idea he wasn't here." He appeared to talk to himself. "Scotland Yard must have followed him... ." He felt the bile rise in his throat. He looked at Anna, realizing what had happened. "Ah ... He went to see you. Thank goodness you came. I wouldn't know otherwise."

"I'm terribly frightened for him."

"When did they arrest him?" Langsford stood, willing his rising panic to cease.

"Over an hour ago by now. I came to Grosvenor Square but I didn't know where you lived, so it took longer."

"You did well—we must act immediately! He's been arrested

for treason and they'll send him back to Germany in no time. We can help while he's in England, but not after he's gone. I must go to Scotland Yard." He rang for his butler. "Do you mind accompanying me? I can explain everything to you on the way."

"Oh yes, I want to see him... ."

"I doubt they'll permit you." Barnes appeared in the doorway and Langsford addressed him. "Have Pelham hitch the horses. It's an emergency." He reached his hand out to Anna. "We should go."

Downstairs by the heavy front door, Langsford donned his hat and picked up an umbrella, while Anna retied her bonnet. Within minutes, Pelham pulled the carriage up to take them to nearby Scotland Yard.

On their way in the coach, he explained to her how Heinrich was originally accused of murder, followed by the allegation of his role in a plot against Bismarck. He gave her credit. Without female hysterics, she listened stoically as he relayed the string of events.

She seemed calmly perplexed. "He cannot possibly be capable of such things. What can we do?"

"*We*, my dear, are doing nothing. I shall handle this. You return home and stay safe."

"You'll get him released?"

"I have a viable chance. Never underestimate a reputation. It can protect you forever or ruin you permanently. My own father's legacy often carries me forward, I've discovered."

"Then surely you, of all people, can."

There it is. People think I can do anything, he recalled thinking. "I shall try."

They rode in silence a spell. "Pelham will drop me off at

Scotland Yard and he'll take you home. Once you get there, stay. I don't want you involved."

She squared herself, sitting straight against the seatback, clasping her trembling hands. "How will I know what happens? Can you please help me explain all this to Uncle Maxwell? Tell him that Henry was leaving to speak to him immediately about our courtship when he was arrested."

"By all means. I'll come directly after I have met with the commissioner."

"Commissioner? I thought the commissioner was ..."

"The head of the Yard. Yes. He is. I know him personally."

"Oh, that is *very* good." She managed a smile at that news.

"Heinrich will be fine." He spoke with a confidence he didn't feel. A poker bluff.

They arrived at the Great Scotland Yard and Langsford exited the carriage. He watched as Pelham clucked to the horses, the landau rolling away from the curb with Anna sitting starkly alone inside. Somewhere nearby, Heinrich, too, was sitting alone, locked up, a package to be sent to a German executioner.

At Great Scotland Yard, Langsford entered the famous back door of No. 4 Whitehall and trotted up a flight of stone stairs to the broad corridor. Here were the offices of The Metropolitan Police, popularly called Scotland Yard. "This is urgent," he declared, immediately requesting to see Commissioner Sir Edmund Henderson. He handed his card to the constable at the long desk. Upon reading it, the man leapt to his feet to take it to the commissioner.

Langsford waited for the commissioner, knowing full well he had no proof that Heinrich was innocent. He felt nervous, knowing he'd have to argue his case well.

CHAPTER 51

Bermondsey, London

Pelham drove Anna on to Bermondsey, across the Thames. As the carriage rolled over London Bridge, she stared at the steely gray water dotted with vessels. Everything around her felt beyond herself, removed from her existence. Unlike her first dreamlike ride in this carriage with Heinrich, this was the edge of a nightmare.

Once home, she walked in the front door, untying her bonnet as she did, and came face-to-face with Robbie. "Where've ya been, Anna? We're worried sick." He blocked her way into the parlor.

She looked around him to see Aunt Bess getting up from the sagging couch, wringing her hands with worry, her normally cheerful face distorted. "Oh dear, Anna." Aunt Bess stepped forward to the door and hugged her, forcing Robbie to step back. "Are you all right? Robbie said a German accosted you and the police grabbed him straightaway." The matronly woman stepped back, a hand on each of Anna's shoulders to survey her young charge. "Are you injured?"

"I'm fine," she said shakily. "Please don't worry, Auntie. It will work out."

"What does that mean?" Robbie's tone was brusque and Anna knew he was angry.

"Everything will be fine."

"Oh dear, Anna." Aunt Bess was prone to repeat herself.

"I want ya to know, Anna," Robbie continued bitterly, "the

police sent a sergeant to talk to us merchants at the market and saw yer shop locked. I told 'im you was too distraught ta work. I also told him ya didn't know that man. I 'ave to protect ya 'cause yer too stupid ta protect yerself. I even posted a note sayin' the shop was closed due to illness. I hope that'll keep ya from gettin' fired."

"I *had* to leave. It was important."

"*What* was so important, Anna?" Robbie was livid. "What? I told ya I'd take care of ya. I told ya that the bludger was a liar. They said he's a traitor for God's sake. So *what* was so important?" He grabbed her arms and shook her. "What?" This was a side of Robbie she had not seen before and it frightened her. He dug his fingers deep into her arms.

Aunt Bess stepped forward. "Robbie, dear. Uncle Maxwell will be home soon and he can sort everything out." She gently put her hand on Robbie's shoulder and he let go of Anna.

Anna removed her shawl and hugged Aunt Bess again. "I could use a strong cup of tea."

"I believe we all could, dearie. Let's go into the kitchen to brew a pot." They left Robbie pacing in the parlor, fists clenched.

CHAPTER 52

The Great Scotland Yard, London

Waiting for the commissioner, Langsford was trying to figure out what he needed to say when the young constable returned. "Sir Henderson will see you now, your lordship." They walked down the broad hall of what originally had been a large residence before the Metropolitan Police took it over.

The constable politely knocked at a door, then opened it for him. Sir Edmund Henderson, sitting behind an immense, ornate desk in the large room, stood. A tall man with keen posture, he was trim and sported stylish pork-chop sideburns. In uniform, he cut a dashing, if older, figure of a man. Smiling and extending his hand, he boomed, "Lord Langsford. What a pleasure to see you. It has been a while."

"Indeed it has. I'm sorry this is not social, but police business."

"Police business is my job." He pointed to the tufted leather chair in front of his desk. "So what brings you here?" He sat back down in his own seat again. His office had once been a parlor. Sofa and divans had long ago been replaced by the officious furnishings of Scotland Yard.

"My friend, whose father was the late Reichsgraf von Dieffenbacher of the Rhineland, needs our help." Langsford pulled out his pipe to fill.

Sir Henderson leaned forward in his leather chair, elbows on the desktop, hands forming a triangle under his clean-shaven chin, mouth pursed. "Yes. I heard of his death. Your father introduced him to me a while back. Nasty business, that murder. Highway robbery is a thing of the past here in England, thank heavens."

"His son, Heinrich, had attended school with me. Unfortunately the German police have falsely accused him of a crime. The Reichsgraf was on his way to Berlin to clear it up straightaway but he was tragically murdered before that could happen. The police still mistakenly think Heinrich's involved."

"Yes, we arrested him this afternoon." Sir Edmond knitted his brows and tapped his fingers against each other.

"Heinrich is not guilty. I have information so you can arrest those who are."

"Heinrich Dieffenbacher. The Germans want him for murder *and* treason."

"He is innocent."

Henderson placed both hands palms down on his walnut desk. "What you must understand is there is no need to find others. No crime happened on British soil. Our only responsibility is to return him to Germany where they confirm his guilt." He stood, as though to dismiss Langsford. "I fail to see how I can be of any help whatsoever. I am sorry."

Langsford didn't budge from his chair. "It might appear to be an extradition case, but its actual scope is wider. At least one British subject is implicated, perhaps more." He replaced the pipe stem between his teeth and waited for a response.

"A British subject, you say?" Sir Edmond said, astonished. "And how do you know, might I ask?" He slowly sat back down.

"I've been looking into it. I have his name... ."

"Which of course you were planning to hand over to us even

if your friend had not been arrested... ." Sir Edmond raised his eyebrows in query.

"Of course. I always obey the law. I just now discovered this information... ." He trailed off, stopping short of a full fabrication.

"I suppose you might not be able to divulge exactly how you obtained your information?"

"In truth, I am in the process of obtaining more. The murder in Prussia led me to evidence of the assassination being planned here in London." Truth be told, he had no evidence of anything, but now was not the time for full disclosure.

The commissioner shook his head.

"Others," Langsford continued, "including an Englishman, are guilty of conspiring to assassinate Bismarck at the Congress of Berlin, November next. I know the identities of most of the individuals, but not all. Not yet."

"My God, man!" Sir Edmond slapped the desk hard with his right hand. "You should have come to me immediately. This is serious if we are involved. It can adversely impact our relationship with Germany! What else do you know?"

"I know Heinrich Dieffenbacher is innocent."

"What's the name of the Englishman involved?"

"Harold Summerhill. I don't know where he resides, but he works within the Social Democratic Party, heading a special committee hidden within the party. It's the committee planning the assassination, not the party, based on what I've discovered."

"How do you know all this?"

"Heinrich joined the committee to see what they are up to. I have confirmed the Germans involved." He went on to explain that one had committed the murder of which Heinrich was accused. "I'm convinced that he murdered his own brother and accused Heinrich to cover up. Then he and two friends murdered the Graf. I've tracked them from Bullay to here in London."

"I'll assign a detective to find this Summerhill."

"I must ask you, gentleman to gentleman, for a favor."

The commissioner was knighted, as all commissioners were, and was a retired military lieutenant colonel as well. Langsford, however, had the advantage of a higher social position, in addition to his far greater wealth.

"A favor?"

"Do not extradite Heinrich. He *must* remain here in Britain." Langsford paused, staring intently at the commissioner. "He is the son of a Reichsgraf, after all. It must mean something."

Sir Henderson cleared his throat. "I can do that, but only for a few days. This stretches my authority with international law here."

"I'm somewhat acquainted with the Extradition Acts. I do know you are not required to extradite someone immediately who is a witness for the prosecution here in England."

"My detective will need to find this Summerhill quickly."

"Be careful he doesn't tip his hand or the conspirators will go underground like foxes and you'll never find them," Langsford warned. "No one must know except your one detective." He tapped the contents of the pipe in the ashtray sitting near the ink blotter, the taste of the tobacco no longer appealing.

"The director of criminal investigations must be told. And in that, we have a problem," the commissioner said with a hint of disdain. "Director Vincent is not under my command. He reports to Home Secretary Sir William Harcourt. The Criminal Investigations Department may reside here at the Yard, but not the control of it. I am powerless when it comes to the CID."

"Forgive me, but aren't you the Metropolitan Police Commissioner? The director is your second."

"I'm afraid I have no say over the CID itself. The director's position is strictly a political post. This is an extradition case and it falls under CID jurisdiction."

"Makes little sense, but there it is." Langsford frowned. "Sir William was a friend of my father's."

Henderson pursed his lips. "Don't speak to him. Let's hold this under the purview of the Yard and stay away from the political and international arena. Sir William is definitely not the person to confide in."

"I understand. Better to keep this in the realm of the police for now. I'll speak instead with Director Vincent. Surely he'll be willing to confine this issue."

"He's a political sort so I doubt it very much, but we do have some luck. He won't be back to London until Friday. I have control of the case until then."

"Just until Friday?"

"Correct. Once Sir Vincent returns, everything will be up to him."

"I see. Then we must hurry. In the meantime, keep Heinrich safe."

"I'll do what I can in that regard, and in the meantime we'll search for Summerhill."

Langsford rose, and the two shook hands. "Thank you." He had two days to get proof to the CID or Heinrich would be extradited. Five days until the committee left for Berlin and vanished.

CHAPTER 53

Bermondsey, London

Robbie sat frowning, his fingers drumming on the arms of the chair, his tea on the side table ignored. "Last time I be askin'. Where ya been?"

"Lord Langsford's residence. Then we drove to Scotland Yard …" Anna began.

Aunt Bess gasped, dropping her spoon.

"I didn't go inside," she reassured her aunt. "His driver brought me straight home. The lord is speaking with the commissioner at this very moment, correcting the mistake."

Robbie's scowl deepened, but before he could respond, Lottie burst through the front door. "Hallo …" she called out, seeing everyone in the parlor. "Hello, Robbie," she greeted with her usual exuberance as she hung up her shawl. "I didn't know we were expecting company." She went in to hug her aunt, turning so Robbie couldn't see her face. She grinned and winked at Anna who shook her head in an effort to head off Lottie's enthusiasm.

"Is something wrong?"

Everyone remained silent. She plopped down beside her aunt on the sofa, looking back and forth at the three of them.

"It's best we wait until your uncle Max arrives, dear. He'll be home any moment."

Robbie sulked, his jaw clenched, glaring at Anna.

Lottie turned to Anna. "What is going on?"

Anna heard Langsford's voice outside talking. Uncle Max's, too. Just in front of the house, her uncle's reply was distinct. "Anna will be inside, I'm sure, your lordship. Please do come in."

When they heard the men, everyone stood. Anna, anxious to hear about Henry, ran to the door and opened it wide. Robbie stood rigidly in front of his chair, while Aunt Bess, wringing her hands, walked up with a confused Lottie.

"I see my entire family is here," Uncle Max remarked as he removed his hat. His smile dropped when he saw their faces. "What is it?" He glanced over to see Robbie in the parlor. "Has something happened?"

"Oh dear, you are needing to get everything settled here, my husband," Aunt Bess pleaded. "This is all too much."

"I regret, Lord Langsford"—Uncle Max turned to his guest— "this may not be the best time to call—"

"Actually," Langsford interrupted, "I can explain exactly what happened. It involves Anna."

"Anna? Then by all means, stay." Uncle Max made quick introductions. He touched Aunt Bess's shoulder affectionately. "My lovely wife, Elizabeth." She blushed when Langsford kissed her hand. "My niece, Charlotte." Lottie's hand covered her lips as she gasped. She did a little curtsey and Anna pinched her. "What?" she exclaimed as she jumped.

Uncle Max continued, "And you are acquainted with Miss Anna Boardman already."

"Yes, I am. It is a pleasure to be in the company of all you lovely ladies."

Lottie took his hat and coat, looking back and forth between Anna, Langsford, and Robbie. "Let me put on more tea, and Lottie, you help." Aunt Bess grabbed her young charge by the elbow and ushered her off to the kitchen. Anna stood alone with the men.

Uncle Max led the way into the parlor where Robbie still stood at attention.

"Lord Langsford, this is Robert Wells."

"We met afore." Robbie held out his arm, elbow rigid, and shook hands. "But ya weren't no lord then. Look all different now, all fancied up."

"Yes." Langsford grinned. "A pleasure to see you again."

"Please, make yourself comfortable." Uncle Max gestured to the empty couch.

Langsford settled beside Anna with Uncle Max in a chair opposite Robbie. He turned to her with a smile. "I see you arrived home safely."

"Yes, m'lord, I did. Thank you."

"So, tell me, Lord Langsford," Uncle Max began, "why is my household in such turmoil?"

"I were there and I know what 'appened," Robbie snapped.

"Do tell us then." Langsford sat and pulled the corner of his moustache.

"The police grabbed this bloke who was takin' advantage of Anna. He's a traitor to boot, he is. Good riddance. I warned her. She ran off when I weren't watchin'. Disobeyed, she did and deserves a good—"

"That's enough now," Langsford stopped Robbie.

Uncle Max, alarmed, looked at Anna. "You were taken advantage of? Are you all right?"

"I'm fine, thank you, Uncle."

"She's a bit flustered is all. She came to tell me afterward."

"Remember, Uncle Max? Lord Langsford and Henry escorted me home that evening. Henry would never harm me."

"You saw this bludger while you were courtin' me?" Robbie leapt to his feet. "You hear that, Mr. Miller? She's behavin' like a trollop!"

"Enough of that talk, Robbie." Uncle Max's voice was stern. "I know you're worried, but let's all calm down and find out what's happened." Uncle Max's tone was surprisingly forceful and Robbie sat.

Langsford calmly continued. "Heinrich was arrested today on false charges while visiting Anna's shop. She simply asked me for help. I've just left the commissioner of Scotland Yard and I promised I'd come by to inform her of the results of that discussion."

"You spoke directly to the commissioner?" Uncle Max asked.

"He knows him personally," Anna announced.

"Well, that'll get the criminal loose," Robbie snarled, furious.

"The law encompasses all of us. Unfortunately, he is not yet released—in a day or two."

Aunt Bess bustled in, rosy cheeked. She offered tea and day-old scones, then silently sat down on a small settee with Lottie.

"Mrs. Miller, I'm glad you and Charlotte are here. It's best to include the entire family in what I have to say. And you as well, Robbie. This situation is, at best, unusual, but I know my friend Heinrich would wish me to explain further." Langsford reached for a scone.

"Obviously Anna shared with you that Heinrich visited me here in London last month. That's when he met Anna at her shop and was immediately taken by her beauty and grace."

Robbie leapt up. "She's a shameless flirt ..."

Langsford glared. "Sit and be quiet. I'm speaking." Robbie sat again, sulking. "I assure everyone, the two were properly chaperoned. Everything was aboveboard and proper."

"Robbie," Anna pleaded, "you and I weren't courting then."

"Trust what Lord Langsford says, Robbie," Aunt Bess interjected. "She didn't think Henry would ever be in London again, did you, dear?"

Langsford continued. "Heinrich unfortunately had to leave London unexpectedly." He sipped his tea while everyone sat waiting to hear more, hoping Robbie would calm. Lottie perched on the edge of her seat.

"As it turned out"—he set down his cup—"Heinrich fled Prussia to return for Anna." He turned to Robbie. "Of course she had no way of knowing any of this. I only told her yesterday, so you may not blame her."

Robbie slunk down in his seat, seething.

"Unfortunately, Heinrich crossed paths accidently with an unsavory individual. In short, he was in the wrong place at the wrong time. Without going into details, he's falsely accused of treason, which he only discovered after he arrived in London." Langsford bit into the hard scone. The room was quiet, waiting for him to continue. Lottie held her breath. Robbie remained silent, staring at his boots. "I've known Heinrich since school days. I know he had no involvement."

"How long has he been in London?" Uncle Max asked.

"Not long. He said he couldn't face Anna until he was free of these charges."

"Yet he came to her today still a wanted man," Uncle Max pointed out.

"Yes, unfortunately, it was premature. Apparently he felt compelled to talk to her. He must have thought we were nearly done finding the real traitors. In fact, we are quite close."

"What about Henry, m'lord?" Anna interrupted. "What happened at Scotland Yard?"

"Sir Henderson and I had an honest talk, the result of which is that Heinrich will not be extradited to Germany—"

"Extradited?" Anna cried out. "You mean they'll shoot him?" Her heart clutched.

Uncle Max explained. "It means 'returned.' When someone commits a crime in one country and is arrested in another, that person is legally sent back to where the crime happened."

"We have very clear extradition laws and agreements with our political allies."

"What happens if he is extra—"

"Extradited. He would be returned to Germany where, I'm sorry to say, he could be hanged for treason."

"Good!" Robbie exclaimed.

Anna burst into tears. Aunt Bess moved to sit on the sofa's arm, bending over to console her.

Ignoring Robbie, Langsford turned to get Anna's attention. "Listen to me. Sir Edmond has promised Heinrich will stay in London. At least for now."

Anna looked hopefully at him. "Heinrich will remain safe?"

"Yes." There was an audible sigh of relief from everyone in the room except Robbie.

Langsford had more to say. "I feel, as Heinrich's friend and in his absence, it is only proper to inform you, Mr. and Mrs. Miller, what Anna related to me earlier."

Anna sat straighter and swiped the tears off her face as a smile broke through.

"Before his arrest, Heinrich was on his way here to ask for your permission to court her."

"Oh, yes, Uncle Max," Anna brightened. "He was coming right away. I was so happy." Her eagerness was impossible for her to hide.

Lottie, unable to contain herself, bounced on the seat cushion and grinned from ear to ear.

Robbie gritted his teeth, his upper lip curled.

"I don't like this, Anna. Not one bit." Uncle Max glowered. He turned to Langsford. "Are you positive this man is innocent?"

"Yes."

"You have evidence?"

"We have some facts yet to gather."

"It must not be enough or Scotland Yard would have released him."

"You are correct," Langsford admitted. "The fact is I know who the guilty parties are and they will be arrested soon. He will be released at that point, I'm sure."

"There are several problems regarding this Heinrich," her uncle contended. "He is not officially exonerated, and until he is, he is legally guilty. That's a major block for anyone wishing to court one of mine. Additionally, I have already given Robbie here permission. You are a decent man," he turned to the fuming cobbler, "when you aren't out of your mind with worry. I know you will provide well for a family and keep them safe."

"But Uncle!" Anna interrupted.

"Hush, girl," her uncle replied, using a tone she had not heard before. She sat back, rebuffed. "The other problem is this Prussian is a nobleman while Anna is a commoner. Anna, It is wrong for this German to court you. My decision is no."

Anna gasped and covered her mouth.

"Let me set your mind at ease, Mr. Miller," Langsford spoke up, and Anna realized he was still speaking on Henry's behalf. The "no" might not yet be the final word.

"Scotland Yard will apprehend the murderers and assassins, and Heinrich *will be* absolved." He sat back and crossed his legs.

"As for your other concern, when Heinrich left Prussia, he abandoned any privileges and wealth he had. Here in London he is a commoner in every sense of the word. So the only issue is Robbie, and Anna might be able to address that."

Robbie stood up, blustering with hands on hips. "Well, Anna, I'm a fine cordwainer. I will make a good husband." He walked closer to her, glaring down, seething in anger. "There's nuthin' more ya could ask in a man, but after all this"—he turned and looked at everyone in the room—"I realize she's not a wife I want. She's fickle and cheap."

He turned to Uncle Max. "I won't be courtin' your niece no more, Mr. Miller. She deserves a decent beatin' to teach 'er a lesson for leadin' on that bloody bludger."

He turned back to Anna who, like everyone else, sat shocked at his venomous words. "The flower girl stops by me shop when I work. She ain't no cheap floozy like you."

"Now see here!" Uncle Max stood, spinning Robbie around.

Robbie tore himself out of the man's grasp as Langsford rose to step between them.

"It's best you leave now, Robert," Langsford said, his soft voice carrying a warning for the cobbler. He put his hand on the man's back and walked him to the door, opening it for him.

"Yer all a bunch of liars!" Robbie called back, but Langsford closed the door behind him, turning the lock.

CHAPTER 54

Pratt's Club, London

Young Lord Percy staggered into his friend, Cecil Westchester, and the pair fell into one of the Pratt's Club chairs, which rolled into an adjacent table, sending it crashing to the floor. The two, along with their third drinking fellow, found it hysterically funny.

"Blimey. You've broken the bloody vaaase," the pimply faced Lord Watkins laughed and poured his glass of absinthe on top of the pair, stumbling backward. He landed in the lap of the Earl of Exeter, Lord Edward Stanley. Disgusted, Stanley shoved him off onto the woven carpet.

"I say," piped up Norbiton, laughing at their antics. "You gents are having quite the time tonight."

"We don't lack for entertainment," guffawed Nevel. "A barrel of laughs."

"You sound like you dunked your head into the rum with sailors, yourself, Nevel," growled Stanley. "They should stick to gin. They're addle-brained from the absinthe."

Two Georges swooped in, one helping the inebriated men to their feet and the other righting the furniture.

"Weren't you young once, you old goat?" Percy laughed at the earl. "You could do with some fun, Lord Pain-in-the-arse."

The rest of the men in the exclusive enclave chuckled. Drunken libations were far from rare, especially with the younger set. Westchester and Nevel occasionally joined in.

"Oooh Ge-ooorge. Ober here," Percy sing-songed. "Gib the earl more champaaa-nnne. He's too holy to im-imbibe in a reeeal man's drink."

"Get away," Stanley snarled.

Cecil turned his empty glass upside down. "I sneed another absinthe. Mine is aaaaaalll gone."

Langsford's thoughts had been jarred. He had less than two days to find proof of Heinrich's innocence. Giving up hope for quiet contemplation, he watched the two Georges blot the spilled liquor from the rug.

With much commotion, the three inebriated gentlemen shuffled off in their dishevelled tails, with hats and sword-canes in hand. They were heading for a new venue. "Wid fem-in-ine compaaaanions," Percy boasted.

"I hope they remain in private and don't venture into public houses," worried Nevel.

"If they do, they'll end up in a *Punch* cartoon," laughed Wofford.

The room quieted in the wake of their departure. The remaining members quietly sipped their drinks and puffed their pipes and cigars, gentle smoke billowing about the wood-paneled room.

"I've news to brag," offered Sir Mallaby, a noted diplomat with them this evening. He leaned sideways, elbow on the chair arm.

"Since you obviously want us to ask," Nevel teased, "what might that be?"

"I have been requested to attend the African Conference in Gladstone's stead. He doesn't want to go. You know what he thinks of Bismarck."

"You've just returned from Berlin, haven't you?" Westchester asked.

"Indeed. And because I've experience there, I've been asked to represent the crown."

"Bully for you! We mustn't let Germany get a strong foothold on the 'Darkest Continent,'" Stanley proclaimed. He held up his glass, signaling George for another.

Langsford's interest was piqued. "Who else will attend?"

"The conference is just now in the planning stage, I believe. It will be weeks before anything is finalized," the diplomat explained. "There's not even a set date."

That's odd. Why would the committee plan for November 15 if it weren't a firm date?

"I fear, Mallaby, you've not been privy to the facts," Stanley offered. "Last week several MP's asked my opinion about Africa. They do know where and when it's scheduled—Bismarck's official Berlin residence in mid-November."

"Indeed?"

Langsford idly watched George serve Stanley champagne while the earl spoke, thinking that at least the earl had accurate information.

"On the continent we get information late, in fragments or sometimes not at all," Mallaby lamented. "Here in London you're all in a better position to garner political details. Yet I am the diplomat. Ironic." He shook his head and puffed on his cigar.

"It is," empathized Nevel, but Langsford had abruptly stopped listening. He'd seen George before: the familiar face under the shadow of a cap at the Lamb Tavern during the committee meeting. It was that unidentified man pouring champagne for Lord Stanley, the Earl of Exeter!

Langsford snapped his mouth shut when he realized his jaw hung open. George was the unknown member, he'd bet a team of horses on it. *A spy right here in our midst!* A traitor gathering information for Summerhill. No wonder the committee knew what's being discussed and planned.

Langsford gulped his port, frowning. Had this man served them when he and Heinrich asked about Countess Cross? Had he recognized them at the Leadenhall pub? *Must not or the man would already be reacting to me.* He sat pondering until Norbiton interrupted. "What are you so serious about there, my man? Is there a new investment you are keeping from us?" The rest of the men laughed, the room again merrier, matching the amount of additional drink consumed.

"Oh," he laughed at himself. "No. A wandering mind. I really should call it a night."

"Then you need another drink." Norbiton held up his glass. "Say, George, pour him more. That's what he needs. And so do I." The others agreed.

"A toast," Nevel proclaimed.

Without looking at anyone directly, this George quickly poured more port all around.

They raised their glasses. "To Mallaby for Africa!"

"Here, here!"

It was Nevel's toast that gave him an idea. *Let's upset the apple-cart and make it urgent for the committee to meet.* This was the perfect topic for a red herring.

"You know, gentlemen, I was recently in Germany visiting a Prussian Reichsgraf," he truthfully began the lie. "We spoke of the fall conference. Interesting what you said, Mallaby, about Gladstone not attending. Bismarck won't, either. More pressing matters to attend to."

"What!? How do you know?" The room instantly quieted.

"Because this Reichsgraf is to represent the German government in his stead."

"Is that so?" Nevel laughed. "This all-important conference will have neither Gladstone nor Bismarck?"

"Perhaps Gladstone will be persuaded to participate after all, knowing that Bismarck won't," Norbiton suggested.

Langsford laughed and glanced around the room, taking note that his George showed no reaction. The servant stood quietly along the wall, white-gloved hands at his sides, looking blankly at the opposite wall.

"Well, isn't that news," exclaimed Sir Mallaby, finishing his champagne.

"Bismarck is unwise not to attend," Stanley remarked. "All the better for us, though."

"Indeed," agreed Langsford. He enjoyed the way everyone took what he said as fact. Again, the legacy of his father added weight and credibility to everything he said or did. No one doubted one word of it.

Now it was up to George to deliver this misinformation to Summerhill post haste.

There it is. Tonight he would follow this servant.

CHAPTER 55

St. James's Street, London

Langsford was waiting with Pelham, parked at the end of the street. The fog had rolled in but not so much they couldn't see a good distance.

"The unknown man in the cap is a George; he's our spy," he'd informed his coachman when he left Pratt's earlier.

"Bloody hell!" the coachman exclaimed, "Pardon me, my'lord," he apologized for his language, opening the door for Langsford. "But to think a wait servant—a spy."

"We need to wait and follow him."

"I'm right with you, m'lord. Imagine ..."

It wasn't long before the man emerged from Pratt's. "There he is!" Langsford pointed. Pelham hopped up in the driver's seat. "Keep a discreet distance."

Cabs and omnibuses were still available this time of night, and within minutes, George boarded a bus on St. James's Street. *Ah, good*, Langsford thought. *He won't be aware of a carriage behind him.*

They followed the omnibus to Charing Cross where George disembarked and waited by the stop. Pelham rounded the corner and halted the horses so they could secretly watch.

"He's walked over to that brick building," Pelham reported, after getting down to talk with his employer inside the landau.

"Which building?"

"By the stop. He's leaning on the wall there."

"If he walks on, we'll follow on foot."

"So far he's just standin' there."

They waited a few minutes, and then George stepped back to the stop to board an arriving omnibus.

"He's taking another bus." Pelham jumped up into the driver's seat, picking up the reins. They continued to follow the vehicle down to Whitehall, where it stopped on Victoria Street. George got off and walked down Artillery Row. Pelham drove on, halting a brief distance beyond.

"Turn around," Langsford ordered. "Walk the horses slowly so I can see out the window."

The team wheeled easily, turning in time for Langsford to see their man enter a house partway down.

"Stop," he called in a loud whisper.

"There are lots of boarding houses around here. Did he enter any?" Pelham asked.

"I think he went into the fourth house on the right."

"It might be hours before he leaves," Pelham said, halting. "Why don't I watch while you rest, m'lord. If this man goes anywhere, I'll follow. We'll trade off, like we did when we had to watch for that bloke at the messenger house."

"Yes, that was a messy business, wasn't it?" Langsford remembered. He'd once helped a friend who was suspicious of a man wishing to court his daughter. After following the potential suitor, Pelham and Langsford had confirmed his friend's suspicions: his daughter's suitor was committing sodomy with messenger boys. The courtship was immediately off. That was a matter of marriage. Tonight was a matter of life and death. "We seem to make a good team when we have to sort out wickedness."

"That bludger was fortunate we didn't notify the police,"

Pelham said grimly. "I do find it rather exciting, spying on someone."

"Don't think of it as spying as much as observing. We don't know who this man is. We must follow him, even if we tether the horses and follow on foot."

"Do you think he'll leave soon?"

"He may if he plans to meet with others to pass along what I said tonight."

"Let's hope so, m'lord. Anything to get young Heinrich out of jail."

Throughout the night and into the morning, they shared the task of watching. In early afternoon they took a much-needed break when George left for work.

"He'll be there for the rest of the afternoon and through the evening," Langsford calculated, watching him enter Pratt's. "I'm tired and hungry. Let's go home."

"Will we follow him again this evening? Maybe he'll go some-where else tonight."

"Yes. Let's hope he goes to Summerhill. We're running out of time."

Late that night, they again parked at the end of Park Place on St. James's.

"He's not come out yet," Pelham said, tucking a bridle strap into its keeper as he stood by the near horse.

"If he's on the same schedule as last night, he should come out soon."

"I was wondering, if you don't mind me askin', why we don't just knock on the boarding house door and ask for the man who works at Pratt's?"

"The best we could do is learn his name and that isn't enough. I need to confirm he meets with Summerhill or a committee member."

When George emerged, they followed his omnibus again but he didn't get off as before. He continued directly on to the Victoria Street stop near his boarding house. Again they drove past, as he walked to his house. When the door closed behind him, Pelham wheeled the carriage about.

"Park on Artillery Row tonight. I want to keep a closer eye out."

"Yes, m'lord." Pelham drove down the cobblestoned street and parked a few doors down.

Tonight they didn't wait long, for in minutes, George, no longer in his servant tails but wearing the same worker's clothing he had at the pub several nights back, exited the house and walked toward Victoria, away from them. At the bus stop, he crossed the street.

"He's not taking the bus," Pelham quietly jumped down to report his observation.

"Tether the horses. We'll follow on foot."

Pelham hurriedly set the brake and tied the team.

Together they walked at a brisk clip, following George. They stayed in the shadows, keeping him in sight as he turned along Great Chapel. In no time they were up Broadway to Queen Street and crossing Birdcage Walk to St. James's Park.

Breathless, they entered the fog-shrouded area.

Trees hovered over them, providing dense shadows as they moved up the path. George walked deeper into the park and slowed down. The footpath forked where the trees thinned, and they caught sight of his shadowy figure taking the right-hand path.

Another figure in a cloak and top hat emerged within the fog, and George stopped to talk with him. Langsford and Pelham scurried off the path into the shrubbery, unable to creep closer without rustling branches. While the fog served to obscure them, it unfortunately dampened sounds. They heard only muffled, unintelligible words.

Suddenly a third figure, a tall man, appeared, and George called out. "'allo, Mr. Summerhill!"

CHAPTER 56

St. James's Park, London

Summerhill. Loud and clear. *There it is.*

Summerhill turned to the cloaked man. "We await orders... ." His voice faded as he closed in on the other two, his words now unintelligible. *Damn.*

The three huddled for merely minutes, then broke apart. George turned to walk back the way he came, toward them. Caught off guard, Pelham ducked down, lost his balance, and sat down hard, snapping thin branches. Langsford rustled bushes as he stepped behind a large oak beside him. He held his breath.

George stopped and looked toward the noises. Scanning the wooded area a couple times, he continued walking when there were no more sounds.

Langsford peeked carefully from behind the tree as the cloaked figure walked away in the opposite direction. He saw Summerhill head deeper into the park on a different path. He signaled Pelham, who brushed leaves off his bottom. "Follow Summerhill," he whispered, pointing.

Pelham nodded.

Langsford rushed up the path after the cloaked man who was now out of sight. Who was this man?

There! Up ahead. The man in the cloak. The fog favored Langsford again, dampening the sounds of his footfalls. He rounded a bend in the path, closing the distance. The man's pace was almost leisurely as he walked to the park's eastern gate. The cloaked traitor turned right and quickly climbed into a waiting cab.

The devil! Langsford clenched his fists. *I need the carriage, dammit!*

The hack rolled off.

He did not see another parked nearby. He didn't dare lose the man but he couldn't keep up on foot. He saw a cab coming up the other side of the street and he hailed the driver. The cab had a fare and wasn't going to stop. "Halt!" Langsford yelled, running in front of the cab to grab the bridle on the horse. Hanging on as the animal half reared, he yelled to the driver. "Scotland Yard business. I need you to drive me."

The driver, uncertain, sat with his whip raised, ready to come down on Langsford. "Wot's 'at ya say?"

"Scotland Yard. I need you to follow that cab that just pulled out—it's over there, see?"

The cabbie hesitated.

"Now!" Langsford climbed in, finding himself next to an older man who scrunched against the far door, his eyes wide.

"Hello. Just a quick detour, then you'll be on your way." He fell back against the seat as the cab lurched forward, wheeling to turn around.

Chapter 57

Langsford, engulfed in his jacquard silk dressing gown, padded in his plush slippers to the library window. He watched as the pale light tinted faint color on the fading darkness, still shocked by his discovery only hours before. The man in the cape had entered No. 20 St. James's Square. He knew who lived there: his friend.

Whoever the top-hatted man was, he had to be a spy within the household. *The man I followed had a build similar to Lentz, the German.* That thought meant it couldn't be his friend, who was a larger man. Or did the cloak deceive?

Pelham, whom he'd summoned, entered the library and stood by the double doors, interrupting his train of thought. His coachman looked damp and exhausted.

"Ah, good morning, if it is yet quite morning." Langsford gestured for his driver to enter. "I've had the better night of it, it seems, just from the look of you, and mine wasn't easy. You discovered where Summerhill lives?"

"Indeed, your lordship. He wasn't difficult to follow. It wasn't far. Went on to another boarding house, he did." He handed his employer a slip of paper with large simple numbers and letters on it. "I wrote down the address."

"Fairly near St. James's Park and Artillery Row." He pulled on the end of his moustache.

"I watched a bit in case he'd leave, but as I'd left the horses behind, I was worried. Went back to drive the carriage home and just now bedded down the team. Wanted to do it myself to make sure they were fine. I hurried, though."

"Well done, my man. Have a seat. You certainly look bushed." He folded the slip of paper and looked at the clock as it chimed four. He was tired himself. "Well, now we know where both George and Summerhill are. Information for Scotland Yard. Excellent."

"Where'd your bloke go?" the driver asked.

"A home on St. James's Square."

"Oh, those are elegant ones, they are."

"I know the man who lives there."

"No! You do?"

"A member of Pratt's. Was with me the other evening."

"That's a blow, now, isn't it, m'lord?"

He felt a chill creep into his bones. "There it is."

"First George and now a gentleman? That's a coincidence."

"And I don't believe in coincidences, but I do believe the man in the cape is a servant, for he seemed a different build."

"Well, at least you know he's not Summerhill or George. It could be the German, Lentz."

"Here's what worries me: either my friend has no idea a traitor is in his household or he knows and is in on the plot."

"Wonder who the servant could be if it isn't Lentz? Maybe another German?"

"Have you heard if any Germans have been hired in the stables around there? A foreign worker could easily infiltrate a residence to hear what is said."

"No, I've not heard anyone speak of it, and you know they would. There's always gossip when we park waiting outside your social events."

Langsford laughed. "If you call having a pint or two at a nearby pub 'parking outside.'"

"That's only when it's going to be hours." Pelham laughed. "It's just a bit of our own social gathering."

"These spies have their own social gathering. With George at Pratt's and a traitor in the midst of the earl's household, the two would have access to all kinds of British information."

"Which earl, my lord?"

"The Earl of Exeter."

"Great Scott!" Pelham gasped. "You've a dilemma, you do."

"The question is: Is this person working with Lord Stanley, or hiding within?"

"I don't see how it could be *with* him, your lordship. It seems to me if a traitor is in his midst, it's because he's spying *on* the Earl. That's my take on it."

"Except my father once told me that he felt the earl to be duplicitous and not fully trusted. That and what we heard Summerhill say, 'We await orders… .' He was talking to someone in a superior position."

"That isn't soundin' so good, then, is it?"

"No."

Barnes entered, asking if the lord wished an early breakfast, and Pelham left for his own quarters above the stable.

"Breakfast? No. Not at this ungodly hour. I only need a note delivered, post haste." He was curt and immediately regretted his tone. "I apologize. I'm tired and feel an urgency about this."

"I understand, m'lord," Barnes reassured his employer.

Langsford walked over to the desk and penned a short note. "Here." He closed the envelope with wax and his seal. "Have this sent to the Earl of Exeter immediately."

"Yes." The old man made a stiff little bow, turned, and left.

Langsford, exhausted from his lack of sleep, returned to his own room and crawled into bed. He faced a busy day in a few hours. He happily pulled the down comforter up to his chin and instantly fell asleep.

By ten o'clock, he had risen and was taking brunch in the dining room while he read the paper. Barnes handed him a message from Lord Stanley.

"Ah, good. He responded quickly." Langsford set his tea cup in its saucer and broke the seal on the square envelop. Unfolding the note, he read:

> *Lady Clementine and I are having a small dinner party this evening. Although I realize Lady Regina is out of town, I would welcome you. I shall smooth Lady Clementine's Irish feathers about you joining us as a bachelor. We shall be able to talk comfortably afterward about your urgent matter. RSVP*

Perfect timing, he thought. He scrawled his affirmative reply.

He'd be able to gauge his reaction to see if he were aware of any traitor and, if not, warn him of one in his midst. What would happen after that, he had no idea. In the meantime, his first stop this morning was Scotland Yard, to attempt to convince the head of the Criminal Investigation Department to keep Heinrich in London until the traitors were arrested.

CHAPTER 58

The Great Scotland Yard, London

Langsford waited in the office of the director of the CID. Precious days had passed since Heinrich's arrest and he still had no solid proof. Today was Friday, the deadline to hold on Heinrich's extradition.

He walked around the spacious throne room, so to speak, of the second most influential man in Scotland Yard, but one whose political power came directly from the home secretary instead of the Metropolitan Police.

The desk was large and ornate. The chair behind it was soft leather. Windows shed dim light on the flat plane of the tidy desk, interrupted by three neat stacks of paper. Books shelved along a side wall were alphabetized. Along the paneled wall facing the desk, a row of four leather chairs lined up as though they themselves might be interrogated.

Sir Vincent, a tall, slender man with thinning hair and a drooping handlebar moustache, energetically swung open the door. He wore no uniform but instead was dressed in traditional morning coat and trousers, his starched collar held in place by an ascot. His bearing matched the formality of his dress. Here was a politician, not a policeman.

"Lord Langsford," he enthusiastically greeted.

"Sir Vincent. A pleasure."

"Do sit, do sit. I know why you've come." He went around the desk, unbuttoned his coat, and sat, the chair squeaking in protest.

"Then I need only to bring you up to date." Langsford described how he'd discovered another British traitor who worked at Pratt's. "There is possibly one more."

"Well, this is interesting," Sir Vincent responded. "You have done right to come to me. We can certainly take over from here. All I need are the names of the British subjects involved and we can arrest them all straight forth."

He knew Sir Vincent would not be easy to sway about Heinrich. "I regret that this case is not quite that simple. While I have information about the committee, it is led by an as yet unknown person who may be British. It is important the leader himself be arrested, and that won't happen if you arrest the others first."

"I believe we here at CID know how to proceed. While you have been helpful, there is a danger involved, and I need to insist that you do not proceed any further. Initially I was concerned you were being used by your Prussian friend and were in danger."

"I certainly appreciate that." Langsford did not like how the conversation was going.

"We had no other information other than you were Dieffenbacher's acquaintance. Thus I had an inspector follow up on this one clue. Reluctant as I was, I gave him permission to inquire about you."

Langsford suddenly felt angry and defensive.

"You'd just departed for the continent, with a cousin, it seems. A Westphalian. I wasn't concerned because it would be idiotic for anyone wanted by the Prussian police to go back. Yet from time to time, the inspector checked on who was coming and going from your residence, as that was the only lead he had."

Langsford willed himself to hold his poker face and check his anger. How dare someone watch who came and went at his home. "So you followed me... ." His hands wanted to grip the chair arms, but he forced himself to stay relaxed. That explained how the police found Heinrich at Anna's.

"The inspector's fine police work led to Mr. Dieffenbacher. I considered questioning you at the time of the arrest but, well, no need to bring the British into this. It's strictly a German affair."

Alarm registered loud and clear. With Summerhill leading the assassination committee, the British are already involved, and the director knows that. He just contradicted himself about involving the British. *Sir Vincent wishes to wrap everything up,* Langsford thought. A loose end to be snagged and returned to Germany for both the county's good will and his glory as the head of CID. Case closed and the home secretary impressed. A politician's move.

"You don't have the information I've gathered," he remarked forcefully. "You'll need what I know in order to make further arrests," he said, wanting to force the director's hand. "And if you arrest only the men I've identified so far, you will have accomplished little except to arrest a handful of criminals. You must find the leader, otherwise he can easily create a new committee and you would never be the wiser until an international incident."

"Interesting thought." Sir Vincent sat further back in his chair, tenting his hands.

"And the British are already involved: the spy at Pratt's, Summerhill, not to mention the head of the committee, possibly British." He avoided mentioning the earl for now, desperately wanting it not to involve him.

Sir Vincent showed his displeasure. "So you have said. I really have no time to go into this further now. Give the information to the constable at the desk and I'll have a detective assigned. That should allay your fears." He frowned and rocked his chair back, showing impatience.

"We are way ahead of any detective." Langsford sat forward, his face serious. "Heinrich worked his way into the committee under the name 'Gerhard' and convinced the others that he was a German farmworker. He can identify these men who murdered his father and the man in Bullay. If you release Heinrich, he can help you, but you must do so now. The Prussians return to Berlin on Tuesday to get set for the assassination."

"We can arrest the criminals by Tuesday, *if* there is evidence against them." He stood up. "I'll have the detectives look into it. We will take everything from here."

"Heinrich remains in London?" Langsford failed to budge from his chair.

"He goes back to Germany first thing Monday. The papers are being drawn up now."

"My God! You send an innocent man to his execution?"

"Germany decides if he's not guilty. We've kept him too long as it is, as a favor to you, I understand. Frankly, this is a simple extradition case, but I thank you for bringing more to our attention." He walked from behind his desk, a sign the meeting was over. "I cannot release a foreign traitor. Not enough justification to risk an international fuss."

Langsford could tell the director was rigid in his decision. Standing, he made another attempt. "Then use Heinrich to gather evidence. I can advise him."

"No."

"Let me speak to him."

"He's not permitted visitors."

"Keep him here at least."

"There's no reason to permit him to remain in London. As a

barrister myself, I am keenly aware of the law, and the law ties my hands."

Langsford continued pressing his case. "Look, I am so close to finding out who the leader is. In fact, this evening at a dinner party I will learn just that." He prayed his bold claim would prove true. "I say we meet again in the morning and if I fail to have what you need to keep Heinrich in England then I shall give up the fight."

"Fine, then," the director sighed in resignation. "Just this one time shall I allow you to proceed. I am shorthanded already and you are tenacious. *And* your father was my friend." He glared at Langsford. "Don't take my gesture lightly, for there are few people I would do this for."

I am in your debt, Sir Vincent." He had until tomorrow morning to absolve Heinrich.

He donned his top hat and left the office, walking past the long outer desk. He had no intention of handing over information to the constable or to anyone at Scotland Yard. He headed straight down the steps toward the door leading into the yard when a woman rushed through the door, colliding into him.

He recognized the bonnet that sat askew on her head before she even looked up at the man who accidently barred her entrance. "Why, Anna!"

Recoiling a step, she put her hand on her hat in time to gasp, "Lord Langsford!" She wore a deep brown dress with a high neck, her skin all the more porcelain in contrast.

He laughed a smile at her as she stood flustered.

"I trust you are here to inquire about Heinrich?"

"Yes. Have you spoken with him?"

Langsford took her by the arm to escort her up the stairs from the busy entrance. "No," he said, stopping at the corner of the police counter. A white globe perched atop a metal post stood vigilant, while queues of civilians waited to speak to one of the two constables behind the desk.

"I'm afraid he isn't allowed visitors."

"Oh no!"

"I'm sure he's comfortable."

"To be so close and not be able to see him," her voice cracked.

"Some good news," he offered cheerfully. "I'm following up on new facts this evening."

"Good," she managed a small smile.

"Pelham is here with the carriage. Let's give you a lift back to your shop, shall we?" He began escorting her back to the door.

"No need. I no longer work there."

"No? That's a surprise."

"I took money from the cash drawer," she admitted frankly. "For the cab fare."

"You did? Cab fare?"

"Two shillings. It was wrong, I know, but taking a cab was the fastest way to you... ."

"To tell me about Heinrich's arrest," he nodded, understanding now.

"I paid it back from my savings, but Mr. Thompson said he could no longer trust me. That I'm a thief. I don't blame him one bit."

"That's a shame. I'm sorry. Shall we take you home then?"

"No. Everyone is in a tizzy over what I've done."

"Where to, then?"

"I don't wish to be a bother, m'lord."

"Never. I enjoy your company, as I enjoy Heinrich's." He laughed, glad she was there so that he could laugh, and wanting to cheer her up as well.

"I don't know what to do now that I can't see Henry."

"Ride along with me, and I'll fill you in on what Pelham and I have recently discovered. It should give you hope." He was determined to lift her spirits. "In fact, why don't you plan to accompany me at dinner tonight. It will lighten both our moods."

"Dinner?"

"Why not? Heinrich's been my Westphalian cousin of late. Come as his fiancée. Consider it practice," he said with a smile. Inwardly he chided himself for being impulsive. Would there be anything to gain? Probably only amusement and fun. "My hostess will be more comfortable if I do not come as a bachelor without my wife and will therefore forgive me for escorting an 'almost relative.' With Lady Regina away on holiday, you will be kind to be my guest." *There it is.*

Panic widened Anna's eyes. "I don't have anything to wear. I—I don't know how to act or speak... ." Her hands fiddled with the small drawstrings on her purse.

"Never you mind." He chuckled. "It's always good to have new experiences."

Anna stood speechless.

"Come, let's go out to the carriage. We can't keep our Pelham waiting, now can we?" He escorted her back outside to the yard. Pelham helped them in and closed the carriage door before climbing up into the driver's seat.

"I'll have Lady Regina's maid find something for you. It will be a pleasant evening." And, he hoped, a productive one, for everyone's sake.

CHAPTER 59

No. 20 St. James's Square, London

Anna felt regal in the rose satin-silk gown overlaid with lace. She sat in the carriage next to Langsford, who was quite handsome himself in white tie. She felt safe with him; still she wished Heinrich were there with them and the nightmare over. At least he was still in London.

They pulled up to a rusticated stone house with a solid ground floor supporting two stories above with Corinthian columns. The numerous windows tucked inside their arched recesses made Anna think of a kind uncle with bushy eyebrows.

She lifted the long skirt of her gown and, on Langsford's arm, gracefully made her way up the bowed steps to the double-doored entrance. The butler escorted them through the elegant tiled entry, passing a hall with a grand staircase and directly into a large, ornate room. Anna took a deep breath and held onto Langsford's arm tighter.

"Langsford," Lord Stanley exclaimed as they entered. "So glad you could come, and with a beautiful lady as well." The middle-aged earl began introductions. "You know Lord and Lady Mallory, Lord and Lady Pembroke. I don't believe you are acquainted with Lord Arthur Talbot or his wife, Lady Mary." Three other couples in all.

"My pleasure," Langsford greeted. Anna nodded with a trembling smile.

"Yes," Lady Clementine added. "The Talbots are down from Warwickshire, so I thought we'd have this little informal gathering to welcome them. I'm so pleased you could attend, Lord Langsford." Incredibly beautiful with red hair and white skin, she was only a few years older than Anna, and Anna couldn't take her eyes off her.

Anna perched on a brocaded settee and Langsford in an adjacent French armchair. She tried not to gawk at the furnishings, but the large Italian alabaster vases standing stoically beside the marvelous marble fireplace drew her attention. While the others talked and she automatically nodded and smiled, she stole glances around the room. She loved the walnut-framed screen and its embroidered panels of beadwork behind the countess. When Lady Margaret Pembroke spoke, it gave her an opportunity to stare at the leafy ferns within huge oriental pots that fanned around a marble pedestal holding a Greek bust on her right. Once she glanced down at the slippers on her feet and found herself admiring the fine wool carpet; loomed with a delicate pattern of pineapples, it stretched nearly wall to wall.

When the butler announced dinner, she followed everyone to the dining room through two fluted columns beside a double-leafed door, as if in a dream. One of the servants held the chair out for her and then gently scooted her in closer to the table. Langsford, seated opposite, smiled at her through the centerpieces of silver candlesticks woven with roses. She seemed to float within unreality.

She couldn't help but gawk at the furnishings around this oval room. Greek friezes skirted the lower half of the walls. Above the chair rails, pictures of flowers and angels floated in molded panels. In the large center panel, cherubs lifted their lyre to the heavens. She felt as if she were lifting upward with them.

"I see you like the room, my dear," Lord Stanley smiled at Anna.

Above another marble fireplace, a relief of Apollo and the nine Muses was centered with tall mirrors on either side. She tore herself away from that to reply. "It is lovely," she spoke in a near whisper, embarrassed.

"It was once a music room, as you can see, but we much prefer to dine here." He spread out his arms as though to encompass the room. "We have the ballroom on the next level for music."

"Perhaps you and your fiancé shall join us the next time we have an occasion to dance," the Lady Clementine invited.

"We should like that." Anna demurely looked down, wishing to avoid further conversation, when she saw the gold-edged china. The crystal stemware prismed light from the gas chandelier and made faint rainbows dance on the damask linen. It was all so elegant, she could hardly breathe. She forced herself to focus on what Lady Regina's second maid had explained to her earlier that evening. "Pick up the spoon or fork that is on the outside. Wait until the hostess eats first. Simply watch her to see what to do." The little old woman had been helpful not only giving advice, but with selecting and altering the gown she now wore.

Hours earlier, Anna had tried it on in Lady Regina's dressing room, the maid fastening it up the back. The old woman stepped back, smiling approval. "It's from Paris. The House of Worth."

"The ladies in my shop talk about Worth gowns. I never dreamt I'd ever wear one."

"My lady hasn't worn this for several seasons, but it's not out of style." The old maid motioned Anna to turn around. "Well, the bustle is on the small side, but I think it will do."

Anna completed her turn. "You're kind to help."

"Nonsense. I'm too old to travel with her ladyship, so when I'm left behind, I'm thrilled to have something beautiful to work on. Now hold up your arm; it fits fine except for right here in the bodice and the waist." She spoke with pins in her mouth, taking one out to mark the fabric. "I'll just take it in here and add another dart there. It will look as though it were sewn just for you." The short old woman stepped aside so Anna could admire herself in the mirror.

"It's beautiful."

"It is. You are too, m'lady."

"Oh, thank you—but I'm not a lady."

"You are as of now."

"But," Anna stressed, "the low neckline. And short sleeves."

"'Tis a formal dinner gown. Your neck is supposed to show. Here." She fastened a velvet neck piece she picked up from the dresser. "This lovely choker matches."

She walked to the bureau and opened a drawer. "You'll wear these gloves."

Anna took a glove to slip on. "I suppose."

"Let's remove the lace here and add a silk ribbon trim to change the look a bit. We don't want anyone to recognize the dress." The maid quickly finished sewing in spite of her gnarled fingers, and the dress fit like a glove.

Wearing it now at dinner, Anna graced the room with her own elegance, although she didn't realize it.

A waiter handed her a menu, bringing her back to the present, and as the maid had forewarned, it was in French, which she couldn't read. If that were to be the case, the maid suggested she should select the first choice for the first course, the second offering for the second course and so on, to appear as though she understood. She ended up with courses of salmon, lamb, pâté, and several other foods she didn't recognize. Much to Anna's relief, the hostess ignored her and spoke primarily to the men at the table of ten.

After dinner, the ladies rose to adjourn for coffee in the front parlor. Uneasy that Langsford would no longer be nearby, she was grateful when he walked over to kiss her hand before she joined the rest of the ladies. "What if I say something wrong?" she asked with panic in her voice.

"You'll do fine. Keep answers short, then ask questions or change the topic," he coached. "You deal with ladies like these every day in your shop." He ushered her through the columned doors, sending her on her way. She tipped up her chin and entered the parlor.

CHAPTER 60

Langsford caught up with the men as they settled in the drawing room across the hall.

Two servants carrying trays offered drinks as the earl turned to his other three guests. "Gentlemen, if you would be so kind as to excuse us. Enjoy your smokes and do imbibe. Langsford and I have something to discuss briefly, but we shall rejoin you shortly." The older man escorted him through a door and into an adjacent study.

Langsford sat in the ante room and spotted a porcelain regimental pipe on the side table. "That's the second such pipe I've seen in a month. It represents a German regiment?"

"It does." Stanley sat in the matching tapestried chair, leaning forward. "Take a close look at the detail."

"What craftsmanship."

"Lady Clementine's close friend married a German, Rolf Nebelung. That was his regimental pipe from the Austro-Prussian War. How long ago was that, do you know?"

"I believe in sixty-six, so eighteen years is my guess."

"That sounds right. We became good friends." He paused, remembering. "During Bismarck's war on Catholics, he was arrested one night."

"Arrested? Why?" Curious that Bismarck's name came up.

"Because Rolf taught at a Catholic school. He was jailed for several years." The earl shook his head. "You fight for your king or queen and then find yourself arrested for teaching religion to children. An accepted religion, nothing barbaric or pagan."

"A sad state of affairs."

"When Rolf was released from prison, he was so ill he only lived another month. My Clementine said he died in his wife's arms. Afterward, his widow sent his pipe to me. She knew how I respected her husband—a man of honor."

Langsford set the pipe back in its stand. "Sounds like a man of fine character."

"I find it impossible to respect someone as vile as Bismarck," the earl opined.

Interesting remark considering everything else I know, Langsford thought. "You are not the only person who dislikes the Iron Chancellor."

"That you may put in your pipe and smoke it," Stanley punned with a laugh since Langsford had pulled out his own pipe to light. But Langsford felt a warning in the pit of his stomach. *Could Stanley be so anti-Bismarck that he would head a committee to assassinate the man?* Did the man in the cloak work for the earl or was it the earl? His instinct told him to watch Stanley closely. He would have to find out tonight.

Stanley continued. "It's bad enough that the economy is ruined in Europe, but Bismarck's laws are breaking the backs of German businessmen."

"I heard talk of that on my last trip to the Rhineland."

"We have family in Europe, you know. My wife's half-brothers. My marriage to her caused some uproar at the time—you did know that she was not peerage?"

Langsford did know, but chose to claim ignorance of that scandal. "I had no idea."

"Difficult to believe given her beauty and spirit. She appears well bred," he said with great pride. "I was willing to do anything to have her as my wife."

Langsford wondered if the earl was willing to do anything *for* his wife and her family. She was, in fact, one of the most beautiful women Langsford had ever met. She had a beguiling ability to create total weakness in the knees of most men. With her auburn hair, porcelain skin, and flashing green eyes, men would do anything simply to be in her presence, much to their wives' annoyance. "She *is* a classic beauty whom everyone adores," he said. "Especially Lady Regina." He smiled, remembering the two women together, filled with excited talk about her upcoming wedding to Langsford

"Yes, she's a beautiful thoroughbred."

Langsford steered back to the topic of Bismarck. "So you've family in Germany? What do they think of the chancellor?"

"My brother-in-law, Samuel, is there. A mere businessman, I know you understand. You dabble in business for fun, but he's a commoner and must work. We don't bring that part of the family to the attention of anyone here in London. Unfortunately he's lost much of his business due to the German tariffs. Everyone there is affected, which in turn affects English trade, I'm told. It's ludicrous."

"I've heard bits and pieces."

"But," he chuckled hard, "at least Samuel certainly escaped the Kulturkampf. He's definitely not Catholic."

"He's English, so the odds are he's not."

The earl smiled and took a large sip of port. "If the family business fails, I must step in and save them. It's what's expected but it galls me to think that I might need to throw my sterling their way or, worse, bring the family to live under my roof. Yet what am I to do?"

"All countries are intertwined with business and investments these days," reminded Langsford. "Whether we wish it or not, we are tied to Europe, to Argentina, and the United States. The world is no longer small, either physically or financially."

"It has always amused me that you enjoy investing. Few would dare be so bold to pursue such an unseemly venture. Your father would not have approved."

Langsford puffed on his pipe, ignoring the insult with a laugh. "I look upon it as a game, much like poker or chess. There is both skill and luck involved in all three, and I enjoy them all."

Langsford tried to figure out what to say next. *If Stanley is leader of the committee, I dare not warn him about a traitor.* He needed to find another way to explain his urgent message.

But Stanley abruptly brought the conversation to its original point. "You had something important you wan—"

CHAPTER 61

No. 20 St. James's Square, London

While Langsford and Stanley sat in the ante room, the ladies sipped their coffee and chatted in the parlor. The countess sat in a French-armed chair, with Anna directly opposite. Lady Margaret Pembroke sat along the side, with Lady Jennie Mallory and Lady Mary Talbot in between.

Anna's heart clutched when the hostess spoke directly to her. "You look elegant, Anna. Your gown is reminiscent of a Worth I've seen somewhere."

Anna blushed, self-conscious. She softly replied, "Thank you, Lady Clementine. Yes, it is a Worth." She hoped the newly ribboned bodice was enough to disguise the original look.

"Well," Lady Clementine conceded, "this one on you is stunning. No one could wear it as well, not even your soon-to-be cousin, Lady Regina."

"Thank you." Silence was safe, Langsford had reminded her, so she offered no more.

"Tell us. Where did you meet your intended? I did not know Regina had a Westphalian cousin. What surprises there are!"

"He is related on the Langsford side. We met here in London, not Germany."

To her huge relief, the countess immediately turned toward Lady Margaret. "Speaking of Germany, I hear you recently traveled to France and Germany. Do tell, how was the trip?"

Anna listened politely as Lady Margaret recounted her journey. Her respite, however, was not long lived. "But I'm curious to hear, Anna. Exactly how *did* you meet your intended?" Lady Margaret asked.

Anna tried to hold her teacup steady. "He came to London. On business."

"Was für ein Glück für Sie."

Anna did not understand.

"You do not speak German?" Lady Margaret asked.

"No, but I suppose I shall learn soon enough."

"La langue d'amour est le français!" Lady Clementine added.

"I am terrible at languages," she confessed, blushing. Her school taught sewing and arithmetic, not languages.

"How can you travel abroad if you don't speak the native tongues?" Lady Jennie looked concerned. "Everyone should speak not only French and German, but Spanish and Italian as well. Am I right, ladies?"

The other three agreed in turn, with a "Yes," an "Indeed," and a "Oui."

Anna forced a laugh. "You are all right. I am sure my fiancé will be a big aid in helping me overcome my inadequacies."

"This is a—" the lovely Lady Clementine began, interrupted when the massive explosion slammed the room. Clouds of heavy smoke and debris blasted through the parlor, leaving gaping holes where windows were a split second before. The world hung suspended in a loud, frozen silence.

CHAPTER 62

No. 20 St. James's Square, London

In a shattered instant, Anna was launched across the room, turbulence shoving her within flying shards of glass and splintering wood. Propelled by the unseen force in an instant, she suddenly found herself on top of her hostess, draped at an angle and clinging to the back of the chair. She couldn't breathe.

The countess herself was flattened under Anna and against the chair's back, which was shoved, tilted backward into the far wall. Anna saw blood running down Lady Clementine's face. They both gasped and instantly began coughing in roiling dust.

The air turned into a slightly lighter cloud and Anna saw the room strewn with broken vases, cracked pottery, and damaged sculptures, the pineapple rug buried. Lady Jennie sat lopsided beside her seat, her face contorted with screams Anna could not hear. Lady Mary lay sprawled face down on the floor. Lady Margaret, cowering in her corner chair farthest away, violently trembled her empty saucer from her lap to the floor. It silently smashed.

Anna's ears screeched with a ringing pain that crushed in on her skull. Her knees buckled and she desperately gripped the back of the chair.

Seconds trickled by until the men, panic driving them forward, raced to the ladies. Coughing as they entered the thick dust-air, they took the women one by one, holding them, picking pieces of debris off them, attempting to soothe them while at the same time burying their own fear as their minds scrambled to answer the question they all shared: *What happened?*

In quick succession, two more explosions ripped through the square outside. Screams and cries swelled and yells resounded.

"Oh, dear God!" cried the Earl of Exeter. "Clementine, my love!" His dazed wife could not hear him. She was sobbing, tears mixed with the blood flowing from her cheek. A gaping slash with hanging skin was an inch below her eye, incongruous with her elegance.

Langsford reached for Anna, still clinging tight onto the chair's back. A long shard of glass stuck from her torn gown at the top of her shoulder blade, blood seeping through the fine fabric into a widening red.

"Get her off my wife, Langsford!" Stanley squawked.

Langsford focused on Anna. "I'm here." He gently touched her, realizing that if he held her, he might drive any glass deeper into her. Unlike Lady Clementine, she had faced away from the blast, partially protected by her chair which now lay on its side, its back shredded.

Langsford wanted to get her out of the room. He gently released her fingers one by one from the chair and steadied her step by step over sharp fragments and splinters of debris, back into the undamaged dining room. "Sit here, Anna. You have glass in your shoulder. Don't move." She looked at him, questioning and dazed. He realized she couldn't hear. He mouthed his words, "Stay here. Do not move." She nodded and yelled, "What happened?"

He shook his head. "I don't know," he mouthed. "Stay here."

She reached out and grabbed his coat sleeve, her eyes pleading. She started to shake.

He reached into his waistcoat and pulled out a small silver flask. "Here. Drink. Whiskey."

Eyes wide, Anna shook more violently. He helped steady her hand, and she swallowed a large gulp then instantly coughed.

"Once more."

She obeyed. She seemed to calm.

"Th—thank you." She yelled, handing him the flask. He put it in his pocket and moved out into the hallway. He needed to see what was going on and figure where it was safe. He shoved a large piece of shattered wood to the side and climbed out over debris in the opening of what had been the front door.

Pandemonium.

People screaming and crying. Panicky horses lunging and rearing against the braked wheels of cabs and carriages. A horse with a driverless hack galloping headlong into a lamp-post, falling to its knees as the cab whipped around and landed on its side. People were running, unsure of where to go. "Are you all right?" a cry in the night. Shock kept most men strong and manhood kept them brave. Langsford had counted three explosions. So far.

Police arrived. *At least Scotland Yard is near.* Men were gathering in front of the house. Langsford stepped down to join them. Bombs, the police said. A bobby reported an explosion at the Army and Navy Clubhouse. "The building's got no windows left. No lights."

"Junior Carlton Club house!" cried out a witness, running to join the group. "On the corner!"

Langsford turned to look at the earl's home. The stone had held against the bomb, but like the Junior Carlton Club only two doors away, the blown windows and doors were dark holes. He worried more bombs would blow up.

He rushed back inside, concerned he'd left Anna too long, wanting to get her to safety.

The ladies in the ruined parlor were now hysterical. Stanley sat holding his shaking wife's hand as a servant dabbed at her cheek with bits of cotton. "That's enough for now," the earl ordered the young maid. "You're hurting her. Leave her be."

Langsford asked the maid to come with him.

"Of course, m'lord." She obediently followed with her bowl of warm water and cotton.

Anna sat rigid, just as he'd left her. "What was it?" she said, her voice still louder than it needed to be, her hearing obviously still compromised.

"Wot did ya see, m'lord?" the maid asked.

"Bombs went off. A good bit of damage, but all the buildings are standing and it appears people are mainly frightened," he replied, doing his best to downplay the scene. "Let's remove this piece of glass and get a bandage on her, shall we?" He hovered over Anna's shoulder. "This maid will help, won't you?"

"Yes, m'lord." Gently she tore the gown from the protruding glass. "Why, that 'n's like a small knife blade, 'tis. I can take it out easy."

"Mind you, it'll come out clean, but we must staunch the blood flow quickly."

The maid handed him her cotton pieces and quickly yanked out the glass. Anna yelped and Langsford immediately pressed the cloths tight on the wound as the blood gushed onto the white fabric. He pressed hard to stop the bleeding, and gradually, it slowed.

"Good," he said, relieved.

The maid rinsed more cotton in the water and cleaned the wound.

He handed Anna the flask one more time, and she gratefully took another, longer, drink. He knew the burning of the alcohol in her stomach would take her mind off her painful shoulder. She coughed again as the whiskey did its job.

"This is going to burn, Anna," he warned, unsure she heard. He poured the rest of the whiskey onto the wound, making her yell.

"It's clean now."

The maid tore more clean cotton. After pressing a piece tightly over the wound, she wrapped strips around Anna's shoulder, tying the ends. She took the pieces of the dress and tied those together with the now-convenient silk ribbons the old maid had sewn earlier. Wordlessly, she curtsied, leaving with her bowl of blood-tinged water.

"How do you feel?" he mouthed.

"It throbs." She tried to look at her shoulder. "I want to go home... ." She trembled again, her eyes wide.

"Of course." He mouthed his words slowly. "Pelham parked the carriage on the other side of the square." He wasn't sure how much she understood. "Too much debris in the street. We need to go to him." He stood up. "Can you walk?"

"Yes." She yelled, and rose, steadying herself for a moment, her balance off. "I think."

He helped her maneuver from the oval dining room into the blown-out front entry. Pieces of the once-elegant doors and glass side panels were strewn all over the tiled floor, spreading as far as the grand staircase. They picked their way through to find the Earl standing and staring at the destruction.

"I must take Anna home, Stanley." His host made no reply. He kept moving Anna toward the gaping hole where the door had been. He had to get her out of there, and hung onto her as they walked through debris and out onto the street toward the north side of the square where Pelham waited.

Suddenly without warning, the air ripped apart. Another horrendous boom seized the night, crashing in on them. Horses reared. A team, breaking from its traces, bolted coachless down the cluttered street. People screamed and ran, pushing one another out of the way in panic. A passenger fell from a phaeton on the south side, and on the east, a cabbie lost his reins and hung onto his seat, helpless to control his bolting steed.

Langsford and Anna halted dead in their tracks. He wrapped his arms protectively around her while chaos churned around them. Frantically, he looked about. Uncertain where the danger was, he stayed his ground, holding her. Someone galloped up from the southeast with booming words that carried through the sudden silence. "Scotland Yard! Bombed!"

Everyone's attention turned toward the latest calamity, merely a half mile distant.

Dear God! Heinrich's there! Shocked, he repeated aloud. "Scotland Yard!"

Anna read his lips. "No! No, no, no!" she screamed.

In an instant, she tore out of his embrace and raced south down the street. A fire engine pulled by madly galloping horses thundered around the corner, but Anna did not hear it. Langsford caught her and pulled her to the curb. They jarred to a rigid halt as the fire brigade blew by.

"Come! The carriage." He carried her toward the north side where Pelham yelled.

"Looord Laaangsford! Heere!" Pelham bellowed, both hands gripping the bridles of his two frightened horses. The coachman stood in front of the team, nearly lifted off his feet as the animals tried to rear.

Langsford willed his own panic still. He had to get Anna to safety.

They got to Pelham, who hung onto the reins with iron-tight fists. "I can't let go." The team tried to pull their heads from his grip, their eyes wide with fear, hooves beating a frantic dance in place. The carriage brake held.

Langsford shoved Anna up onto her seat.

"I can't let go to raise the tops," Pelham tilted his head at the landau's double tops, down from earlier.

"No matter. Get us out of here!" He swung up into the landau that rocked hard against its brakes, slamming the door shut.

Pelham leapt up to his seat a split second before the horses stood on their hind legs. He released the hard-set brake and instantly the team jumped, but one horse bolted sideways, bringing the other to its knees. Pelham wrestled with the reins as more than a ton of horseflesh panicked. He got the fallen horse up and headed the pair in the same direction. Once underway, he could barely steer and needed to work the brake to slow for turns. They galloped headlong toward Piccadilly. People jumped out of their way and drivers without crazed horses yielded the street. The team automatically barreled onto Old Bond, knowing the way home. Pelham let them race while his passengers hung on.

"It's rough, m'lord," Pelham tried to shout over his shoulder. "Sit tight!"

"Just get us home," Langsford hollered.

They galloped the short mile in record time. Pelham swung his weight hard to pull the team left toward the front of the residence. Once on Brook Street, the horses winded, they slowed to a trot and impatiently halted, blowing and snorting. Langsford and Anna stepped out on their own.

"Nice job of not letting this turn into our runaway deaths."

"Yes, m'lord," answered his tremulous driver.

Quickly inside, he told Barnes to call the old maid to come assist, but Anna protested. "Scotland Yard. I have to go... ."

"No. Too dangerous."

Anna stood forlornly in the foyer, her dress hanging lopsided, the hem torn. She tried to speak, but her words drowned in convulsing gasps. Langsford held her tight, knowing full well there was little he could do to comfort her.

The old maid scurried into the large foyer. "My lord in heaven," she gasped, rushing when she saw Anna. "She's bleeding!" She turned her gently, taking her from Langsford's arms. "What happened?" she asked, her eyes wide.

"A bomb. She'll recover in a day or so."

"'Tis not good for her heart."

"Take her upstairs and get her comfortable, then bring her into the library by the fire. I'll see that she gets a strong sherry. She'll stay the night."

Nodding, the old woman gently took Anna. "I'll tend to her." The maid ushered her up the stairs.

Langsford's thoughts whirled. During the wild ride home he recounted the number of bombs he'd heard. At least four. Maybe more. All exploding within minutes of each other, the last at Scotland Yard. He wearily hauled himself up the staircase. So deep in thought, he hadn't noticed he had no hat or gloves. When he realized his servant was behind him, he requested a whiskey be brought to the library. His man instantly turned about to descend and oblige. Langsford continued up to the hallway. *Why St. James's Square? What prompted the bombings?*

Tweed trotted out of the library, tail waving a grand hello. His master automatically stroked the dog's head as they entered the room together.

"Tweed, I'm a befuddled mess." He sat in the closest wingback while the dog panted agreement. "I don't know if Heinrich was injured or killed tonight. Even if he's alive, I have no proof of his innocence for the CID director in the morning. Anna is injured. And the bombs. Why? Who?"

The room was still except for the crackling of the fire and the steady ticking of the mantel clock. For minutes he sat surrounded by comparative silence.

Could it be an act of the committee? If so, then the Earl of Exeter couldn't be involved. But there were other bombs... . It didn't make sense.

"Your whiskey, m'lord," Barnes's voice broke into his reverie.

"Thank you," he said, taking the glass from the tray. "Bring a large sherry, a *Jerez Dulce*, if you would, for Anna. She'll be joining me shortly."

"Is she all right, your lordship? I understand there was a bombing of such?"

"Indeed, there were several." He sat back and sipped his drink. "Anna shall be fine but her heart is hurt more than her person. Friends were injured, and one in particular may be severely injured or killed."

"Most terrible. Dreadful. We all heard what we thought were cannon shots," Barnes explained. "Being Friday and the like, we thought it might be a ceremony near the War Office or the Army and Navy Club house. But they were *quite* loud, even for cannons."

"Very loud."

"I shall have the sherry here post haste."

Langsford stared into the flickering fireplace.

The Army and Navy Club—so near the earl's residence. Why blow up other buildings? Why blow up Scotland Yard? The War Office across the street from the Junior Carlton Club filled with government officials. The earl and Mallaby both together at dinner. *There it is.* He sat upright. The Border Collie jumped up, eager to participate. The bombs were directed at Britain's government and important individuals. Acts of terrorism!

He rose and walked closer to the fire, feeling a chill. It couldn't be the German government. "What would Germany gain, instigating a war?" Tweed cocked his head as his master spoke aloud. "Germany strives to be like us, with trade, power, and colonies. Bismarck isn't stupid. He knows that unlike France or Austria, we can't be defeated." This made no sense. Could it have something to do with Summerhill's committee and not the German government? Wanting us to blame Bismarck? "No, Tweed," he told the dog who sat on the hearth listening with ears perked. "They want to *assassinate* him, not incriminate him. Unless … they *want* to incriminate Germany… ." Too far-fetched.

Who else, then? "The Irish? They bombed us in February. Tonight was much more severe … still …"

Deep in thought, he hadn't noticed the sherry had been served until Anna entered the room, a warm knitted shawl over her shoulders and injury. Her eyes were sunken and dark.

"Come, Anna. Sit. Have some sherry."

Silently, she obeyed. She took the crystal stemware from him and sipped. "Can we go to Scotland Yard now?" Her voice was still loud. "Henry might be injured. He has no one except … except us. Surely they'll allow us to see him?"

He thought it best to warn her. "From the size of the explosion at Scotland Yard, you should be ready to accept the worst."

She shook her head. "No. He is strong. Nothing could harm him… ." Her sherry spilled over the rim of the glass and he gently took it from her.

"It's too dangerous to go anywhere tonight."

"I don't care." She stood up, her voice odd and loud. "I'm going to Scotland Yard if I have to walk."

The old maid stood silently by the door and caught Langsford's silent, nodded request. She gently went to the exhausted girl.

"Come on now, miss, off to bed. There's a cozy room ready, and I made up the bed with lavender-scented bedding. Come mornin' you'll be better," she twittered and escorted Anna out of the library.

Come morning, thought Langsford, *and I have nothing.*

CHAPTER 63

No. 12 Grosvenor Square, London

People moved around their city, fear on the fringes of their lives the next morning.

The paper told the story. After the bombing of the Earl of Exeter's residence, a bomb exploded on the windowsill of a crowded room at the War Office inside the Junior Carlton Club. Another simultaneously detonated in the basement. The next blast hit the Army and Navy Club on the corner of Georges Street and Pall Mall, two doors from the earl's home.

The final discharge, the largest, had been placed in a public urinal outside detective offices in Scotland Yard. The corner of the building, which was composed of thick brickwork, was blown off to a height of thirty feet. A brougham standing opposite the point of the explosion was wrecked and the coachman injured, the horse killed. A policeman standing nearby was blown across the yard and severely injured.

Another bomb planted at the Yard had failed to explode due to a defective fuse.

Later during the night, bobbies discovered sixteen packets of dynamite in Trafalgar Square at the base of Nelson's column. They frantically yanked the fuses free.

Sixteen persons so far were injured by the explosions, five of them seriously, though there was no final tally yet. Military sentinels guarded government buildings. Everyone entering was thoroughly searched, including all bags and parcels.

"Terrorism," people cried. Never had so many bombs exploded so close together in time and distance. Someone wanted to destroy London.

Scotland Yard was thrown into complete consternation. They not only had failed to protect British subjects, they failed to protect themselves—a dark blemish on their capabilities. Scotland Yard inspectors were frantically talking to witnesses and sorting through the debris for clues.

Langsford put down his "Extra" edition of the paper, absorbing all he'd just read while at the breakfast table. He wasn't surprised his message to Sir Vincent, inquiring of Heinrich's well-being, had gone unanswered, given the circumstances. The director of the CID most surely was consumed with the bombing investigations. Commissioner Sir Edmund Henderson, however, did reply.

> *All efforts centered on bombings.*
> *No time to discuss Prussian's extradition.*

Langsford read the note immediately when Barnes brought it in. He folded it in half and creased it sharply several times between his thumb and forefinger. At the very least he'd hoped for word on how Heinrich was. Nothing. If everyone was focused entirely on the bombings, did that mean Heinrich, if he were alive, would *not* be extradited Monday? Langsford had only questions and no answers.

Pelham had driven Anna home earlier. "Stay home and recover," Langsford said, closing the carriage door. "You've had your nerves shattered and you need rest. I'll let you know what I find out." She looked like a broken doll as the carriage rolled away from the curb. He was not sure he felt much better than Anna. The chances of getting the police to arrest the committee members now were nil.

He left the table and walked through the house toward the stable yard, Tweed padding behind him. Pelham had already returned from Bermondsey and stood chatting with Mike the groom, who was tying one of the horses to an iron wall ring. He pulled up the wooden chair.

"How are you after last night, m'lord? Quite a time."

"No worse for wear. Thank you, again, for getting us home safely."

"The ponies were wild, they were." He tilted his head toward the large horse. "They got some bumps and scrapes, but nothin' that won't be healin'." He sat on a hay bale and Tweed went over for an extra pat.

"How's it goin' about Heinrich?"

"I don't know. I've made no progress. The police are busy with the bombings."

"Not good, then."

"He'll be extradited on Monday, if he's even still alive after the bombing."

"Oh, bless the man." Pelham looked down at his dusty boots.

"If the committee is set to leave Tuesday and Heinrich isn't there, they'll be suspicious."

"They'd likely disappear, I reckon."

"That can't happen. If only I could discover their leader." Langsford was at a standstill, and that annoyed him. He reached for his pipe, but didn't have it. Gads, he'd dropped it somewhere. He certainly was rattled.

"What if we cornered George and made him tell us?"

"He hasn't committed a crime. He'd be a fool to confess to the plot." He stroked his moustache and stared blankly as the groom smeared a white salve on the black horse's skinned knee. "I could force the issue. What if we found a way to get George to the Earl of Exeter's residence? There's a good chance the spy will give it away when he recognizes whoever the servant is. We will watch closely, then know who the last traitor is."

"Spy George is the only one besides Summerhill that we know for sure can do that. And we can't ask Summerhill—too risky," Pelham reasoned, petting the dog.

Silently Langsford worried what he could not voice, that Stanley might be the leader with the money behind the plot and had a bomb planted to make him appear uninvolved. If so, this was doubly horrific, risking his own wife as well. He, himself, conveniently was not near the bomb when it exploded ....

Pelham walked over to inspect what the groom had done, and Tweed again circled the tied horse. "Put 'im back in the stall," he told Mike. "Walk 'im out again in a couple hours to keep that swelling down." He patted the horse's rump as he walked by, returning to sit by Langsford.

"How will you get George to the residence?"

Langsford started, his thoughts interrupted. After a second he answered. "I've an idea, Pelham. A bit far-fetched."

"A far-fetched idea is better than no idea, m'lord." Tweed came over, his tail wagging agreement.

CHAPTER 64

Pratt's Club, London

Pelham hitched up the two horses reserved for occasions when a four-in-hand team was required, one over twenty years old and the other only three. Langsford sat in the open carriage, thinking how the semiretired horse teamed with the younger, less experienced one matched his far-fetched scheme—both unbalanced. At least he needed no disguise for this bit of detective work. He only needed to obfuscate.

They started at Pratt's, where Langsford gave a brief description of George to the head steward, a nervous little man who stood stiffly in his tailed suit as they spoke in the entryway. The surprised man replied, "A most unusual request." He thought a minute. "I can't imagine why you shouldn't know his real name. Of course you would never use it here. Jack Marston." The man appeared concerned. "He's not here now, I'm afraid. He works later on Saturdays. Due here by three."

"I need to borrow him and can't promise he will be here on time. If he's late, or doesn't get back at all, put the onus on me. I need his help." Langsford made everything up as he spoke. "This is related to last night's bombing, in a manner of speaking," Langsford bent the truth. Sometimes he surprised even himself. "He may have witnessed something of import."

"I see," the steward replied, though the frown on his face said otherwise. "Lives at a boarding house. Wait here while I obtain his address." He disappeared into a side room where Langsford could see a desk. After a few minutes, the steward returned, handing over a piece of paper. "His address, then. Very well. I won't count on him." He walked him to the entrance, remained standing at attention and closed the door behind him.

Langsford returned to the carriage. "Confirms the boarding house—11 Artillery Row," he told Pelham. "Let's hope he's there."

Pelham opened the door for his employer. "Did you find out his name?"

"It's Jack."

"Jack. Funny, I've become rather fond of calling him George."

The perplexed Jack hesitantly entered the seedy boarding house's sitting room. His trousers were well worn and his shoes scuffed. His coat was hastily buttoned with one not all the way through its buttonhole. His wrist bones showed below each cuff, the ill-fitting coat too small. "George here, at your service, your lordship. You requested me?" He was clearly uncomfortable.

"Yes, may I call you Jack?"

The young man nodded.

"You have, uh, impressed me with your work at Pratt's and I have a favor to ask."

"I am at your disposal," he replied, standing erect.

"I'd like to borrow you for a bit."

"I am afraid I must be at work before long," he answered formally.

"I've received your leave from Pratt's head steward. I'm willing to pay you three shillings for your efforts."

"Then by all means, m'lord," he replied eagerly. "As long as it is permitted by my boss, I mean 'employer,' I am pleased to oblige."

That was almost too easy, Langsford thought, like handing candy to a baby. This fellow had no idea what was about to happen. But then neither did he, truth be told.

"There's a servant I'm interested in hiring. I'm told you know him, so I need you to point him out."

"That's an odd request." Jack tilted his head, then as an afterthought added, "What's his name?"

"I don't know. His employer is reducing staff, so if you can identify him it would be useful." Langsford couldn't think of any other reason to take Jack to the earl's residence. Hiring staff was something a butler would do, but Jack didn't necessarily know that. Far-fetched or not, it would have to suffice. He had to get Jack face-to-face with Lord Stanley's servants.

"Which household is it?"

"The Earl of Exeter's." *There it is. The first moment of truth.*

"The earl? Why, I dunna think I know anybody there." Jack's face registered surprise, not suspicion. *Maybe he doesn't know the man he met with the other night works there. What a shock it will be when he sees him.*

"Perhaps your friend has recently come into his employment without your knowledge. Why don't we go see."

"All right, then. As long as you've cleared me at Pratt's. I wouldn't care to lose my job."

"You need not concern yourself about your job," Langsford assured him. No, his concerns should be about other activities.

CHAPTER 65

No. 20 St. James's Square, London

The landau with Langsford and Jack rolled up in front of No. 20 St. James's Square. Much of the debris from the night before had been swept into piles of rubble to make the road passable. The house stood solid, its scorched and blackened stones undamaged but the windowless ground floor appeared vacuous. Carpenters worked at replacing the wooden jambs at the gaping hole where the front door belonged. Other workers were beginning to glaze one window.

Langsford got out, whispering to Pelham as the coachman opened the door. "Let's see if my far-fetched idea works."

"Still better than no idea, m'lord," he repeated, turning to tether the horses.

Langsford watched Jack hop down from the landau. He was unsuspecting. *For a couple bob, he could easily be bought for any spy job.*

The three walked through the open doorway directly into the hall. A maid, coming from an adjacent room, startled, uncertain as she looked at the odd trio. "May I help you, uh, gentlemen?" she greeted. "Let me find the butler for you."

"Not necessary. I'm calling on Lord Stanley. My card."

"Yes, your lordship. May I ask you to wait, uh ... Usually guests wait in the parlor, but after last night, the room is in much disarray." She hesitated a moment, then suggested another venue.

"Shall you follow me past the stairway into the drawing room? I will then have the butler alert the earl."

She deposited them in the same room where the gentlemen had adjourned following dinner less than twenty-four hours ago. The door to the small anteroom off the side was open as it had been left when he and Stanley rushed toward the front of the house split seconds after the explosion. Langsford spied his tobacco pouch and pipe on the floor beside the chair where he had been sitting. The porcelain pipe remained in its stand and instincts that warned him last night from discussing the committee resurfaced again. *In a few minutes we shall see.* He stood with his companions, waiting.

Stanley appeared in the doorway, surprised to see his friend with two men he did not recognize. He scowled at the driver and the other in his ill-fitting clothes.

It was clear he didn't recognize Jack. Langsford had half expected them to know each other but they didn't. He was disappointed and relieved at the same time.

"Good afternoon." Langsford gave his widest smile. "Thank you for seeing us without an invitation." Pelham and Jack stood silently along the wall. "May I have a brief word in private?"

"This is a rather inopportune time." He stared keenly at the other two. He looked back at Langsford. "The workers have this house disheveled almost as much as that blasted bomb did, so make this quick." The earl escorted him into the anteroom as he had the previous evening.

"How is the countess today?" Langsford inquired once the door was closed. "Have her nerves settled?"

"Yes, finally. The doctor managed to give her something." Stanley remained standing, his expression rigid. "She is worried that dreadful cut has marred her beauty. Hopefully all will heal without any trace." He shook his head in dismay.

"I'm sure she will heal fine. But that is not why I have come unannounced—for which I extend my apologies."

"I would hope. Why are you here with those two?"

"We didn't finish what we were discussing prior to the bombing."

"Yes. Something was urgent, though nothing hardly seems so now." He stayed next to the door, impatient.

"I must be so bold as to request a favor, and it involves those two men out there."

"A favor? What sort of favor?"

"Your safety might still be in jeopardy, even after last night." He bluffed. "I'd like you to assemble your entire staff into the dining room. One of the men accompanying me can help identify a suspicious individual. Someone perhaps connected to the bombings."

"This sounds stupidly dangerous."

"The other man is my coachman and he will stand guard. The younger man is not aware of why he is here. I doubt there will be any fuss," Langsford lied.

"This is unacceptable. I think not."

"Originally, Scotland Yard was to pursue my concern today, but the bombings have discombobulated everything. So I am following up myself after discussing it with the commissioner, Sir Henderson," he spun a version of his tale. After all, he *had* discussed the case with the commissioner. Just not this particular action. Still, it couldn't hurt to add weight to his request.

The Earl of Exeter stood glaring at his friend. "Have you gone daff?"

"I'm afraid not. I need to be sure that this man is *not* covertly connected with any of your staff members. That's all. It will take more time for you to gather everyone than it will for me to see if that man out there recognizes anyone."

"My staff—I can vouch for them. I have very high standards." Stanley, indignant, took a step toward the door.

"Of course you do. So that is why, by having them meet this individual, it will be possible to clear all of them of any suspicion. If you and I do not do this today, then eventually Scotland Yard will come and do it," he fabricated. He wasn't sure Scotland Yard would follow up on anything, except to extradite Heinrich, *if* he were alive. "It's best to get this done and over with now before they come in and disrupt your home far more than I."

"Very well," Stanley growled with an ever-increasing scowl. "Let's get this charade over with. I'll have my butler gather everyone." Saying nothing more, he marched directly through the drawing room, past the two waiting men. In the entry hall, he yelled for the butler.

Langsford requested Pelham and Jack to stay put while Stanley's staff noisily assembled across the hall. He walked over to the dining room entrance, watching as they chattered on, wondering why they had been called from their duties. "It must have sumthin' to do with the bombin's," a footman surmised. The upstairs maid complained that she had plenty of work to do and had no time for foolishness. The scullery maid smiled and replied, "I'm glad fer the break." The butler hushed them all.

A few minutes later, after the stable hands had pulled off their dirty work boots and hastily yanked on cleaner ones, the outdoor help entered. Most from the stable yard had never been inside, let alone in this oval room with its gilt and grand ceiling. They stood silent, awkward and uncomfortable, gawking at the cherubs and

Apollo. Once the butler confirmed all were present, Langsford walked across the hall and motioned for Pelham and Jack to join the group in the dining room.

Together the three men walked opposite the line of household staff. *Which man was it?*

"Point out your friend, Jack," Langsford urged. He and Jack perused the staff while Pelham kept his eye on the wait-servant, braced for anything once Jack recognized the hidden traitor. They walked past every servant in the line. Several nodded, unsure when Langsford walked by. No reaction either toward Jack or from him.

"Aye. I told ya, I never knew no one who worked in this grand 'ouse." He'd slipped again into his lower-class dialect. The staff, still in the dark as to why they were standing there, shifted uneasily, looking at one another.

Disappointed, Langsford turned and nodded to the earl who was standing in the doorway watching. "Thank you. We are done." He turned to the staff. "Thank you all for gathering here." The butler dismissed them back to their stations and tasks at hand, and with bustling talk, they noisily filed from the room.

"You are correct about your staff, Stanley. They are trustworthy."

"As I told you," he smugly retorted.

"Breathe easy. You have no security issues here."

"Except for last night's bomb," the earl sarcastically replied.

"True. Let me ask you. Have you ever seen this man, Jack, anywhere? At Pratt's?"

"I couldn't tell you that I have seen him ever. I'm not involved with my servants here. I certainly pay no attention to the wait staff there."

Langsford was forced to conclude there was no connection

between Jack and the earl or his staff. He was stymied. *Then who came back here that night?*

Thanking the earl for indulging him and apologizing again for the intrusion, Langsford and Pelham led Jack from the dining room. His mind kept churning. *There must be someone living here who isn't on staff but is hiding within the household.* He was thinking through different scenarios where he might investigate the servant's quarters personally as Stanley escorted them closer to the front entrance. *If only I had a Scotland Yard inspector with me, we could search the entire place.* Once he left, Stanley wouldn't permit another search.

Her sweet voice preceded Lady Clementine as she and her maid descended the staircase. "Oh, our home. Just look... ." She was pale, her high cheekbone covered with a bandage. It was obvious the bombing had taken its toll on her, and he felt her agony. Cuts on her face or not, she was breathtaking. His companions stopped, caught in her beauty—Pelham inhaled abruptly and Jack stood wide-eyed, bemusing Langsford with their reactions.

"There, there, my sweet," the earl soothed as she walked toward him.

"The house is fast getting repaired, m'lady," comforted the maid beside her.

The maid! She'd not been in the dining room, Langsford realized with a shock. The maid? Could it be? *Disguised in a cloak and top hat.* He caught his breath.

The countess looked at her husband as tears rolled down her flushed cheeks. "I shan't rest until ..." She paled. "You?!" She gasped in horror. "What are *you* doing here?"

The earl, exasperated by the strange events in his once-tranquil, elegant home, had reached his limit. "Now you've upset my wife! Enough! All of you! Langsford, take your men and leave!"

Langsford ignored the earl, keen on this new interaction. He followed the countess's accusing finger—pointed straight at Jack. He and Pelham looked rapidly back and forth between the two, completely dumfounded.

"How *dare* you follow me!" the countess spat.

"I swear. I never knew ya lived here. I swear. These blokes just brought me here. I swear. I didn't. I—"

The earl unleashed his anger. "Go!" he commanded the three men. "All of you! Leave!"

Not listening, Langsford looked at Pelham. "The servant is no servant."

"What shall we do now, your lordship? I cannot strong-arm a lady... ."

"You won't have to. Simply see to Jack, here."

Jack stepped backward.

"Jack, go with Pelham."

"Like 'ell I will. You trapped me!" With that, Jack bolted like a wild hare toward the front entrance. Pelham's grab narrowly missed Jack's coat as he leapt through the opening and beyond, startling the workers. Pelham raced close on his heels.

The leader of the committee: not a man, not a worker, nor a servant, but the exquisitely beautiful, red-haired Countess of Exeter, Lady Clementine.

CHAPTER 66

No. 20 St. James's Square, London

The countess shrieked and began to swoon causing Stanley to leap forward and catch her in his arms. Stanley carried his wife into the parlor that had been swept, its furniture repositioned in the corner farthest from the disarray. He placed her on a settee in the middle of a jumble of chairs and glared at Lady Clementine's maid. "Do something!" The woman rushed for smelling salts.

Langsford followed. He had to take advantage of the lady's surprise and couldn't let the countess regain her wits. He was sure she'd feigned this swoon not only for her husband's benefit but to buy time. "It's unfortunate the countess knows the lad who ran out, but since she does, she most likely is a part of an international conspiracy."

"That dreadful man," she moaned, coming to, "dreadful, dreadful ... he must have followed me home. I saw him begging on the street.... He frightened me so just now!" She began heaving sobs in her husband's arms.

"There, there," the earl soothed. He turned at Langsford. "The bomb has addled your mind."

"That man, Jack, is not a beggar. He's a George at Pratt's—spying on you and others."

The countess sobbed louder. "Nonsense!" the earl bristled. "Do I need to have you thrown out? I don't care if your father and I were friends!"

"No, you won't do that," Langsford countered, hoping he was right. "I followed this spy two nights ago when he met with a man named Summerhill and another individual whom I personally followed back to this house. The meeting, to refresh your memory, Countess, was in Saint James's Park. I am sure Summerhill will be willing to confirm you were there."

"You've lost your mind!" the earl snarled, attempting to soothe his wife.

Ignoring him, Langsford continued to speak to the countess. "You wore a man's cloak and top hat. You returned here and entered through the servant's quarters." He turned to the earl. "That was what was so urgent last night. I needed to warn you because I thought you had a servant who was a threat. But it wasn't one of your servants after all."

"That could be anyone, you fool."

"None of your servants recognized Jack. Nor he, them. But when the countess came downstairs and saw him, they both reacted—the reaction I had been looking for with your household staff in the dining room. The only person Jack reacted to was you, Countess." He paused, letting his words sink in. He hated this. He hated it was she. "I'm so sorry I have to do this."

Her sobbing lessened, her face buried in her hands.

The earl stood, his tone threatening. "Get out, Langsford!"

"Do you own a dark cape, Stanley? Send for it and prove me wrong. If I am, I'll leave."

The earl's face was red with rage.

"On my father's grave, I swear," Langsford continued, "I won't mention this ever again should I be wrong. I would love to be wrong, for it to be a servant. Anyone but her ...."

"It couldn't be her, you idiot! The night before last I was gone;

was in Kent. Clementine would never have gone out alone." The man was emphatic.

"The cape?" Langsford spoke softly.

Sitting back down and holding his wife, the earl slowly responded. "Yes. I own a cape. I haven't worn it in some time, but it would be far too large for Clementine... ."

The maid returned with the smelling salts. The countess reached out for them. "Oh ... I feel so faint... " she started to swoon.

"Oh m'lady, do take a big whiff of the salts."

"Let's prove you wrong once and for all," Stanley sneered at Langsford. He ordered the maid, "Bring me my black cape."

"You mean the cape we altered for the countess? That cape?"

Chapter 67

The parlor immediately fell silent as the earl dismissed the workers. They gathered up their tools and departed, leaving an empty quiet to sit heavy around the pair Langsford confronted.

Lady Clementine, tears streaking down her pallid cheeks, looked at her husband. "I've done nothing wrong. Do believe me."

"Of course you haven't, my sweet." He held her close, glaring at Langsford. "She's the Countess of Exeter. How dare you put her through this!"

"Forgive me. I wish I didn't have to, but she has broken laws even if she doesn't realize it. She's involved, in fact she's in charge, of a group planning an assassination."

The countess sat up, indignant now, staring him down. "I have done absolutely nothing wrong. How dare you insinuate that I have? I've only spoken to some people. That's no crime."

"What people? Clementine! What are you talking about?" The earl frowned.

"I had to help my brothers because you wouldn't?"

"What are you talking about?" he repeated. "Did your brothers get you involved in something amiss?"

"No. They have no idea. I am simply helping them, along with thousands of other people. I'm doing it for the good of the German people and Britain's trade with them."

"Now you don't know what you're talking about. That darn bomb has made everyone go daft!"

"No, my husband. I'm helping the world." She looked up at Langsford who had been standing still, listening. "You are right. You followed me that night."

"Why? I don't understand. Why would you plot Bismarck's assassination?"

"It's a long story," she brushed tears from the unbandaged cheek, a sob escaping, "... been stewing for years." She took a big breath and looked defiant. "I'm the Countess of Exeter and no one dare accuse me. I am beyond reproach."

"That you are, my dear. You needn't say another word," the earl frowned. "Someone got you entangled in this—put you up to this—"

"Let her explain this long story."

Color came back into her face as she glared at Langsford. She wiped away a final stray tear. "I am quite familiar with Germany and what is happening there."

"You?" her husband sat back astonished. "You're a woman with no idea—"

"My brothers. Their business," she hissed.

Langsford didn't understand. "Your brothers?"

"Her insufferable brothers—" Stanley muttered to himself.

"Yes, my brothers," she answered Langsford. "My father's first wife, Rebecca, was German. They had two sons, Benjamin and Samuel. Rebecca died when my brothers were eight and ten and father sent them to Germany to be raised by their aunt."

"What does that have ...?" the earl sputtered. "This is not the time or place—"

"Go on, Lady Clementine," Langsford encouraged, wondering

what on earth she was talking about. Maybe she was unbalanced after all.

"Five years later, Father married my mother, an English girl with Irish ancestry. She felt I should know my older brothers so I visited often. I adore them both. Even though their aunt wasn't mine, I came to think of her as a real aunt. They were a second family to me. A loving one."

"She's close to those brothers. So what?" The earl clenched his teeth.

"They began a cotton import/export business. Benjamin, the younger one, returned to London and lives here now so I see him often. He buys cotton from a Manchester mill, then exports it to Germany. Samuel is the official German importer for the cotton dye plant there. The dyed cotton is exported back here or to other countries. It has been a very successful business."

"A very lucrative one, I'm sure, but not now—not with the tariffs," Langsford's financial mind mused. "Now, it is failing. Am I correct?"

"Yes."

The earl interrupted. "Am I expected to help poor relatives because Bismarck breaks their backs? I ask you! German laws crippled their business so I have to pay?"

"Bismarck did this!" The countess raised her voice, nearly screaming at her husband. "To them. To everyone! And I hate you for not helping." Her anger was overt. Then she buried her face in her hands again. "I cannot bear for my smart, wonderful brothers to fail." Her shoulders trembled.

The earl failed to comfort her and sat stiffly beside her. "So you ask me to either throw more pounds into the sinking ship, make a foreign investment like a common businessman, or support them and their families for eternity? Hardly something someone of my position should even consider. Ever!"

Langsford realized this was a discussion they had had before, probably more than once. The earl still failed to recognize the seriousness of what the countess had done with her committee of traitors. Rather than interrupt them, he opted to let the conversation play out.

"I know you won't help my brothers," she accused, spitting her words at him. "They aren't peerage and they aren't blood relatives. I came from the working class, so I understand how hard it has been for them, but you ... you don't dare ..." she sputtered in her rage. She turned to Langsford. "If something happens to Bismarck, the Social Democrats would take over. Everything would be normal."

"A rather extreme method to stop the Iron Chancellor." Langsford frowned, attempting to understand why a failing business was motivation for assassination. "Is there more?"

The earl stood, facing him chest to chest. "You've heard enough. She doesn't like Bismarck and neither do I. What of it?"

"Can you explain further—" Langsford was interrupted when three uniformed police entered, clambering around a pile of debris swept in a pile by open entrance.

The tallest officer faced the three. "Lord Stanley, I am Commissioner Edmund Henderson of Scotland Yard. Lord Langsford's man summoned us after he turned in a spy he nabbed. What have we here?"

Relieved the police had arrived, Langsford began to reply to Sir Henderson when he was interrupted again by Lord Stanley.

"I am afraid you are not needed. There was a misunderstanding about the Countess of Exeter," he indignantly greeted,

referring to his wife in the third person. "She has not done anything wrong, and there is no issue here."

"I believe it best for me to be the one to determine if there is
an issue here or not. Let's just sort this situation out, shall we?
Thank you, Lord Langsford. Your man, Pelham, gave me a quick
briefing. We'll take over from here."

"Certainly, Commissioner," he nodded, ready to leave. Still, he
felt something was missing in her story. A ruined business is not
reason to want someone assassinated.

CHAPTER 68

The Great Scotland Yard, London

Two days had passed, but it was far from over. Where was Heinrich? Langsford was worried sick not knowing more. Sir Vincent had ignored all his messages since the bombings. He had heard nothing. Today was Monday, the day of Heinrich's supposed extradition. Langsford began to plod his way through the piles of broken bricks and mortar in the Yard, heading toward the Whitehall building's back door, Pelham right behind him. The gaping hole in the building rose thirty feet, metal rods and beams sagging in a broken mass. Even though the bomb blew two nights ago, police still dug, searching through the debris.

A little man in a short coat and cap stopped the pair. "It'll be thruppence, sirs, if'n ya want ta see the bombin' site. That includes a tour of the Rising Sun public house 'ere." The adjacent pub had also been damaged and the pub's proprietor was determined to turn an extra profit. "You won't find a more famous spot in all of London town." He grinned.

"Don't exploit this horror, man." Pelham stepped in front just as a bobby came over.

"You 'eard the governor," the policeman said to the pub's owner. "Move on."

The little man walked over to some gawkers standing at the edge of the Yard.

"I need to see Sir Henderson," Langsford told the bobby.

"Go in. I 'remember ya from afore, squire."

Nodding thanks, they went in the back door and up the stone steps into the building which stood unharmed. Inside, Scotland Yard was a continuation of the chaos outside. While there was no physical damage to this particular building, the Whitehall offices were abuzz with police scurrying up and down the halls, ushering witnesses in and out of rooms, and piling papers up in tall stacks on the long desk.

Langsford and Pelham walked unchallenged into the commissioner's office. Sir Henderson sat behind his paper-laden desk, hair rumpled and head resting on his hand. He looked up at his visitors, red-rimmed eyes telling of his sleepless nights. He rose when he saw Langsford.

"Hello, again. I fear you have caught me at a bad time, though we have made considerable progress. Do sit"—he interrupted himself, gesturing at two chairs—"with the bombings and your assassination case."

"Excellent. I don't mean to delay you. I've only come for news regarding Heinrich. I'm worried he has been already extradited. I need to talk to Sir Vincent."

"He's not been in his office since the bombings. In fact, no one can reach him. He's disengaged from this entire mess and sent me a message to handle the bombing case while he huddles with the home secretary. A show, a pretense that he is accomplishing something, I fear." Henderson leaned back in his chair, worry etched in his face. "I'm sorry to say, your friend is missing. He should be here at the Whitehall Division station, but we can't find him."

A sharp pang cut through Langsford. "Do you think his body is in that rubble out there?"

"The poor devil," Pelham said. "To be under all that stone ... maybe alive ..."

"I don't know where he is," Henderson continued. "I've put the word out for everyone to look for a Prussian prisoner and report to me immediately if he's found. Or if they locate paperwork that shows he *was* extradited. There would have to be at least that."

"If he were already sent back, then Sir Vincent broke his word to me."

"That wouldn't be unlike him, I'm afraid. He's a political sort."

"Either way, neither prospect is good."

"My hands are full with these bombings or I would be searching personally."

"Who set the bombs?" Langsford shoved back thoughts of Heinrich, worried the bombs were part of a greater plot by the committee.

"Your committee of terrorists are in league with the Fenians. Irish bombs made with American dynamite and planted by Prussians. There'll be hell to pay. The Irish want to destroy England and the Prussian terrorists want to end Bismarck's Germany. By creating a series of attacks and finally assassinating Bismarck, they planned to instigate a war between England and Germany."

"Two factions incapable of destroying an entire country on their own so they tried to set a war in motion. Good God!"

"We already got confessions from the Prussians and we're arresting some of the Irish now. Bad business. Without knowing about the party's special committee, we would have had no leads whatsoever, so I thank you. Scotland Yard is in your debt."

"The party members confessed?"

"They did. The first was Jack, who was scared silly. Admitted he spied on everyone at Pratt's. When he learned Bismarck wouldn't be at the Berlin Conference, he needed to signal his compatriots straightaway."

"And he left a signal at the bus stop?"

"He did," Sir Henderson confirmed. "One of my detectives found it yesterday afternoon. A chalk mark on a brick wall to alert the man named Summerhill. They met the following night at the park."

"That was the meeting we watched, m'lord," Pelham declared.

"Summerhill then contacted everyone to meet at a pub Saturday night, the night after the bombing. It couldn't be sooner, because they were busy Friday night setting the bombs. It was imperative they meet to alter their plans for the assassination."

"They had to rush. The Prussians planned to leave for Berlin tomorrow. Now I understand why they needed to get to Germany so soon. To leave London after the bombings."

"My inspectors were ready for them. I had to take a few of my men off the bombing case, which was a difficult decision at first, but this had the potential to be more devastating to England. I'm damn glad I did. We arrested all the terrorists at the pub."

"Let me guess. It was the Lamb Tavern in Leadenhall Market."

"How did you know?" The commissioner was nonplussed. "Never you mind. It's best I don't know and definitely better for you."

"So you arrested Summerhill, Lentz, and the three Prussians?"

"They gave up without a fight, except one pulled a knife."

"Let me guess again. Karl Gülker."

"I tremble at how much you know, Langsford. And I suppose you know he murdered his own brother ..."

"I also know he murdered Heinrich's father. Send a telegraph to the Prussian police that he's arrested. There's a man who worked at the Dieffenbacher estate, Hans, who can testify."

"You certainly seem to know a great deal about what those three have been doing." The commissioner shook his head. "I'll see Prussia is notified right away, then."

"I didn't know enough until I found Lady Clementine."

"Once we got the lot of 'em back here to Scotland Yard, this Summerhill confessed he'd been hired by Lady Clementine."

"No one would have ever suspected the beautiful countess," Pelham lamented.

"I certainly didn't," Langsford confessed. "She was in a perfect position to learn a great deal from ambassadors, diplomats, and MPs whom she frequently entertained."

"Ultimately, she was the 'brains' behind the operation, planning every detail. She thought she did no wrong if others committed the actual crimes she planned." Sir Henderson stood and looked blankly at the street outside his window.

Langsford broke the small silence. "What the countess did still seems extreme to me. Are you sure there wasn't something more than trying to protect her brothers' business?"

"Astute of you, Langsford. Yes." He turned around. "Hatred. Hatred of those who hate the Jews."

"I don't understand. She isn't Jewish."

"No, but her brothers are, as is their family in Germany. She's very sensitive how ill-treated they were there," Henderson explained.

"No wonder her brother wasn't arrested with the Catholics ... and the earl kept quiet about them." It began to make sense now.

"Do you recall the barbed exchange between Bismarck and Disraeli a few years back?"

"The one about Africa and Jews?" Langsford pulled on the corner of his moustache.

"Yes. Most of us remember what Bismarck said. It created

quite a stir throughout London—something along the lines of, 'The Germans bought a new country in Africa where Jews and pigs will be tolerated.'"

"And our Benjamin Disraeli, born a Jew, so succinctly replied, 'Fortunately, we have both in Britain.' The perfect retort from a civilized gentleman." Langsford smiled.

"The countess let her hatred rule her. She hates Bismarck far more than he hates the Jews. She said it was fitting to have the chancellor come to the end of his reign at the African Conference." The commissioner sat on the edge of his desk. "She also contacted the Irish, offering the assistance of the Prussians with terrorist attacks. She knew if Prussians set bombs here and if an Englishman was responsible for the chancellor's assassination, then war was likely; England favored to win although the Irish would prefer a difference outcome, if asked."

"She bombed her own home!?" Langsford was incredulous.

"A villainess disguised as her own victim. The bomb there was much smaller than the rest and placed on a window ledge farthest from the parlor where she knew she would be. She didn't figure on it being as strong a blast as it was."

"What she didn't figure on," Langsford observed, "is that one of her Prussian traitors would falsely accuse Heinrich of murder. Had that not happened, then most likely Bismarck would have been assassinated, the bombings would have continued, and ultimately, England and Germany would be at war."

"Indeed," Henderson replied. "With what Jack and Summerhill confessed, Scotland Yard had enough information to arrest her, which we did early this morning."

There it is. It was ever so much more than just protecting her brothers.

CHAPTER 69

The Great Scotland Yard, London

A constable knocked on the door, opening it partway. "Excuse me, sir, there's a reporter from the *Daily Telegraph* and two artists, one with a camera contraption from the *Graphic* and the other, the *Illustrated News*. I rounded 'em up and detained them so you could see 'em first. I wasn't sure if you'd approve of them here at the Yard."

"Quite right, Hayward. Tell them I'll have someone come speak with them, will you?"

"Yes, sir." Constable Hayward closed the door.

"I don't envy you dealing with the press." Langsford stood.

"They are asking why Scotland Yard couldn't protect Scotland Yard, let alone London. I ask myself the same."

Langsford thought the commissioner looked extremely burdened and fatigued as they walked out into the hall, and did not envy him his position. "Is the press probing into the assassination plot as well?"

"I doubt it since nothing came of it. Should they ask, there won't be mention the Earl of Exeter, of course. He is extremely distraught over Lady Clementine."

"He'll have to get good legal counsel," Langsford said sadly.

"No. She's brought disgrace upon the earl's name, even without any newspaper story. He decided that her actions prove she's feebleminded. He declared this morning that she committed

fraud when she agreed to marry him without disclosing her mental state. He's pursuing an annulment."

"Quite the volte-face."

"A high price to pay to remain honorable, plus the destruction to his home and its injured occupants. I understand your cousin was one of those?"

"Yes. She isn't my cousin, but she will recover quickly."

"Not your cousin? No. I simply won't ask."

Sir Henderson called over an inspector who joined them. He spoke quietly to him, "There are three newspapermen outside wanting to talk to someone here at the Yard. Can you handle it, Blake?"

"Yes, sir. Straight away."

"Good. Give them a little tour around the destruction here. I'll talk to them afterward."

Pelham decided to tag along with Inspector Blake, curious to see the camera contraption.

The commissioner and Langsford followed a short distance behind. They walked outside where the piles of blown bricks filled the majority of the yard, and men painstakingly stacked broken bricks, attempting to make a wider path for wagons to come in and remove the debris. The shattered growler, its shafts still pointing skyward, was untouched, but the body of the horse had been removed, the leather traces cut with a knife.

The two stood on the steps outside the door, surveying the scene. The extent of the destruction was far worse than at the residence on St. James's Square. The pit of Langsford's stomach ached, his thoughts on Heinrich.

"Were other jailed men injured or killed here?"

"No prisoners, but one constable and the driver of that growler there were badly hurt. That building is CID offices and the Special

Irish Branch Headquarters, which is why it was a target. I doubt your Prussian lad was in there—why would he have been there at night? At this point, I tend to believe he was sent back to Prussia."

"You're probably correct. Which means at least he's still alive."

"The whole of London could have looked like this if we ended up at war with Germany over an assassination. I owe you, Langsford, for informing me about the traitors."

They walked to the bottom of the steps and over toward the broken carriage, watching as the photographer set up a wooden contraption and an odd square box. The artist sitting beside it was sketching the scene.

A constable walked up to report to the commissioner. "Sir, I have gone through all the extradition paperwork, and there is nothing about a prisoner going to Germany, either today or in the last week."

"You've gone through everything in Sir Vincent's office?"

"Everything. Unless his papers were in the CID offices there," he pointed to the crumbling walls. "It will take time to find all the papers left that haven't been destroyed."

"Thank you. Just keep looking, though. In case."

If he isn't back in Prussia, then where the hell is he?

Chapter 70

The Great Scotland Yard, London

The commissioner bid Langsford good-bye and walked over to the newspapermen to face the damage to his reputation—damage as great as the damage to the building in front of them. Langsford felt sorry for him.

"It'll be thruppence, miss, if'n ya want ta see the bombin' site." The greedy little man was still charging an entrance fee. "That includes a tour of the Rising Sun public house 'ere. You won't find a more famous spot in all of London town."

Langsford turned, irritated by the audacity of the greedy proprietor, then recognized the tipped bonnet of a girl as she stepped around the unofficial gatekeeper. "No, thank you," he heard her say. "I am here on police business."

A bobby came to her aid. "Leave her alone. If we have to keep warning you, you'll find yourself behind bars."

Langsford walked over, tipping his hat. "Anna." His heart was heavy.

"Where's Henry? Is he all right? Is he with you?"

"I'm afraid you've made this trip in vain."

"What? *No!*" Anna staggered, covering her mouth at the unspeakable.

"No one knows where he is at the moment. He just isn't here. He seems to be, well, lost."

"Then where is he? Is he in a hospital?"

"No."

"I don't understand."

"He may have already been sent back to Prussia, I'm afraid." Langsford was reluctant to talk of the possibility of death. At least until it was confirmed, he wasn't inclined to mention it; she stood and sobbed. He held her for support and called over to Pelham. "Take her home and see that she's settled there. Come back for me in a bit. I want to speak to the commissioner again when he's finished talking to the newspapermen." The coachman helped Anna back over to the coach on the street, while Langsford waited in the Yard.

The commissioner finished and started back to the Whitehall building's back door.

"Wait a minute, Henderson." Langsford caught up. "Do you still have your original telegraph from Prussia about Heinrich?"

"I imagine it's been filed, but yes. Oh, I see, you want to tele-graph the sender."

"Yes. They should know if they have their own prisoner back by now."

"Good idea."

"Then I can at least travel over ..."

"It'll be thruppence if'n ya want ta see the bombin' site. That includes a tour of the Rising Sun public house 'ere. You won't find a more famous spot in all of London town."

Annoyed still by the sleazy man, both Henderson and Langsford turned to glower at him.

"Step back! An' stay away from here, you!" barked a constable. "Let 'em pass." A man in a derby and long coat walked through, another man behind him.

"Commissioner Henderson!" the man called out. Langsford didn't know him.

"Inspector Abberline. Good. Did you ...?"

"I did, indeed."

Langsford squinted at the man's companion. *"Heinrich?"* He saw no cuffs on his friend. He didn't appear to be under arrest, but he looked drawn, eyes sunken with dark circles. His clothes were rumpled, torn, and dirty. Langsford sprinted down the steps and clapped him on the shoulder, glad beyond words. "Here you are, old chap! We thought you were either dead or sent to Prussia!"

"Well, aren't they the same?"

"Where was he all this time?" the commissioner asked.

"He was right where Sir Vincent sent him first thing Friday morning," the inspector explained. "The Bow Street Station. Wanted him there ready for extradition."

"Always politically minded." The commissioner grimaced. "He wanted to make sure to garner a lot of attention from the press that are always at Bow Street."

"My guess is, Commissioner, Sir Vincent forgot about him in light of the bombings."

"I had no idea you had been put there," the commissioner apologized to Heinrich. "We were looking everywhere for you, which is why I pulled Inspector Abberline off the bombings. I asked him to find the man he arrested last week."

"Am I released, as the inspector said?"

"You are free!"

Heinrich blew out a deep breath, "Gott sei dank!" Thank God! "I was convinced I would be executed and sent to hell for not being a priest."

"No, Heinrich." Langsford laughed. "I doubt this was a divine punishment. Only a plot."

"The plot! Have you arrested Karl Gülker and the rest of the traitors?"

"They did. Including three British who were also involved. Confessed to the assassination plot and more, including aiding with the bombings."

"*Three* British?"

"The committee grew in your absence." Langsford chuckled. "Much more pervasive than we originally thought."

"They also confirmed another Prussian named Gerhard," Sir Henderson added with a laugh. "Seems he was with an English cousin, both with the Social Democrats. That I would have loved to have seen."

"Fun while it lasted," Langsford admitted, "but our detective days are over."

"Thank goodness!" Heinrich exclaimed. "I'm not keen to work for Scotland Yard. Ever."

"We'll find you a job elsewhere. Somewhere safe. In the meantime, Pelham is due back for me and you will get cleaned up and have some decent food."

"But Anna ... where ... ?"

"Not until you are presentable. Love can just wait a bit longer."

In the library a few hours later, Langsford stood by the fireplace, Tweed at his feet. Heinrich gazed out the windows overlooking the square. "I could work in a bank or teach German at a school. Either would be respectable positions."

"I'll speak to the heads of several banks. As for schools, I know William Rutherford, headmaster at the Westminster School. I'll have a word."

Barnes opened the library door. "M'lord, Mr. Maxwell and Miss Boardman to see you."

Uncle Max entered with a vengeance. "Lord Langsford, I

certainly don't appreciate being dragged here by your damn driver and I refuse to let our Anna come here again without someone to see to her safety. The last time you placed her in the middle of a bomb... ." He stopped to catch his breath, Anna trailing behind him. Barnes clicked the door closed.

"Anna," Heinrich whispered. "My dear, blessed Anna."

Uncle Max stopped and stared at the strange man at the front of the room. Anna stood quietly as Langsford spoke next. "Uncle Max, it's time you met Anna's Henry. Cleared of all charges and as common a man as you could wish for."

Langsford watched as she walked over to the window and Heinrich. Slowly they embraced as Heinrich whispered, "Oh, Anna." He lifted her chin with one hand and gently kissed her lips.

There it is. Langsford grinned and nodded to Uncle Max. The sun broke through the gray skies, brightening the trees in the square, turning the couple into a single silhouette.

Langsford had crossed many boundaries lately, rubbing elbows with spies, killers, and would-be assassins to seek murderers and traitors. He'd lied to the police and probably broken more than one law. But unlike Heinrich, he could never be with the person he loved most. Still, he was glad his school chum could.

The End

Background:
1884 No Boundaries

The history is real—it is the setting for all main characters in which to play their parts. Many of the people in the tale are also real, although the members of the committee, the guests at Pratt's, Langsford and his household were born of my imagination. Henry and Anna are based on real individuals and yes, Henry actually did flee Germany the night before he was to receive his robes in the church, and arrived in London to fall in love with Anna. I know their story well because my grandmother told me about them. They were her grandparents.

In 1884 the economy throughout Western Europe, Great Britain, and the United States struggled through a long depression. During the years between 1873 and extending, some claim into the 1890s, countries fought for financial stability.

The London bombings May 30, 1884, did happen as described, and I happily took the literary license of adding one additional bomb at the #20 Saint James's residence so I could share the blame of all the bombings with the fictional "committee." In actuality, the Irish Fenians get all the credit, without help from anyone.

I did my best to make sure everything was in the correct year—whistling tea kettles had not yet been invented, I discovered. I learned, however, that dynamite had and the United States was happy to supply it overseas.

It was an interesting decade, leading into the better known "Gilded Age" and the "Roaring 90s," as the world economy recovered and danced its way toward the new century and all that it would bring. The 1880s was a pivotal time not only for Langsford but for the Western World.

Sources

Herbert Fry, *London in 1880,* Scribner, Welford, and Co. London, 1880

Bertrand Russell, *German Social Democracy*, Simon and Schuster, New York, 1965

Edgar Feuchtwanger, *Bismarck,* Routledge, Taylor & Francis Group Ltd. Oxford, 2006

David Cannadine, *The Decline and Fall of the British Aristocracy*, Vintage Books, New York, 1990

Alan Moss & Keith Skinner, *The Victorian Detective*, Shire Publications, Oxford, 2013

Cowen & Cowen, *Victorian Jews through British Eyes*, Vallentine, Mitchell & Co, Ltd., London, 1986

Clarkson & Richardson, *Police!*, Scribner and Welford, New York, 1889

John Basset Moore, *A Treatise on Extradition Vol. I*, Boston Book Company, Boston, 1891

ACKNOWLEDGMENTS

An author's journey with a book begins as a solitary one, but along the way others join the path, contributing ideas and encouragement, arguments and kudos. This book began with a family legend, with notes made years ago lying quietly in the recesses of a box, pages already turning yellow. Finally the time was right for this story to be spun. The late Richard Warren Field, one of my early readers, was the first to tell me to go for it, introducing me to the Historical Novel Society. Authors Jeri Westerson and Danny Kemp provided honest, and yes, often brutal but accurate, advice. Michele Russell-Tsiotsias, a total believer, along with Eddie Conner, my enthusiastic cheerleader, and beloved Kathy Woodhill, a stickler for perfection, kept me on my path. Editor Chuck Sambuchino held my feet to the fire while Helga Schier, with her graceful corrections, ushered me on. Finally, William Curry and the entire team at Archway escorted this novel into print. To each and every one of them, I extend my deepest gratitude. The largest thank you goes, of course, to my husband who has always, patiently, been my rock, and who has whispered to me, "have faith" in all things— especially myself, and never permit boundaries to stop my own dreams.

ABOUT THE AUTHOR

 The daughter of a newspaperman, A.E. Wasserman grew up in a household filled with books and stories. At age 14, she wrote her first novella and never stopped writing. After graduating from The Ohio State University, she lived in London, then San Francisco. Currently she resides in Southern California with her family and her muse, a Border Collie named Topper. She recently received top honors from *Writer's Digest* for one of her short stories.

Visit the author's web site at www.aewasserman.com

CPSIA information can be obtained at www.ICGtesting.com
Printed in the USA
BVOW03s1205080515

399475BV00001B/2/P